The Petting Zoos

the

PETTING

ZOO

a novel

K.S. Covert

DUNDURN
PRESS

Publisher: Scott Fraser | Acquiring editor: Russell Smith
Cover designer: Michel Vrana
Cover image: hands: istock.com/artpipi and istock.com/Delmaine Donson
Printer: Marquis Book Printing Inc.

Library and Archives Canada Cataloguing in Publication

Title: The petting zoos : a novel / K.S. Covert.
Names: Covert, K. S., author.
Identifiers: Canadiana (print) 20210287411 | Canadiana (ebook) 20210287446 | ISBN
    9781459748804 (softcover) | ISBN 9781459748811 (PDF) | ISBN 9781459748828 (EPUB)
Classification: LCC PS8605.O9235 P48 2022 | DDC C813/.6—dc23

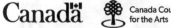

We acknowledge the support of the Canada Council for the Arts and the Ontario Arts Council for our publishing program. We also acknowledge the financial support of the Government of Ontario, through the Ontario Book Publishing Tax Credit and Ontario Creates, and the Government of Canada.

Care has been taken to trace the ownership of copyright material used in this book. The author and the publisher welcome any information enabling them to rectify any references or credits in subsequent editions.

The publisher is not responsible for websites or their content unless they are owned by the publisher.

Printed and bound in Canada.

Dundurn Press
1382 Queen Street East
Toronto, Ontario, Canada M4L 1C9
dundurn.com, @dundurnpress 𝕏 f ⊚

For Jack, who loved petting zoos
And for the guy on the rollercoaster,
who touched but did not feel

Glossary of Terms

From the Diachronic History of the H9N9 Pandemic,
ed. Lily King

BLT laws — Early in year two of the pandemic, the regency government passed the *Laws Against Behaviour Likely to Cause the Spread of the H9N9 Virus*. This was quickly shortened to "Behaviour Likely To laws," or BLT laws, in the common parlance. The laws were at least partly in response to an evangelical sect (see also: *Sickos*) that deliberately spread the virus in an attempt to bring on the Rapture. Among other restrictions, the laws made it illegal to be in any public space without an approved mask and gloves; to engage in any activity that could become a super-spreader event, such as gathering in nonfamilial or familial groups of ten or more people without protective coverings; and to wear clothing or use textiles that had not been treated with Impermatex (see also: *Impermatex*™). Despite the long-term availability of a vaccine, and its widespread use, the laws remained in place more than a decade after the height of the pandemic, although there was a growing public outcry against them (see Chapter 20).

Bonnell, Arthur D. — Arthur Bonnell was a dentist whose wife and children died in the early stages of the pandemic, after which he spent several years as a near recluse, as dentistry was at first suspended and later shunned as unsafe (see Chapter 8 for arguments for and against this premise) in the years immediately following the height of the pandemic. His solitude — and his seeming inability to do anything about it — caused a psychotic break. He shot four members of a family — strangers to him — because, according to him, they had deprived him of mental and physical affection when he'd broken in to their home and demanded it from them. He later shot himself. His is the first known example of a person driven to desperation by the lack of physical contact that is the long-lasting impact of measures used to prevent the spread of the H9N9 virus. (See also: *Bonnelly*.)

Bonnelly — A person or event in which someone experiences a psychotic break owing to lack of physical contact. This almost always ends in suicide, but is differentiated from traditional suicide in that it is generally done in public and the triggering event is the person's need for physical contact with another human being. It will sometimes involve the deaths of innocent bystanders at the hand of the person experiencing the break before his or her own death. These events started becoming more common about nine years after the height of the pandemic, as the Behaviour Likely To laws limited interpersonal contact. (See also: *Bonnell, Arthur D., BLT laws,* and *Therapeutic Touch Clinics.*)

H9N9 Virus — H9N9 was the fourth and most deadly of a series of global pandemics that struck within a two-decade period. Its source has never been traced officially, but anecdotally it is believed to be a variant of an earlier pandemic virus that escaped from a U.S. biological warfare lab (see Chapter 1, "Origins"). Its mortality rate is attributed to its rapid mutations, as well as the delay in discovering that it could live for weeks in natural textiles. The virus could be killed if the fabrics were washed in hot water with soap, but would otherwise lie dormant for a still-unknown period. This uncertainty contributes to an ongoing and widespread fear of natural, untreated textiles. The combination of the deaths directly attributed to the virus, along with those caused by the lack of food, medical assistance, and medications, as well as political unrest and violence immediately after the outbreak (see Chapters 3–5), is believed to have reduced the world's population overall to pre-Industrial levels, though as of ten years following the outbreak no official global census has been completed.

Henny Penny — The H9N9 virus was first referred to as "Henny Penny" in a right-wing online news article three months after the initial outbreak. The author, trying to downplay the seriousness of what was just coming to be recognized as a pandemic, had wanted to evoke the children's story character who protested that the sky was falling, and erroneously used the name Henny Penny. In fact, it was Chicken Little who worried the sky was falling. Despite the error, the name stuck and is now widely used colloquially to refer to the virus.

Impermatex™ — A treatment for textiles, developed after scientists discovered that H9N9 had a long half-life in woven fabrics. Fabrics treated with Impermatex are stiffened, as with starch, and are impermeable by the H9N9 virus, which lives for less than twenty-four hours on a hard surface.

Light-Emitting Sanitation Device — A motion-sensing device housed inside a silicone strip. The strips are fitted inside doorways. A blue light travels from top to bottom and back while a person stands in the doorway, a process that lasts about five seconds. The device was invented by Arnold Taylor, a year after the outbreak began, to kill free-riding virus molecules. To give people confidence that the virus would not be carried from public to private areas, a regency law declares that each public-private doorway shall be fitted with this device to irradiate people and goods passing through it. (See also: *Nuker.*)

Nuker — Common name for the Light-Emitting Sanitation Device invented by Arnold Taylor.

Petting zoos — Believed to have begun as an underground phenomenon three to four years after the passage of the Behaviour Likely To laws. In the petting zoos, strangers go without masks and gloves in order to experience skin-to-skin contact. Petting zoos violate the BLT laws in several ways — lack of protective equipment in public and size of public gatherings, for example — and are the target of regular police raids. They tend to be described by police and the regency as unhygienic sex clubs, which are illegal under both the Behaviour Likely To legislation and the public decency section of the *Criminal Code.*

Regency — Those elected officials who survived the pandemic, along with prominent citizens with proven expertise in areas of need who were invited to join them to maintain governance and order until such time as the population had recovered enough to hold elections.

Regency Hours — Instituted shortly after the regency formed, when the workforce was at its lowest. Each citizen is required to give the regency eight weeks of volunteer service a year, according to their skills and abilities.

Going Back to Work

THEY SENT US back to the office when the bonnellies became a social hazard.

Much as the idea of just travelling to and from the office scared me — my brain was still having a hard time convincing its inner lizard that I could be safe around other people despite the vaccines — I felt the relief of someone who'd been stopped in the nick of time from doing something irrevocably stupid. I mean, I could shake my head with the best of the net pundits at the people who couldn't handle the solitude, voice my scorn at their weakness, and vow I'd never show that fragility of character myself, sure. But when it came down to it, I had walked right up to that line and stood with my toe hovering over it.

The only thing that stood between me and the bonnellies was cowardice, and lack of access to opiates. And an enduring fear that I'd kill myself and no one would notice. I shuddered to think of people coming to investigate the smell and finding my body a bloated mess on the floor.

There was also the tiniest smidgen of fear of missing out: a curious certainty that the day after I killed myself, things would get better and I'd have just missed it.

As soon as I heard about the third bonnelly in a week — and those were just the ones that were reported — I expected a call, and sure enough, a day or so later, there it was: Everybody into the office.

It was probably time — past time, really, but I'd become so used to working at home that the rigamarole associated with actually leaving my apartment and making my way into an office threw me. I didn't know how offices worked anymore — how did that many people occupy one space without killing each other?

But the bonnellies were getting out of hand and the word from the regency was that this was the way to combat the madness. The last one, a woman, had set herself on fire in the middle of a downtown sidewalk, but she had killed only herself, which was a blessing. Men always took someone with them, like Arthur Bonnell had.

But if anything was going to change for me, I needed to get over my fear of people.

For starters.

Solitude, loneliness, lack of contact with other living beings — the things that drive the bonnellies mad — had been nibbling away at the corners of my psyche for a long time, even before Henny Penny, to be honest. But back then, I had hope.

And even if Nietzsche was right about hope being the cruel-lest thing, I knew better than some that lack of hope rips you apart. If you're lucky — or, like I was, somewhat inured to it, having gone long periods of my life without the touch of a loved one — you can shut down enough to continue anyway. For a while, at least. If you're not, you go insane. Maybe not Bonnell insane, but mad enough to matter.

Funny how when there's no official scarcity, you can live without touch for years — perhaps not fully, perhaps not hap-pily, but you can do it because the prospect is always right outside your door, or at the very least, right around the corner. Theoretically, you can always find a likely somebody and invite that person to touch you and they'll take you up on it and life is fine and you go on with it — maybe with that person, maybe not. That wasn't precisely how it worked for me before Henny Penny, but something like that happened often enough that I never exploded with despair. Now that it couldn't happen, now that I could barely open my door and go through it, it was all I could think about — if I let myself think about it, so I didn't often let myself consider the lack, the absence. Ten years after Henny Penny was wrestled to the ground, people were still dying because of it, but this time for want of physical contact. I didn't want to be one of them.

But that first step was a doozy.

And it was going to have to be a literal step. I had gas ra-tions, but needed a new tire for my car, and my bike chain was broken, and neither was going to get fixed any time soon. I couldn't bring myself to book one of the extra cars the regency had put in the taxi fleet to accommodate the influx of at-home workers needing a ride, couldn't commit myself to sitting in a closed space with another person.

That was one of my guiding paradoxes. Did I trust the vaccines? Yes. Did I think the masks and gloves were effective at preventing the spread of the virus? Yes. Was I terrified of people and public spaces anyway? Yes. It wasn't rational, but fear never is. I read a lot of articles, particularly in the early days, about the fear-anxiety feedback loop that a lot of people experienced: being afraid of Henny Penny, and then becoming more anxious about things as their body responded to the fear itself instead of the actual situation on the ground. Knowing I was probably on a loop didn't make me less afraid, though. The only thing that would cure me was behavioural modification, and I wasn't strong enough to impose that kind of therapy on myself.

The day the order came down, I looked at myself — judged myself — in a way I hadn't bothered to do in years. My hair, my nails, the full pelt on my legs and under my arms: all of them proclaimed me an at-home worker. I cut my hair myself when it got long enough to annoy me, and the result was as could be expected. I'd started to go grey but had never really paid attention to what it looked like — we see ourselves at least partly through others' eyes, and when no one you care about is there to see you, you become a bit blind to the things you care about others caring about. Some people go grey in a pretty way. I am not one of them. A carb-heavy diet proclaimed itself from my middle and thighs. I continued to moisturize my face when I could find creams, but otherwise my skin was dry and flaking: the soap I could buy at my corner store did me no favours, and I thought about lotion only when my skin grew so dry it hurt. My clothes were an uninspiring mish-mash: either well-worn items that were comfortable but made of illegal, untreated fabric, or the ill-fitting Impermatex clothes that I wore when

I had to go outside. I had to order new Impermatex outfits to wear to the office.

I thought about makeup, but my eyeshadows were all dry and cracked, and my foundation smelled vaguely rotten. Just as well: no one was going to see my face under the mask, anyway. Or my fingernails. I'd never been a girly girl, although I suppose if I had been, maybe I would have found a way — or a reason — to obtain cosmetics. I'd grown up in an all-male household after my mother left, where femininity was not celebrated. If I ever displayed the slightest hint that I thought I was special — if, for example, I wore makeup — that idea was quickly and roundly quashed. And most of my friends were like me: shy, unassuming mice, by nature or by nurture. Until I met my friend Sophie, I'd spent the better part of my life trying not to draw attention to myself. Even now, wearing makeup felt like putting a big neon sign on my face, saying, "Look at me!" I only ever wore it when it seemed inappropriate not to.

• • •

"For god's sake, Lily, I'm not going out with you when you look like death." It was Sophie's twenty-first birthday, and she had come to my room in our dorm to pick me up on the way to her party.

"This is how I look, Sophie." I was wounded, to have made an effort and still not pleased her. It was Sophie in front of me, but I heard my mother's voice. My best had never been enough for her, either.

"You keep insisting on wearing grey. You can't wear grey without makeup — I don't know how many times I have to tell

you that. It washes you out. Sit down, let me fix you up." She pulled her makeup bag from her purse. "You're so pretty, I don't know why you don't flaunt it a bit."

"If I'm so pretty without makeup, why do I need to wear it? Besides, no one's looking at me."

"Stop being childish. Call this my birthday present. You're going to look nice because I want pretty people around me."

. . .

On back-to-work day, I slid the elastics of my regency-issued disposable surgical face mask behind my ears, pulled on my gloves, shrugged into my backpack — which held my laptop, ID, and lunch rations — took a deep breath, and opened the door. And screamed in fright, in turn scaring the hell out of the neighbour I hadn't expected to see walking past at that moment. I'd never laid eyes on her before, and I tried to apologize as she scurried by me. Another person not used to the morning commute — or at least not used to it including me.

The thing about being an at-home worker is that you — obviously — don't get out a lot. But because you move easily around your own environment, you don't consider the ramifications of that lack of activity: how the length of your stride shortens to match the available space; how your ever-efficient body packages energy into apartment-size boxes and then doles them out grudgingly if you ask for more. I hadn't gone much further than the corner market in ages. Every so often, I'd get an urge to go further afield, but the panic attacks — or if not a full-on attack, the endless second-guessing about the wisdom of my actions — would always start within a few blocks and I'd high-tail it home again.

I don't know why I thought I'd be fine walking the two miles to the office, or that it would take me only half an hour. After the first five blocks, I was miserable.

It wasn't just the exertion, truth be told. The noise of the traffic was a full-on assault once I'd left the side street I lived on and stepped into the stream of people heading to work via the main artery through the city. The sounds of motors and horns and brakes echoed off the flat surfaces of tall buildings and the plywood covering former storefronts. I felt terrorized by the number of people on the sidewalk with me, even though by pre–Henny Penny standards it was a quiet day. I jumped into the street as one man barrelled toward me, giving no indication that he intended to veer away from his logical trajectory, which would have taken him far too close to my left shoulder. My heart pounded at this near miss, but he continued as if he hadn't noticed me at all. When a driver honked at me, I scurried back onto the sidewalk and found temporary refuge in the doorway of a boarded-up store, taking deep breaths to try to calm down.

"They can't kill you they can't kill you they can't kill you," I chanted to myself, willing my heart to slow. "It's all right." There were people passing by me, but all I could see were disease vectors. It had been that way for me ever since the Sickos carried out their reign of terror.

• • •

"Do you want something to drink?" the woman asked. "I don't have any coffee, that's hard to get these days, but I have some nice herbal tea. Cold water?"

"Water would be nice, thank you," I said, because she seemed determined to do something for me and I hadn't let her take my coat.

I didn't want to be there, in a stranger's house, with a virus raging outside. I had no intention of touching the glass she placed on the table beside me, let alone taking off my mask to drink the water.

"So in your email, you said you can put me in contact with family members who identify as Sickos."

She looked uncomfortable. "Well, you just get straight to it, don't you?"

"Sorry, I don't have a lot of time."

She was a slender woman in nice clothes, perfectly coiffed hair, but nervous. No mask or gloves, but you didn't expect people to wear them in their own homes. She flitted around the room, minutely adjusting the few knick-knacks and framed photos.

"Are those pictures of your family? Are they the people you want to put me in touch with?"

She picked up one of the photos, brushed some non-existent dust from the frame and showed it to me. A pleasant-looking older couple in a studio portrait.

"My Aunt Leah and Uncle Peter. They became born again a couple of years ago, before the pandemic, and they're convinced that this is the apocalypse predicted in Revelations, that they're going to be Raptured up."

"And they're willing to speak to the media about it? I thought they only spoke through the leader's proclamations."

"Well, they don't necessarily agree with everything Pastor Abraham says," the woman said, coming uncomfortably close, her hand brushing my arm as she flitted past.

"And why is that?"

"Well, it's like you folks in the media are always saying: it's like the Sickos don't trust God to be able to do the job of ending the world, so they have to help him along. But if they trusted in God, they'd let him do it himself."

I sighed. I was burned out from the pressures of reporting while my colleagues kept dying. I was hungry — Sophie hadn't been able to scrounge up more than some bouillon cubes and half a sleeve of saltines yesterday. I just wanted to crawl into bed and wake up when it was all over. And this woman — she'd insisted on meeting me here instead of talking to me over the phone, she kept touching me, or trying to, and now she was just spouting net-pundit talking points at me instead of telling me what her contacts might say.

"So do they belong to Pastor Abraham's church, then? Has he been predicting the end of the world for a long time?"

"Oh yes," she said, fluttering past me — and managing to touch me again.

I was about ready to crawl out of my skin. With social distancing rules, I hadn't been that close to a stranger for a long time, and I didn't like it.

"Pastor predicted Henny Penny before it happened — didn't call it by that foolish name, of course, but he said a pestilence was coming that would raze sinners from the earth, and now it's here. A lot of people are believers now who weren't eighteen months ago. The church has grown." She said it proudly.

Suddenly I realized she was one of them. Exhaustion was no excuse; I should have known. I'd been beyond stupid to put myself in harm's way by coming to her house. But the promise of the scoop, to actually talk to Sickos, had been too tempting.

I stood up. "I have to leave."

"But I haven't given you the information," she protested.

"You can email it to me, but let them know I will not meet them in person. If we have an interview, it has to be over the internet."

"They won't like that," she warned.

"Then they can find another reporter who will do it. Won't be me."

I picked up my notebook and pen and headed for the door. She accompanied me and opened it, touching me again and coughing as I brushed past.

I didn't think I'd touched anything in the house, but I didn't pay a lot of attention to how I stripped off my mask and gloves. I'd always been hit and miss with the whole sanitizing thing, anyway, washing my hands when I remembered to; not worrying too much if I forgot. When I added it all up later, I realized I would have been a walking disease vector by the time I left her house. I could have picked it up on my gloves, and then transferred it to the steering wheel, where it would have lived for another twenty-four hours. She could have passed it on any of the times she'd touched me — it was only later that we learned how long it lived in the weave of fabrics. It could even have come through the mask I was wearing: a single layer then, not the triple-layer masks the health officials were soon to recommend.

Within two weeks, I was on my deathbed, with a fever high enough to bring on seizures, and in agony from the sores that trailed down my left side.

• • •

The fear of strangers getting too close was part of my approach to the world now. My lizard brain didn't give a damn about vaccines and herd immunity.

Finally I was calm enough to move into the human traffic again, but my eyes kept darting around, on the lookout for threats.

True to the nature of the city, no one met another's eye or said hello. Even a world-altering pandemic can't change that kind of ingrained culture — although, to be fair, it was also smart to keep an eye on the ground because the sidewalk was cracked and uneven. Sidewalks were not a priority maintenance item when resources were scarce. And of course the masks meant we couldn't really smile at each other even if we'd been so inclined.

My office was still in its pre-pandemic space on the third floor of a five-storey building downtown. It was a fortuitous floor at a good address, low enough to be easily reached when the elevators weren't working and close enough to the city centre to have enjoyed continued service — water, sewer, electricity — all through the pandemic and its aftermath. The old government had tried shutting down offices altogether a couple of times in the early going of Henny Penny, in an effort to stem the rate of transmission, but when corporate landlords and downtown businesses had complained loudly enough about lost income, they'd instituted protocols for letting people back into the communal spaces, so some people had continued going to work all along. It hadn't been enough to stop the economy from collapsing, and many businesses had had to close, anyway, but it had forestalled complete economic failure. The regency had been encouraging people to go back to the workplace for several years, but hadn't made it mandatory until now.

Another woman walked in right behind me, so I chose to take the stairs in order not to have to share an elevator. My legs started cramping on the first flight and by the time I was halfway up the third flight, I had to stop. I stood panting and waiting for my calves to unclench, hoping no one would come along and see me — or have to brush by me. At that point, I couldn't have said which would be worse.

Finally I had enough control of my lungs and my legs to open the door to the office. I stood still while the blue light of the nuker ran up and down my body, then I stepped inside and greeted the receptionist.

"Hi, I'm Lily King," I said.

"Lily! Hi! I'm Jill," she said, excited, jumping up, and for a minute I thought she was going to hug me, but she stopped herself short of that. "Lovely to meet you."

"You, too," I said. "Good to finally put a face to the name of the person who makes sure I get paid. Half a face, anyway."

But what a half a face. Jill had obviously had no trouble finding makeup — the skin that was visible above her hepa mask was elaborately painted, with dramatic shading and glitter everywhere.

"I love what you've done with your face."

"I did it special for the special day." Jill laughed. "It doesn't always look like this. It's been like a parade this morning, all these people I've been emailing for years, getting to meet them. Bob did an orientation for them, but … You're a little late …"

"Yeah, I didn't realize how long it would take to walk."

"Want me to show you to your office?"

"I have my own office?" My memory of the bureau was of a maze of low-walled cubicles so that Bob, the managing editor, could look out from his office and see who was there to yell at.

"They had them built — the pods really didn't work anymore for social distancing, and we needed doorways for the nukers. Since there are so few people, there was plenty of room to create an office for each employee, in case everyone came back."

"Sure, sure …" Silly of me not to think of that.

I followed her down a long hallway in the middle of what had once been our bustling newsroom. Doors along the hallway were closed.

"BLT laws," Jill said as she led the way to my office. "If the door's open, you have to wear your mask and gloves, so knock first on any door that's closed — give them time to put them on. You have to wear them to walk in the hallway as well, so a lot of us mostly leave them on. Masks, anyway."

She opened the door, shrugging apologetically as she looked around the bare space. "The chair's new and everything's gone through the nuker."

She gestured for me to enter and as I did, the nuker inside my office door ran me up and down.

"The supply cupboard is across the hall and the kitchen is where it always was." She looked around again and nodded as if satisfied that she'd done all she could. "Why don't you get settled, and I'll tell Bob you're here."

I sat in my new chair — leather, of course, because it had been shown to not carry the virus the way textiles did — and surveyed the space. Basic desk, empty drawers. A few new pens for the notepad-sized whiteboard, a pair of reference books that someone — Jill, probably — would have had to painstakingly nuke page by page. I felt bad about that — it was so unnecessary. All of my files were on portable storage; everything I needed to do the job I'd been doing for the past ten years was either on my laptop or in my head.

Henny Penny had done me a favour, in a roundabout way. I'd been a copy editor until the pandemic, when I was pressed into service as the real reporters got sick and died. My gift had been with words and sentence structure; journalism itself had never been my calling. I died a thousand deaths every time I had to talk to a stranger and ask personal questions. Still, I'd done a decent job of it until Henny Penny got me.

• • •

"Lily, turn on your camera. I don't want to talk to your picture."

"Bob, you don't want to see me…" It had been five weeks since the peak of my fever with Henny Penny, but I was still weak and exhausted from fighting it. Hygiene hadn't been my most important consideration.

"Turn on the camera, Lily."

So I did, and watched Bob's face — slimmer now than it had been a year earlier, when Henny Penny was at its height, or even two months ago, before I'd become sick, but still soft and kind. He winced when he saw mine: gaunt, red eyed from crying. Hair lanky and greasy.

"Jesus, Lily, are you okay? When was the last time you ate?"

"I don't know. Today, I think. It takes a lot of energy to get food."

"Don't you have help? A roommate? What's her name …"

"Sophie."

"Isn't she helping you while you recover? You said she had great foraging skills."

"She left."

"She what? When?"

"What's today — Tuesday? A few weeks ago."

"Why the hell would she do that?"

"She said she couldn't take it anymore. She left some food and a note. I don't want to talk about it." Talking about it would have made me cry again; that was what I'd been doing before

Bob called. "How are you? Your family? What are you doing at work? I thought they closed us down."

Bob's wife and both of his adult children had survived Henny Penny. Most of our co-workers had not. For a while, it looked like the pandemic had also killed the news business, especially once the global internet crashed. Even though a good part of it came back fairly quickly, the government — which had just become the regency — had maintained firm control over who was able to publish. For the past few weeks, the only news source had been the regency itself.

"Ardythe and the kids are good. And the regency is letting us open up again, now that they've made sure they got rid of the wingnuts' ability to get their word out. I'm back in the office. Ardythe is our receptionist for now. I'm starting interviews tomorrow, hiring some more reporters — and a new receptionist. Husbands and wives should not work together."

"Is that why you called me? I don't want to report."

"It's not going to be the same ..."

"Ever again, Bob. I don't want to report ever again. If it means taking the regency's guaranteed income until I find a new job, I'll do that." The regency had also promised that everyone who, like me, had been moved closer to the city core during the pandemic would live rent free. I wasn't worried about money.

"Don't worry — that's not what I was going to ask you to do, anyway, though that option is always open for you if you want it. You're much better at it than you think. No, I have another suggestion: the regency has asked us to carry some lighter offerings — fiction, stories, poetry, that sort of thing. I remember you talking about submitting short stories to magazines and how happy you were when they were accepted. Would you be willing to do that full-time? The regency has suggested some parameters,

*but you could write pretty much whatever you wanted to. We'd
syndicate you; it would be a good gig. Hang on, I have to talk to
Ardythe for a minute."*

He muted his microphone and turned away; his wife must
have been standing in the doorway.

"Have you had time to think about it?" he asked when he
came back.

"I'm not ready to come back to the office," I warned. We'd
all been working from home for a year or more at that point,
carving office space out of unused corners of our homes, making
do with whatever computer equipment we had there while our
desktop computers sat gathering dust in empty offices. Even before
I became ill, going back would have been a huge adjustment; in
my recovery, I couldn't imagine being so close to strangers, having
to talk to them, to answer questions.

*"That's okay. Everyone who wants to will continue to work
from home. We'll get you a new laptop and office supplies, and
make sure you have a secure connection. The regency is giving us
whatever resources we need, so it's all easy-peasy. And if you're not
able to start yet, we can wait for you, but if you have any stories
lying around that we can use, so much the better. You can start
when you're ready."*

"Okay." It was a generous offer. No reporting, but for the first
time in my life, I'd be paid to write what I wanted. I'd have been
foolish to turn it down.

*"Great. And listen, I don't know if you heard, but the regency
is starting to make food rations available. Ardythe is going to
send you some information about how to get them delivered. The
regency is prioritizing Henny Penny survivors. Because you don't
have a support network, you should get right on the list."*

• • •

I was the Charles Dickens of the apocalypse. My work, written to government specifications and serialized weekly in net zines and online papers, ranged from ghost stories to science fiction to mysteries and travel adventures, all set in a magical time when the world hadn't lost a huge chunk of its population to a terrorizing pandemic. That didn't take a lot of research.

I'd known war reporters who'd needed more than one brush with death to deter them from their course, but that was all it had taken for me. I missed the newsroom, the back and forth between interesting people who knew interesting things, the adrenalin rush of a breaking story, the feeling of having a finger on the pulse of something alive. But story-telling was safer. My mind wasn't about to kill me — except maybe in the very darkest hours before dawn, and so far I'd managed to best it.

"Lily!" Bob was in the doorway of my office. "I'd give you a hug, but … I'll do this instead." He lifted his gloved finger-tips to his mask, gave a loud smack, then mimed sending a kiss my way.

"That's the best kiss I've had in years," I said, returning the gesture.

Bob stood for the nuker, then came in and sat down in my leather-covered guest chair. "So?"

"This is very weird."

"Ten years is a long time, kid. You should have come back ages ago."

"Yeah, well … you know."

"I know. How've you been keeping? What are you doing for fun these days?"

That was a strange question from Bob, the one person I'd spent any time talking to while I worked at home. "Did the regency tell you to ask that?"

"Yes, as a matter of fact, though you weren't supposed to be able to tell. I'm also interested."

"You're the only person I've been in constant contact with since ... " I waved my hand to encompass the past decade. "Believe me, if I'd had anything to tell, I'd have told you. I stay home, I eat pasta, I read, I write stories on deadline, and I binge-watch old TV shows on the net."

"What about a social life?"

"What about it?"

"Do you have one?"

"No. Who would I have one with? I have no idea how to meet people anymore — and Henny Penny killed all the dating sites. People are afraid to move outside their own bubbles. What would anyone do on a date now, anyway? There are no restaurants, there's no theatre, no one's making movies ..."

What I didn't say, the words that lay between us on my perfectly bare desk: *and everybody's dead.* I didn't tell him I was too scared to leave my apartment most days.

"Why, what do you do?" I asked him.

"I come to work, I see people ... Ardythe and the kids — we have a small circle of friends. People we trust."

"Yes, well." I shrugged.

"You can't have no one," Bob said, appalled. "What about ..." and then that penny dropped. Not only were all my old friends from the newsroom dead, but I saw the moment he remembered my best friend had simply disappeared after I'd recovered from Henny Penny, saying she couldn't take the restrictions anymore.

"You never found her?" he asked, finally.

"No."

"And you haven't met anyone since?"

"See above re: everyone being afraid to move outside their bubble. My bubble burst ten years ago."

"Jesus, Lily …"

My throat clenched and my bottom lip started to tremble, but I was damned if I was going to cry and embarrass us both.

I waved away his pity and forced myself to be glib about it. "Living alone, no social life … What else does the regency want you to find out about me?"

"Well, that was actually it." Bob slapped the arms of the chair as if to clear the threat of emotion from the air. "And now that I know it, I have to send you to a therapeutic touch clinic. A TTC. And you're going to have to go at least twice a week."

"What's a therapeutic touch clinic?"

"The regency just finished a pilot program. I'm surprised you didn't hear about it. They're rolling them out across the country now. It's essentially a massage."

"You're kidding me."

"Nope. A massage by a licensed practitioner, courtesy of the regency. Everyone without a partner is required to attend at least once a week; people who've had no intimate contact in the last year or more must go twice a week."

"They think that getting strangers to rub people down will stop the bonnellies?"

"The results of the pilot project were very promising."

"Jesus, Bob."

"Jesus, Mary, *and* Joseph, Lily. You're going. And you're going to write about the experience for me."

"Am I?"

"The regency wants us to get the word out."

"So even if I don't like it, I can't say so?"

"I don't think it will be a problem. I even went to one. It was nice."

"So first I do an advertorial, then you'll ask me to start reporting again?" A little chill of dread ran through me at the thought.

"Not unless you want to. Your stories are still the most popular thing we run, so I'm in no rush to put an end to them. That one you did last summer, about the fishermen who hauled in the treasure chest? I'm still getting requests from other outlets for that one — it's sending our syndication stats through the roof."

I smiled. I wasn't allowed to write sad stories, or anything critical of government. But a good mystery, where the underdog wins, was welcomed by the regency and the reading public alike.

"On the other hand," Bob continued, "I have an idea for a feature series, and I do want you to write that. We'll talk in a few weeks, after you've settled in."

"Okay," I said, not bothering to argue yet. We'd talk in a few weeks and I'd talk him out of it then. I still wasn't ready to report again.

Bob got up to leave.

"How many came back today?" I asked.

"You're one of ten people who's been working from home more or less full-time. We've had five or six in the office all along."

"Anyone I know?"

Bob shook his head. "A couple of bylines you might recognize, but no one you've ever worked with." He walked to the door. "Settle in, and I'll take you around to meet everyone later. And Jill will let you know when your first touch clinic appointment is. There's one in the building, so it's all easy-peasy." Bob shut the door on the way out.

All those closed doors. This was supposed to be less isolating than being at home?

I sat back in my chair and closed my eyes. Between the walk and its terrors, and talking to Jill and Bob, I'd had more interactions with people in the past two hours than I'd had in a decade, and my brain was wrung out from the effort. And I was going to have to meet more people later. And I was going to have to do this every day. I nearly cried at the thought.

On my walk home that night, I started thinking about visiting the TTC — what it would be like to be touched again. The last touch I remembered was when I was recovering from Henny Penny, Sophie helping me back into bed after a walk around our apartment left me drained. That was the night before she left. That made it a little more than ten years since my skin had come into contact with another's.

Where had those years gone?

I had told my Grade 12 yearbook committee that my favourite saying was *le temps passe inexorablement*. It wasn't anything close to my favourite saying, which was probably obscene and unpublishable, but it sounded erudite and adult and, above all, French, which epitomized erudition and adulthood to my teenaged self. It was a line from a pop song I'd learned that summer, and to me it spoke of the futility of fighting time — no matter what I did to stop it, or to hurry it along, time would pass at exactly the rate it wanted to and no faster, but it would in fact pass, and so, too, would "this," as promised.

If I had a guiding philosophy, I suppose that was it. If I waited out the bad things, they would pass; if I failed to enjoy the good things, they would pass. No matter what I did or didn't do, in fact, it would all pass, regardless of my having done or not done. And letting life grind on carried far less risk of failure or rejection than fighting against the inevitability of it all.

So that was essentially how I'd lived for ten years, waiting for it all to pass, for some invisible hand to change my lot. Honestly, when I tell you the better part of those years went by in a blur, that I couldn't remember them in minutes or hours, I'm not being disingenuous. Time was being itself, passing inexorably, and my life — my existence — was marching in incidental tandem. I could say that passivity was one of the scars left by the virus, along with decreased lung function and a series of pockmarks down my left side, except that it was also the story of my life. Fear of being shot down when I stepped up; coming of age in a house where boys were the stars and girls were surplus to requirements, being told I was making a spectacle of myself if I stood out for any reason, had left me loath to come to anyone's attention. I waited to be noticed, to be told to act. When I had wild impulses, I tamped them down until impulses stopped appearing, or until I stopped acknowledging them for what they were. Time didn't notice me, and I wasn't surprised that I passed under its radar.

It wasn't that I didn't keep track of small time. I did. I had a job; the job had to be done. I woke up each day, bathed, ate, sat down at my desk, logged in, and two or three times a month, when I submitted my latest instalments, I talked to Bob. Sometimes we had long conversations, although never about anything personal — that wasn't our way. He usually had to remind me to turn on the camera; I had no interest in showing my face to the world.

I worked for hours on end every day. Writing, researching, reading my fan mail: I didn't get a lot, but I got some, especially in response to family dramas, which the readers loved; or stories about people showing strength of will and a can-do attitude. Both would bring a stream of mail from readers, along with their own stories — some of which I borrowed with impunity. I rarely responded. I idealized contact to the point that I would rather go without than settle for something imperfect. I dreaded the possibility that I'd enter into correspondence with someone who didn't interest me, just for the sake of having someone to talk to. I wanted contact *and* meaning.

Between regular updates to the history of the pandemic — I'm one of the contributors, it's how I fulfill my mandatory volunteer hours for the regency — and my day job, I kept busy.

We all mark the passage of time in our own ways, but mostly we do it by the changes in people and things around us, whether it's green grass or snow on the ground; when the tree that used to be shoulder-high has inched above the roofline. Children have measurable benchmarks — they can lift their heads, sit up, crawl, walk, run, speak, argue, reach puberty, become adults — and there's twenty years. Ask parents where those years went and see if they can answer you.

I stopped looking in mirrors. Growing up, I had been discouraged from thinking much about my looks, and now that I was alone, I stopped bothering about them at all. There hardly seemed to be any point. At first, all I'd see in the mirror was this sad woman, wasted by her fight with a disease that had killed almost everyone she'd ever cared about. Although the initial sadness passed, that lingering, low-level grief never went away. In the ensuing years, mirrors would have told me that time had gone by — the increasing amount of grey in my hair, the new wrinkles on my face and weight on my body — if I'd bothered to consult them. Every so often, on one of my quick, fearful trips for food and supplies, I'd catch a glimpse of myself in one of the few plate-glass windows that hadn't been smashed or boarded over and would stop and stare, startled by the middle-aged stranger I saw there. But even that would just tell me a good deal of time had passed since the last time I'd looked. In the moment-to-moment time, in the day-to-day time, I would see no change. I only saw it in retrospect.

But ten years, you ask. Ten years without significant human contact? How can anyone not notice that?

Well, I wasn't living years, was I? I was living days. One day at a time. And I was filling those days. I had a purpose, a mission. I had a reason to get up in the morning — even though I wasn't on a clock anymore, I forced myself to observe the normal workday, just to give my life some structure.

Evenings were harder, especially once the electricity became reliable and I didn't just go to bed when it got dark, but stayed staring into my empty rooms, if there was nothing to write just then, or to read, or to watch: nothing to occupy my mind. I'd pull out my album of memories — swatches of fabric that told the story of the people I'd loved, the me I'd been. I'd touch the forbidden textures and remember that I'd once known joy and love. That was when I'd feel the absences bite; that was when they crawled into my head and slithered around, and I'd allow myself to cry — not too much, just enough to let off some pressure. Sometimes I'd make a plan to actually go into the office and see someone I knew, someone who knew who I was. Because I did see people, every time I left the apartment, although that wasn't often, but strangers didn't meet your eye. They didn't want to know. And I didn't want to know from strangers, either.

So those nights when I stopped long enough to notice the time passing and leaving me alone, to see the bare walls of my apartment, a place that was stark and impersonal because anything else was too painful, I'd either succumb to the gloom as much as I ever allowed myself to, or make plans. But in the light of day, there was always a reason not to follow through — I didn't have the right clothes to go outside, or my hair looked awful, or I didn't know anyone at work anymore except Bob, so what was the point. The distance between my home and the world outside became increasingly unbridgeable. I ordered a painting once, after one of those nights, to break up the beige of my rooms, but that was the only time I acted on one of my midnight plans. Three tulips rampant on a field of green were my one act of defiance — or maybe hope — against the void.

Time also passes at a different rate when you're living in your head, as I was. The worlds I created on the page contained fascinating people in exotic places, golden sunshine, the tinkle of ice in tall glasses, and interesting conversation. I made myself a vibrant character near the centre of each one of them. A person with a good imagination can be alone, but not lonely for — well, years on end, apparently. I'd lost all interest in what was going on around me, but I cared deeply about what happened in my alternate universes, where the people were more real to me than those I met on the street, had lives and dreams I could understand — and direct to my liking.

I guess I assumed that everyone else was in the same situation as me, or close enough. I knew that some people, like Bob, hadn't lost everyone, but they were a definite minority. And I figured the rest of us were sitting alone in our apartments, working, waiting for the world to get better, but needing someone else to take the first step.

If I'd thought about it, if I'd asked the right questions, I would have realized that the world could simply not have continued to function, could not have stabilized, if everyone had holed themselves up in their homes the way I had. I had electricity, for crying out loud. I had running cold and sometimes hot water. Most of the time, I had heat when I needed it, and working internet, and after the first couple of years of scrounging and food riots and then lining up for rations, reliable access to food. Outside, there were people walking, biking, driving cars — I could see that the world had continued to turn, even if my own little part of it was standing still.

What I hadn't realized was that people's lives had kept moving, too. I've always had that kind of blind spot, an inability to imagine people doing things if I'm not implicated in their lives, as if I expected them to go into stasis until the world spun them my way again. I'm always amazed by how much can happen when I'm not there to bear witness.

And despite their fear, despite the ludicrous masks, other people had continued to find ways to meet and fall in love and talk into the night, becoming 3:00 a.m. philosophers over shots of bootleg vodka. One of the reporters I'd been introduced to today had met his partner two years earlier at a dinner party thrown by friends. I was stunned when he told me that, as much at the thought of having friends who gathered together in the same room as at the idea of meeting and creating a relationship with a stranger. People continued to die, too, and they were mourned, and life went on.

That life could be different: that was what I hadn't seen. All my stories were set in some idyllic time when people met and talked and loved and *did* things — heroic, interesting, risky, ridiculous things like colonize Mars or take flimsy canoes down uncharted rivers, or slip into the Sun King's bedroom to steal the gems from his shoes. They didn't mourn populations lost to a pandemic; they took action to improve their worlds. Avoiding reality was part of my job description — and my work was my life. So time just kept passing. Inexorably.

That's how ten years happens. The blink of an eye.

Going to the TTCs

THAT WAS NO massage.

I'd had massages, used to get them regularly: nice, long, deep-tissue explorations of my shoulders and back — sometimes the gluteus maximus, if I felt like shaking it up a bit. I'd get off the table an hour later a little trembly, a little spacey, blissed out from the endorphin release and smiling every time I moved and it felt like my muscles were bruised. That, to me, was the sign of a successful massage.

This left me aching, but not in the same way.

I sat in my new leather chair behind my desk in my new office and tried to write about the experience I'd had at the therapeutic touch clinic, and I collapsed into tears. I'd never been violated like that, ripped apart and exposed in all my vulnerability, all my tendernesses open to the air. My psyche was bruised. I couldn't imagine putting anything in my stomach, and yet I was beyond empty.

How the hell was I going to write about that?

I'd had to go up to the fifth floor for my appointment. A receptionist showed me to a beige room with a sink, a massage table — just the leather-covered table, smelling faintly of the alcohol they would have used to wipe it down after the last client, no sheets or pillows. The dim lighting and soft music were the only holdovers from my massage experiences in the past.

The receptionist told me to leave my mask and gloves on and when the technician came in, she was similarly covered.

"I'm Bethany," she said. "I just need to ask a few questions before we start. How long has it been since you've been touched by someone else?"

"Ten years."

"So you haven't seen a loved one or even a doctor in ten years?"

"No. Loved ones are dead. My doctor died shortly after I recovered from Henny Penny, and I've never looked for a replacement."

"You've had no medical check-ups in ten years?"

"No."

She wrote something down with a stylus on the tablet she carried. "How do you get your vaccine?"

"I get the needle at the vaccine clinic they set up in my building every year. We inject ourselves."

She nodded, made another note. "And you're healthy?"

"Yes."

"When was the last time you had a cold?"

"Eleven years ago, I guess. I couldn't say."

"Tell me, how do you touch yourself?"

I frowned, taken aback. "You mean masturbation?"

"Well, we'll get to that, but let's just start in general. Do you touch yourself?"

"Nnnnnooo," I said, as I realized that I actively avoided it, touching my skin only when absolutely necessary for cleanliness.

"Why do you think that is?"

"I hadn't thought about it at all until just now. I guess because it is … unsatisfying," I said, groping for the right word. *Alien. Painful.*

She made another notation and set the tablet down on the desk.

"I'm going to hug you," she said, and I nodded but I tensed up, too.

I'd never been much of a hugger. Hugging was what you did with grandparents and boyfriends, never strangers. My family was not affectionate, and for the most part, what friends I had were likewise observant of WASP-y boundaries. Sophie was, of course, as always, the exception. She respected no boundaries — was always hugging and kissing and touching, her nature truly tactile. I had learned to accept it from her, even to appreciate it eventually, and missed it when it was gone.

Bethany approached me and put her arms around me and held me close for a torturous, excruciating minute. To be that close to another human being, to share her warmth and the lingering aroma of her lunch and her laundry detergent, was bizarre. I wasn't prepared for the rush of sensation. Unable to decipher all the unfamiliar messages it was receiving, my brain responded by hitting me in the stomach, where I always experienced anxiety and stress. I couldn't tell whether I'd enjoyed it or hated it. I felt scalded.

"How was that?"

"Confusing," I said, after a minute, and she nodded as if that was the answer she'd expected.

"Take off your shoes and lie down on the table, on your back, please."

I did as instructed.

"Close your eyes," Bethany said, and I did that, too.

And then she touched me.

And it wasn't a massage. She just touched me. Bursts of warmth against my clothes and whatever bit of skin they left exposed. At first it was simply a laying-on of gloved hands: she'd rest them in a spot, let that spot grow warm, and then move them to another spot, which might or might not be adjacent, and warm it up, and then move again.

I'd been ready to bolt after the hug, but with each little warming, I relaxed a bit more; I opened a bit more. I did that. I laid myself bare. I was so taken aback by the unfamiliarity of it all that I let down the walls that had been inviolate for a decade, the protective tissue that had shielded me from the reality of my situation, from the true extent of my loneliness and my unwanted solitude. I let her touch my weakness.

She had me roll over and started again on my back, where she stroked lightly, rhythmically, hypnotically, from the middle of my back to my edges. I started thinking, *This is where I begin, and this is where I end. I go this far and no further. I am here.* And that was a mind-blowing thought. I mean, I'd been me, and I'd been there all along, but somewhere I'd lost of my sense of "I" and the physical context of my being. I was being reminded that I was *I* and I was *there* and that someone else had taken note of my presence. Even though I'd spent most of my life avoiding attention lest it harm me, receiving it in this gentle way felt like a wonderful, cruel gift. *I am noticed, therefore I am.*

It was too much. I forgot my inner rule about crying in front of others — or, at least, I couldn't make myself obey it. I just curled up into a ball and ... bawled. Cried like I hadn't let myself in years — not the controlled burn of my lonely nights, but with all of my newly exposed heart and soul. I never allowed myself to cry like that because once those walls cracked, there was no holding back the deluge. Once that surge of emotion took you by the neck and started wringing, you could strangle on it. And I did. I was a great, big, heaving, choking mess of self-awareness.

Bethany told me later she always makes first-timers her last clients of the day because there was no telling how long the appointment would take. My reaction was a little extreme, she said, but not unusual.

"I don't usually cry during a massage," I said, sniffling. I had finally managed to sit up on the table, while she'd taken a seat at the desk.

"The psychologists call what you have 'skin hunger.' There are all these little nerve endings close to the skin, called C tactiles, that exist to tell the brain you've been touched. When someone you trust touches you for long enough, those nerve endings send a message to the brain, and the brain responds by releasing oxytocin, which makes you happy."

"Do I look happy?" I asked, choking back another sob.

She nodded. "Muscles store memory. They'll avoid the bad memories — if you were hurt, say, on the lower left of your back, you might find yourself unable to bend over, to avoid activating that particular muscle memory," Bethany said. "Being touched for the first time in a decade brought back good muscle memory for you, but it also released the trauma of the memory of not having been touched. Think of it as your muscles suddenly releasing after you'd been holding them clenched for a long time. There's relief and also pain. While the touch is good for you, mentally and physically, your brain and body are at war with each other right now over what you're feeling and how to process it."

It hurt to get up from the table, but as soon as I was on my feet, my legs buckled and I grabbed the table to hold myself up.

"I don't know if I can stand," I said. "What did you do to me?"

"I showed you what was missing, that's all," she said. "How are you getting home?"

"I was going to walk."

"I'll call a car for you. I'm going make another appointment for the day after tomorrow. Same time. And I'm going to refer you to a doctor. It never hurts to get a check-up."

Despite my fear of getting into a car with a stranger, I could only nod. At the thought of being touched again, I started to cry once more.

"Will this stop?" I asked her, embarrassed, accepting her offer of another handkerchief in a sterile wrapper.

"Eventually, but it may take a while," she admitted. "I have you down for twice a week, but that may not be enough. You've been out of the game for a very long time."

She hugged me again before I left. It felt a little better this time.

I managed not to throw up until I got home, which was one small blessing.

I spent a lot of time in the next few weeks, tossing around the idea of skin hunger. We all used to laugh — back in the early days, when Henny Penny still seemed controllable and we could still find things funny — about how odd it was to watch movies made before the pandemic, where people gathered in large groups and touched each other casually: a quick, one-armed hug; pecks on the cheek on meeting and goodbye-ing; a hand on the shoulder to demonstrate support. A decade of solitude later, it was as foreign as watching apes groom each other, picking off lice and ticks.

My skin could still feel warmth and lack of warmth, it hurt when I cut myself, but I never experienced tenderness or ecstasy — those are sensations others create for you. I couldn't imagine sitting close enough to someone for our legs to touch, let alone formulate a memory of experiencing bliss at another's hands. I didn't just have skin hunger, I had chronic malnourishment, the kind that diminishes one's humanity. Everything was dull, one note. Someone whose skin had never starved for affectionate contact could never entirely understand it. I had never tried to understand it myself — I was just living it — until Bethany gave it a name.

The second visit was as bad as the first. And the third was only marginally better. I was skinned and gutted, hypersensitive to the elements. Everything hurt: soft rain pierced my face, a light breeze harrowed the back of my neck. My Impermatex-treated clothes grated where their roughness touched my body. My brain processed every sensation as pain, as if it couldn't tell anymore.

"Where's that article?" Bob started asking when we passed in the hall.

I had a list of excuses. Story deadline. Editing to do for the regency pandemic history, which would always trump my deadlines for Bob. Couldn't find the lede.

I didn't want to tell him about the great heaving pile of emotion that I became each time I went. Bob and I were work friends. The closest he'd ever come to seeing me as myself — the closest I'd ever let him get — was when he'd called me after Sophie left, to offer me my current job, and even then, I'd deflected his attention from my misery as much as I could.

"It's an advertorial, for chrissakes," he'd say impatiently. "Just write something nice about the experience."

I couldn't tell him that that was impossible for me.

"Why isn't this getting any better?" I asked Bethany in despair after my tenth visit, as I lay curled in the fetal position on the table, snivelling and snotty, with all the dignity of a three-year-old whose blankie is in the dryer.

"'Better' is subjective," she said, maddeningly vague. "You have a lot of trauma stored in your muscles. A lot of pain, a lot of suffering, a lot of rejection, a lot of refusal to admit there's a problem. Every time you come here, a little more of that is released. This could be a long process." She shrugged. "Do you have anyone to talk to?"

"You think I need psychiatric therapy, too?"

"Don't you? You're functional, but your body is telling me you're deeply depressed — the way the muscles resist, flinch away from me. Even if you didn't spend half of every session crying, I'd know. I suspect there's a certain amount of rage, too — most women have a store of it. Society has never taught us how to express it safely, so we hold it in and drink too much or eat too much or bite our fingernails to the quick. It might help to talk to someone. I'll give you a couple of names."

We talked only at the end of these sessions, which allowed me to concentrate on the sensation. It was surreal, being in this intimate space with another person, and giving that person the freedom to explore my body, however fully clothed. And once my brain stopped telling me that every touch was painful, it started telling me it was something else. Although there was never anything remotely sexual about the therapy — even if I'd been in a headspace to be seduced by a woman in surgical mask and gloves — my body reacted as it would to a touch with far more seductive intent.

"Tell me what's going on with your body," Bethany said about a month in. I blushed and she nodded knowingly. "That means we're making progress," she said. "Are you normally attracted to women?"

"Not as a rule," I answered.

"Your brain is still figuring it all out. You're a sexually healthy woman. When no touch is sexual, all pleasant touch is sexual, whether you'd normally be attracted to the person doing the touching or not. There's a false intimacy here, but when it's the only one you have, it's powerful nonetheless."

"Is it transference, then?"

"Not really, because I don't think you're falling in love with me. You would likely have that response no matter who caused it. I see a lot of this. It's normal."

· · ·

Bob appeared at my office door. "Where's my story? I need three hundred and fifty words. You making a life's work out of it?"

"No, it's just harder than I expected."

He came into my office and sat down. "It should be a gimme, Lily. What's hard?" He looked at me sharply. "This isn't about you not wanting to report, is it?"

"No, it's not that. Let's just say my reaction has surprised me. Not the therapist, who's seen it all before, but me. I'm finding it hard to process."

Bob clearly didn't understand. Like any good editor, he wanted more detail — and in this case, I was going to have to give him information that we'd both prefer I kept to myself.

"Bob, when was the last time you went to bed without a goodnight kiss?"

He rolled his eyes, but didn't answer.

"For me it's been more than a decade. Not just Henny Penny, but before that, too. You can't even imagine it. Neither could I. But every time I go to that damned clinic, I'm forced to confront that reality, and it hurts."

"Fine. Don't psychoanalyze your response on the page, then. Write, 'I go to this place twice a week and this is what it looks like and this is what happens …'"

"And then I go home and throw up because it upsets me so much."

Bob was taken aback by that — not only the idea that I'd throw up after what, to him, had been a totally benign experience, but because we simply … didn't share deep personal confessions, unless it was well after the fact and telling all was in aid of a good story over a drink. Didn't particularly want to hear the other's deepest secrets, or at least had never broached the subject. I'd just given him too much information.

"Jesus, Lily …"

"Sorry. You didn't need to know that."

"No, I think I'm glad you told me. I thought maybe you were just having trouble getting back in the saddle. I had no idea this could actually be hard."

I shrugged. "Neither did I."

"Okay, so write about it, with as little or as much detail as you want, but I need to have something, and I still want you to write it."

"Why?" I asked in a more pitiful voice than I'd intended, and I swallowed hard against the tears that came far too easily these days. "Surely some of the others who came back …"

"Yeah, but … well, remember I said there was a feature series I want you to write? This article is required writing for the regency, but it's also a stepping-off point for the other thing."

"What's the other thing?"

"All in good time."

So I wrote my piece; formulaic, probably not as enthusiastic as the regency might have wanted for its star program, but not as dark as it could have been. What little journalistic instinct I had wouldn't let me make up details, and it would have been irresponsible to allow people to think it was all sunshine and lollipops behind the closed doors of the treatment rooms, but the private person I'd always been didn't want to expose too much of my personal torture, either.

And eventually it did get better. I started stepping into the hugs. I was able to get off the table without experiencing pain. I stopped crying like a baby before she even touched me, and best of all, I no longer threw up after sessions. But I never did seek therapy, because I already felt like I was giving away too much of my inner self to Bethany, who continued to preside over my flayed soul twice a week. I didn't want to open another vein for another stranger.

Meeting Eleanor

IT WAS AROUND this time, when the TTCs were starting to work for me and going to the office every day was gradually becoming normal, that I became friends with my neighbour. She and I had scared each other at least three more times before I worked up the nerve to say hello one day as we walked down the corridor to the stairs, she slightly ahead of me. She said hello back but barely turned her head to do so. She got to the stairwell door first and bolted.

I had no idea how long she'd been living on my floor — the building was well soundproofed, and when you leave your apartment as rarely as I did, you miss things. But now that I knew there was another woman approximately my age living nearby, I was consumed with curiosity about her life and was determined to get to know her better. And she seemed equally determined to avoid me.

Knowing about what time she left, the next day I waited for her. But she never showed.

The day after that, I got ready early so as not to miss her, but did so anyway. No way to tell whether it was by chance or design.

The third day she was in the hall, not quite at my door, when I opened it. "Good morning," I said. "I'm Lily."

"Eleanor," she replied. While I still had to stifle my impulse to shake hands, she didn't appear to do so — people who'd spent time in the world were better at that than I was — but there was still an awkward lull where the handshake would have gone.

"Nice to meet you," I said. She nodded. I couldn't tell whether she was shy, afraid, or just unfriendly.

She started to walk toward the stairwell again and I blurted out, "Eleanor — you want to get a drink?"

She stopped, and it looked like she might be smiling under her mask. "A bit early," she said.

"Tonight? After work? There's a bar down the street ..."

"My Happy Place," she said, and I answered, "Really?" and a little ice broke.

"Four thirty?" she asked.

"I'll see you then."

"I have to run," she said, and I waved her on, smiling at having successfully made my first approach to a stranger in years.

The bar looked like an old-fashioned ice cream parlour, with black-and-white checkered tile floors and bold pink and turquoise paint. It was furnished with chrome kitsch — chairs covered in vinyl and tables topped with Formica. It was all miles away from the look of an average pub, or a bar for serious drinking. The patrons were almost entirely female, women leaving work at the end of a long day and having a giggle with a girlfriend. Not that there were many patrons, maybe half a dozen women in business suits drinking the kind of drinks that used to come with an umbrella.

"Where do they get the sugar?" I asked Eleanor after we'd ensconced ourselves in a booth with a tall glass of the bar's signature rum punch in front of each of us.

"Mostly from fruit, probably." Eleanor shrugged. "My husband, Dan, swears every kind of alcohol these days tastes like apples or peaches on some level." She pulled a metal straw from her purse, dropped it into her glass and slipped it under her mask to take a drink.

I made a mental note to buy one — I had to use the waxed cardboard straw the bartender had given me, and as soon as I removed it from its paper wrapper, I could tell it wasn't going to hold up.

That first drink was a disaster, of course. Neither of us knew what to say to each other, and I'd never been good at small talk at the best of times — always the person in the corner, listening, rather than the one with something to say. And she seemed at least as bad at starting or maintaining a conversation with someone new. There were a lot of awkward silences that first day. But we promised to do it again, and I knew I had to try harder. People were still living and making lives, I'd just discovered, and were going along fine without me. I had a lot of catching up to do. I had questions to ask her — *When did you meet your husband? Before or after the flu? How do you live? Do you have friends? What do you do to keep from giving in to the despair?* That kind of thing.

The next time we went, it was better.

I got there first and was already in a booth with a drink in front of me when she arrived, her cheeks rosy from the chilly October evening.

"What are you drinking?" Eleanor asked, dropping her coat onto the opposite bench.

"Singapore Sling. Well, not a real one, but as close as we're going to get these days."

"That looks yummy. I'm going to get one, too."

Eleanor went up to the bar and, moments later, came back with her own.

"Cheers!" we said, clinking our glasses together before slipping our metal straws under our masks and taking a drink.

"That's lovely," she said. "I don't think I've ever had one before."

"This isn't exactly a textbook Sling," I said. "It's missing the grenadine, so it's not nearly as sweet as it should be, and the gin is iffy."

"You're a Sling expert, then?" she asked.

"I'm a girl-drink drunk," I admitted. "I hated the taste of alcohol even before they started making it in bathtubs. I had a traumatic experience as a child — I came downstairs one Christmas morning and there was this cute little glass by the sink that I'd never seen before, and of course I had to use it, so I poured some water in and drank it and nearly threw it back up. I later learned that it was a shot glass and my parents had had a drink or two while wrapping presents."

"Moral of the story: using clean glassware prevents life-long trauma."

"Precisely."

"Was Christmas a big deal at your house?"

"Within limits. My mother made a big production of it, but she left when I was nine. My father pretty much left the celebrations to the grandparents, and when they died ... well, we'd get a tree if my brothers went out and got one; we had Christmas dinner if I made it. Presents, at least for me, were strictly practical."

"But not for your brothers?"

"No," I said, taking a long drink. "No, my brothers were kings — they got special things. They would share with me sometimes."

"You sound like Cinderella."

"Do I? Maybe. Dad was deeply hurt when Mom left. He never talked about it, and neither did his parents. We lost complete touch with Mom's family. As far as I know, they never tried to contact us. But he never remarried, and was bitter toward women, including me, for the rest of his life. Women are meant to do work without being seen or heard. But that's enough of that. What were the holidays like at your house?"

She told me about her mother's embrace of Halloween, and even seeing only the top of her face, I could tell the delight she took in the memory of spooky decorations and elaborate costumes.

"I feel sorry for today's kids who are never going to experience that kind of licence to be absolutely silly," she said. "Imagine a world where people open the door to strangers."

"I wonder if it will ever come back."

"Halloween, Christmas, Valentine's Day, Easter — those chocolate feasts of our childhood are probably gone forever. What would people even put in the treat bags? There's barely enough sugar to make alcohol; no one's making candy anymore. And chocolate is like unicorns — you hear about it, but you never see it."

"Ah, chocolate, we knew ya when," I said, and we clinked glasses again and drank.

Eleanor caught the bartender's eye and wagged her glass at him, then held up two fingers.

"This is sooo much better than last time," she said, sitting back in the booth and looking at me.

I nodded. "Introductions are always awkward. Plus it's hard to know what to say to someone you've never met — you don't know what questions are too personal, or what will be a trigger."

It was Eleanor's turn to nod. "You're such a mouse, I didn't even know you lived on the floor."

"I didn't even think about who might be living on my floor," I admitted. "I was never agoraphobic in the clinical sense, I don't think, but until we were ordered back to work, I didn't really go outside unless I had to for food."

"I was afraid of the Sickos for a long time," she admitted.

"I was infected by a Sicko —"

"Holy shit!"

"Yeah. I'm getting better, but I still panic walking into crowded places. The unknown unknowns."

We started meeting every Friday for cocktail hour. We were more likely to talk about the perils of online shoe-shopping than to dig deep into each other's souls, but Eleanor was easy to be with. There was no drama, just a sly and dry sense of humour that made me laugh. She wasn't a social convenor, like Sophie had been, creating excitement and demanding that I participate in it, but she was the friend I needed to ease me back into the idea of society and spending time with other people.

I started to feel almost normal.

I remember the first time I noticed that the world once again had colour in it, and pretty noise. It was the end of

October as I walked in the late-afternoon dusk along a tree-lined street to my apartment. Dry leaves rustled underfoot and the air was filled with the scent of earth hunkering down for winter, the decay that would bring new life in the spring. It was as if the grey pall of desolation that had covered my eyes for years had been lifted. I was becoming interested in the world around me, starting to feel the tingling of regeneration, new growth in places long dormant.

Even at the TTC, for a small period of grace I felt calmed, gentled, as the healing warmth of Bethany's hands knitted the broken parts of me back together. Between that and my new friendship with Eleanor, I was rejoining the world in some small but important way. I started paying attention to my surroundings, the colours in the anti-BLT graffiti on downtown walls. I stopped thinking of people I passed on the sidewalk as potential Sickos and started noticing what they were wearing, whether they were talking to other people. It was as if I'd dropped acid and was seeing everyday things through new eyes that found them strange and fascinating. I was interested in something outside myself for the first time in a long time.

But of course, as soon as everything in my life started getting better, I began to notice how unsatisfying it all was.

"Why do we keep our masks and gloves on?" I asked Bethany. "Why am I dressed? We've both gone through the nukers. We're both vaccinated. Wouldn't this have more impact if it were skin to skin?"

"It's a protective measure," she said.

"Protecting whom from what?" I asked.

"You and me from each other," she answered, then shrugged. "And until the regency changes the law, it's illegal to take them off because, in legal terms, this is a public place. Have you gone to the doctor yet? Or done any psychiatric therapy? You really should."

I started to crave the feeling of flesh on flesh in ways I hadn't allowed myself to do when there was no touch at all. I itched with it and unconsciously scratched myself just to feel something, not noticing what I was doing until I'd drawn blood. I resented being unable to see Bethany's entire face when we spoke after the treatments. Her touch-stroke routine did not vary from session to session. I started timing each touch: it was a remarkably steady thirty seconds everywhere except on my face, where it was twenty. I wondered why it was different for my face. I wondered if she was counting, too.

I was distracted. Whenever I get distracted, therapy, no matter what it is, stops working for me.

I experimented with going to other easy-to-reach clinics, to see if a new therapist could bring back that initial feeling of release. The regency was offering the service for free, so there was no reason not to. Male, female, old, young: the technicians had all learned at the feet of the same master. All offered the exact same service. It wasn't enough anymore.

When I started noticing other people noticing me scratching, I made an appointment with the doctor whose name Bethany had given me during my first session.

"What can we do for you today?" she asked, sitting behind her bare desk in her spare office, only her framed diplomas on the stark white walls.

"I've been scratching myself a lot," I said. "I itch everywhere. I'm worried I have eczema or something. And I'd like to discuss tranquilizers. I'm feeling ... unsettled."

"Do you have a rash of any kind where it itches?"

"No."

"What does the itch feel like?"

"Like bugs crawling on or under my skin."

"Do you take drugs, or have you recently stopped?"

"No, not at all."

"Okay, well, I'm going to do a basic check-up, since you haven't had one in so long, and we'll see where to go from there."

She left me alone in the examining room to strip off my clothes and put on a paper hospital gown.

The doctor gave me a full physical, from blood pressure to Pap smear, before telling me to get dressed again and join her in her office.

"Pending the results of your tests, I'd say you're doing well. You should maybe vary your diet a bit — hard to do at this time of year, there's not a lot of fresh food out there, but a few more veg, a bit less pasta."

"Okay."

"I don't see any sign of a skin condition, but I'll prescribe a lotion for you. Your skin's quite dry and that might be at least one source of your problem. You can pick it up at the front desk on your way out." She tapped at the keyboard of her laptop for a minute, then hit enter.

"What about a tranquilizer?" I asked.

She sat back in her chair and looked at me, appraising.

"I had a look at your records. I see you've been going to the TTCs," she said.

"Yes."

"What do you think of them?"

"They've been helpful," I said.

"You worked from home until the regency sent everyone back? That was what, ten years?

"Yes."

"Is there anyone in your life now?"

"No. Well, I've started making friends, but no intimate friends."

"So your only physical contact is at the TTCs?"

"You just touched me more intimately than anyone has since well before the pandemic," I said.

She nodded. "You've been going a lot. Maybe a bit too much?"

"Maybe." I was wary. Where was this going?

"Want to talk about it?"

"Not really." I'd come for tranquilizers, not talk therapy.

She raised an eyebrow at me. "Try."

Resigned to having to give her something, I told her about my TTC experience, and how instead of filling in the gap left by physical contact, it had exposed the void.

"And now, I guess I'm bored. I keep looking for that reaction — not the extreme reaction I had on my first few visits, because that was unpleasant, but ... now I feel no different afterward than when I went in. Does that mean I'm cured?"

"When did the itching start?"

"I started noticing it a month or so ago, maybe. It's been getting worse."

"How would it make you feel not to go back to the TTCs?"

My stomach lurched at the thought. What would there be if I didn't go back?

"Sad, I guess. For all that I don't really feel the same therapeutic value, it's touch, you know?" *I crave it,* I thought. *My skin cries out for it. It has become consumed by its hunger. I gouge my flesh with my fingernails in order to feed it something.*

"I think your itch is psychological," she said. She closed her laptop and leaned forward, elbows on the desk, eyes unblinking above her mask. "I'm going to suggest something, and I'll deny ever saying such a thing if I'm asked, but if you're not in a position to meet anyone to fill that intimate space in your life — and I know it's harder than ever these days to make meaningful contact — you should consider going to a petting zoo."

I was shocked. "A what?"

I'd heard of petting zoos, everyone had, but no one I knew would ever go to one — for one thing, they were illegal, both for having too many people in a public place and for defying the mask and glove laws, not to mention social hygiene and basic human decency. We'd all read reports of the busts, of the people who crawled around naked, begging to be touched, and the perverts who stood outside the corrals and did as requested. We'd all read the salacious true confessions by various people named "Anonymous" who talked in veiled euphemisms about the disgusting things they'd done, and we'd all snorted in prurient derision at their weakness. Nodded in satisfaction at their harsh sentencing to work on farms or other physical labour.

And yet. I was almost curious enough to give it a try. If asked, I would say that I was put off by the taboos — the dirt, the indignity, the ickiness of crawling in front of strangers.

But in truth I was deeply intrigued by the idea of being free enough to overthrow whatever social mores I'd been raised with and seek out what I needed without caring that anyone might think it was uncivilized. That was what I desired almost as much as the prospect of contact itself — the possibility that I could shut off the finger-wagging part of my brain and just do the thing that I wanted to do, no self-flagellation, no chagrin.

I had had the occasional random desire to be homeless, and I made the mistake once, long before the pandemic, of telling someone about this craving, the mistake not so much in the telling as in the context. I said it to a friend whom I didn't know had spent two winters living on the street, addicted to heroin; for whom the idea of homelessness had lost its romantic cachet.

"You don't want to be homeless, believe me," Chris had said.

I'd been shocked by his appearance when we reconnected on social media years after graduation. He'd looked decades older than he should have, his once-almost-pretty face pockmarked, his lanky body much too thin. I'd been bewildered by his insecure employment, his seedy address, and his apparent comfort with both, but didn't feel that a loose connection on the internet gave me the right to ask about it. Like me, he hadn't come from money, but unlike me, he'd learned somehow to get along happily on very little of it. I was envious of his equanimity with not having.

Homelessness and heroin would explain how he'd won his peace with it.

"Okay, you're right, I don't want to be homeless." I was embarrassed by having said it in the first place, having opened up in the intimacy of a late-night chat room, and desperate to explain myself. "What I want is to be unencumbered by things and the desire for things and the responsibility to maintain those things, which for me is all wrapped up in the idea that I have to live a life that fits within a certain social hierarchy and idea of morality.

"I want to be like you, in a place where want doesn't frighten me."

"You want to stop being middle class," he had said know-ingly. "The rich are arrogant enough to think they'll stay that way, and the very poor have nothing to lose. The middle class have just enough that they can't bear to let go of any of it, for fear they won't get it back."

Through the food riots, the mass unemployment, and the near collapse of the economy, before the regency was able to restore order, we'd all learned more than we'd ever wanted to know about want and need, but even so I had never reached Chris's depths of indigence, or his level of freedom. Sophie's foraging skills and a steady job had buffered me from the worst of it — if I had nothing, it was because there was nothing to have — and once I recovered, I simply resumed my previous position in the social order.

Sophie had managed to slip the lines, although whether her escape route was unencumbered life, or death, I didn't know. But I remained tied, never able to divest myself of my self, the one that obeyed laws and did the right thing and sought approv-al for having done it. Sophie didn't care what anyone thought of her. It was part of what I had liked about her, of course. I've always been drawn to those who personify my secret desires.

Despite my inner *bourgeoise*, there were times in the past ten years when I might have gone to a petting zoo. But I knew about the zoos the way white bread knows about heroin or S&M dungeons — we'd heard about them, but they were so far from our reality we'd never encountered them. I wouldn't have had the first clue where they were, and even with clear direc-tions, I would probably have been too timid or embarrassed — or afraid of my reaction — to have gone through with even a first exploratory approach.

But this was a doctor telling me to go.

"Hear me out," she said. "I know of a zoo that's clean and well run — one that I might go to myself, if I needed it. I've sent other people in your position there, and they've been very pleased. I think you should consider it. Frankly, in my opinion the TTCs have done as much as they can for you; from now on, they're only going to frustrate you more. You need a deeper level of contact, and this is a way to get it. And it's a far better cure for what ails you than pharmaceuticals."

She stood and came around the side of her desk. "Think about it." She left a business card with a phone number on the edge of the desk, then left the room.

I picked it up and put it in my purse. I didn't look at it. I was pretty sure I already knew where it was going to lead me — the same place the letters were telling me to go.

• • •

When the first letter had appeared on my desk, it was eerily as if someone had taken a peek into my brain for the best way to appeal to me. My name was written on the front in black ink by a someone with lovely penmanship, although the letters were just slightly off — as if the English alphabet was not the writer's first.

The envelope itself was art: linen texture, in the colour of new cream, handmade with precision. I'd always had a bit of a fetish for nice paper. I loved scenes on TV where someone got a letter and the paper would have an audible presence — you could hear its thickness; it crackled importantly as it was folded and unfolded, passed around. I sometimes used to buy high-quality paper just to hold it, run my fingers over it. I'd never use it, never risk defiling it with my imperfect handwriting or unworthy sentences. I just wanted to have it, to admire it.

And the letter inside — it seemed like the author knew, not just about my love for fine paper, but also that the touch clinics would provide inadequate sustenance for my skin hunger. The author only ever signed a single initial, but I decided after the first few that a man was writing to me.

The first letter had come a few days after my piece on the TTCs was published, telling me about a different kind of experience at his petting zoo, which sounded luxurious and inviting. Over the course of months, I received several letters, one every couple of weeks. The writer addressed me as a friend, despite the fact that I never responded.

Dear Lily,

I hope this letter finds you well. I'm enjoying your latest adventure, your evocation of midwinter in an age when people could gather in numbers for days and weeks on end. I'm looking forward to learning the secret contained in the ornament. Am I perhaps assuming too much, however, when it seems that your heroine's dissatisfaction with her life might mirror your own desire for something more?

Of all of Henny Penny's deprivations, the loss of Christmas saddens me the most. I miss the colours, the feeling of camaraderie, the one time each year when you could walk down a street and have strangers smile at you and wish you peace with good will. It was a time of magic, of giving from our hearts. Even for those who didn't observe the religious occasion, it was hard to escape the sheer joy of the season. And now it is just dark and grey. I still get a little tree and put lights and a few baubles on it. It both warms my heart and creates a haunting sense of melancholy.

Winter is often a time for drawing closer to oneself, for introspection. The short days encourage us to look into our souls to gauge the levels of light and dark and determine what we might need to balance the two. It is so hard to make contact of any kind in this world. I would make a gift of it to you. Something between the sterility of the TTCs and the squalor of the petting zoos you've read about — something that offers dignity and beauty as well as the touch that we all need to remind us of our humanity.

To hear from you is my fondest hope. I wish you a pleasant Yule.

K

The letters compared the therapeutic touch clinics to early medical marijuana — a watered-down version of a highly potent black-market cure. And some of the letters didn't mention the zoos at all. They talked about philosophy and life and the nature of the human condition, and I was growing more and more intrigued by the writer. Whether he knew it or not, he was seducing me — by the level of the argument, by the beauty of the writing, by showing me glimpses of his humanity. And also by bothering to try to engage me in discussion at all.

All those years I'd avoided responding to my fan mail, knowing instinctively that it would leave me wanting more, like the TTCs. K seemed like the correspondent I'd been waiting for. But his intellectual challenge was accompanied by something that frightened me — not the thing itself, but my need for it — and for that reason, I was reluctant to respond, afraid of that need overtaking me. There was no question that the letters fed into my dissatisfaction with the TTCs. Letting me know there was something more, if only I had the nerve to reach for it.

As shocked as I'd been by my doctor, I was more surprised by the source than the suggestion itself. Because by then I'd been seriously thinking about responding to the letters — K had outlined a way of communicating. No expectations, no expiry date. Any time I wanted.

And then, just after New Year, Bob came to me with his little pet project, completing the triangle of desire, opportunity and licence. We should have both known it was irresponsible for him to offer it to me — him because, as my employer, he would have known I was spending an unhealthy amount of time in the clinics. And me because by then, I knew I was behaving like an addict looking for my next high, and he was ordering me to go to the warehouse where they kept the drugs. Neither of us could resist.

"I want you to check out a petting zoo," Bob said when he came to me a day or so after my doctor's visit and asked if I was ready to do some real writing.

Jesus. Did *everyone* think I needed to go to a zoo?

"Haven't they been done?" I asked as calmly as I could, although in his hands I could see the bright glimmer of the key to my desires.

"Yes and no." He got comfortable in my guest chair and I settled in for a story. "A few years ago, it occurred to me that while we hear only about the sort of grubby, trashy zoos where perverts go to play, the world has all kinds of different people, and it made sense that there would be other kinds of zoos. The places that get busted by the cops are the grotty alleys where skid-row junkies shoot up, say, but we know for a fact that there are addicts with money getting high in nicer spots, right? So I've had my ear to the ground for years, and I've been listening for any mention about the possibility of a higher class of petting zoo."

"And you found one?"

"I can help you find someone who could help you find someone who could get you into a high-class zoo."

"You just want me to go and check out the fancy zoo? Tell you what I see?"

"More or less. One of them, anyway."

"One of them? How many are there?"

"That's the thing — you hear about one zoo and you think that's not so bad, and then you hear something else, and you think that can't possibly be the same zoo. God only knows how many there actually are, or what they're actually like."

"Just a bunch of consenting adults feeling each other up."

"Well, there's some scuttlebutt that not everyone is consenting." Bob shifted in his chair, uncomfortable. "Some people — loners, with no family to raise a hue and cry — are getting caught up in something bad."

"Like ..."

"Maybe human trafficking. No one really says."

"And you would send me, a loner, into the lion's den? Thanks, Bob."

"I don't think the zoo I'd send you to is the one you need to worry about, let's put it that way. I've been collecting information — rumours, impressions — for a while. I'll give you my file. But I'm fairly certain it's a different operation."

"Why are you sending me? I'm barely a journalist, let alone someone with investigative skills."

Bob sat forward, elbows on his knees, to make his pitch. "The thing is, I don't want a news item — I want a feature, a magazine piece, with a few sidebars. The regency is gearing up for its annual crackdown on the zoos. I want something I can splash, an alternative to every other zoo story out there. All we hear about are the shooting alleys. It'd like us to be the first to talk about the opium dens, and you're my best writer."

"Opium dens?" I asked, raising an eyebrow.

"Whatever. Something more opulent than an alleyway. What do you think?"

"Hmm."

"Hmm?"

I dithered for a moment, then opened a drawer in my desk and pulled out the top envelope from a small pile.

"What's that?" Bob asked.

"An invitation."

"To?"

"I think to the kind of petting zoo you want me to try out."

"Uh-huh ..." Bob's face showed puzzlement. He hadn't expected this.

"I walked in one day and it was on my desk. Jill didn't know how it got there. I ran it through the nuker a few times and then pulled out the letter inside and ran it past the nuker a few times, and then I read it."

"And?"

Bob held out his hand, but I was strangely reluctant to give it to him. Not only would it have been obvious that this was far from the first letter, but this had been my secret, my little dilemma — to answer or not to answer — and I didn't want to share it. The person who had written the note was at the centre of one of the most illegal games in town and was inviting me to come and play. Just me. And I was tempted. So tempted.

"Lily?"

"I got it after I wrote my piece on the Therapeutic Touch Clinics for the regency"

"And you didn't think there was a story in it?"

"I didn't know if it was a story I wanted to tell," I said honestly. It was a story I'd wanted to live.

"Who's the writer? A concerned citizen looking to expose them?"

"No, I think it might be someone who works there, or maybe even the owner. They don't specify. I'm not sure what the motivation for writing to me is — whether they want publicity or what." The invitation had sounded personal, and certainly the successive letters had been, but behind it all, I sensed a yearning to be understood and accepted.

"Well, that's that, then," Bob said, slapping his gloved hands on his legs. "We have our way in. That was way easier than I expected."

I shrugged. "Sure."

"No?"

"I'm not really interested in reporting again. I've told you that. And undercover's not my thing."

"So, don't be a reporter, be a storyteller. And don't be undercover. They wrote to you, they invited you, knowing where you work and who you are. Be up front about why you're there. Maybe that's what they want."

"Maybe." I was torn. Going in on a professional level would satisfy my inner censor by deflecting responsibility for my actions, but the need to be an observer would put me at a remove from the process. I was afraid I'd be neither as satisfied by the experience as I wanted, nor as objective a reporter as I should be. But I knew I wouldn't say no. My show of reluctance was *pro forma*; I'd known I'd go the minute Bob suggested it.

"RSVP to the invitation and get something started. Work your source. If you can walk in through the front door instead of having to make up a story to get in, so much the better. If we think there's stuff you're not seeing, or if you find anything that points to a trafficking operation, I can send in someone else to do undercover. If you need credits, we're good for that. Arrange to meet in a public place. I'll send a bodyguard with you just to be sure this is on the up and up."

"A bodyguard? That's a bit much, isn't it?"

"For the first meeting, at least. I insist. And make sure it's in a place where there will be other people. That's a nice envelope, but you can't tell a person's character by the quality of their paper."

And just like that, it was done. After all those times in the years since Henny Penny, when I'd wished I could find a petting zoo to go to, I now had an invitation, a prescription, and an assignment to do so. A trifecta of legitimacy to overwhelm any noise from my bourgeois conscience.

That was how in early January, I found myself in a booth at a pub near the office, with a heavy-set guy sitting at the bar ready to protect me if I needed it. Both of us kept an eye on the people walking through the snow and slush outside, twitching to attention if anyone came near the door.

Bars and restaurants had all been closed in the early days, victims of the BLT laws, food shortages, and a faltering economy, but the rules surrounding public gatherings had been relaxed in the last year or so, allowing bars to open under strict occupancy conditions.

The Cock and Bull had been a grotty little pub before the pandemic, and nothing much had changed in the intervening decade: the greasy red carpet had been pulled up, flags taken down from the walls. The bathrooms were cleaner, because fewer people used them and the inspectors checked for hygiene compliance far more stringently than before. The kitchen was long closed, so the pub's former fug of boiled cabbage mixed with cigarette smoke was gone. But it was still an airless basement, its grimy windows showing just the footwear and pant cuffs of the passing crowd, and it still had so few customers that I wondered how it stayed open. I used to assume mob money propped it up, but I didn't know whether the mob had survived Henny Penny. Probably. Crooks and cockroaches always endure. I'd chosen it for its proximity to the office, not for the ambience.

When I walked in with my bodyguard, there'd been an old guy nursing a drink at the bar, and a pair of lovebirds at a table in the corner, sitting closer than I was used to seeing, making eyes at each other as they sipped their drinks through straws, gloved fingers touching.

The bartender was watching some decades-old show on the internet as he polished glasses. Bottles behind him sparkled in the pot lights embedded in the ceiling, different shapes and sizes holding fluids of various hues, all the progeny of some bootlegger's bathtub and bearing only passing resemblance to the alcohol they purported to be. It was hard to get good stuff these days, but lack of quality didn't seem to stop people from drinking this swill. I'd gone on a bender or two myself in the early years, trying to find solace or oblivion, depending on the day, but my one real bit of self-care was to stop drinking in any volume. It made me maudlin, made me vomit, and gave me a headache. And it didn't solve any of my problems.

I had my laptop open on the table in front of me, but my eyes kept darting from the screen to the bodyguard to the door. All my life I'd been early to appointments. Always being early means that everyone else always seems late, even when they're on time. The moments that pass between my arrival and anyone else's are excruciating chasms over which I must make repeated leaps of faith that the other will show up.

Mid-leap, I saw a man enter, look around. Tall and slender in a navy pea coat and grey scarf, dark hair peeking out from under a matching toque. His eyes found me at my booth and he nodded, and then he went over to the bar, where he ordered a drink and spoke quietly to my bodyguard, who shook his head, said a quiet word or two in return.

When the drink came, the man took the glass in one hand and a paper-wrapped straw in the other and walked toward my table. My bodyguard watched him but was visibly relaxed. Whatever he'd said, the guy hired to protect me trusted him.

That's interesting, I thought as I closed my laptop. And a bit worrying.

The man placed his toque and winter gloves on the table and sat down across from me. He unwrapped his straw, plunked one end into his drink and slid the other under his mask. He winced slightly at his first sip — it obviously had a rougher edge than he was used to.

"That bad?" I asked.

"*A*, you should never drink whisky through a straw …"

"And *B*, that's not whisky," I said, and he laughed.

"Hello, Lily," he said. "My name is Kaz." His voice was deep, lightly accented. Whatever his original language was, he'd learned English from a Brit.

He shrugged out of his coat. He was wearing jeans and a blue V-neck sweater with a white shirt underneath, all looking more natural than any Impermatexed fabric I'd ever seen. I wondered for the first time whether different grades of it were available at different prices. My own business suit felt rough and poorly made in comparison. Getting dressed that morning, I'd uncharacteristically hesitated over what to wear, and had finally chosen the black suit and a red blouse, the nicest outfit I owned, legal or otherwise. I'd wanted to make a good impression.

"Hi, Kaz."

"I was pleased to finally hear from you."

"It took me a while to figure out what I was going to do with your invitation."

"What made you finally decide to answer?"

"My editor asked me to write about your zoos."

"So you answered because you want to write about us?"

"Let's get this straight right now — my quandary was whether to respond in a personal capacity. My editor assigned me to write a story to which you'd serendipitously given me the entrée. So I will write about the experience, but I'm also a potential client."

So odd, trying to read half a face, to gauge sincerity by eyebrows and eyes alone, without the additional subtleties of lips and chin. I couldn't tell whether he was disappointed by my answer, or pleased.

He took another sip of his drink, and I took a sip of mine, and we both sat back on our benches, relaxing a little now that my cards were on the table.

"Was the bodyguard your editor's idea?"

"How did you know he's my bodyguard?"

"George? He's done some work for me. But don't worry, he's a professional. If I were to threaten you in any way, he would protect you. He owes me nothing."

"That's not entirely reassuring. That's how you knew he's a bodyguard ... how did you know he was here with me?"

"I know what he does for a living and I know this isn't his bar. I made an assumption."

"What did you ask him?"

"Whether there was a photographer or police waiting for me."

"You expected police?"

"I was more worried about a photographer. Although this would be an excellent chance to set me up."

"Except I'd probably do it after I saw the zoo, not before," I pointed out.

"Touché," he said, acknowledging the logic of that, and took another sip of his drink, wincing with it.

"But you sent me the invitation. Why would you do that if you were worried I'd answer just to set you up?"

"I'm a fisherman. I bait the hook hoping for one fish, but am aware that something less pleasant might bite. I sent my letters to Lily King, writer of short stories, but I know you work for a news organization."

"I'd thought maybe you were writing because you wanted me to write about your zoos."

"I wrote because I think you'd find my zoos a far more satisfying experience than your TTCs, and I hope you'll consider joining. But you're not wrong — I've recently decided it might be time to tell the zoos' story, and so I also wanted to determine whether you should be the one to hold the pen."

"And how will you do that?"

"We must first establish trust. I need to know who I'm dealing with before I start spilling my secrets."

"Okay. What do you want to know?" My directness seemed to take us both by surprise.

He considered my question for a moment before answering. "What was your life like before the pandemic?" he asked, his dark eyes searching mine.

"Normal," I said finally. "Good job, decent social life, nieces and nephews who I didn't see often but who loved me and whom I loved."

"Friends?"

"Sure." Sophie's face flashed into my brain.

"Who was that just now?"

"Where?" I looked behind me, puzzled.

"The friend whose face you just saw, who was that?"

"Sophie," I said carefully.

"Lover?"

"No. Best friend."

"You miss her more than your family?"

"No … it's just …" How to explain that empty spot? "She didn't die — she disappeared."

"You can't mourn her if she might still live."

"That's right."

"So what do you do?"

"You know what I do."

"I know what your job is, but I'm trying to find out about you."

"Why?"

"Curious. Interested. I need to know where you're coming from before I can know where to take you."

I started to feel a little angry, and a little trapped. As I wrestled with the urge to just leave, I looked over at the lovebirds in the corner, practically on each other's laps now, cheeks touching as they whispered into each other's ear, maybe. I wondered if the bartender would try to break them up, or call the police. That was definitely prohibited under the BLT laws.

Kaz turned to see what I was looking at, then turned back to me and shrugged. "Do you disapprove?"

"I thought you were taking me to your zoo," I said, finally. "You said meet me here and we'll talk about going to the zoo. This isn't supposed to be about me."

He took off his scarf, folded it neatly, and placed it on the table beside his hat.

"If we were just going to the zoo, I'd give you an address, set up an appointment —"

"Why didn't you?" It was rude to interrupt, but this was interesting. "Do you ask all your prospective clients to meet you for a drink first?"

He looked a little abashed; a touch of red crawled up his cheekbones from under his mask.

"Not all of them — just the ones whose motives are open to scrutiny. And it was a fair guess this time, as we've established. I also have another agenda, so we are on the same page. But if I'm going to open up to you about my business — and, for reasons I will explain to you, I do hope to do that — I need to know who you are. I know you're a writer, but I don't know anything about you otherwise."

"I'm a person who lives alone and eats too much pasta," I said. "I read books and I drink tea and write stories about better times."

"Take me to your place," he said suddenly.

"What?" That was completely unexpected.

He shook his head. "Don't worry, I'm not going to hurt you."

"Said the prime suspect in any number of slasher films." I laughed nervously.

His eyes crinkled at the corners; maybe he smiled.

"I don't know what seeing my place will tell you about me, or how it could tell you more than I can sitting right here."

"Look at it this way — I know I reached out to you first, but you're in the power position. You could report me at any moment. For all I know, anything you say to me is a lie. By seeing your place, I will get a far better idea of who you are and what you might do with the information I'm prepared to share."

"Or you know where I live if I report you, and you need to exact your revenge."

"I don't need you to show me where you live to know your address," he said, and while I heard no menace in his voice, I felt that he could be menacing if he wanted.

"Well, if you can find that out, you can find out anything else you want to know about me, too."

He shrugged. "This way of learning is more instructive."

"Why do you assume I'll lie?"

"I have to assume it. it's less dangerous for me that way. So take me to your place. We can take off our masks, look each other full in the face, and talk about what we can do for each other."

I hesitated.

"You can bring your bodyguard," he said.

"You seem to have turned him," I pointed out. "I'm not sure he's still on my side. Plus, I don't want him to hear our conversation."

"So park him outside the door." He looked me straight in the eye. "It'll be fine."

"It's about a mile and a half away."

"I have a car."

We left the bar and started walking, Kaz at my side and George a discreet ten paces behind us. I had a quick vision of myself running through a graveyard in heels.

Ten years ago, the bars along this strip would have been hopping even on a weekday evening, packed with university students and civil servants celebrating the return from Christmas holidays, the start of a new year. My fellow reporters and I used to congregate at a place that was closed now, although I thought I could see ghosts of us, and the politicians and bureaucrats who used to come out to play with us, as I passed by. My current co-workers and I just went home at the end of the day.

Tonight it wasn't yet dusk and the streets were empty. The odd pedestrian walked by, hunched over, eyes looking strictly at a point in the middle distance and not at fellow travellers. As if germs were subject to ocular spread.

Taking a stranger home was madness; taking two didn't feel any less so. I wasn't sure why I trusted Kaz — probably because he'd been talking to me for months, telling me his thoughts, and he would have been playing a very long con if he was a different person from the one he'd presented on the page. I felt like I knew him.

As we arrived at the car, I turned to George and said, "I think I'm good. You can go. Bill us for the full night."

"You sure?" he and Kaz asked at the same time.

"I'm sure," I said to George. "If he's going to kill me, he'll do it whether you're there or not. I feel silly taking you with me."

"Said the victim in any number of slasher films," Kaz murmured under his breath, surprising a laugh out of me.

"If anything happens to her, you know where to find me," Kaz said, and with one more searching glance at me, George went on his way.

"So was that the stupidest thing I've ever done?" I asked.

"We'll find out," he said, unlocking and opening the passenger door of his high-end SUV for me to get in.

We drove in silence. Just like my first cocktail night with Eleanor, I found I didn't know how to start a conversation with a stranger I wanted to get to know. I'd been imagining for months who and what the writer of those letters might be, building a story around him and the things we'd say to each other. I wanted to have a conversation with him about real things — not something you could cover in a five-minute drive. I didn't know where to begin to talk small.

We passed nearly empty storefronts, crumbling sixty-year-old office towers and solid hundred-and-sixty-year-old low-rise retail buildings in the city core. All of them were covered in graffiti. Lately, a group calling for an end to the BLT laws had been spraying its message all over the downtown; I saw it everywhere on my walk to and from work.

The building where I lived was six storeys high, my condo on the fourth floor. The elevator was working for once, and the short ride to my floor was as silent as the rest of the journey had been.

I stepped inside the apartment first to be scanned by the nuker, and then he followed. I left my wet boots on a mat and directed him to do the same before I hung up our coats. I took off my mittens but kept the gloves that were underneath, and reached automatically for my mask, the way I would any time I came home, but stopped myself. I wasn't ready to go bare with a stranger. He left his on as well.

"Can I make you a cup of herbal tea? I'm afraid that's all I have to offer."

"Sure, that would be nice, thank you."

He looked around at the room. Tile floors, a little hardwood. No carpet, of course. Wooden table and chairs in the dining area, leather couch and armchair on either side of a plain coffee table. Walls unrelentingly beige. My tulips on the wall over the couch, but no pictures, no photos of family.

"Have a seat. I'll be with you in a minute," I said, heading for the kitchen.

Instead of making himself comfortable, though, he followed me to the kitchen, and while I filled the kettle and put it on the stove, he looked through the cupboards, opened the small fridge, and peered inside.

"Hungry?" I asked, surprised at his snooping.

"No," he answered, before continuing his tour of my apartment.

I followed him as he went to the bathroom, looked through the medicine cabinet, sniffed my shampoo, surveyed my linen closet, peeked briefly into Sophie's old room, which was empty except for a bed with a bare mattress and a few dust-covered boxes, then came into my bedroom. He opened my bureau drawers one by one, touching the odd garment, and then repeated the exercise in the wardrobe.

"What the hell ..." Bemused by his inspection at first, I was growing furious at this intrusion.

"I'm looking for you. Where are you in this place?"

Irritated as I was, I didn't bother pretending not to know what he meant. I went to the bedside table, opened a drawer, and pulled out a photo album. The kettle started whistling. I slammed the drawer shut, put the album in his hands, and returned to the kitchen to make tea.

He took it into the living room and sat down on the couch.

I carried two mugs in and handed one to him before sitting in the armchair opposite him. "Sorry, no milk, no sugar, and nothing to snack on, as you probably noticed on your tour."

"This is fine," he said. He held out the album. "Show this to me."

I had to get up, sit beside him on the couch, close enough to feel the heat from his body, smell a light cologne.

I took it from him and held it for a moment, my hand on the cover, a garish photo of Niagara Falls. I looked down and realized that I was still wearing my gloves.

I pulled them off and hesitated for just a second before I removed my mask. I was afraid to expose myself — to him as much as to the virus. I hadn't been in the same room with another person without a mask on in more than a decade, and I breathed deeply to control that anxiety loop — fear feeding on fear — as it tried to kick in. This was what I was going to have to do in order to build trust with him.

A glancing rush of cool air from the room hit my over-heated face. He put down his cup and followed suit. I couldn't help staring at him as he stripped off his mask. What a wonder to see another living face this close: not Bob on camera or an actor in some twenty-year-old movie. Nostrils and lips and five-o'clock shadow, teeth and chin. Light olive skin close enough to touch. The gloves came off. He had long, slender fingers, lightly dusted with dark hair; tidy, buffed nails. A thin gold bangle slightly bigger than his wrist, watch, no rings.

He lifted a hand to the book and I came out of my reverie. Our eyes met.

"Hello, I'm Kaz," he said, his voice husky and soft, and even though he'd introduced himself at the bar, it didn't seem strange that he'd do so again. Without the masks, we were different people.

"Lily," I said, wanting to touch his face, the brush of grey in the hair at his temples. What was he, maybe forty-five, fifty? Maybe a little older than me, but not much. "Nice to meet you."

We studied each other's faces for a moment, and as I drank his in, I wondered what he was seeing in mine. Cheeks reddened from the cold outside, maybe, and from my earlier anger. Skin that was starting to lose the elasticity of youth. I wondered if he felt the same overwhelming impulse to touch a cheek, stroke an eyebrow. Lean in and sniff where shoulder met neck.

"What's in the book?" he asked, and I watched as his lips and teeth formed the words. What wonder there was in a face in motion, in the act of speaking.

Finally, I shook myself minutely and looked down at the album. What was in it?

I opened the cover and revealed scraps of fabric, glued on one edge to the pages so they could be lifted and appreciated from both sides; swatches of colour and texture representing my former life. "When we moved here during Henny Penny, I was able to bring only a certain number of boxes. I created a memory book with pieces of things I had to leave behind."

"Tell me about them. Teach me about you."

The first square was navy-blue corduroy. I fingered the familiar thick nap as I told Kaz the story. "I was pretty sure Matt was the person I was meant to spend my life with. He got assigned — he was a war correspondent, and he was assigned to cover something somewhere, it doesn't matter now, and he didn't come back. And then six months later, Henny Penny." The pants had been baggy in the ass, but he'd loved them. He'd torn a hole in the knee just before going on his last assignment, so he'd left them behind. I'd promised to mend them.

The next piece was thick cotton flannel. "This was a night-gown I took the first time I went camping with Matt. He laughed at it and then ... rearranged it into something more to his liking." I smiled to myself at the memory of him ripping it strategically in the dark tent, saying I wouldn't need flannel to keep me warm.

Kaz watched my face as I remembered, but didn't push for more detail.

A silk square with alternating matte and shiny stripes in a rich purple was a scarf I'd borrowed from Sophie and kept for myself. We had different taste in clothes, but what we liked of the other's wardrobe we borrowed freely.

There was worn blue gingham from an apron my mother had made for me when I was a young girl eager to help in the kitchen. I had few memories of my mother and happy mem-ories of her were fewer still, but this was one I'd held on to.

"This is from my nephew's favourite bear. He gave it to me to keep me company after Matt left ... and then never came back for it."

A piece of rabbit fur from the warmest mittens I'd ever owned, a gift from a quirky aunt. I stroked it with my finger-tips, each individual filament lighting a fire on the sensitive pads. I closed my eyes and lost myself in the pleasure for a moment.

"You're not afraid of catching something from this fabric?" he asked as he ran the rabbit fur between his own fingers.

I fought the urge to pull the book away, to protect my memory. "No." I shook my head. "This has all been washed and nuked. No free riders here."

I closed the book before he could see that I'd put one of his letters in it, so that I could admire the textured paper at will and think about the person who'd written it. I set the book on the coffee table, then picked up my mug and sat back on the couch. "That's my life, in there. All the memories that matter."

I blew on my tea and took a drink, obscuring my face for as long as I could. I felt indescribably naked.

Then I looked up. "So? Now you've seen me."

"I'm the first person you've had in here since the pandemic, aren't I?"

"Since I nearly died, yes. Sophie lived here for a while."

He looked around the room, assessing it. I felt anger mixed with shame bubbling under my skin, at his boldness and his pity.

"Cut to the chase, Kaz. You wanted to see my place, now you've had a look around — this is my life, what there is of it. Here it is and here we are."

"Can I ask just one more question? Why did you agree to meet with me?"

"I told you. Because my editor wanted a story and because I was curious about your zoos. Can I ask *you* a question?"

"Of course."

"Why did you write to me in particular? Everyone was doing articles about the TTCs; did you write to all of them?"

He shook his head. "I've read your stories. One of the things I like about them is the empathy you show for the human condition — no matter the condition. I thought you might have the imagination it took to see my zoos as something other than criminal." He laughed, suddenly self-conscious, and said somewhat shyly, "I pretended I was writing to a character in one of your stories. I enjoyed it."

"I enjoyed them, too," I admitted. "And you convinced me that I shouldn't dismiss out of hand something I had no first-hand experience of."

"Tell me, do you still go to the therapeutic clinics?"

"Yes."

"What are they like?"

"Have you never been?"

"That surprises you?"

"Well, yes. You've been telling me not to judge the petting zoos without going — but you were very judgmental about them in your letters."

"I'm not completely unfamiliar with them. I want to hear what your experience of them is." He took a sip of his tea and relaxed into the couch, watching me.

I weighed my response for a second or two, but quickly decided there was no value in not telling him the truth. I wanted him to understand why I would seek out what he had to offer without a hidden agenda.

"Well, you read the sanitized version. The unsanitized version: for the first few months, I cried every time, then came home and threw up. It hurt in ways I didn't expect it to, mentally and physically. I hadn't been touched in ten years. That's a long time."

"Had you ever considered going to a petting zoo?"

"I'd heard about them, of course, but there were a lot of things stopping me from going. A fear of going bare with anyone, let alone strangers. I'm still not sure I can. I haven't been maskless with another person in years, and this, right now, is freaking me out a bit, to be honest."

"That's not unusual," he said. "Masks are safe, so mask-less is unsafe. You have to learn to be in the world again."

"That's it. I spent nearly ten years barely able to leave my apartment because I was afraid of the virus. Between going back to work and going to the TTCs, I'm getting better about that. Six months ago, I wouldn't have been able to go into that bar without having a panic attack, much less go bare with you here. Plus, what I read about the zoos was unpalatable, to say the least. The lack of hygiene as well as the lack of dignity. So for a while, the clinics were giving me what I needed, but in a safe way, a way I could trust."

"Were?"

"I don't know how often people go to the zoos ..."

"It varies."

"I started going to the clinics twice a week, regency mandated ..."

"Because you hadn't been touched in a long time ..."

"Yes. And before, even, before it stopped hurting to go, I started going more often, because once I'd allowed myself to feel anything, the hurt was better than the not hurting. And then when it started feeling better, I started going more often still, days when I felt sad, or days when I felt happy, or days when I just needed a little tweaking. I go about five times a week, trying different places, different practitioners ..."

"And it's not working anymore?"

"I've been testing it, to see if different technicians or places will give me a different experience, or a better one, and none of them do. I feel like I've built up a tolerance to it."

"And the masks and gloves."

Grateful that he seemed to understand, I peeled away another veil. "It's so stifling, so oppressive and invasive, this person touching you and you can't see their face, don't feel their fingers on your skin … there's contact but no release." It makes me want to scream.

"Are you ready to go bare in a room full of strangers, to be this close or closer to people you don't know?"

"I don't know. I think I need to be."

"What do you know about the zoos?"

"Only what I read about in the news when clubs get busted."

His scowl would have told me what he thought of those clubs, even if his letters hadn't already done so.

"That's why I never seriously considered going to one," I said. "But I'll tell you that in the middle of the night sometimes, I find them appealing because there is contact, however it happens."

"Despite your fear."

"Fear's the thing that stopped me. But one day, something was going to be stronger than fear."

"So when I told you there was another option …"

"When my editor approached me, I was about to contact you. You were offering to show me what I'd been looking for and didn't know how to find." I took another drink of my rapidly cooling tea and set the mug on the table in front of us. "So that was my motivation. What's yours? Why are you thinking about telling your story now?"

"I'm tired of hiding. That's the quick answer." He looked at his watch. "I have to go now, but," he reached into his pocket and drew out a card, "come to this address tomorrow at two, and I'll introduce you to one of our vanilla zoos. You can decide then whether you're there as a journalist or as a prospective member, or both."

"They have flavours?"

"There are various levels. Everyone starts out at what we call a vanilla zoo. You'll also have a medical exam and a psychiatric assessment."

"Psych assessment? Really?"

"We try to weed out potential problems — unwanted behaviours. The zoos are as safe as we can make them, which is something that the ones that get busted can't say. Tomorrow you can do the tests. I'll make the arrangements. If you pass them and decide to join, we'll process your membership and book you in for a zoo later in the week. I'll give you a tour and tell you about the operation then."

I hesitated.

"What's wrong?"

"It's just ..."

"What?"

"I don't even know how anybody really goes to any of these places. Don't people worry about getting sick? Don't they die?"

He reached out a finger, held it near my cheek. "May I touch you?"

My breath caught in my throat and my jaw clamped shut. I nodded.

His finger drew a path of fire down my jawbone, the nail softly scratching. Every fine hair it touched stood on end.

He said, gently, "This is what you get at my clubs, Lily. It's as safe as possible. No one gets sick. Nobody dies."

"But it's still illegal."

"It's a victimless crime. It's been ten years. It's time to throw some of your caution to the wind."

Talking to Kaz

THE ADDRESS ON the card was in what had once been the city edge of the suburbs, where the office buildings stopped and closely packed look-alike houses had once clustered around streets that led to nowhere but more houses in the same subdivision. Those houses had been derelict for a decade, if they hadn't already been destroyed by cleanup crews, so there was no reason to service the streets. Fortunately, the main road out of the city was kept in relatively good condition, potholes patched and regularly plowed.

I drove to the meeting — I'd finally had the flat tire fixed after a long run of rainy weeks late in the fall and was starting to use up some of the gas rations I'd been stockpiling. It was still strange to be behind the wheel after so many years of not driving; there just had been no place to go in my tightly wound life. I only ever got in the car when I couldn't face having to come into contact with people on the sidewalk.

There was almost no traffic, but I braked out of habit at a stop sign, where I was distracted for a moment by city workers in hazmat suits carrying a velour sofa to a dumpster that was already loaded with the detritus of a life: upholstered chairs, clothes, a mattress. I assumed that, like me, everyone had untreated textiles at home — the regency might send you to a work farm for wearing untreated fabrics in public, but it wasn't going to bust anyone for sheets or towels. I was a little surprised that furniture upholstered in fabric was still being destroyed, though I supposed it was because after spending years in derelict houses it was mouldy and riddled with vermin. I remembered big bonfires in the streets years ago as people burned books and furniture — anything presumed to carry the virus. And even now society didn't trust untreated fabric, though any virus it might have harboured should have been long dead. Suspicion ran deep.

I hadn't realized how big the job to clean out the city's sprawling suburbs would be, or that it would still not be complete after all these years. Everything that was salvageable and useful was sanitized, nuked, and sold on.

One of my new co-workers had written about the warehouses where the things the cleanup crews found were stored. They were full of reclaimed lumber, copper wiring, pipes, and ductwork — even pink insulation for repairs and the rare new construction. He'd described buildings with rows and rows of mirrors of every size and description, twinkling crystal chandeliers hanging from the rafters; pottery and sculpture; and hundreds, maybe thousands of glass-fronted cases full of crystal, china, and silver, all of which could be bought for a very reasonable price. My tulip painting had come from just such a warehouse. I'd shopped for it and ordered it online. It was on board, not canvas, so had seemed safe enough. An artist I'd admired but whose work I could never have afforded before.

Once the houses were stripped, whatever was left was burned, and nature was allowed to take its course. As I drove on, I saw after-burn birches, alders, and poplars that had already put down roots in many of the old neighbourhoods. In the summer, there would probably be blueberry patches. An entire ecosystem was re-evolving as people turned inward for once in their history, shrinking into communities their own size instead of forever encroaching on new territory.

I gripped the steering wheel as I drove through an unseasonal rain, the logical part of my mind trying to convince me to turn around, and the irrational part, the part whose language Sophie had spoken so fluently, daring me to keep going. The windshield wipers seemed to take sides in the debate, swished go, don't go, go, don't go, in a hypnotic rhythm as I wrestled with the implications of what I was about to do. For all that I was justifying this as my job, just another reporter meeting a somewhat sketchy source in a secret location, I was also deliberately setting myself on a criminal path, something I couldn't have contemplated even a year ago.

I'd looked into the penalty for being caught at a petting zoo. There was no trial, no recourse. People were arrested and immediately sent off to work at some sort of labour — forestry camps, mining camps, road crews, far away from civilization; such was the taboo of seeking physical contact outside one's safe social bubble.

But Kaz's fingertip on my cheek haunted me. That drizzle of honey on my hungry skin.

I was struck by a flash of panic as I pulled into the nearly empty parking lot of the address Kaz had given me. My heart started racing and my hands trembled on the steering wheel. I was miles from the safety of my home. I'd come without a bodyguard, and I'd taken a personal day from work, not wanting to tell Bob about it until I had packaged the experience into a narrative that felt safe to me. I hadn't wanted to share the anticipation, hadn't wanted to give him a glimpse of my excitement, my need. So no one knew where I was, and I didn't know anyone here, except for Kaz.

"You're about to become a criminal, Lily," I said to myself, trying it on to see how it felt.

I was a little taken aback when the chill of fear became a thrill of excitement. For most of my life — and certainly for the past ten years — I had not surprised myself in the slightest. I had done nothing where the outcome was unknown, where I hadn't analyzed every action's possible reaction and compensated for it on my mental balance sheet before taking a first step. I hadn't felt this excited since the first time Sophie took me by the hand and, with a twinkle in her eye, said, "Come on, let's do something crazy."

I was about to do something extraordinarily irresponsible, and while I still cared about what people might think about me for doing it, I was willing to go ahead anyway. The thought was exhilarating.

"Here's one for Sophie, then," I said, as I turned off the ignition and slid the elastics of my mask behind my ears before gathering up my purse and gloves.

From the outside, the building was a squat, nondescript

cube, the relic of some short-lived city-planning attempt to move offices out of the downtown. Inside it was warm, with dark wood panelling and the kind of floors that I'd always loved, charcoal-grey slate with rusty traces of oxidized iron, a touch of cobalt, and the occasional yellow flash of sulphur.

I looked up from the floor to see a young woman sitting at a reception desk, a tag bearing the name "Jane" on her chest.

"Hello," I said.

"Hello, and welcome," she replied, her eyes kind above her mask, which was painted with a winter scene: pine trees and a snowman. She stood and walked over to me. "Let me take your coat. I hope you don't mind, but I'm going to ask you to leave your boots here." She showed me a selection of footwear I could put on to wear around the office: comfortable felt slippers in various sizes. "None of these have been worn," she said as I hesitated.

I put the slippers on and then followed her back to her desk.

"Kaz told me you'd be coming," Jane said, the skin around her eyes crinkling to show me she was smiling. "Your real name is not something I need to know. I do need something for our records, though, so give me a pseudonym, something you'll be able to remember."

"Kate Matthews," I said after a moment. Kathryn is my middle name.

"Thank you, Kate. I'll start a file for you. Have a seat. You've been told what's happening today?"

"Medical check-up, psychological assessment."

"That's right. And Kaz will give you a tour of the zoo. Do you have any questions?"

"Not right now, no."

"The doctor will be free in about ten minutes. Would you like a coffee while you're waiting?" When I hesitated, she said, "Real coffee."

"Real coffee?"

"Real coffee. Au lait."

I nodded vigorously. More than once I'd wished Henny Penny had left me stranded in a country where either coffee or tea was grown. I'd have picked it myself. The inscrutably flavoured liquid that had been passing for coffee for the past decade wasn't worth the cost of heating the water. Tea was moderately better, if only because many kinds of leaves can be steeped for a refreshing drink, but I wouldn't have cared if I never saw another cup of mint or chamomile tea in my life. And fresh milk was nearly as precious.

Jane brought my café au lait in a kind of sippy cup, with a spout that could go under my mask. I smelled it long before she reached me, a rich, heady aroma, tinged with hazelnut, that took me back to lazy afternoons spent arguing and whispering and laughing with interesting people in trendy coffee shops. I took a quick sip, feeling the warm liquid flow down my throat to my stomach, the caffeine spreading its long fingers out through my veins. And something else beloved yet almost unfamiliar, something that danced on my tongue.

"Is that sugar? Oh my god, that's ..." It was as if individual crystals were pinging themselves at my tastebuds, at the pleasure centres in my brain. I felt a sudden, inexplicable joy to be alive. I closed my eyes and savoured the aftertaste. Refined sugar was nearly impossible for individual consumers to come by, and had been for years. "I shouldn't be surprised that people who can get their hands on coffee can also find sugar, but still ... Where?"

"We know people who know people," Jane said enigmatically. "I should have asked if you took it with sugar, but that would have ruined the surprise. No one ever says no when they know it's available."

She walked back to her desk, leaving me in my comfortable armchair, sipping coffee and drinking in the colours of the floor.

Finally, her phone buzzed and she stood. "Okay, I'll take you to the doctor now."

I finished my coffee, and she took my empty cup and set it on her desk.

Jane led me down a corridor lined with colourful art to a room outfitted as a doctor's office, where an older woman took my blood pressure, drew blood, and questioned me about my medical history — specifically, about my experience with Henny Penny. Then she led me to another office, where a man sat behind a desk, reading a book.

"This is Kate Matthews," she said. "Have a good afternoon, Kate."

"Thank you, doctor."

The man behind the desk directed me to sit.

"So, how are you today?" he asked.

"Good, I guess. A little anxious about doing this, but otherwise good."

"What makes you anxious?"

"Well, meeting strangers, being touched by them. Doing something illegal."

"All pretty reasonable. And yet you're here."

"Everyone seems to think it's a good idea. My doctor even told me I should."

"And why would your doctor think that?"

So I told him about my experience with the TTCs.

"Have you ever been addicted to anything?" he asked.

"I was a smoker for a long time."

"How long?"

"I found a pack when I was about fourteen and a friend dared me to light one up. I took one drag, accidentally inhaled, and I can still feel the way it hit some pleasure centre in my brain that made me feel dizzy and happy. I was addicted immediately. I smoked until about eleven years ago, when the bottom fell out of the tobacco industry," I said.

"How do you feel about smoking now?"

How did I feel about it? I still dreamed about smoking. I wouldn't think of it for months and then I'd be hit in a dream with a vision of myself laughing over a drink with some anonymous someone, taking a deep drag on a cigarette, letting the feathers of hot smoke tickle the back of my throat, sucking it into my lungs and feeling that little rush of nicotine in my brain before I blew it softly back out. When I woke up, my brain would be convinced that I had never quit smoking and I'd have to remind myself for hours that there would be no cigarettes that day or the next or any day after that.

So even though it had nearly killed me, the virus had probably saved me from death by lung cancer.

· *The cruellest jokes are the funniest, right?*

Look at me laughing.

In the dreams when I'm smoking, that's when I recognize myself — or at least the self I wanted desperately to be and hoped I might be projecting: confident, self-assured, fuck your Surgeon General. It had been my one true act of rebellion, the thing no one would have expected of me. Cigarettes were part of my makeup, part of my concept of self. I'm naked without them. In more than a decade, I have figured out to live without many things, including cigarettes, but I still don't know what hands do in the absence.

"I don't miss the smell or feeling like a social pariah," I said. "And I don't miss spending a big chunk of my income on cigarettes. But if there was tobacco, and if I could have a cigarette every now and then without becoming addicted again, I'd still smoke. I enjoyed it."

He asked me how I'd come to be alone for so long and about the depression that accompanied my solitude. We talked about the TTCs and my reaction to them. I told him about everything, except how I ripped my skin open scratching at phantom itches, like a junkie too far from her last fix.

"What do you do when you're angry?" he asked.

Repress it, I thought. "I live through it," I said. "Sometimes I throw things."

The hour passed quickly. I had expected tests, but there were none, just gentle questions and non-judgmental responses to my answers.

When the time was up, I asked, "What are you looking for?"

"Problems," he said. "We need to know you're relatively sane, that you have empathy for others, that you don't have issues that will be triggered during a zoo."

"And that conversation we just had told you all those things?"

"Pretty much," he said.

"Did I pass?"

"I think so. I have to write up my notes, but I will tell Kaz he can go ahead with the intake."

A nurse led me back down to the lobby where Jane sat. She showed me where the washroom was and offered me another coffee while I waited for Kaz. It was every bit as delicious as the first one, although two doses of unfamiliar caffeine and sugar left me a bit jittery. Finally, she led me to Kaz's office, down a different hall on the same floor.

"This is Kate Matthews," she said before shutting the door behind me.

"Hi, Kate. Nice to see you again. Have a seat."

Like any executive, he had two guest chairs at his desk in a large office that also held a more comfortable seating area, leather armchairs facing each other across a low coffee table, with floor lamps for reading. The office was panelled in dark wood, with paintings providing splashes of bright colour on the walls.

"Who's your decorator?" I asked, taking one of the chairs opposite him.

He looked around him as if assessing the office for the first time. "Some of this came with the building, some of it my partners and I did. We figured if we were going to be spending time here, the surroundings had to be pleasant."

"You did a good job," I said.

"Thanks." He pointed to his computer. "You passed the medical and the psych exams, so if you want to become a member, we can go ahead with that. Otherwise, I'll give you the visiting journalist spiel instead."

"Are they so very different?"

"I don't know — I've never done that one before."

"I want to become a member," I said, feeling certain about nothing but bowing to the seeming inevitability of it.

"Okay, from now on, you'll be Kate inside these doors. Your anonymity won't be complete — I'm going to take your picture and attach it to your real name in a coded file. It won't go online, so there is no chance of it being hacked. There is a very small and trusted circle of people who know where and what the file is. It's to protect me and to protect you."

He spoke obliquely, but I understood — it was his insurance policy.

He held up one of those cameras that makes instant photos, and waited.

"You need to take your mask off," he said finally, and it was only then that I realized I still had mine on — and I'd been too nervous to notice that he wasn't wearing one at all.

I unhooked the mask from around my ears and he took the picture, catching the print when it shot from the camera before placing it on his desk.

"All right, now we talk about money."

I blinked when he told me what it cost to become a member. I didn't say anything, but I momentarily considered taking Bob up on his offer to cover my expenses.

The fee, paid monthly, gave members unlimited access to what was officially on the books as a private club, a type of organization where it was legal for people to gather in small groups, although going bare inside one was not.

"You will have to undergo regular check-ups, including a finger-prick test at the door to check for active H9N9 antibodies in your blood every time you come to the zoo."

"Really? Do people ever not pass the tests?"

"The virus is mutating all the time, and sometimes the vaccine doesn't catch the new variant. We've turned a few people away over the years. But it's also a psychological thing — as low as the chance of catching the virus is, it calms people to know we're looking for it. So we do finger-prick tests and if there's any chance you're carrying an active virus, you will not be allowed to enter. The premises are as sanitary as possible. We ask all our clients to self-identify for each visit as fauna or tactiles —"

"As what?"

Kaz smiled wryly. "It's a petting zoo. Thus, fauna — it sounds better than 'animals,' doesn't it? Those who are there to be touched. Tactiles, or tacs, are there to touch. Pretty much everyone starts as fauna."

"Okay, let's back up for a minute. Why are they called petting zoos? Where did that come from?"

Kaz thought for a moment. "The only explanation I've ever heard came from the person who set up what I think was the first-ever zoo, about seven years ago. And he just saw the resemblance: putting people who wanted that sort of tactile experience in a room with people willing to give it to them. Plus, I imagine he derived a certain amount of gratification from thinking of at least some of his patrons as helpless baby animals set out for the pleasure of others." Kaz sneered at the thought. "Anyway, it's like calling the virus Henny Penny — people liked the analogy, and it stuck."

"Huh. But the animals in a petting zoo don't touch back. Is that why your ... fauna ... don't participate? That seems weird."

"That's what we thought, too," Kaz said. "I can get more into the history later, that can be part of my visiting journalist tour, but for now I'll just say that the original petting zoo, at least the first one in this city, was an S&M club before the pandemic."

After the pandemic, Kaz said, the owner noticed people coming not so much because they were into that scene, but because it was an opportunity to experience touch. While the business model changed, the dom/sub ethos remained. "My partners and I set out to provide a different experience, but what we quickly discovered is that there are some who tend to be more submissive and prefer to be — or need to be — touched, while others are more dominant and they prefer to be in charge of the touching. In order to ensure that everyone who comes here is satisfied, we ask our members to self-identify. In a perfect world — and a few zoos on — it's a more symbiotic relationship, with both participating equally."

"'A few zoos on'?"

"As I said, this is what we call a vanilla zoo. G-rated. For some, this is enough; for some, it's not. It's how we started out, but we later diversified."

"Why?"

"Demand, primarily." He shrugged. "We give the customers what they want."

"Will you be showing me those other zoos, too?"

"Of course. As a member, though, you have to work your way through them in stages."

"At the clinics, you're always a … fauna," I said. "And you're assigned a therapist, or at least, at the clinic I started going to, I always had the same therapist. Sessions last an hour."

"We ask you to make an appointment if you want to attend a zoo, and when you do you will be asked which role you would rather play. Everyone showers beforehand, and we give you a bodysuit — a dancer's leotard — to wear. They're extremely lightweight and have not been treated with Impermatex, so they are form fitting, cover the torso, but won't dull the sensation."

"But people are coming here for a skin-on-skin experience. Why bother with clothes?"

"Modesty, to a certain extent. Not everyone is comfortable being naked with strangers — our members range in age from eighteen to eighty. And at the vanilla level, they're just looking for simple, non-sexual physical contact, and that's all we're offering. Nudity would blur that line."

Kaz gave me a tour of the vanilla zoo, which in its earlier life had probably been a large conference room, able to hold about fifty people comfortably. More of that panelling covered the walls, but in here there was no furniture, just baskets containing small bottles of lotion scattered around the floor, set among piles of blankets and cushions covered with soft fabric in muted colours. The floors were thick with hand-knotted carpets.

"One of my partners knows people who ran an imported rug business," Kaz explained, when I asked where they'd all come from. "We nuke these daily. And the cushions and blankets are all cleaned and sanitized daily."

"Heckuva cleaning bill," I said. "And a lot of staff."

"That's what your dues are for. We want this place to be as safe and as carefree as it can be. But it's also one of the reasons why there's no furniture."

"There's no corral," I said. "I expected a pen or something."

"You get those in some of the original zoos," he said.

"So how does it work? Do you just throw everyone together and have a free-for-all?"

He laughed. "No. The fauna come in through that door from their changing area, and lay out a blanket on the floor. Then they line up and put on blindfolds. Then the tactiles come in through that door from their changing area." He pointed to the other side of the room. "They're blindfolded, too. They walk past the fauna until they choose one, and that's how they're paired off for the evening."

"That's ... bizarre. How did you come up with that process?"

"Trial and error. Believe me, it's the best way I've seen," Kaz said. "Our guiding philosophy was to make this zoo a warm embrace for everyone who entered it, welcoming to all. You touch with your eyes, too, and sometimes that kind of touch can hurt. Blindfolds limit the variables. Nobody is rejecting or being rejected because of physical appearance. Blindfolded, tactiles have to rely on a more primal sense that ultimately takes them to the fauna who will be satisfying to them. An eighteen-year-old man might think it's odd to have a grandmother for a tactile, might prefer the beautiful woman beside her, but sometimes an eighteen-year-old man needs to feel the years of care in a grandma's hands. Or a big brother's."

"You put a lot of stock in the power of pheromones," I said, and he shrugged. "Do the blindfolds ever come off?"

"Somebody has to see where they're going." Kaz laughed again. "The blindfolds come off once the choice is made. Or not. The participants may choose to leave them on, or one or the other might ask for that."

"But what if the fauna or the tactile aren't pleased with the person they end up with?"

"Strangely, it doesn't happen all that often, or not as often as you'd think — at least, we get very few complaints, and no, we don't screen for physical attractiveness. We welcome all shapes, sizes, colours, and conditions here. When you sign your membership papers, you will be asked to agree to remain open to the experience, whatever that experience might be."

"So this is a G-rated zoo, but you must have people who go too far. How do you deal with sexual touching?"

"Tactiles who deliberately cross the line are barred. That said, sometimes a hand is going to land in a place you're not expecting, and sometimes the male tactiles and fauna can become obviously aroused. It's a human response. Women can become aroused, too, of course, but — well, men can pee standing up and women can hide their arousal. It's a trade-off." He smiled again. "It's up to you how you handle it: you can go on with what you're doing, you can call a time out. If it's an ongoing and unwelcome problem, or obviously intentional, you can end the session and report him — or her, because we've had some aggressive female tacs — to the office."

"I thought all zoos were sex zoos."

"Is that why you wanted to come? Or is it what kept you from coming?"

"Both." I looked around me at the opulent surroundings, picked up a pillow to stroke the satin binding, enjoying the cool smoothness of it under my fingertips. "This is going to sound like a stupid and sexist question, but why would men ever come here? What do they get out of it?"

"Are you thinking all men are ever interested in is sex, that any touch has to be a means to that end?"

"I wouldn't be alone in thinking that men who come to a place to touch or be touched, wearing a light bodysuit that hides nothing, might find it a bit of a preoccupation, sure. It sounds a bit cruel to deny that."

"Do you think it's also cruel to deny women sexual release, or do you think women are not preoccupied by the same thing, so that only they are capable of appreciating what we offer here?" He smiled. "I'm a little surprised to be taking this side of the argument. Men who are looking strictly for sex can find it elsewhere, at our zoos or someone else's. The men who come here, to this particular zoo, are looking for human contact, looking for the possibility of human warmth. Sometimes that's all even men want. I think it's a very old-fashioned way of thinking, to assume that all men are rampant sexual creatures for whom every physical encounter must end in ejaculation, who can't appreciate other levels of contact."

I held up my hands in protest. "Okay, okay, I was just asking. You apparently cater to a more evolved subsection of the species than I've had the pleasure of dealing with. But obviously, if you went on to open zoos that were more overtly sexual ..."

"It was because both men and women asked for it. As you've discovered for yourself, it can be hard to meet people and form relationships — everyone's afraid of strangers. We all stick to our own little bubbles because we feel safe there. But the body needs what it needs. I never wanted to run a sex club. But I like the thought that I can provide the opportunity for contact in a safe way."

Kaz led me to one of the changing rooms, with numbered lockers lining the walls. Each locker was stocked with towels and toiletries.

Guests were expected to be at the zoo, showered and dressed in their bodysuits, at 7:00 p.m., when the zoo opened, and could stay until it closed at 1:00 a.m., or leave earlier if they wanted.

"Who decides when it's over?"

"In a perfect world, it's a mutual decision. But either partner can decide at any time. We try not to send anyone home unsatisfied, but it happens sometimes. And if you want to go longer, you can always arrange to hook up with your fauna or tac outside the zoo."

"You don't have a non-compete clause for things like that?"

"God, no. We're unfortunately not in danger of running out of clients. If someone can find pleasure outside the zoo, I'm happy for them."

Kaz took me back to Jane's desk, where I filled out my membership form and paid my dues — refundable if I didn't enjoy my first three sessions.

Original Zoo

THERE WAS A three-day cooling-off period before I could go to my first zoo, so before I left that first afternoon, I asked Kaz to take me to one of the original zoos, the kind I was used to reading about in the papers, to show me the other side of the coin. I'd need to do it for research, but also saw it as a way to safely feed my curiosity.

"I can't write the story without having been in one, and I have no idea where to find them," I said.

"You have no idea where to find one?" he repeated.

"No."

"How hard have you looked?" His tone and the look on his face expressed bemusement.

"Well, I did some internet searches, but they just told me they existed in the city — gave me no idea where. Sometimes there was an email address you could use for more information but I always worried that it was a regency trap, or a scam, so I never followed through. I was too afraid to wander the parts of the city where I thought I might find one."

"There's one at 289 Pine Street," he said.

I stopped still. "That's next door to my place."

"Yes."

"How long has it been there?"

"It's the original one — the one I was telling you about. It was the first one I ever went to, so at least seven years."

"I had no idea."

"Well, it's never been busted, and the clientele is pretty discreet. It also helps to know people who know things."

"Everyone I knew who knew things died a decade ago." I shrugged.

"Did you never wonder about people wandering in and out of the place at all hours?"

"Well, no, because I'm not out at all hours, and how would I have known whether they belonged there or were just visiting?" I didn't tell him that looking at the world outside my window made me sad, so I looked inward instead. "I wouldn't have guessed there was one in my neighbourhood, though."

"Where did you think they were? They're everywhere, not just in seedy, rundown places. And there aren't as many seedy, rundown places as there used to be, anyway."

Holy cow, I thought; there had been one next door all the time. Could it really have been that easy?

"Would you have gone if you'd known it was there?"

"I don't know. Probably not. Maybe."

• • •

I hadn't gone to church in years, not since I'd graduated from Sunday school, and had never been in an evangelical church where the minister paced the wide altar like a tiger in a cage, and a full rock band played drum and bass–driven hymns that sounded more erotic than devotional.

I was on an exchange trip with my senior class, visiting our partner school on the other side of the country. Mr. and Mrs. Leeuwin, the parents of the girl with whom I'd been billeted, swayed quietly to the music. They didn't shout their responses to the minister's calls the way others in the congregation did, but their soft responses were nonetheless enthralled.

Sometime in the third hour, when I was deeply regretting not having taken up another friend's offer to include me in her family's plans for the day, the minister got down on his knees in front of the congregation and started talking to me. Or at least it felt like he was talking directly to me.

"I know you are hurting," he said. "I know there is a big, empty place inside you, wanting to be filled. I know you don't believe you can be loved, but let me tell you can be loved."

"Praise Jesus!" a woman behind me called out.

"There is a love that will welcome you, will wrap you in light. Will give you what you've been looking for. Are you ready for it?"

"I am ready, Lord! Amen!" the congregation said as one.

"I can feel you wanting to come to me, wanting me to bathe you in the blood of the lamb. Don't be afraid — it's what your soul is crying for. Stand up now and come to me and receive Jesus in your heart. It will make you whole."

Maybe it was fatigue, maybe it was low blood sugar, but I

*felt the altar reaching out, the charismatic preacher exerting a
magnetic pull on every fibre of my being.*

*I was halfway to my feet when I felt Mrs. Leeuwin's light but
firm touch on my arm.*

*"This is not for you," she said quietly, and I settled back
into my seat in the pew, spell broken. I felt oddly empty, and
disappointed at possibly having just missed the miracle cure for
my ills.*

· · ·

I knew I was susceptible to the allure of things that seemed
like they could fill the emptiness inside me even though, in the
light of day, they were spiritually incompatible. My personal
rules for survival stated that if there was a chance I could give
in to that kind of attraction, there had to be a Mrs. Leeuwin to
hold me back. It was why I couldn't have gone to a petting zoo
alone all those years. As much as I craved the dropping-away of
awareness, I feared it in equal measure, worried that the reality
of self-abandonment wouldn't quite match up to the fantasy;
that I could be free and still in some sort of chains.

I shrugged. "In ten years, Kaz, a lot of things appeal. Acting
on that interest is another thing altogether."

"My partners and I discussed why people would go to
these things in spite of the danger from Henny Penny and the
police."

"And what did you decide?"

"One of my partners suggested it was the breakdown of
the social order. I thought it was desperation for contact moving people into a sort of post-religious, post-moral world —
because once the virus was regulated, other than hygiene,

religious-based social mores are the best reason to go against our biological programming, our need to be touched and loved." Kaz stopped and thought for a moment. "And then my other partner was just concerned about how we could get in on the action in a more aesthetically pleasing way."

"Do you all still work together?"

"We were three, now we are two. One has gone her own way."

"Is that a good thing?"

"It was the best thing."

Where once a prospective client would have needed a referral from a regular patron, Kaz said that now all it took to get in the door was to show up.

We met at my place just before 8:00 p.m. that night. We walked halfway down the block to another nondescript condo building much like mine, a place I passed every day. Over the years a couple of businesses had tried to make a go of the ground-floor commercial space, with no luck. They would have been the only reason I'd paid the building any attention at all.

One quick glance to make sure the sidewalk was empty, and Kaz led me down an alley to the service entrance.

Kaz nodded to the bouncer at the door, who stood up straighter when he saw my companion.

"Kaz."

"Harry."

"There's no orphans here tonight."

"I'm not here for orphans."

Harry looked me over. "You don't usually bring a date. She in the corral or out?"

"Just here to watch."

"The Colonel's going to want to know you're here."

"Tell him if you have to. But we're just stopping by — we're not staying long."

After a second, Harry let us through with a nod.

"What are orphans?" I asked.

"I'll tell you later."

It was a basement, dark, with the odour of mildew. Like in the zoos I'd read about, there was an actual corral. Bales of straw were placed both inside the fence for the "animals" to display themselves on for attention, and outside the fence for the audience to use to get comfortable if that was what they wanted. The corral, holding a dozen or so naked people, of a variety of ages and physical conditions, was in the middle of an otherwise empty space. The floors were bare concrete, dotted with mysterious dark spots. There was a small bar along the wall, selling alcoholic drinks and paper bags of popcorn to feed to the animals.

We joined about twenty patrons standing near the corral, all of us still wearing our winter coats, having declined the services of the cloakroom attendant. My coat felt like a protective carapace and I was one of the few observers wearing a mask. It was strange to be so fully clothed in a place that existed to give people the skin-to-skin contact that had been missing from their lives: no masks, no gloves, no prophylactic material to protect from any of the diseases that could be spread by contact or body fluids. I'd expected mud and there was none, but the place was none too clean, inside or outside of the fence. I was repulsed.

Kaz must have seen something in my face, because he said, "Even if cleanliness was a priority, it would be hard to do here. This place runs twenty-four-seven."

"How is that possible?"

He shrugged. "Supply and demand. I don't have the numbers, but believe me, if it wasn't a sound business model, they'd shut it down. The first time I came here, several years ago, it was evenings only, but now they have enough clientele on both sides of the fence to keep it going all hours."

"So this place is free?"

"Pay at the door. The animals — the people inside the corral — pay a small, nominal fee, maybe one credit for the night, at least until they become trusted or popular regulars, and then they come in for free. The more animals, the bigger the audience, so management keeps the prices low. The audience members pay to play. Admission is six credits per hour, twenty credits for the night." He pointed out the lights pinned to people's clothing, programmed to turn off when their time was up, and the bouncers circling to make sure people left when they were supposed to — or paid more to stay. It wasn't an exorbitant price, you'd have to spend a lot of nights here to match the cost of a membership at Kaz's zoo, but it could buy the better part of a week's rations. "People use prepaid cards for anonymity. The bar is where they soak you, about seven credits for a beer, more for alcohol. They don't really want people to drink too much — that causes problems."

"I didn't see you pay."

"Professional courtesy. I know the guy at the door, and I know the guy who owns this place. There are more zoos in this city than you'd think, but there aren't that many of us, all in all, who run them. You get to know each other."

"Do you come here a lot?"

"I've been here a few times."

"Looking for orphans."

"That's right."

Kaz didn't offer any more information, and I filed away more questions to ask later. He got us each a drink — paying this time, with a prepaid card — and together we approached the fence.

I could see a woman taking a breather in an inaccessible part of the corral. On second glance, I realized she wasn't taking a rest — she was answering a call of nature on what I hoped was an artfully disguised chemical toilet and not just an open bale of straw.

"Oh!" I said, surprised that anyone could or would relieve themselves in public like that.

Kaz followed my gaze and said, "They don't take breaks. Once an animal is in the pen, he or she is there for the night. If they come out, they have to pay to go in again."

"So they can't even come out to use the bathroom and go back in?"

"No. Some really don't want to come out, and frankly most don't seek privacy."

We watched quietly for a while. Some of the animals stayed close to the fence, eager for whatever contact they could get, rubbing up against legs or extended hands, shamelessly seeking attention, while others played a game, forcing onlookers to entice them closer with popcorn or bottles of water, the former nibbled from open hands, the latter sucked on through nipples hanging around the animals' necks, which could be attached to the mouths of the bottles. Only after being seduced by these enticements did they offer themselves up, allowing audience members to lean over, or reach through the fence, to caress a thigh or a breast, or stroke their hair.

"What are the rules for touching here?"

"Move back if you don't want it, on both sides of the fence," Kaz answered simply. "There are no real rules. The audience isn't allowed in the pen, isn't allowed to touch with anything but hands, and must remain fully clothed." He nodded toward an area of the pen where a woman was being masturbated by an audience member, presumably with her permission, and said, "Most of the people here are voyeurs, and that's what keeps them coming. Any woman or man willing to allow that to happen a few times a night gets in for free, and those who will perform sexual acts with each other inside the pen might even get a credit card tucked into their clothes when they leave."

"Can a spectator become an animal if they decide halfway through that they want more?"

Kaz shrugged. "It doesn't really happen. People tend to play the role they choose, and not everyone inside the corral is prepared to have sex."

I nodded toward the woman being masturbated. "Is she free to say no?"

"Yes. This place is a lot of things, but it's not a front for prostitution."

"So she's not just doing it because she needs the credit card tucked into her clothes …"

"Well," he said, "there's no shortage of jobs if you need credits. I can say that as far as I know, payment for services is not guaranteed, and there would be a nominal amount — maybe twenty-five credits — on a card."

"And other zoos?"

"Some have a more official employment relationship with their animals. Contracts are signed, but entering knowingly into bondage is, as you say, not necessarily the same thing as entering willingly."

There were two ranks of onlookers — one group standing at the fence, actively taking part, and another group standing farther back, watching everything.

"Do you allow voyeurs at any of your zoos?" I asked.

He laughed. "We have security and sometimes I think the people who really like that job are there for more than the credits. But no, never at my zoos are you ever allowed in strictly to watch, though of course sometimes you can be excused for doing so."

"So are all of the original zoos like this one?"

"No. This grew out of a completely different experience. Most zoos that I've heard of have some sort of dom/sub model — not as extreme as this one, maybe. They all fill a certain need. Like human beings, the variations are endless."

Suddenly Kaz tensed, and I looked away from the corral, following his gaze to a tall, whip-thin man walking toward us. Like most of the people in the zoo, he wasn't wearing a mask. I would have put his age around sixty, maybe. His skin was relatively unlined, his salt-and-pepper hair in a neat military brush cut. His eyes were pinned to me. Kaz lifted his arm as if to put it protectively around me, then dropped it again, but moved closer and slightly in front of me as the man reached us.

"Kaz," he said, looking briefly at my companion.

"Colonel."

"What brings you here tonight?"

"Sightseeing."

"Been a long time since you came as a tourist. Introduce me to your friend." It was an order, not a request.

"Colonel, this is Kate. Kate, Colonel. This zoo is his … creation."

So this was the dungeon master who had found a new business model? I would have expected a lot more leather.

"Good evening, Kate — welcome to my little enterprise."

He took my right hand from where it rested by my side, removed my glove, and kissed the centre of my palm before letting it go, an act of terrifying intimacy. He watched for my reaction with cold brown eyes. I felt violated, but knew on some level that that had been his aim, so I was determined not to let it show.

I retrieved my glove from his open hand and put it back on before I said, "Good evening."

"It's unusual for Kaz to bring anyone with him. Are you in training to be a saviour of souls like him?"

"She's new in town. I thought I'd show her some of the sights," Kaz said.

"What do you think of my zoo?" the Colonel asked. "Don't I have some exciting specimens? Are you enjoying the show?"

"Why the feeding rituals?" I asked the first thing that popped into my head. "The popcorn and the nipples?"

"Did you ever go to a petting zoo when you were a child?"

I shook my head.

"I used to take my children," he said. "It was always a special treat for them to feed the animals, or give them a bottle. And some animals came to like it very much, like these ones here — they would approach only people who had enticements." His eyes gleamed in the dim light. "It's a dance — the submissive animals in the pen get to exercise what little power they have by demanding an offering, and the audience on the outside can appease them by offering it, or make them beg by denying it. It's interesting to watch the transaction play out, don't you think?"

His eyes never left my face. I felt like he was mentally stripping off my mask to see me more clearly.

Clearly, Kaz had had enough. "I think we'll be going." He took my drink and handed it, along with his own, to the Colonel, who finally broke eye contact with me to look in bewilderment at the bottles he was suddenly holding. "You'll take care of those, right? Goodnight."

Kaz took my arm and led me quickly up the stairs and past Harry outside. We walked down the alley to the street and then turned in the opposite direction from my building.

"Where …?"

"It's a lovely evening for a walk, don't you think?" he asked, looking casually behind us.

"Do you think he would follow us?"

"I'm not sure, but if he does, I'd rather not lead him to your door. We'll just go for a little stroll."

It was a nice night, for January, cold but no wind, and the rain had stopped hours before, leaving a clear sky bright with stars.

"He didn't seem like a particularly nice man," I said.

"No."

"And you two don't like each other much."

"No."

"I'm guessing it has something to do with orphans."

"That's part of it. He's … a vile human being. And his influence is one of the reasons my former partner is my former partner. She followed him down a path and at a certain point stopped following."

"She developed her own ideas?"

"They're more of a team these days."

We did a full turn around the block, which was a new experience for me. I almost never left the house after dark, even now, when I was less afraid of being outside. Streetlights were erratic, and while the crime rate was nothing compared with pre-pandemic times, I was a product of an upbringing that discouraged women from walking alone at night in poorly lit areas with little foot traffic.

My cheeks were rosy but I felt warm and alive when Kaz dropped me at my door, having finally persuaded himself that no one was watching us.

"I've cleared my mornings for the next few days," he said. "Come back to the zoo tomorrow any time after nine. We'll drink coffee and I'll tell you everything you want to know."

Back in my apartment, I put on my pyjamas and thought about what I'd seen as I warmed my hands around a mug of hot tea.

Artists are the world's voyeurs. It is the job of writers to observe the human condition and make note of what we see — and sometimes to make sense of it, and make conclusions based on those observations. While I lacked the killer instinct of the true journalist, I'd always enjoyed knowing things I wasn't supposed to know, watching people as they furtively went about their secret business. I'd been creeped out by the Colonel's appropriation of my hand, but also fascinated by him, curious about what he got out of the transactions he facilitated. I would also have loved the chance to talk to the animals in his corral; I wanted to know what human parts of themselves they'd lost to be able to enter freely into that position.

Of course, the parts they'd lost might have included shame, fear of public ridicule, maybe even self-awareness: that original sin that calls on us to clothe ourselves or be damned. Maybe these people weren't lost — maybe they were free.

I was less clear about the audience. The active participants were enjoying themselves, performing a service — doing what was asked of them, in fact — but their faces, what I could see of them, their postures, breathed scorn on the animals. For the most part, the voyeurs exhibited pure ennui — or, in Kaz's case, and I suspect in mine as well, a mixture of pity and disgust.

• • •

The next day, Kaz told me that his orphans were fauna who never became tacs, for whom touch was a drug and the zoos the supplier.

"I don't understand addicts," he said, playing with the cuff of his white shirt, which peeked out from the sleeve of a black cashmere sweater — no Impermatex this time. My fingers itched to touch it. "I understand needing to touch and be touched, but I don't understand and will not pander to that narcissism, that self-involvement, at the heart of every addict."

"You're pandering to me," I pointed out, speaking as Kate the zoo member and not Lily the journalist. I leaned back in my leather armchair, facing Kaz, who sat in the matching chair across the coffee table in his office. "I've admitted to being all but addicted to the TTCs, which are like a gateway drug. You know that and you're still offering to introduce me to much stronger stuff."

He thought for a minute, choosing his words. "Our psychological testing is designed to weed out addicts. You're right, there are red flags all around you — you almost didn't pass. But the testing suggested that you have the will to self-correct when what you're doing is not working for you. You know that the zoo isn't going to be the answer to all that you're asking for.

I don't think you'll keep chasing the dragon if it's not paying off for you. I think you'll know when to stop."

"You have precious little evidence that that's the case, and quite a bit of evidence to the contrary."

He shrugged. "I have a feeling. And a very good psychiatrist who hasn't been wrong yet."

"What do you do with the orphans when you find them?"

"Most of them don't have a social network or anyone to care for them, so I take them someplace safe, help them come down. Orphans, like any addicts, may know that what they're doing has become dangerous for them, but the need to do it is stronger than their instinct or their will to quit. They stop taking care of themselves, they stop eating properly and sleeping, they stop going to their jobs. All they can think about is the next fix — in this case, someone to touch them, to give them that rush they're seeking. They can do themselves a lot of harm, and become targets for the kind of people who like to exploit the vulnerable. I put them in touch with people who can help them get healthy enough to find what they're really looking for."

"And what are they really looking for?"

"More connection than they can find in the zoos."

"Where do you find that for them?"

"It depends. I sometimes try to get them jobs on farms, where they can re-establish connection to nature, to plants and animals. It can be very grounding to have to take care of something outside of yourself — even plants."

There was a knock at the door, then Jane entered with a tray holding a small carafe of coffee, two mugs, spoons, a jug of hot milk, and a dish of raw sugar. She smiled at me as she placed it on the table between us, then left.

Kaz reached for the coffee pot and raised an eyebrow at me.

"Yes, please," I said eagerly.

"Helping orphans is something I do because I unintentionally contributed to a situation that harms some of the people I thought I was helping," he said as he poured hot coffee into our cups and added milk and sugar. "It's good corporate social responsibility. I didn't create the environment for the zoos, but I'm profiting from it and from people's need for connection. It is, very simply, both incumbent upon me to clean up my messes, and the very least I can do."

"You said there were a lot of zoos but not a lot of owners. Can you explain that?"

"There are quite a few zoos, both the original kind, which take all comers, and ones like mine, which are members-only clubs. Some are strictly sex clubs, some are strictly vanilla, some are strictly gay, and some aren't strictly anything. If you're going to make a real go of it, financially speaking, you have to offer a range, so most owners have more than one zoo. Mine is an elite, national syndicate with zoos in other cities across the country, and there are maybe one or two more of those."

"Who are your customers? It sounds like half the people in the city would have to go to zoos for all of them to be profitable."

"There are a lot of people who are alone, or even if they're not alone, they're missing physical connection, or not getting the connection they want, for whatever reason. I have about five hundred members here; another two thousand or so across the country."

"Active members?"

"For the most part. People stop coming when they find something else, but I get about five new members a week, so it balances out."

"And are all the owners as altruistic as you?"

He shrugged. "If I was altruistic, I'd probably have only vanilla zoos and I'd offer them at cost. Money's not my primary objective, but I am in it for the money, too. I just care about my impact on the world. Some of the owners are like that; others, especially the ones who run the original zoos, I'd call opportunistic entrepreneurs, looking to make a buck by exploiting the needy. At least one of the elite zookeepers also runs one or two that are more like the zoo where we went last night. They're very profitable."

"Aren't all entrepreneurs opportunistic in one way or another? You all exploit a need."

"Not all. Yes, my zoos are making money from people who want what we're selling, no question, but we allow the needy some dignity when they come here — safety and security. I think that puts us in a class above."

"And the people who go to those other zoos are people who don't have the credits for dignity or safety," I challenged him.

"Some of them. Some are people with plenty of credits and also a need to feel something, anything, twenty-four hours a day. Some are people who've been turned away by responsible zookeepers because they can't or won't obey the rules. Some people start there because they're the most easily accessible, and try to work their way up the ladder, but once they've become conditioned to those zoos, they find it difficult to accept this kind of experience. It seems to harden them in a way, or maybe they're naturally more prone to the kind of risk-taking that those clubs require."

"So why aren't people getting sick if those clubs are so risky?"

"They are — you just don't hear about it. First of all, it's probably not Henny Penny —seasonal colds and flu are often deadly these days because no one has any sort of immunity. But people hide it because to get sick means they broke the BLT laws, which could get them sent to a work camp."

"And people who come here don't have or don't get colds and flu?" I let my skepticism show.

"My zoos don't really attract risk-takers. Risk-takers say, 'Screw your medical check-ups and psych evaluations, you're not going to prick my finger every time I come to see whether I have the virus.' You're taking a risk to be here, but you're not a risk-taker at heart. Neither are the rest of my members, which means they're careful about washing their hands and about when and where they take off their masks and gloves, so there's much less chance they'll have picked up Henny Penny or anything else that could be passed on here. People who get sick at a zoo are far more likely to have gone to one of the original zoos. And they're usually lost by then, anyway."

"Orphans."

"Yes."

"Who are the tacs at those zoos, then, if the orphans are all fauna?"

"Some of them are there for the same reason as some of the fauna — it's what they've heard of, or they don't have money for the better-regulated zoos. Some are risk-takers. But there are also quite a lot of people who get off on that kind of scene, and others are collectors."

"Collectors?"

"Some people, like the Colonel, have private collections. They seek out fauna who are ... *exquisitely submissive* is a term I've heard used. And quite often what they find are orphans."

He paused. "I really don't want to talk about them. I'll tell you about my zoos and what they do."

I filed that away to be pursued later. He was an odd bird, Kaz, opening some parts of his world to examination while drawing the curtain on others.

"So is this a purely entrepreneurial venture for you — you saw a niche and filled it?" I asked him on another day, back in his office with more café au lait, which still felt like a revelation every time I took a sip.

He shrugged. "Does it have to be more than that?"

"You tell me."

He paused for a minute, then said, "The three of us had different reasons for starting the zoos. Making money was down on the list. It was primarily a challenge — we were looking for something to do. For me it was almost an experiment, a social experiment. But it was also fun, it was living on the edge because it was illegal, so that was a thrill. And we were subverting the order of things, finding a better way of doing a thing we could see a need for but thought was being done badly. I also liked watching how people reacted to the zoo, how they acted within it. It's almost boring now; it's so fine tuned there is no real spontaneity. Those early days, though — they were exhilarating."

"Is that why it's such a weird setup? The tacs and fauna and blindfolds were the results of your experiment?"

"The provable results," he amended. "The ones that provided the same results on repetition."

"What did you do before the zoos?" I asked, and he looked away, didn't answer.

"Seriously," I pressed him. "You say you didn't need the money. Are you independently wealthy? Family money? The

regency requires everyone who can to work at something —
why were you different?"

"That's not really germane …"

"The hell it's not."

He thought about his answer for a while, and finally I suggested, "Were you an axe murderer?" and he laughed, startled.

"You can think of me as a displaced person," he answered
finally. "I arrived in this country in the middle of Henny Penny
and I never registered. I had a friend here. He and I decided
it would be better — safer — if I lay low, to see how things
would fall out."

"Yeah, I remember, newcomers were being turned back. But
that was eleven years ago."

"And I'm still deciding the best course for me. The regency
is doing its first post-pandemic census ahead of the elections
next year. I've decided to decide by then whether to leave or
to figure out how to become official without being deported."

"What's home like? Would you be in danger if you were
deported?"

"It's hard to say what kind of reception I'd have if I went
back. Better not to find out," he said, and offered no further
information.

First Zoo

I'D SEEN THE ZOO during the tour, of course, but there was no way to prepare my bare toes for the shock of soft silk carpets, or the gentle roughness of wool.

Textiles had been enemy for so long, surfaces had become so hard and unyielding, that I'd all but forgotten about carpeting, how velvety it could feel against the soles of your feet, how you sank into it gently and it worked a plush resistance against forward progress — not pulling back like sand or snow, but offering a subtle suggestion that you might stay for a moment and enjoy.

I wasn't as naked as I felt, but it was as if there was nothing between my skin and the air. All the people in the zoo — fauna and tacs — were given a feather-light, silken bodysuit to wear. Just enough coverage for modesty, it was cut away like a tank top, leaving shoulders and arms bare, and the legs ended just at the top of the thigh.

That beautiful, permeable fabric was, of course, as illegal as anything else in the zoo. As far as I knew, manufacturers weren't even making anything like it anymore. Kaz said he'd been able to source them from a defunct dance company. I accepted that as the beginning of the story, if not the whole of it. In order to service the zoo's clientele, the bodysuits would have to be available in a lot of sizes that a dance company wouldn't normally stock. But as far as I knew, all textile manufacturers in the country had been pressed years ago into producing masks or basic rough fabrics made from indigenous plant and animal sources — and even if they had access to silk, they'd be forced to coat it with Impermatex.

Fauna and tacs were always exactly matched, based on the number of fauna who booked the zoo on any given night. "There are always more tacs than fauna seeking appointments," Kaz had explained. "Eventually most fauna transition to tacs — they become tired of the passivity."

The zoo was dimly lit and comfortably warm, but I still had gooseflesh up my arms as I anticipated what was coming next. I breathed deeply, trying to relax, to tamp down my fear of being in a room with the twenty or so people who were already here, and all the people to come, without protection, without my mask to hide behind.

I stood, rigid, listening to myself breathe, and trying to see through the dark cloth covering my eyes as the blindfolded tactiles filed toward us, wondering who would pick me. I couldn't decide whether I was surprised when a tac claimed me by touching my arm, and I removed my blindfold to see Kaz, barely visible in the low light, not wearing a blindfold of his own.

"Hello," he said, smiling.

"Hello," I replied, puzzled. We'd spoken that morning in his office; he hadn't said he would be here. "I wasn't expecting you. I thought this was supposed to be anonymous."

"It is, but sometimes I claim *droit de seigneur*. Is that okay?"

I nodded, though I wasn't sure it was. We'd established an open, professional relationship over the last few days, and while I enjoyed talking with him — and had exposed a certain amount of my private self to him already — I wasn't sure I wanted to meet him on this physical level. It would have been easier to be vulnerable with a stranger, baring my soul as I might in a confessional to a priest who would never know me outside of it.

I led him to the blanket I'd laid out earlier. We sat cross-legged, facing each other. He may have eschewed the blindfold, but he wore the same bodysuit as everyone else, exposing a lightly muscled body covered in fine, dark hair.

Deep scratches on my forearm caught his eye as he reached for my hand.

"What were you scratching at?" he asked.

"The numbness," I said.

His expression was sad as he began exploring my hands with his fingertips, the pads of his thumbs. Except for the Colonel's cold kiss a few nights earlier, it was skin that hadn't been touched by another's ungloved hand since the pandemic. I could touch myself the same way and never feel the same thing. A nerve in my cheek jumped as he traced a path down the inside of my wrist.

Going years without deliberate, purposeful, respectful, loving, laying-on of hands wears away the skin, creates pockets of longing. Touch isn't bump, isn't shove, isn't "Oops, sorry." Touch is "your skin is soft," is silky smooth and whisker rough, is "please" and also "thank you."

The ancients used to disagree on which organ held the soul. Some said it was the heart; others were convinced it was the liver. For me it has always been the stomach. Fear and excitement, boredom and anger, love and hate: they all make themselves felt first in my gut. So I felt a familiar punch to my abdomen when he ran his thumb along the bone in my wrist, slid his fingers between mine. My breath caught when he softly, gently, scratched the length of my lifeline with his thumbnail. I could hear others around me talking, but I lost all awareness of them. Kaz and I were in a bubble; outside it, nothing existed that I needed to concern myself with. It was him, and me, and his hands on my skin.

It seemed that I could feel each individual whorl of his fingerprints bump slightly as the pads of his fingers slid across my arm, the back of my hand, my palm, hundreds of individual points of contact that made my nerve endings spring up like flowers in the desert after a rain, each sending signals of approval and pleasure to my brain, which I could feel unravelling — not because of conflicting messages, this time, but because it was all excruciatingly wonderful.

"The gloves make our palms hyper-sensitive. The skin is so constantly protected from the elements," he whispered. "Have you ever had acupuncture, or acupressure?"

"No." I fought to find that one syllable.

"There are meridians in the hands that affect other parts of the body ..."

"Please," I said, my voice ragged. "Don't tell me what you're doing, or how, or why. Just do it, okay?"

"Close your eyes and let go of your brain, then," he said. "Trust me."

And I did. For most of the night we sat face to face on my blanket. He took a bottle from a basket and spread lotion over my hands and arms, shoulders and neck. Lightly touching, gently stroking, a contemplative and respectful meeting of flesh that made me feel acknowledged in a way that the TTCs never had. It was the closest I'd come to a loving touch since Matt left, and I drank it in until the last part of the wall I'd been building for more than ten years, the wall that the TTCs had started to wear away, collapsed. The touch itself was nourishing; touch plus care was almost my undoing. My ego destroyed, I became all id, hungry for the sensation he was providing. As if he had sensed that shift, Kaz lay down and pulled me to his body and held me until the zoo closed, opening up yet another door of awareness as my naked skin touched his, as I tucked my head into the crook of his neck and absorbed his warmth. I cried, but for once it was an expression of release, of happiness. I felt like a person who deserved to be noticed, to be appreciated, even loved. I had come home to my skin.

Coming Alive

FOR DAYS AFTER my first visits to Kaz's zoo, I was filled with a giddy joy, like Ebenezer Scrooge on Christmas morning when he realized he'd lived through the night. I smiled and laughed at inappropriate times, skipped on my walk to and from work.

And once that wore off, an odd calm came over me. My focus on my work was razor sharp, and I started creating a plan for the articles about the zoos, although the actual writing was still some time off.

My senses overwhelmed by the opulence of the zoo, I'd had less need to pull my scrapbook of fabric out of its hiding place to remind myself of how it had once felt to be a human of certain means, able to afford the richness of texture. I stopped scratching myself raw. I slept better, was more refreshed on awakening.

However, if my mind was at ease, I found my body less so. It twitched with the need to move; even after I walked to and from work, I buzzed with energy. Walking more didn't seem to be the answer — I still had the occasional panic attack if I found myself in the middle of an unexpected crowd, but otherwise I was getting much better about manoeuvring around others on the sidewalk.

My building had a gym that had been closed by order of the regency years ago, though it still contained all of the equipment.

It occurred to me that if any of it was still in working order, I might be able to move it into my place and use it there. I asked my building supervisor if I could take one of the rowing machines to my unit.

"You want to what?" he asked.

"I want to take one of the rowing machines to my condo."

"They belong to the condo association," the pinch-faced little man said. I had never had much to do with him, but that suited me fine — he was far too parsimonious with his good nature. "We're not allowed to move them."

"I am part of the condo association. I could go out and buy one, I suppose, but then I'd have to trouble you to deal with delivery people. So I thought I'd see if I could get one that's already in the building."

"I could get in trouble."

"Tell you what, I'll pay you fifty credits to bring one up to my place. I'll write to the condo board and offer to pay for a new one. They can buy a replacement or not, up to them."

Another fifty credits on top of that for his brother-in-law
to help, and one cold and blustery evening in January, the two
of them managed to get the machine in and out of the elevator and install it in Sophie's old bedroom. Soon I was skim-
ming forward and back, back and forth, feeling the pull of the
cord on my arms and shoulders, while my legs stretched and
bent. Pull and be pulled. Sweat formed on my forehead and I
laughed. When was the last time I'd sweated for any reason
other than the heat of the day? As I continued, sweat began
trickling down my back. By the time I stopped, the ache in
my arms and legs having transitioned from sweet to deep, my
entire body was a clammy mess, my clothing soaked. I poured
a glass of ice-cold water from a pitcher in the fridge, drank it
quickly and promptly threw it back up.

"Slowly," I admonished myself as I wiped the sink and
rinsed out my mouth. I stripped my clothes off, dropped them
on the bathroom floor, and stepped into the shower, turning
the head to deliver short, sharp, massaging needles.

Every nerve ending seemed hyper-sensitive. I swore I could
feel each loop of thread in my terry facecloth, every bubble of
the soap suds slipping over my skin.

After my shower, I reached for one of the towels on the rack,
a leftover from before Henny Penny that was thinned with use,
but then I dropped it, despising its meagreness. I had packed
away Matt's favourite bath sheets in the linen closet and never
used them. I pulled one out and that night it didn't hurt my
skin to wrap myself in the plush fabric, the way we used to do
when we got out of the bathtub: swaddle ourselves in one towel
the size of a blanket and then sit in front of the fire, skin on
skin, unable to keep our hands off each other. I'd put them away
but hadn't quite been able to bring myself to dispose of them.

I took the bottle of lotion the doctor had prescribed and spread it over my body. The strangeness of the sensation made me think about how I hadn't really touched myself in years — avoiding it like I avoided anything that wasn't going to be perfect, wasn't going to be the exact thing I needed. By not applying lotion to my dry and hungry skin, I'd starved it of even the crumbs of touch I could have fed myself.

I opened up a drawer and rummaged around to find a silky nightgown that I hadn't worn since Matt left. The cool, slick fabric against my warm skin made me shiver. My nipples hardened as I remembered what it was like to be young and healthy and sexually alive.

I lay down on my bed, and for the first time in years found something more than the utilitarian pleasure I'd been providing to myself on the rare occasions that my libido raised its head in a way that couldn't be ignored. My fingers were rusty, but soon the old rhythm came back to me, the fantasy that had always worked magic for me. I came quickly, and after a minute started again, playing out a longer scenario, teasing myself until my breath came in short gasps, and I came again.

I was clean. I smelled good. I was sexually calm, if not satisfied. I was exhausted. I slept.

The next day at work, I felt like I was going to die. Breathing was agony, walking was agony. I called a fleet car to take me to work. I couldn't face the stairs to the office, but lifting my hand to press the "up" button on the elevator panel was agony.

Delicious agony. There was pleasure in feeling something in my body other than the dull numbness that had been my constant companion for so long. This pain was sharp, but it was of my own creation, and it would pass.

Going to Market

EVERY TIME I went to a vanilla zoo — whether the one in Kaz's office building or, more often, his downtown zoo closer to home, which was convenient when I didn't want to drive in bad weather — the experience was new. The tacs were often, but not always, male, and ranged in age from early twenties to seniors in their late seventies or older. Fauna, by nature of their role, followed the tac's lead: some liked to cuddle; some, like Kaz that first night, would concentrate on delivering sensation to a certain part of the body — back, arms, legs — while others would work their way from top to bottom, touching every bit of bare skin along the way. There was no urgency in this place — people came for quiet companionship and a reminder of their humanity. The rule that there was to be no sexual touching was set, and every tac I ever met complied. It gave the zoo a sense of peace and quiet contentment.

On one particularly poignant night, the tac who chose me had to have been eighty. Still tall and sturdy, but with translucent skin and a tonsure of pure white hair. I led him to my blanket.

"Do you mind if we move this over to the wall?" he asked, pointing to an unoccupied space.

"Sure," I said, and he picked up the blanket and spread it out in the spot he'd chosen. He lowered himself, slowly, carefully, onto the blanket, and arranged a cushion between his back and the wall. He spread his legs into a wide V and said, "Would you sit here, please?"

I dropped to the floor and scooched in to sit between his legs, my back against his chest. I was short enough, or he was tall enough, that he could rest his chin on the top of my head. He wrapped his arms and legs around me, encasing me in a cocoon of his body.

"My wife died two years ago," he said softly, his voice adding to gentle murmurs around the room. It wasn't really the thing to talk in the zoo, but some people liked to do so, and as long as it didn't get too noisy no one seemed to mind, especially at the beginning of the evening or the end. "We were married sixty years. High school sweethearts, we were."

"That's nice," I said.

"We had a passel of kids, brought them up right, then they moved on and started their own families, and we had the best years of our lives, travelling, grandchildren, friends ..."

He was quiet for a moment, his hands moving from my shoulders, down my arms, and back again.

"We used to sit like this when she was pregnant. I'd rub her back and we'd talk about the new baby, and what it would be like, and how our lives would be enriched. And even after there were no more babies, she said she liked to feel like I was her suit of armour. She said she felt safe like this, and loved."

"It does feel safe," I said, "and I'm sure she felt loved."

We sat like that for hours, both of us lost in thought.

I wondered what it would have been like to sit this way with Matt, cradling my pregnant belly, knowing we had love and a lifetime ahead of us. I met Matt through Sophie. She'd brought him out one night, planning to make him her next conquest. She had a habit of leaving her marks with me while she socialized, coming back for them when it was time to go home. They rarely protested. Matt was the exception — after spending the evening talking to me, he turned down the opportunity to be with Sophie, instead asking me out the next night. I never forgot that he'd originally been attracted to her, and I was fearful for a long time that he'd grow tired of my quiet ways, yearn for a brighter light. I had just started to feel confident in his feelings for me, had started to believe he might not disappear as soon as he saw something better, when he told me he was going to a war zone and I realized that women weren't the only bright lights I needed to worry about losing him to.

Walking down the hall to my apartment that night, already hungry for something I couldn't quite put my finger on, I was struck by the most mouth-watering smell, something rich and beefy, but fresh and inviting, too — cilantro and cucumber.

I was still buying the regency's ration packs — they were quick and easy, nutritionally balanced and proportioned for appropriate calorie intake, two minutes in the microwave, or eaten cold if the power was out. The quality and assortment were far better than they had been a few years earlier, when food was still scarce and the regency worried more about providing nutritional balance than delicious meals, but it had been years since I'd smelled anything like this.

I walked up and down the hall until I finally pinpointed the source of the aroma. To my surprise, it was coming from under Eleanor's door. Surprise, because when we had talked over Friday night cocktails about the kinds of food we missed, I had assumed she was eating the same rations as me. Instead, the aromas around her door suggested far more colourful tastes and interests — and access to better food sources — than she'd ever mentioned. So much for getting to know her.

I had my hand up to knock on her door, to ask where she got her rations, when I remembered the time. It could wait.

As I let myself into my own dark apartment, I wondered why I'd never smelled my neighbours' cooking before, and realized that for one thing, I wasn't generally in the hallway in the evening: I came home and stayed in.

But it was also true that since I'd started going to the petting zoos, my body and my senses were undergoing a renaissance — I had a new energy, a brightness, and a renewed sense of smell.

For ten years I'd sat uncomplaining at my desk for hours at a time, and now I wanted to skip and dance. The rowing machine helped me use the pure energy that was ricocheting through my body. And the trek to and from the office had become a welcome way to wake up to the day, to see the world around me — really see it. Despite the slush and snow of winter, I was noticing colours and life and movement where before I'd seen everything through a dystopian grey lens. Had seen it that way for so long I'd forgotten there was an alternative. Becoming bolder as my fear of public spaces abated, I ignored sidewalk protocol and began to meet the eyes of the people I passed on the street every day. I started looking forward to recognizing them, meeting their eyes, and nodding "hello." It seemed like such a small thing, but it was a continuation of the thought that I'd had at my first TTC: "I go this far and no further." Having someone notice me was an acknowledgement that I was in fact there and that I now extended outside my body because I had inserted myself into someone else's day, however briefly. I go here and also there. I am … in someone else's eyes.

I even dug out my old MP3 player, which I'd packed away years ago and hadn't sought out, even after the cloud crashed, taking all my favourite music with it. When every song is a memory you can't bear, listening to music is a form of self-flagellation. I'd given music up, stored it away in an unused part of my brain with all the other memories of things that had once given me pleasure, but since Henry Penny only provoked thoughts of people and things whose absences were an exquisite, continuing torture. People and things that I'd never replaced, so I'd never been able to move on from them. The vanilla zoo helped me heal enough to start listening to music again, and dance around my apartment when the feeling overtook me. I even wrote a story about living in a world where people moved together because dancing made them feel good.

The city was blossoming into spring and so was I, coming alive again, bursting with energy and optimism and the desire to see and taste and do.

• • •

"Where do you buy your ration packages?" I asked Eleanor the next time we met in the hall on our way to work. "The cooking smells from your place are amazing."

"Ration packages?" she asked, surprised. "Do you still eat those?"

"Me and a lot of other people, I guess, or they wouldn't still be making them. I didn't know there was another option."

As we walked down the stairs together, she said, "I shouldn't sound so superior — I haven't been going there long myself. Meet me at the front door at four thirty and I'll take you. I need to pick up a few things."

I am part cat, in that I am a creature of habit. I find the shortest or most pleasant or most convenient route between two points, and unless I am drawn off my path for a specific errand, I never seek another. A circus might be going on two streets over and I would never know it was there because I wouldn't have thought to go that way.

Two streets east and one block south of our condo building, there was what had once been a mid-sized grocery store — a downtown store, not a suburban supermarket, but boasting an impressive square footage nonetheless, especially now that most of the original fixtures had been torn out.

I panicked a bit at the door. My fear of other people was waning, with going to work every day and, of course, going to the zoos. I still had to fight back that initial jolt of fear every night, but comfort came with familiarity. I didn't know this place, and I had no idea how many people would be there, or how closely they'd be packed.

"Lily, it's all right," Eleanor said, knowing me well enough by now to understand my hesitation. "I've been here. There's someone at the door, counting — the regency won't let them have more than fifty customers in at a time, anyway. It won't be that crowded. You'll be safe."

She pushed open the big front door and we entered a magical garden of delights. A few dozen vendors had staked out positions, like stalls in a market square. There were tables loaded with fresh fruit and vegetables, meat and fish laid out on trays of snow and ice. Pickles, preserves, and condiments. Bread in a dizzying array of shapes and styles. There were more people than I was strictly comfortable with, but not too many to handle if I didn't think about anything beyond the person in front of me.

Eleanor handed me a couple of her Impermatex shopping bags and cautioned me that I shouldn't try to buy everything at once — I would be able to come back for more. Storage would be an issue; I just had a small fridge, so anything that needed refrigeration had to be purchased in moderation.

Even so, I was like a kid in a candy store, going from stall to stall, taking it all in. The smells were overwhelming; cucumbers and spring onions were a full-on assault on the senses. I bought them both, along with new lettuce and herbs and greenhouse tomatoes.

I nearly wept to find a vendor selling olive oil. I spent a lot of credits on a small, precious bottle of it that the seller dipped out of a vat and filled through a funnel, then capped with a cork. "Bring that back for a refill," he said.

A piece of salmon — how had it arrived fresh from the Atlantic? The vendor just smiled inscrutably, but it was the real thing, and it was indeed fresh. A small steak. Butter. Eggs. My mouth was watering so hard it hurt by the time I added my final purchases to my overflowing bags: a paper bag holding a half pound of loose black tea, a bottle of cherry preserves, and another of heavy cream.

"Thank you for taking me shopping," I said as we walked back home. The smell of fresh bread was in my nose. I ripped a piece off the loaf and chewed on it as we walked.

"Do you remember how to cook?" she teased.

"I guess I'll find out."

"It took me a bit of time to get the knack, the timing, back."

"When I do, maybe I'll invite you over for dinner — I love to cook for people, or at least I used to."

"I'll look forward to it."

"Where does this all come from?" I asked her. I honestly couldn't remember the last time I'd seen a fresh vegetable, and yet here was this market abundance, varieties of food and people I had forgotten how to be able to imagine in the real world, although I wrote about them all the time in my stories.

Fairy tales.

"Local farms, I guess." She shrugged. "They must have recovered enough to have extra to sell once they fill their regency quotas."

"How did you find out about it?"

"Honestly, Lily, it was in the news."

"Yeah, well, I don't read the local news."

We walked on in silence. I'd been an editor on the world desk, and I was a bit of a snob about that — I was far more interested in the way the international dominoes fell than I was in the ones next door. And when the world has died around you, you can forget to look for signs of life — or in my case, you invent them and stop paying attention to the things that flutter outside your mind, for fear those are imaginary, too, and acknowledging them might drive you insane. I didn't expect to see anything interesting in the local news, so I didn't bother to check there for interesting things.

When I got home, I looked up the market — it was one of several in the city that had opened in the past few years, as power and water supply grew less erratic and, as Eleanor had suggested, farmers started producing surplus to sell after fulfilling their regency requirements. Transportation systems were also coming back to strength, allowing for some goods to be once again imported — at ridiculous prices, of course. I'd spent a couple of days' pay worth of credits on that beautiful green olive oil, and I was sure it would be worth every one of them. I'd been banking the bulk of my credits for years — what was I going to spend them on? — so I could indulge myself for a very long time before having to worry about a dip in my savings.

Supper was a dissertation on delectation — poached salmon that flaked neatly away from my fork. A salad of tender new lettuce and dill tasted vibrantly green, and the cucumber was a fresh crunch between my teeth, with a sprinkling of olive oil providing an unctuous note. Cream helped temper the unfamiliar sweetness of the syrup the cherries had been preserved in. And tea — real orange pekoe tea, which had disappeared after the pandemic, when supply lines from tea countries dried up — was a smooth, hot, bitter finish to a perfect meal. A finish that kept me up half the night because despite the many cups of café au lait that I'd enjoyed while interviewing Kaz, my once-famous resistance to caffeine had not returned.

On a whim, after supper I went down to the basement locker where Sophie and I had stored all of our inconvenient belongings, and where I had packed away memories I couldn't bear to face after she left.

I piled some quilts my grandmother had made, and which I'd carefully cleaned and nuked before packing, into a small two-wheeled shopping cart, along with some cotton sheets and towels. There were boxes of books I'd never unpacked, and old papers, CDs, some of Sophie's clothes and some of mine, pretty things that had had no place in a stay-at-home, Impermatexed world. I made a mental note to come back for those. There were even a couple of sewing projects — a love of sewing was one thing Sophie and I had had in common. But I was looking for pictures and art. Kaz had stung me when he'd said there was nothing of me in my home, but it was the truth. It wasn't for want of art — I had it, but had put it away. Paintings that I'd bought in happier times for happier homes were like music: it had hurt too much to enjoy them. It was easier to survive if I forgot — or at least wasn't constantly reminded — that life could be better.

I found a photograph of me with my brothers and their families — one that we'd taken at a gathering after Matt had left but before he'd been killed, so we all looked happy — and a nice frame to put it in. I chose a painting to hang over the dining room table, a multimedia mandala in a colour wheel of blues. It was too big for the cart, so I took it up separately and hung it on the wall, running my fingers over the thick swirls of paint, feeling the rough textures of fabric and wood that had been worked into the piece. Tonight I'd actually sat at the table to eat instead of standing at the sink, spooning rations out of the cartons they'd come in. When I went back down to the storage room, I rooted around and found placemats and napkins — I intended to eat at the table more often.

I opened another box, which turned out to be one Sophie had left behind. On top there was a photo of her from university. She looked tall and strong, like the farm girl she'd been before running away to join the circus — or at least that was the story she told to make herself sound more mysterious and daring. She hadn't run away, she'd gone to circus school with her parents' support, but the intent was the same, she always said. Get away from the mundane, shine on a stage. An injury put her circus dreams to bed, and that was when I met her, when she came to my dorm at university.

Looking at the picture, I could almost smell her — she carried a particular scent that I've always associated with sex: a little tangy, a little vinegary. I used to think that it was this that attracted men and women to her, this hint of a promise of fantasies fulfilled.

· · ·

"Well, hello," she said, sitting at my table in the cafeteria where I'd been eating alone, reading. "I'm Sophie."

"Hi, Sophie." I knew who she was.

"Mind if I sit with you?"

"No, go ahead."

"Is that an interesting book?"

"Yes, sort of."

"Well, put it down. I'm more interesting than it will ever be."

I put the book down a little resentfully and looked across at this girl with hair dyed a shade of red that didn't occur in nature, cut into one of those severe styles that reminded me of modern architecture, all angle and affect and no softness, although it suited her face and compact, slender body, toned and muscular from years of gymnastics and dance training. Her softness came from her clothes, today a blue velvet dress trimmed at the neck and wrists with what might or might not have been real fur. It looked like something a sixties go-go dancer would wear — an illusion underlined by her orange tights and green suede booties. It was a ridiculous outfit, but she wore it with such nonchalance that it seemed normal. I wondered what she wanted with me — people like her always wanted something from people like me; otherwise, we were beneath their notice, in my experience.

I waited for her to continue.

"You live on my floor," she said.

"Yes."

"Your roommate's a bit of a bitch. Are you friends or did the university match you up?"

"Barb's all right when you get to know her. But no, we met when we moved in." Was this what she wanted? She and Barb were marking out battle lines; was this her incursion into enemy territory?

"She called me a skank."

"She finds you ..." I searched for one of the nicer words I'd heard Barb call her. "Obnoxious."

"Does she talk about me much?"

"Only when you've been particularly obnoxious."

"But I'm not ..."

"Barb likes people who fit into her pre-labelled boxes. She doesn't have one for you. You don't have to do anything for her to find you obnoxious."

"What's your name?"

"Lily."

"What's your story, Lily? Do you have pre-labelled boxes, too?"

"No story, no boxes. First-year English major." I held up my book as proof. "You?"

"First-year arts. I'm about to change my major to fine arts."

"Are you an artist?"

"No, but I like art, and artists. Don't you? They're always doing something, or thinking about doing something. What do you want to be when you grow up?"

I laughed. "Writer, probably. You?"

"I want to be rich and surrounded by beautiful things and host salons where all the interesting creative people come and talk and drink and argue all night. And dance."

"Didn't that kind of thing fall out of fashion a few centuries ago?"

"I'm going to bring it back."

"You need a certain amount of money for it."

"Mm, I need to find a sugar daddy to bankroll me."

"That's a legitimate strategy, sure," I said, skeptical, not knowing then that it was essentially how Sophie operated; she was one of those people to whom other people gave things — tickets to sold-out events, designer clothes, high-priced meals in fine restaurants. A batted eyelash was an invitation to drop bills of large denominations in her handbag, seemingly with no quid pro quo.

...

I don't know why I had captured her attention — maybe it was her way of making Barb upset; maybe it was because I didn't pay her any. I mean, I had noticed her, of course — it was impossible not to; her clothes and hair screamed, "Look at me!" — but I just hadn't done anything about it.

Every society has its niches, and every niche has its own stars. In university, bright political lights run for student government; star athletes become captains of the team. Sophie wasn't one of the cool kids, exactly; she wasn't laid back enough and her interests weren't mainstream enough. But she was an influencer. She exerted a gravitational pull on interesting people — and people intrigued by interesting people — and they orbited around her like planets, secure in the knowledge that if something worth experiencing was going to happen, it would happen because she was there. Most people either loved Sophie or hated her; I might have intrigued her by not seeming to care either way. I had neither deliberately shunned her nor hung around her edges, hoping people would think I was part of her entourage. She was unused to being ignored.

People used to complain that I was aloof, but that was just fear of rejection — you can't reject me if I don't ask you to include me. In truth, I am a middle child; my heart has always been available to anyone who will treat me like I'm the only other person in the room. And I'd always yearned for a big sister. Sophie was my age but far more worldly. I assumed she was responding to what she thought was my lack of interest when she made a concerted effort to befriend me — coming to talk to me without her usual entourage; engaging me in conversation about things that interested both of us. She wooed me onto her hook, where she played me like a fat trout, pretending to let me swim my own way all the while training me to choose hers by rewarding me when I did: introducing me to some interesting new artist or writer she'd met, or taking me to gallery openings and after-parties. She found a couple of sources for my honours thesis that impressed my profs and helped me earn a post-grad scholarship.

It's hard to resist someone who's working to make you like them by doing things you're interested in, and I was entirely seduced by it. Even when I started realizing how manipulative she could be with me, I couldn't push her away — not far, not for long. She might have had her own reasons for doing so, but she made it her job to understand me. She got me in ways few people had bothered to try.

Her joie de vivre sparked something in me, too. I loved the bright, shiny world of artists and entertainers that she moved in but I would never have had the courage to seek it out, or the gall to expect it to welcome me. Sophie entered it fearlessly as if by right and took me along with her. Once she'd claimed me, there was no more standing back — she pulled me out of my shell. If I ever did anything exciting in my life, it was because Sophie gave me the nerve to do it, or at least showed me that I had the nerve, if only I'd use it.

In turn, I was her biggest cheerleader, urging her on in whatever she did. She saw her whole life as a performance. She never did open the salon she'd dreamed of as an undergrad, but she had found a way to keep interesting people around her — ran a gallery where performance artists, painters, and sculptors exhibited their latest work. She planned events that drew creative souls, and people with mysterious pasts and arcane secrets, the way she'd drawn me. We were all moths trying to find ourselves in the light of her flame.

When the regency began to relocate everyone to the city centre, where they'd been able to maintain essential services, they assigned me to this two-bedroom condo and Sophie decided to move in with me because it was nicer than the one they'd given her. The walls had been sanitized, then repainted a flat beige. The furniture was covered in treated leather — not a porous surface to be found — but it was certified disease free, and as long as the two of us were there, with a constant stream of her colourful friends and clients coming and going even when we were all supposed to be social distancing, it had felt like home.

I probably would have died of starvation, like millions of others that first year, except for Sophie, who saw the food riots as a challenge to be overcome. She turned out to have marvellous foraging and bartering skills. Sometimes she'd come home with no more than half a box of crackers, but she always came with something.

Sophie refused to wear a mask and gloves before the regency passed the BLT laws. She railed against the restrictions — not just masks and gloves but Impermatex fabrics, nukers at every outside door, and the ban on public gatherings.

To say the BLT laws cramped Sophie's style is to understate the effect they had on her soul. All of her favourite things were suddenly illegal. With no restaurants or bars, she had nowhere to perform socially, nowhere to meet the dangerous men with whom she had her wild, short-lived affairs. Everything she lived for was considered behaviour likely to spread disease. It didn't matter to me that I couldn't go out to see and be seen — I was still grieving for Matt, and it was also in my nature to be happy at home with a book. But without a space in which to be her fabulous self, Sophie became unsustainably life-sized. The virus nearly killed me, but it almost destroyed her.

When Henny Penny got me just a few months before they approved the vaccine, Sophie nursed me through the worst of it. But one day, shortly after I'd recovered enough to stand up and walk around, I woke up from a nap and she was gone, a few scattered belongings — things she'd forgotten or couldn't carry — the only sign she'd ever been there. I later realized she must have been moving her stuff out a bit at a time while I was sick. She left a note telling me there was food for three days and after that I was on my own. She had to get out.

Henny Penny left absences, in splatters, in drizzles, and in big, Sophie-shaped splotches that I tried not to look at because thinking about what was no longer there hit too hard, hurt too much.

When Henny Penny was done with us, when everyone had retreated into the sanctuary of nuclear families and close friendships, I was alone. Everyone who'd ever populated my world was either dead or gone. Any remaining members of Sophie's entourage disappeared with her. They hadn't been my friends. She must have told them she was leaving because they never came knocking again, and I had no idea where to find them even if I'd been so inclined.

For all I knew, she'd wandered off and died on an ice floe. But I hoped she'd found a community of fellow travellers, people who were similarly unprepared for post-pandemic life, and they were off living without gloves or masks, sitting on the rim of the abyss that we all looked into during Henny Penny, and daring the edge to crumble.

I wondered sometimes who I'd have been if she'd stayed. Sophie would never have allowed me to become as isolated as I was. She needed people around her — they were the air she breathed. I was still trying to figure out who I was without the woman I'd for years jokingly called my personality.

"I still miss you like crazy, and if I ever see you again, the first thing I am going to do is punch you for leaving me behind," I said to her picture.

I put the photograph back in the box, rolled my cart filled with illicit fabrics out, and locked the storage room door. Baby steps. I was re-entering the world in baby steps. I wasn't ready to invite Sophie back into my life. For the first time, it occurred to me that I was no longer certain she belonged there.

...

"What the hell are you eating?" Bob asked a few days later, the blue light of the nuker washing over his face as he stuck his head around my office door.

"Oh, no, is it bothering you?" I asked. I hadn't thought about how people would react to the smell of fish and garlic.

"Only in the sense that it smells delicious," Bob said, "and it's a big departure from the usual fare around here."

I waved him in and he entered somewhat reluctantly, staring at my face for a moment before awkwardly removing his mask — I'd already taken mine off to eat.

"Well, hello, stranger," I said, and he smiled.

"Hey."

"So tell me," I said, leaning forward and moving my dish to the side, "do you still eat regency rations, or are you back on real food?"

"A little of both," he said. "Ardythe does the shopping, so it's whatever she can find. Fresh food isn't all that plentiful in the winter, though greenhouses are starting to change that, of course, and we're seeing more affordable imports."

"My neighbour, Eleanor, introduced me to a market near us the other day. I couldn't believe all I found there."

"I'm glad to hear you're getting out a bit, meeting people. I worry about you."

"You do?"

"Sure. You survived Henny Penny, and then you stopped living."

I stared at his once-familiar face. He had more lines and wrinkles than I remembered, his eyebrows were starting to get a little out of control, but the laugh lines were rich and genuine

and his blue eyes sparkled, although now he looked concerned
that his words might have been a bit too pointed. A couple of
months earlier, they would have wounded me to the core, and
as it was, I'd probably go home and turn the words *stopped living* over carefully, looking for thorns and testing them against
my skin to see if they'd pierce me, but I couldn't deny the truth
of what he'd said.

"You're not wrong," I said, finally. "Damned if I can explain
it. My TTC therapist said I'd been in a deep depression —
maybe that's part of it. Shock, grief — everything going on at
once. But ... this is going to sound trite, but I'm starting to feel
reborn. Renewed, anyway. It's a good thing. And so is this," I
added, taking a bite of my salmon.

"And what's brought this about?" he asked.

"Being forced out of my cave." I shrugged. "Having something interesting to work on."

"I'll make a reporter out of you yet," he said. "How's that
going, if I might ask? When will I see a draft?"

I'd been playing my cards pretty close to my chest on this
story, and taking far longer than I really needed to. I didn't
want Bob to know how involved in it I was. I didn't tell him
that I'd become a member of Kaz's zoos in my own right, or
had started going a few times a week for less-than-investigative
purposes, just like I hadn't let on to Kaz how much of what
he was telling me was likely to appear in the final piece. I'd
stopped taking notes when we talked, and I thought he'd
stopped thinking of me as a journalist.

The truth? I was deliberately playing it out. The assignment was still providing legitimacy, in its weird little way, for
my trips to the zoo. Once I handed it in, I'd have no more
excuse to talk to Kaz, which I was enjoying, and I'd be out of

justification for going to the zoos beyond the pleasure I found in doing so.

"It's good," I said. I told Bob I'd gone to the original zoo near my apartment as an observer, and that I'd had a tour of Kaz's zoo.

"Are you going to go to that one?" he asked, and I lied and said, "Maybe. Just to see."

"So how do they work?" he asked. "What makes them different?"

"Hygiene, for one," I said, explaining the cleaning protocols in the room itself, the flu tests, the bodysuits and blindfolds.

I fed him some details about the original zoo: the corral, the audience, and the animals.

"What a weird setup," he said. "Why would anyone do that?"

"I think the zoos look a lot like the owners — that one has its origins in a particular BDSM scene, and the owner gets off on a high level of submissiveness, so he's set his zoo up that way. My contact's zoos are more refined hedonism than dungeon," I said, leaning forward as I warmed to my subject. "It is a symbiotic relationship. You have people who want to touch and those who want to be touched. Nobody just stands around and watches. My contact tells me that there are levels of zoos, starting with the vanilla one, which is what I've seen. Others have more nudity, more overtly sexual activity."

"So it's not just sex?" Did Bob sound a little disappointed?

"Not at a vanilla zoo. Anyone who makes a pest of him- or herself that way is kicked out. I suppose if a pair felt like they were in the mood for more, they could leave and get a room, but that doesn't seem to be the way it's happening. And although everyone's in couples, it's not just hetero. Everyone has to be open to giving or receiving from anyone."

"Wow. Who goes to these things?"

"Anyone with enough credits and a need to touch or be touched. People at the vanilla zoo range from eighteen — minimum age — to eighty or older."

"It'll be interesting to see whether there's anyone you recognize in the zoos," Bob said.

"It can't be part of the story if I do," I warned. "I've been wondering — you said, back when you asked me to write this, that you knew someone who knew someone who might be able to get me in. Who's your source? I'd like to interview him or her for the piece, get someone else's perspective."

"My source never actually went. He said his doctor gave him a number to call."

"Really. Do you know the doctor's name?"

"I can find out."

"Do that. It would be interesting to know."

"Okay. Easy-peasy." Bob shrugged. "So has your contact told you why he's letting you in on all the secrets? These zoos have been operating under the radar for a very long time. It's almost beyond comprehension that they'd end up contributing to their own exposé."

That was a question I'd also asked on one of those sun-drenched mornings over café au lait in Kaz's office.

"You know how dangerous it is," I'd said. "Do you want to be caught?"

Kaz had hesitated. "Not exactly."

"Not exactly?"

"I don't want to be caught. Given my irregular status, I could be in deep trouble for that alone, even if my business were strictly legal. But …" He sighed and gazed into my eyes, as if judging how much of the truth I could be trusted with. He looked out the window for a minute, got up, and paced to the door of his office. He came back and sat down, swiped with his thumb at a mote of dust on the arm of his chair. "One of my original partners, Violet, has branched off in a venture that has convinced me it's time to stop. It's a logical continuation of the zoos' … entropy, but to be connected, however remotely, to Violet's endeavour — it's too much. What I really want is to put an end to the need for the zoos. I want the mask and glove laws repealed. I want people to go back to living normal lives and stop needing the zoos just to feel human."

"What does this new one of Violet's do that yours do not? Is she one of the collectors you talked about?"

He was visibly uncomfortable with the question, and his answer was oblique. "During any period in history, when social mores have loosened or tightened, either extreme will bring on a slide into the degradation of other humans — it's the ultimate kink: when you're allowed everything, it's taboo enough to give you thrills, and when you're allowed nothing, that's the one place you have power, because everyone is more powerful than someone else at some level. And of course, usually it's the authority figures who are indulging in it the most."

"Sounds like your average day in a dungeon."

"If it stopped there, it wouldn't bother me. It's BDSM skewed to the current reality. Which takes it too far down an unpalatable path."

"And you think getting me to write about luxury zoos where people get their kicks like kings will encourage the regency to repeal the BLT laws? That's a bit of a bank shot you're playing there, Kaz."

"Yes and no. I think the regency is holding on to the mask and glove laws for reasons that have nothing to do with hygiene and everything to do with control. Until the country is back to normal, they can put off having elections, they can delay being truly accountable."

"A lot of people seem to be wondering why the BLT laws are still in place, why we're still wearing masks and gloves years after the vaccine. Why do you think we are?"

"I don't know. Some people in remote areas still haven't been vaccinated, and some people are still dying, because the virus is still mutating. It's reason enough for people to be afraid, and I think the regency stokes that fear for its own purposes. I personally think people who are profiting from the fear are going to milk it for all they can get until the sheer ridiculousness of the situation forces them to stop."

"I think that's a cynical view of the regency, but say you're right — I'm still not seeing how talking about it to a reporter is going to change anything."

"The regency is counting on citizens to be snobs. As long as only a certain class of people is seen breaking the law in a certain class of zoo, they can perpetuate the myth that it's something only the poor and weak-willed would do. We both know that's not true. If respectable people start talking about the zoos in respectable circles, the regency will know the party is over."

"And what then — you'll close the zoos and go legit?"

He chuckled. "I don't think of myself or my partner as criminals — at least, not the way we started. We thought of ourselves as providing a service made necessary by the misplaced laws passed by governments. Or maybe not misplaced — there was a time when the BLT laws were absolutely necessary. But they'd outlived their usefulness by the time we set up our zoos, and all they're doing now us keeping us isolated from one another. I'm happy to subvert those laws. I'd be less happy to be caught and branded a criminal for doing it — I'm not crazy. But it's time for them to go. And when they do, so will the need for petting zoos, and I'm okay with that. So I'm courting disaster purposefully." He smiled at me. "Strategically."

• • •

"He's kind of hoping to be put out of business," I said, and Bob raised a skeptical eyebrow.

"I know," I said, shrugging. "It's a long shot, but he seems serious."

"So when am I going to see some copy?"

"Soon. I have more research to do."

"Start writing and figure out what you don't know," Bob countered. "I suspect you have more than enough for a series. In the meantime, you owed me a chapter in your latest saga four days ago."

"Sorry, I've been working on my Henny Penny history. The regency's deadlines trump yours. Tomorrow?"

"If not sooner." He got up and headed for the door.

"Bob?"

He stopped.

"Let's do lunch tomorrow. Invite a couple of the others to join us. Do you think they would?"

He smiled as he put his mask back on and nodded. "I think that's a great idea. I'll send out a message. Lily's office, noon, bring your own."

Going to the Zoos

THE VANILLA ZOO had been good for the first couple of months. But as with the TTCs, once it started being enough, it stopped being anywhere near satisfying. I found myself analyzing my responses, playing with the paradigm — for example, standing sideways in the line, or leaning out a bit, to see if that would make someone pick me more quickly. But unlike with the TTCs, when I just kept going more and more often, to try to surprise myself with a change in the pattern, this time I knew there was somewhere else to go, and I knew someone who could tell me where it was.

"Chocolate zoos?" I'd laughed. "That's hilarious."

"I didn't name them!" Kaz had protested.

"What defines milk chocolate?"

"It's vanilla with a hint of sin," he said. "Like necking on a date when you're a kid — kissing, touching through the clothing only."

"What comes after that?"

"After that is semi-sweet. You can be naked — or not, but if you don't want to be, it's best to make that clear up front. No intercourse, but sexual touching is allowed. And then dark chocolate, where there's no more fauna and tacs, and it is expected that sex will be enjoyed by all."

People had to spend a mandatory five nights at any zoo before progressing to the next level; there was no jumping the line. People tended to stay longer at milk chocolate, and the least amount of time at semi-sweet, Kaz said.

"Once they go that far, they're often ready to go all the way, either at home with someone they've met at the zoo, or in the next zoo. Semi-sweet can be tremendously frustrating."

"Sounds like a tantric experience — the sensation is the point, taking it as far as you can go without climax."

"Well, climax is allowed, just not penetration. But you're right, and not a lot of people have the patience for tantra. So they either stall at milk chocolate or jump as soon as possible to dark. Milk chocolate and semi-sweet are the only chocolate zoos that run every night of the week. Dark chocolate is only twice a week. We just don't have enough demand at that level to make it any more frequent."

"Anything after that?"

"Mocha. Group sex. Free-for-all. Once a week. And that's where mine stop."

"No bittersweet?" I asked and he laughed wryly.

"Isn't it all bittersweet, when you think about it?" he asked.

"No, really, though — where else is there to go?" I asked.

"Nowhere that I want to take it. Places where it's less about the pure experience of touch, and more about the ... I don't know what you'd call it, curated kink."

"I'm curious. Accepting that some are looking only for the vanilla experience while others want more intimacy, why don't you just go from one to the other? Why do you have intermediate levels?"

Kaz sipped his coffee and thought about his answer for a moment. "There are a couple of reasons. First of all, it's kind of the way they happened. People came to us and said, 'Touch isn't enough, we'd like to kiss,' and then they said, 'Kissing's not enough,' and then they said, 'We'd really like to be able to come here and have sex.' So we made all of these variations, but we kept the other ones open because people still use them."

"You'd close them down if they weren't making money."

"Or providing a worthwhile service to people who want them, yes."

"So what are your other reasons?"

"I think of it as foreplay," he said. "Sex isn't just penetration and ejaculation, and physical pleasure doesn't begin and shouldn't end there. I think it does us all good to be reminded every now and then that pleasure is more nuanced." He leaned forward and put his empty cup on the table.

"Believe it or not, I'm a bit of a romantic. I think there should be some element of mystery, of anticipation. You don't get that — or you don't get primarily that — in the sex zoos, but I think it's important to experience it before you get to those zoos, so in my world, it's a requirement."

"More of your social experiment?"

"Sure, if you want to put it like that."

"So have you participated in all of these zoos?"

"All of mine, yes."

"Quality control?"

"Partly. Partly to see how they work, especially in the early days: if they work, what doesn't work. And partly because ... I'm no angel, never was, not going to pretend to be one. They can be a lot of fun. I need to touch and be touched, too."

"And it saves you the bother of meeting a nice girl and taking her out to dinner ..." I grinned.

"Well, there are no restaurants anymore," he responded with his own smile.

As we became easier with each other, these sessions became less about the interview and more about getting to know each other. He seemed so serious most of the time that I took particular pleasure in making him smile, and I gave myself points when I managed to coax a laugh out of him.

Kaz had primary charge of the vanilla zoo, and oversaw new member intake, while his partner, Aziz, was in charge of milk chocolate. They managed the other chocolate and mocha zoos together.

"Will I be able to meet Aziz?" I asked.

"I'm not sure," Kaz answered. "I'll ask."

"And are the chocolate zoos all over the city, too?" I'd been going to a vanilla zoo downtown.

"Milk chocolate is downtown, but the sex zoos are here," he'd said, meaning the zoo in the suburbs where we had all our interviews. "That's about quality control, too. People who are willing and able to travel this far are less likely to make trouble once they get here."

I used the number Kaz gave me to book my space at a milk-chocolate zoo.

"Hello, Davina speaking, how may I direct your call?" The voice on the other end of the phone was pleasant, middle aged. I imagined Davina with a sleek chignon, wearing a well-fitted dress in a subdued colour and sensible heels.

"I would like to make an appointment," I said, not sure what I should be asking for.

"For which service?"

"Milk chocolate."

"I see. Is this your first time here?"

"Yes."

"And how did you find out about us?"

"Kaz gave me your number."

"I see. Kaz referred you." I heard computer keys clicking. "Does head office have your records?"

"Yes. The name is Kate Matthews."

"Thank you, Kate. Are you interested in participating as a fauna or as a tac?"

She could have been the receptionist at my doctor's office, asking me questions to which the answers were deeply personal, in a tone of professional boredom.

"Fauna."

"Excellent. When would you like to join us?"

"Tomorrow," I said, thinking I needed time to prepare myself for a more intimate experience than the ones I'd had at the vanilla zoo. It might only be necking, but it had been a long time since I'd done even that. I was eager to start, but also apprehensive.

The apprehension won. I cancelled the appointment an hour before the zoo started. Davina sounded resigned, and not surprised. Maybe a lot of first-timers got cold feet.

Wanting to take that next step, and being able to imagine doing so, were worlds away from picking up a foot and advancing.

I was old enough to have been thoroughly indoctrinated in the things good girls did and did not do, but young enough to have seen all those norms partially fall — although the double standard held firm, leaving me uncertain of which was the correct path. I'd been in awe of Sophie's ability to take her pleasure where it pleased her, but had never been able to emulate her. I had always had that little voice calling "Shame!" in the back of my head.

I knew what my brothers — not to mention my father — would have had to say about women who offered themselves up to be pawed at, and that was how they'd see going to the zoos, even the vanilla one. The milk-chocolate zoo might involve relatively innocent necking, but that slight permissiveness removed any plausible deniability about what I was seeking out, all my cover story about needing simple human connection blown. If I came home juiced up and buzzing, it would be because that was the point, and not because it was an accident or a side effect. Blatantly seeking intimate attention from a stranger was a no-no for good girls.

So instead of going for vanilla with a hint of sin, I went back to my usual zoo the next night. The peaceful innocence of that experience, which I'd found both energizing and calming at the beginning, left me edgy and frustrated. Having someone delicately stroke my arm might appease my skin hunger, but other appetites were entirely unsatisfied.

At work for the next few days, I was cranky with everyone, snapping and impatient to the point where attendance at the lunches in my office dropped off sharply.

But when I snapped at Eleanor after meeting her in the hall, she snapped back.

"What the hell is your issue? You're about as pleasant as a dead fish."

That stopped me in my tracks. "Come on over for a glass of wine and I'll tell you all about it."

Eleanor popped her head in at home to tell Dan where she'd be and then stepped into my apartment.

"Homey," she said, looking around my place for the first time. Even with the touches I'd started to add, it was still bare.

"Well. This is where I live, but it's never been my home," I said, stepping out of the kitchen with a bottle of wine, two glasses, and a hastily assembled tray of cheese and crackers.

I poured the wine and we clinked glasses, then laughed uncomfortably when we realized we were both still wearing masks. When was it going to become normal to take them off in front of others? We'd been friends for a few months now and we'd never seen each other without them. It was becoming ridiculous.

We looked at each other for a moment, as if waiting for the other to go first.

"Dear god. I feel like I'm about to lose my virginity," Eleanor said finally.

"I'll go first," I said, reaching for my mask.

"No, we'll do it together, on three," she said. "One, two, three," we counted together, and both pulled off our masks at the same time.

Today was one of those days where she had some sort of intricate face paint, the whole scheme of which was revealed when she took of her mask.

"That's the solar system!" I said, blurting out the first thing that came into my head, looking at the delicate whorls of colour. "How long did that take you?"

"Actually, Dan does it. He's quite artistic."

"Are you blushing?"

"How can you tell?"

"Saturn just took on a reddish tinge. Why are you blushing?"

"Don't you think it's weird that my husband paints my face?"

"Hell, no. I think it's nice. A lovely little bonding ritual."

"Bonding ... foreplay," she said, blushing again. "Speaking of bonding rituals," she held up her wineglass and we clinked again, then drank.

"So what's been on your mind, Lily? Who is he?"

"What?" I sputtered.

"There's always a 'he,'" she said confidently. "When I met you, you were a quiet little country mouse, new to the world, but in the last few months, you've started moulting — working out, eating good food, and looking happy. Next thing you know, you'll be getting a decent haircut. Women don't just do that spontaneously. The transformation can come before the sex or after, but there's always a he involved."

"There's no he."

"Okay, she, then."

"Nope, no she."

"Well, something's been pushing your buttons. Got a robot in the bedroom?"

I laughed, then took the plunge. "I'm writing an article about this secret ring of elite petting zoos," I said. "And I've started going to them."

"Well." She put down her glass. "That's news. How long have we known each other — six months? And you never told me I've been drinking with a criminal."

I couldn't tell whether she was upset. "Well, I guess, but that wasn't my point. You don't sound that surprised I'm going to a zoo."

"I've heard of them, though given your track record for paying attention to the world around you, I'm surprised you have. I thought you said you weren't reporting anymore."

"It was a special project for my editor. But hell, my doctor told me to go. The TTCs weren't doing it for me anymore."

"You went to the TTCs, too? You never mentioned that."

"Yeah, I know. It felt weird to talk about. It would have been like telling you what medications I was on. I was ordered to go because I live alone."

"Right, I think I knew they were doing that. So how long have you been going to the zoos?"

"Since January."

"So tell me about them." She picked up her wine again and sat back on the couch.

"They're really quite nice." I described the luxurious, sensation-rich zoo, how it worked. "I'm at the vanilla level, no sexual touching. After that, they get progressively more intimate."

Eleanor eyed me knowingly. "And you're looking to progress."

I nodded. "I made an appointment a couple of nights ago at the next level, milk chocolate. And I couldn't go."

"Why not?"

I took a big gulp of my wine and topped up my glass. "Because ... I felt like a bit of a slut, frankly."

"Seriously? What would happen there — a bit of kissing, a grope in the dark?"

"Yeah, but nice girls — please don't cringe — nice girls aren't supposed to just put themselves out there for that."

"Oh, please, you put yourself out there for that every time you go to a petting zoo, and don't give me that crap about it not being about sex. It's always about sex, one way or another."

"I disagree. I've had partners there who don't interest me at all sexually, but it feels good to have them touch me. One night I went in with a headache and my tac gave me a facial massage, I felt reborn."

"If you say so." She took a drink of her wine and thought for a minute. "But seriously, I don't know what you're getting worked up about. Did you ever play that game when you were a teenager — you sit in a circle and you spin the bottle and whoever the bottle points to goes in the closet with you and you stay in there for five minutes?"

I shook my head. I'd heard of it, but was never invited to the parties where people played it.

"Well, we played it all the time when I was a kid. One party, you might end up in the closet with five different guys. Now two of those guys might be too shy to talk, let alone touch you, and another two might not make it past a sloppy kiss, but maybe the fifth guy would rock your world just a little. The point is, you probably weren't dating — and weren't going to date — any of them. It was all just a bit of fun."

"And the moral of the story is you don't think there's anything wrong with me going?"

"Oh, I think there's plenty wrong with you going. I think you should just invite the next partner you get at the zoo who's the slightest bit interesting to get to know you a little better. But failing that, if you accept that going to the vanilla zoos is a viable option, then it's a logical next step to the chocolate zoos."

"And what about when that's not enough? Because my pattern seems to be that they stop being enough pretty quickly."

"Well, in a perfect world, by then you'll have met yourself a nice man and will have invited him home to continue the party. But frankly, Lily, I've never met a woman who needed to get laid quite as badly as you, and if that's where you can get it, then that's where you should go. No retreat, no guilt, just surrender. Be sure to use protection."

I laughed. "Protection, sure. Protection is what I'm trying to get rid of by going."

She laughed, then said, seriously, "I wouldn't do it. Can't imagine a world where I would do it. And I'd rather you not do it, or feel you had to. But you've been without for a long time. That's not good for the soul. Or for your mood. Or for your skin, for that matter. Just tone down that nonsense about what good girls do and don't do. Smart girls do what's good for them."

We drank a toast to smart girls.

Eleanor bit into a piece of cheese. "That reminds me — I've heard about this farm about forty miles outside the city, where they make feta. We have to go."

We ate our cheese and crackers and drank wine and talked and laughed, but all the while I was turning what she'd said over in my mind. The milk-chocolate zoo was spin-the-bottle, not a sign of depravity and dissolution. My new friend — and at least one of my old friends — wouldn't have thought twice about it, so why was I hanging myself on pejorative words for relatively innocent acts?

The next day, I called Davina back.

The milk-chocolate zoo that I went to downtown was as richly upholstered and just as dimly lit as the vanilla zoo I'd been to before, and as in that zoo, the tacs went to one changing room and the fifteen or so fauna to another. I entered the zoo first along with the other fauna and prepared a spot with blankets and cushions close to one of the walls. I did that at all the zoos now, finding that I liked the sense of boundary the wall gave me, a line that couldn't be crossed. At the cue — a

brightening, then dimming of the lights, as in the theatre —
we formed a line in front of the door to the tacs' changing room
and put on our blindfolds. I stood trembling, eyes shut tight,
listening to the tacs file in, hardly daring to breathe, waiting
for a hand to fall on my head or shoulder.

My tac that night was forty-something, a man with
smooth brown skin; shiny jet-black hair; and an air of complete self-satisfaction. He took my hand and I led him to my
blanket.

".This is your first time here," he said.

"How can you tell?"

"You're trembling."

"I don't know what to do," I admitted, feeling once again
naked in my bodysuit, even though I'd become used to wearing
it and seeing my partners in the same attire. I was painfully
aware of how minimally we were covered.

"Let me show you."

He dropped to the blanket and took my hand, drawing me
down to him. We lay side by side, inches apart. "Close your
eyes," he said, and I did.

His lips met mine and began a kiss that lasted for hours.
Occasionally our mouths parted, lips landed on a cheek, a chin,
the base of a throat. The pressure was light here and firm there,
but the essential joining lasted for hundreds of long, delicious
minutes.

I realized later that although we'd moved around, rolling
this way and that, he'd barely touched me; the brush of a palm
against the side of a breast was as close as he'd come to exploring me with his hands, which for the most part had stayed at
the small of my back, in my hair, or on my shoulders, as mine
had on him. Our bodies had never really met, and certainly

not below the waist; I couldn't have told you whether he'd been aroused. We'd kissed. Just kissed.

"You're quite lovely," he said as I rose to leave. "This has been a pleasure."

"Yes, it has, thank you," I said. Blushing, trembling a little still, as I left.

I didn't go back the next night, but I didn't wait for long. Again, there was no problem getting a reservation, although there had been relatively few couples the first night, and I worried that this zoo might be harder to get into because it had fewer patrons.

I did wonder how representative my first experience of the place had been — it had certainly not been what I was expecting, and the more I thought about it, the more bewildered I was. The tac had kept his hands and everything else to himself. In a *petting* zoo. But he'd kissed me as if he couldn't imagine anything more intriguing, as if there were worlds inside my mouth that he couldn't wait to explore, a universe on my lips, galaxies exploding outward on my face and neck, like Eleanor's face paint the other night. It had been such a sensual thing. I'd never experienced anything like it. Even in the early days of my relationship with Matt, when we'd spent days in bed together, touching, learning, experimenting, a kiss was always understood to be a prelude, never an end in itself. The fact that this one had gone nowhere robbed it, in some strange and inexplicable way, of its sexual power. Pleasant? Of course. Affecting? No question. Sensual, but not, all in all, sexual somehow. And I wondered why this man had drawn in his horns, so to speak. Maybe because I was new, and a little scared.

I hoped it had had nothing to do with a lack of sex appeal — it was so hard to tell, after all this time, whether I still had the thing that made men look twice. I'd never had such an ample supply of it, anyway, not compared with someone like Sophie, who had had men clamouring at her heels and trailing after her down the street. It would be horrifying to rejoin the world and discover I had no place in it as a sexual being.

Two days after my first trip to the milk-chocolate zoo, and two before my second, Kaz finally sent a note to say that Aziz had agreed to meet with me late that afternoon, if I could make it to the office.

Jane brought me a coffee. "So you're going to meet Aziz?" she asked.

"Yes. What's he like?"

"He's a good guy, bit of a trickster — not in a bad way," she rushed to clarify. "Utterly charming. But watch yourself around him a little. He tends to ignore boundaries."

I was a bit taken aback, and her eyes crinkled and she said, "He's my brother-in-law and I adore him, so I'm allowed to say that about him."

"Ah," I said, smiling back.

Kaz came out and led me to his office, where a tall, dark-haired man stood, looking out the window as he waited.

"Aziz, this is …" Kaz said, and his friend turned and smiled broadly when he saw me.

"We've met," Aziz said, taking my hand and kissing it. "Your Kate made a trip to my zoo that I forgot to tell you about," he said to Kaz, who looked at him intently for a moment, then said, "Bastard."

"My lineage is well established, Kasimir, as you know. And your friend is a delight, as you also know. I didn't know she was also the reporter to whom you've been spilling all of our secrets." Aziz spoke English like someone who spent most of his day speaking a different language. His English was perfect, with a scent of something foreign.

"Aziz, my business partner and oldest friend," Kaz said, presenting him to me as I blushed, speechless.

"I'm delighted to see you again."

"You …" I sputtered at Aziz.

"Aziz has an interesting sense of humour," Kaz said, then looked back at Aziz.

"I was a perfect gentleman," Aziz said.

"And you knew who I was, too," I said accusingly to Aziz, still processing the fact that it was Kaz's partner who had kissed me all night without touching me. "So much for blindfolds and anonymity. Do you claim *droit de seigneur*, too?"

"Kaz makes a special recommendation, I can't help but be curious, and to satisfy my curiosity. And when Kaz's special recommendation displays cold feet by making a reservation and then cancelling it, I think it might be nice to make her first experience a gentle one." Aziz smiled.

"But I didn't make a special recommendation …" Kaz protested.

"I told the woman making the reservation that you'd given me the number," I remembered.

"Ah," they said together, nodding.

"Well, that almost explains that, then. I wondered how I could possibly go to a petting zoo and not get petted … thought maybe I'd lost my mojo."

Both men laughed. "Never fear," Aziz said. "Your mojo is intact."

"How do you two know each other?"

"We've been friends since we were children," Kaz said.

"If there's anything you'd like to know about him, Kate, just ask me. You know where I can be reached. I make superlative espresso and would be very pleased to share a cup with you."

They led me to a part of the building I'd never seen, through an empty zoo to a darkened alcove behind an intricately carved wooden screen. There were comfortable armchairs where one could sit and watch the activity inside the zoo without being seen. I remembered a similar screen in the milk-chocolate zoo. I'd thought it was decorative, hadn't guessed there was anyone sitting behind it.

We sat. "Quality control?" I asked. "You told me there were no voyeurs at your zoos."

"Well, except for Aziz," Kaz answered.

"I'm not a voyeur — or not just a voyeur. I need to know things are going well and I don't always think it's fair to make others watch when they can't participate. So while we have security, I do like to be a little more hands-on."

"But why this setup? Why not one-way glass, or video cameras?"

"Both are too obvious." Aziz shrugged. "No one gets close enough to the screen to suspect my presence, and this keeps me honest — I must sit here quietly, and pay attention. And if there's a problem, I can act immediately."

"What he's not telling you," said Kaz, "is that there are, in fact, some cameras, and there are always guards in a nearby room who are ready to act if there is trouble."

"Does that happen a lot?"

"Enough for it to make sense for us to watch occasionally, and take part every now and then."

"Your *droit de seigneur*."

"I don't always pick the new member — that's a judgment call. It's being in the room that's important," Kaz said.

"I take it you have fake blindfolds, then?"

"Those are Aziz's specialty."

"We participate in each of the zoos about once a month — separately, as a rule — to observe that all is continuing to go well," Aziz said. "You must understand this about us: we are serious about these zoos not simply as a money-making enterprise, but also for the experience we offer our guests and the service we are providing to those who have nowhere else that is safe to go for a human connection."

"To get back to your question about trouble, most of the people who come here are just looking for what we have to offer," said Kaz. "There's enough variety in the zoos now that once they're plugged into the network, anyone looking for some specialized kink can find it."

"This might be a dark-chocolate zoo, but it's still pretty vanilla in that all anyone will get here is straightforward, one-partner sex — no bells, no whistles, no whips, no chains," Aziz added.

"What happens at mocha?" I asked.

"There's no pairing off for the evening, it's just everybody in one room," said Kaz. "If you're approached for an activity that doesn't interest you, you are allowed to decline, respectfully, but we expect people to be there because they are interested in experiencing the full scope of the human condition."

I turned to Aziz. "Kaz was saying there's less of a need for dark-chocolate zoos because people tend to stall at milk chocolate?"

"Not everyone has a taste for dark chocolate," Aziz agreed. "The pandemic has robbed many people of their inhibitions — once they've looked death in the face, once they've lost everything, it seems, many people find their former sexual mores superfluous. Still, it's a big step to go from public petting to public nudity, and a huge step to go from there to public sex, although I suspect that when our ancestors lived in caves, they managed it fairly successfully."

"Though not, as a rule, with strangers, I suspect," I said, and both men nodded.

"As you say," Aziz said. "I'd like to see statistics on pre-pandemic swingers' club membership and post-pandemic mocha club regulars. I'm guessing that proportionally speaking, our numbers are better. Henny Penny survivors seem to have lost some of their pre-pandemic moral hang-ups."

"Why don't you have privacy at this level? Or at any level? Surely it would be easy enough to divide this space off into cubicles ..."

"We actually tried that at the beginning — not cubicles, but strategically placed curtains," Kaz replied. "But it felt ... tawdry, like a really low-rent brothel. And there was too much abuse. When everything's out in the open, the group is self-policing. There is very little unwanted groping in the vanilla zoos — 'no' means no when the whole room is watching."

"We also enjoyed the prospect of ripping away inhibitions," Aziz added. "There is something infinitely more hedonistic about being the fauna — or the tactile — in an open zoo, where others can see and hear you, than there is in being behind closed doors. In the dark-chocolate zoo, when someone is having a good night, quite often everyone will ride the wave with them. We decided we liked the idea of breaking down that barrier, literally and figuratively — requiring our members to see and be seen, and in that way, allowing them to admit to themselves and to the world that they are needful human beings."

Going to the Farm

LILY'S LUNCHES HAD begun with me, Bob, Breaking-News Steve (as opposed to Politics Steve), and Jill. We brought a table and some chairs into my office, but by the next week, we had too many people, so we started eating in Bob's office, which was a bit bigger, and finally graduated to an unused boardroom, and anyone who wasn't off on assignment came. We usually had more people in the boardroom than the ten allowed under the BLT laws, but if anyone else noticed we were eating lunch like criminals, no one said anything.

"Jill, what time do you have to get up in the morning to paint a puss on your puss?" Breaking-News Steve asked, pointing to the realistic cat face Jill uncovered fully when she took off her mask to eat. Everyone around the table nodded — her makeup was becoming more and more detailed as lunches went on, as if she were painting her face in anticipation of the reaction she'd receive.

"What's your secret?" I asked, shaking my small container of dressing before pouring it over my lunch salad — spinach, boiled eggs, and mushrooms.

Jill laughed and shook her head. "Just time," she said, opening the lid of her bowl. "Okay, I'll start today. I'm having pasta with a pan sauce of tomatoes, basil, and mozzarella. Cheese comes from the little market on Switcher Street, where I also found this," and she held up a barely ripe mango.

"Yum!" said Steve. "I'm having leftover chicken and twice-cooked potatoes. I found the sour cream for the potatoes at the market near where the old Beechwood subway stop was, the one I told you about last week, where I found the avocado. I also have peas, and for dessert, there's a hand pie made with reconstituted dried apples."

Bob had carrot soup with a buttered ciabatta bun. "Our milk guy has started to branch out with cream and butter. He's promised us curds next week, and Ardythe is going to make poutine."

There were a lot of oohs and ahs around the table about that.

This had become our lunchtime routine. We were creating a food map of the city, with markets the new important landmarks.

I looked around the table at all the uncovered faces, people I was coming to know and like and could now see in all their glory. Less than a year ago, I had been eating rations at home, afraid to go outside. This kind of gathering would have been unthinkable. Even now, every lunch was a shock all over again. I had had to reprogram my recognition function, because people were one person with the mask and quite another without.

"I have an idea for a column," I said, after finishing the day's recitation with my spinach salad. "I'm going to call it Lily's Lunches, and share some of the recipes from lunch — with everyone's permission, of course — and shopping information. What do you think?"

"Start with Bob's soup," Maddie, the arts reporter, said. "That smells delicious."

Because of those conversations, I started going farther afield to buy delicacies, overcoming my fear of the monsters lurking in the unknown to change my usual patterns, hoping to discover something new that I could share with my lunch companions. I was starting to resent the need to don the mask and gloves in familiar places, but I appreciated the security they afforded me when I went somewhere new.

It was while I was out walking one sunny Saturday in late April that I noticed a sign for Valerie's Hair Salon and decided to go in. I hadn't had a professional haircut since Henny Penny, in part because salons were closed those first few years — and then later because I didn't really care. I'd never liked getting my hair cut, anyway, the torture of having to stare at myself in the mirror, with nothing to do but catalogue my flaws and make excruciating small talk with the stylist over the noise of hair dryers. I just took out the scissors and chopped when my hair got on my nerves. It was getting on my nerves again now, but I was more conscious these days of how it looked — Eleanor had been teasing me about my bad cuts.

"Do you take walk-ins?" I asked the woman at the counter — Valerie, by the nametag on her blouse.

"Sure! What do you want to have done today, hon?" she asked.

"Cut," I said.

"And colour?" she asked, looking critically at my grey.

"I don't want my hair to feel like straw," I said warily.

"It was hard to come by quality colour for a long time," Valerie said, "but it's coming back now. It's expensive, but it will brighten you right up if you have the credits for it."

"All right, then — let's go crazy."

Valerie showed me a card with a bunch of swatches.

"I'd recommend this soft caramel shade," she said, and I reached my hand out to touch the strands of artificial hair on the card. "And I think you'd look fabulous with copper highlights, some gold to give it texture. What do you think?"

"I think you're the expert, and if you like it, you go ahead," I said. She seemed to know what she was doing and I was willing to let her have a go.

She mixed the colours, then wrapped a towel around my neck and covered my clothes with a gown.

"How long has this salon been open?" I asked. "You don't see many around."

"I've had this place for about twenty years, though I had to close for a couple of years during Henny Penny," she said. "I opened up again ... eight years ago? Of course, many of my clients were either gone or had moved or were too afraid to come in, so I've had to rebuild my clientele, and I'm still not as busy as I was, as you can see. I used to have five girls working for me on a Saturday — now I have just two during the week and I bring them in on Saturday morning, but I cover the afternoon by myself." Valerie paused for a moment while she concentrated on preparing another area of hair to be coloured.

"But I own the place, don't need to worry about paying rent, and I keep it open as much to give myself something to do as to make money."

It was fascinating to watch her work. She separated the hair on my scalp into sections, then subdivided those sections, applied the colour solution, wrapped the hair in foil and then did it again until my scalp was covered. Another person walked in while she was folding over the last foil. "You have a seat, hon, I'll be with you in a minute," she called out, then brought me mint tea in a sippy cup to drink while the colour worked its magic on my hair and Valerie went off to work hers on the other woman's.

A hair salon is such a scent-rich place, with the colouring solutions, peroxide, shampoo, and hair products all warring for space in your nose. The hard surfaces were immaculate, the floors carefully swept, the mirrors dust free, and the windows sparkling. It was a professional salon with a certain amount of style — mirrors in ornate frames, richly coloured wallpaper, and intricate mouldings. It echoed Valerie's own style — despite the slow Saturday, she was carefully dressed in flattering Impermatex pants and blouse, and perfectly made up, at least above her mask. It was a little sad to think of her choosing her outfit and putting on makeup to spend the day looking out the window of an empty beauty parlour, watching the few people walking by and remembering better days, when the place had been alive with snipping and sweeping and the chatter of a dozen women.

When the timer went off, she took me to the sinks in the back. I rested my neck in the dip of the sink while she turned on the water and waited for it to come to temperature.

"We've got some good hot water today," she said. "You're in luck."

To my dying day, I will love having someone else wash my hair. I adore everything about it, but especially being able to lie back and have someone spray water on my head. It is a sensation that even the best shower can't replicate, having that nozzle right against the scalp, spreading hot water droplet by droplet.

Once she'd washed out the colouring solution, she applied a fresh-smelling shampoo and worked that through, and then conditioner. And then came the scalp massage. I'd always dreaded it because it was a crapshoot whether the person giving it would be good at it — and even people who are good at it can have bad days. More often than not, it seemed to be just an exercise in hair-pulling that I could live without.

But Valerie, not surprisingly, was a pro, and the massage eased away tension I didn't know I was carrying. I could feel the muscles in my face and neck release as she manipulated various areas on my scalp, being careful never to pull my hair. I nearly fell asleep with my head in the sink.

Eventually, though, I was back in the chair, sitting in front of a mirror, and she was examining the product of a decade's worth of self-styling — trying, I thought, not to be too judgmental about what she saw.

"What style were you looking for, hon?" she asked.

"Something better than this." I laughed, and she laughed with me. "Get it out of my eyes, and after that, it's up to you — just keep in mind that it has to be something that doesn't need to be styled. I get out of the shower, run my fingers through it, and that's all I'm going to do."

"Well, here's the thing — to do it right, I'm going to have to start from the shortest bad part of the cut, and even it out from there. And that means it's going to have to be pretty short, because whoever's been cutting your hair ..."

"Me."

"Well, it might have helped if you had eyes in the back of your head." She smiled. "Are you game?"

"Have at it," I said, and she began snipping.

We talked about this and that — mostly she talked and I listened, and that was fine with me. She told me about interesting people she saw going by; about the availability of hair products. I asked her about her favourite places to buy food and wine and she shared a few addresses.

When I walked out the door a couple of hours after walking in, my head felt pounds lighter, and I was happy, knowing that I looked good and that I'd brightened up Valerie's day just by stopping in and giving her someone to talk to.

"Nice cut!" Eleanor said over Friday night cocktails. "And great colour. Where'd you go?"

"Valerie's, near the old Greek town."

"What were you doing over there?"

"I heard about a good fishmonger, thought I'd see if I could find some trout."

"And?"

"It was great. I'll take you there."

"Speaking of going places for food, want to go to that cheese farm, where they make feta and pecorino cheese? I've been wanting to go for ages. Let's cash in some gas rations and go tomorrow — what do you say?"

The next morning, we hopped in the car for our great farm adventure.

I'd seen the desolation of the former edge of the city on my way to the petting zoo, but beyond that was miles of empty and decaying houses. The suburban strip malls where people had once shopped lay in ruins, doors hanging, windows broken, and covered in more of the graffiti I'd been seeing downtown, declaring the BLT laws to be long past their usefulness.

As we drove past one warehouse that looked to be in better shape than other buildings in the area, I noticed Eleanor paying particular attention.

"What's that place?" I asked.

She hesitated, and that intrigued me even more than her interest had.

"Off the record?"

"Sure," I said. "Secrets are safe with me."

"Dan and I do ... well, I guess they would have been called raves back in the day. We call them 'events.'"

Eleanor looked at me expectantly.

"What?"

"I'm waiting for you to say you had no idea such a thing existed, or was possible. Honestly, tell me, did you just drop here from outer space? Are you a spy from another country? Just wake up from a coma?"

"Not a coma," I said, "just a severe catatonic state." And that was very nearly true. True in all but the details, anyway. I waited a beat. "I had no idea they still went on," I said, and Eleanor laughed.

"So tell me about your events," I said. "Who comes? Why so far out?"

"Well, we're far out because that's where the building is. Plus they're illegal. Even if there was a licensing system, we wouldn't be able to get one."

"But there's no law against dancing," I protested.

"No, but there are laws about how many people you can put in a space at once. And definitely ..."

"… definitely?" I kept my eyes on the road, but I could feel her looking hard at me, assessing me, wondering whether she could trust me, and I knew. Of course I knew. "Definitely when they're dancing without masks and gloves. You can't be in a public space without them."

Eleanor nodded. "That's the reason."

"And here I thought you were just a quiet office worker."

"Yep, just like you were a little mouse who wouldn't think of going to a zoo."

"So how did you find the space? How do you keep it?"

"Dan was a DJ before Henny Penny," she said. "Some buildings are getting torn down pretty quickly, but warehouses and large industrial spaces are being preserved. Dan was on a team that was cataloguing the spaces, and he knew about this one because it already had a club on the main floor — it had been part of his regular circuit. He talked to the guys on his team and they agreed to keep it off the books. Previous owners are dead, and because this area's already been catalogued, the regency's not looking for it. Anyone who sees it assumes it's been inventoried."

"How do the kids find out about it?"

"Word of mouth. We leave coded messages in the graffiti downtown, and we also have an email notification system for the regulars."

"Was it always a place for the kids to go bare?"

"No, but they started doing it almost immediately, and there's no real way to force them not to without getting too heavy handed."

"Don't they get sick?"

"Last year, a cold went through and I thought it might wipe us out. Some of the kids got really sick, and the regency started looking for us — never found us, and the kids eventually came

back. But we check them more carefully at the door now —
anyone with sniffles has to go home."

"But not Henny Penny?"

"Not that I know of. It's rare to get any cases in the city."

"So it's where all the cool kids go, is it?"

"Pretty much. I still have a job because every able-bodied
person has to work," she said. "But Dan's officially on the dis-
abled list and we're doing really well."

"What do you do with all the credits? Surely you're bringing
in enough that the bank would want to know."

"Cryptocurrency. They don't know what you've got when
they can't find it."

"Is that still a thing? I thought that had disappeared when
the electrical grid blew and the internet crashed."

"Some of it did, but as you know, the internet never died
completely, and neither did the dark web."

"This is fascinating. How many of these places are there?"

"Just one other in the capital. Parents have their kids on a
pretty tight leash, and frankly, there aren't a lot of teens out
there because Henny Penny and the aftermath both hit young
kids so hard. We're either going to have to change the business
model or go out of business soon — the birth rate is so low,
there aren't many coming after this crew."

"Can I come sometime? See what it's all about? I know I'd
stick out like a sore thumb, but it would fit in nicely with my
petting zoos piece," I said, thinking aloud.

"I was talking to my friend Lily, who said this was off the
record," Eleanor said, her voice tight.

I looked over at her; she was looking with great interest at
the freshly tilled field to her right. "Yes, I did, and if you say no,
that's a no, though I'd still like to go and see it."

"I'll talk to Dan. How's your zoo article going? You've been working on that for months now — still all caught up in research?"

"Research is very important," I said, and we shared a conspiratorial grin. "There are zoos downtown I like, but I'm using half my gas rations these days driving to a zoo on the outskirts. That was the first one I went to, where I met the owner."

"So you know Kaz?"

"You know Kaz? You didn't say anything when I mentioned going to the vanilla zoo."

"I didn't know you knew him — he's the only owner with a vanilla zoo on the outskirts."

"I thought you didn't know anything about the zoos," I said.

"The underground in the city is pretty small. Most of us know some of the same people, even if we move in different circles." She shrugged. "I've met him, but I don't know him well. Have you met his partners?"

"Aziz."

"Well, he's all right — Aziz. He and Kaz can be a laugh. I didn't like her at all. Violet. She doesn't come around much. She's a piece of work. I met her once, at a party the other rave promoter threw a few years ago. She's about five-foot-six and ... ropy, like she works out too much and lives on white wine and lettuce. She talks in this arch voice like Katharine Hepburn and she has this way of looking at you that you know she's judged you and found you wanting. I was like, whatever, bitch. I've got a life that doesn't need you in it, either. She's ... I don't know, predatory."

"He tells me they're no longer partners with Violet."

"At one point, they were a threesome in all senses of the word, I heard, and I really don't understand that because, like I said, Kaz and Aziz without her can be fun. We've done a couple of scavenger hunts with them — one of the other zoo owners likes to organize them. They're a blast. I gather the happy trio split up when Violet started her own zoo — shortly after I met her, in fact, so maybe she was just bitchy because her life was going to hell, who knows. Hey, you should ask Kaz out. He's straight and attractive. And as far as I know, he's single."

"Kaz said something about not approving of Violet's latest venture," I said, ignoring her comment about asking him out.

"There are some questionable zoos in this town, and some of them belong to Kaz — though they say his are the best over-all. I've never been in any of them, so I couldn't tell you. But I hear Violet's crosses a line. I don't know the details. You should ask him about it."

"I will. You know, I feel like I don't know anything about you. Today I find out that you run illegal dance parties, you have connections to the city's underground — you have a social life that you've never mentioned to me."

"You thought I was as boring as you?"

"Well, yeah."

Eleanor laughed. "You're not boring — I'm just more used to the world than you are right now. You'll be fine. And I'll see if I can get you invited to the scavenger hunt this fall."

The sun coming through the windshield warmed up the car, so we put the windows down. The air had a clarity that I remembered from my childhood visits to my grandparents' farm — no smog, no fog, no dust in the air, just piercing blue sky, dotted by fluffy white clouds. The same sky as in the city, except more of it.

There were a few cars on the road, the occasional tractor.

The road conditions deteriorated more the further we went from the city; cracked pavement, potholes filled with gravel — or, more usually, patches of grass and dandelions where we least expected.

About twenty-five miles from the city centre, we started hitting true farm country, plowed fields with the first green shoots of this year's crops showing, and cattle, sheep, and horses grazing in pastures covered in tender spring grass.

Whereas the city still didn't look normal — too many things missing, not enough stores or restaurants, not enough cars or people — here the balance was right: not many people or houses, but there weren't supposed to be many. The present looked very much like the past.

"This is it," Eleanor said as we approached a wooden sign painted with goats and sheep.

I turned into the farmhouse yard where goats roamed freely, while sheep and cattle grazed in nearby fields. The sun shone brightly upon an expanse of lawn fronting the freshly painted white farmhouse and weathered outbuildings. I stopped the car and drank it in.

"This is the first time in ten years I've left the city," I said as we put on our masks and gloves. "I forgot what it looks like."

"And how it smells," Eleanor said, wrinkling her nose as she opened the car door.

"And how it smells." I laughed, opening my own and stepping out. Despite the aroma of fresh manure, the air was clean like only country air on a spring day can be. It took me back to happy days in my childhood, those trips to my grandparents' farm.

A bolt of pain hit my stomach and I doubled over, gasping.

Eleanor rushed to my side, worried, but I brushed her away.

I'd thought I'd made it past this. I'd thought I was better, healed. Recovered. But that fleeting glimpse of precious childhood joy had brought with it the memory that everything I loved had been lost, a stealth attack making me aware of the absences in ways I'd forgotten to be aware over the past few months. I got back in the car, put my head on the steering wheel and took deep, shuddering breaths as tears rolled down my cheeks. In the few minutes it took for the pain to go away, Eleanor got acquainted with a friendly dog.

By the time the farmer came out of the barn, I mostly had hold of my emotions, and was able to dry my tears and join them.

"James," he said, holding out his hand, which had no glove. He was young, thirtysomething maybe, wearing a T-shirt and overalls with a hammer in the loop made for that purpose. His face had no mask, and when he saw me noticing, he started digging around in his pockets.

"Sorry," he said. "Not many surprise visitors out here, and the gloves get in the way. And the masks scare the dogs."

The dog didn't look scared at all, but to save James further indignities, I took off my own mask and Eleanor followed suit, and we both removed our gloves.

That was a milestone for me. It was the first time I'd ever taken off that protective gear in such an open space without some prior connection to the person I was with — or the protective finger-prick tests at the zoos. My decade-long horror of getting sick again, the fear of people that had held me captive for so long: it was as if I'd shed all of it with those tears. James didn't seem to think it was odd, nor did Eleanor, but this was a whole new world for me.

Mostly I wanted to pet the dog.

"That's Lizzie," James said. "Phil's around here somewhere. Do you want to see the puppies?"

I am such a cliché: a childless, middle-aged woman coming undone around baby animals. James was lucky that he had puppies and not kittens, or I might never have left.

When the regency set him up to farm sheep, he said, he'd had to import the animals, and the exporter offered to throw in a breeding pair of sheep dogs. James had had to get special permission to have them, but because herding dogs were working animals and not pets, he'd been permitted to bring them on and breed them for other farmers.

I took in only so much of his story, buried as I was under an avalanche of puppies. The sensory overload — fur, farm smell, pink tongues licking and tickling — enveloped me in a state of delight.

Finally the puppies found something else to amuse them, and I looked up to find James smiling at us.

"I haven't seen puppies in ..." I waved to indicate *forever*.

"I know, they're a little bit of heaven, aren't they? We have lambs in the next barn ..." he said with a grin, and Eleanor and I groaned. Lambs might have been too much.

"We came looking for cheese," Eleanor said, standing and picking straw out of her hair.

"What kind?"

"What have you got?"

He showed us what he had in stock and gave us a tour of the dairy, demonstrating how it was made. We both bought feta and pecorino, and promised to come back for cheddar.

"You know, the next guy down the road has a market strawberry patch," James said as we got ready to leave. "By the time the cheddar's ready, the first berries should be ripe."

We added that to the list.

Going to a Rave

NOW THAT I knew they existed, I knew my series on the zoos and the connections people make there wouldn't have been complete without mentioning the raves. The zoos were for adults — I hadn't thought about what teenagers needed or how they were getting it. Eleanor and Dan reluctantly agreed to let me in and write about the experience, but only if I disguised the location and all the players, and any details that could lead to them.

The zoos, good food, and regular exercise had taken years off my face and pounds off my body, but even with a decent haircut and new hair colour, I would still be older than even the oldest ravers by at least two decades, and I looked it. Eleanor told me that the kids who came to the raves were re-creating major art pieces on their faces, and she painted a fairly reasonable version of Van Gogh's *Starry Night* on me, bright circles of yellow on a blue background, which disguised my age to anyone looking at me from a distance. The ravers were still wearing Impermatex clothes — it was really all they'd known; only the very cool kids had fabric like untreated denim. Eleanor instructed me to buy an outfit in a style different from what I'd usually wear — a short skirt and form-fitting crop top whose two buttons both fell below my cleavage. When I raised an eyebrow, she said, "Don't worry, you can pull it off. You've really tightened up since you got the rowing machine."

"I'm not worried about pulling it off — I'm thinking about how little things change. We come through the apocalypse and girls are still dressing to titillate. What do the boys wear?"

Eleanor shrugged. "Whatever they please. A lot of the girls cover up, too, but when you figure that back in the day, they'd be wearing filmy baby-doll outfits and sucking on pacifiers, this is really quite staid and unexciting. Plus, it's fun to see you put it all out there for once." She smiled a little wickedly. "I mean, who knew Impermatex could be sexy?"

When we walked in the neighbourhood, she pointed out to me the coded invitations to the event in what I'd assumed was random anti-BLT graffiti on the sides of buildings. It was illegible to anyone who didn't know the language. A musical note within a lightbulb inside a circle meant the first Saturday of the month; outside it, with devil horns, meant the second Saturday.

"We try not to create patterns for events that anyone can discern, so it's not always the first Friday or the second Saturday — we randomize the choices."

They ran shuttles from downtown. Any teen lucky enough to be able to drive to the venue was instructed to park in the back, where cars couldn't easily be seen from the road. The warehouse itself was well soundproofed, so not a lot of the noise leaked out, in case there were any passerby even in this remote part of town, surrounded by empty houses and derelict shopping malls.

Inside the warehouse was a magical garden, with fairy lights strung around and between tall, leafy plants, creating an intimate atmosphere in the huge space. There were some chairs and tables, a bar selling water and popcorn in what Eleanor called the "chill room." I smelled the skunky tang of marijuana, and looked questioningly at Eleanor.

"Yep, there's pot and harder stuff for anyone who goes looking for it. The kids bring it in. We try to keep the dealers out, but they'll always find a way."

The music was pounding when we arrived, a low, almost inaudible hum when we got out of the car.

"Have you ever been to a rave?" she asked.

"No," I said. "Read about them. They didn't really sound like my scene."

"Back in the day there were all kinds of different raves, different kinds of music, and different experiences. Most of the people who went to raves before the pandemic wouldn't recognize this as a rave, outside of the music and the venue. This is more like a high-school dance set to happy hardcore. Dan misses the vibe from the old days, but he's just happy to be spinning again."

The music blasted me in the face when Eleanor opened a rear door. EDM had never been my favourite, but I couldn't ignore the beat, the life pulse, and neither could the teenagers who crowded the big dance floor. Unlike any school dance I'd ever been to, the dancers at the beginning of the evening were equal numbers male and female, some dancing in same-sex groups, but as the night wore on, there was the pairing-off familiar from any old-timey high school gym, although there were no wallflowers here. This world didn't give teenagers much freedom to be part of a crowd experiencing the same thing at once, and they weren't about to waste the opportunity by waiting for someone to ask them to dance.

Eleanor walked the perimeter with me, checking to make sure that all was well, then left me alone while she spelled the bartender.

I found the lights fascinating. They seemed to move and change colour with the beat. It was hypnotic.

Some of these kids would have been barely able to walk when Henny Penny descended, I thought, looking out at the sea of youthful, exuberant faces, alive with energy and the joy of dancing. If you figure two years of pandemic, then ten years of aftermath, the fifteen-year-old making her high ponytail swing wildly wouldn't have known anything but the post-pandemic world. They wouldn't remember leaving the house in anything but rough Impermatex clothes, gloved and masked, and yet here they were, grabbing hold of whatever freedom they could find.

"Come dance." A young man — late teens, early twenties, maybe — grabbed my hand. "Music's too good to stand still."

I was going to refuse, but then gave myself over to it. When was the last time I'd danced with someone? This wasn't my music, but my hips and feet found the rhythm, and the young man and I lost ourselves in it, the never-ending, seamless blending of tunes, impossible to tell where one ended and the next began. The kid — Chad — kept his eyes on my cleavage. No lie, it was a bit of an ego boost, knowing I was probably old enough to be his mother and still attracting the male gaze to that extent — although of course at that age, tits were tits, and any that found themselves uncovered in front of a teenage boy were going to be ogled. When he pulled me close and started grinding on me, though, I drew the line. I pulled away, laughing, and said, "Thank you, but no." He smiled good-naturedly and waved goodbye, then looked around for another person to dance with.

"You look like you're having a good time, passing as a teenager." Eleanor laughed.

"I'm hoping he was at least eighteen, or I'm probably going straight to hell for enjoying that," I said ruefully.

I danced some more but left long before the party ended. The music and lights were giving me a headache.

I thought about what Eleanor had said about the raves dying out soon because the ranks of teenagers weren't being replenished. Did that mean no one was having kids anymore? Come to think of it, I never saw parents with babies on my daily walks to work, or even on my increasingly longer excursions to markets around and outside my neighbourhood. Now that we were into the longer daylight hours of spring, I'd started taking my bike out in the evenings and on the weekends, visiting parts of the city that I'd once loved. I'd pack a lunch and take a book and sit under a tree by the river, my peace undisturbed by children or dogs.

When I got home, I changed into a pair of cotton pyjamas that were nearly worn through in some places, they were so old, but indescribably soft with it. I made a cup of herbal tea and booted up the computer to look up the statistics on the birth rate. My part of the pandemic history dealt with the pandemic and its immediate aftermath. Someone else was doing long-term effects, like looking at the birth rate. I'd never actually thought about it — the childless don't naturally consider the question of the lack of children, but now I was curious.

The pandemic history talked about places where Henny Penny had hollowed out the population — in the early stages, the virus had killed the very old and the very young, but at its height was also hitting people in the most fertile age group, twenty to thirty-five, in part because they'd been most likely to ignore social-distancing rules and be lackadaisical about hygiene, thinking themselves immortal. They were also more likely to work in occupations where they were constantly exposed to the virus — like retail, or the medical professions. Or the media. I had been lucky enough to survive, but a lot of people in my age cohort had not.

The book quoted the Health Minister, Roger Sweetwater, who at the time of writing was convening a task force to discuss ways of encouraging people to have more children.

"Think about this: the last time the world's population was this low was nearly four hundred years ago, in 1650," Sweetwater was quoted as saying.

Think about what the world was like. Of course, we've developed technologically since then; learned to tap the power of the atom and fossil fuels; we have machines to do the work that in the seventeenth century was done by hand.

And despite all of that, somehow we can't make everything work reliably with the people we have left. Not the way we're used to. Much of the world doesn't

have safe water or access to an uninterrupted food supply. Even here, despite our relatively smooth recovery,
our power grid is subject to intermittent failures in
the cities, and can go down for weeks at a time in the
country. Food continues to be in short supply in the
winter months.

Before Henny Penny, the birth rate had fallen behind the
death rate, to the point where any growth in population was a
result of immigration, Sweetwater continued. But the pandemic had killed immigration, meaning the national population
had continued to shrink even after the vaccine was introduced
and supplies of food and medicine had stabilized.

"I'm looking for ideas, for solutions to this problem,"
Sweetwater said about his task force. "We're looking at it from
all the angles: psychological, sociological, religious, whatever.
We need answers to medical and ethical questions. To wit: is
there a medical reason for this lack of fertility?"

That was the most recent entry, and I couldn't find news
articles that gave me any more information than the book had.
But the bee was in my bonnet. When I went back to work, I
tried to reach a couple of fertility specialists to get an answer
to Sweetwater's first question, at least. Finally, one of the task
force members, Dr. Josie McDuthie, who had been credited
with discovering the Henny Penny vaccine, took my call.

"Sorry," she said, when I asked why no one was having
babies. "Fertility is not my field. About the only thing I have to
offer to the discussion is the certainty that there is nothing in
the original vaccine or any of its iterations that should disrupt
the fertility of any healthy man or woman."

"So people could have babies if they wanted them."

"Presumably. But here's the thing, and I've said this to Minister Sweetwater: If you want more women to have babies, you need to convince them those babies will live. You need to convince them that the world they're bringing those babies into will be safe."

"But how do we do that?" I asked.

"Stop telling them that it isn't," she said simply. "My brother and his wife have recently had a baby — unfortunately, they're repopulating Australia, not this country — so I have something of a bird's-eye view of the concerns that new parents have in this time. How do you keep a baby — a crawling, touching, curious baby — safe? How about the toddler who puts everything that will fit, and some things that won't, in their mouth? How do you make a temperamental three-year-old keep a face mask and gloves on? And what about the nukers? What effect do they have on an infant's tender skin, brain? What about the hand sanitizers and caustic soaps we use to kill bacteria?"

"How are your brother and his wife planning to deal with that?"

"They're both doctors, and they've convinced themselves that they know what the risks are and will be able to handle them. But there are a lot more people out there who are not medical professionals, who are being governed by people who are likewise not medical professionals but are constantly telling them, in one way or another, that this is a dangerous world that will kill them if they're not careful."

"But ... and I know this is going to sound like a stupid question, so forgive me ... but isn't it?" I asked.

"My learned colleagues are undecided, frankly. So let's unpack the problem a little bit," Dr. McDuthie said, leaning toward the camera. "My team and I developed the vaccine for Henny Penny just over ten years ago. We have almost a decade's worth of inoculated people, as well as herd immunity. The virus is constantly mutating, but we have been able to stay on top of it, and in the last five years, there have been fewer than two thousand deaths a year attributed to it in this country. That's fewer than a seasonal flu killed each year before the pandemic."

"But is that because of the vaccine, or because of the mask and glove laws?" I asked.

"At this point, we can't say," she replied. "We still have to figure out whether fertility itself has declined in step with the birth rate. If it has not, the culture of fear we've allowed to grow up around Henny Penny is probably as detrimental to the birth rate as anything. And if you want people to have more babies, I think we're going to have to work on making the world appear safe."

"There's also the isolation factor," I added. "I haven't had a date in a very long time."

Dr. McDuthie laughed ruefully. "Me, either."

I eventually managed to contact the Health Minister and a fertility specialist, who said pretty much the same thing as Dr. McDuthie. I spent a couple of days writing an article about the birth rate, but when I handed it to Bob, he didn't seem that interested.

"Aren't you going to publish it?" I asked, a little incredulous. "I know it wasn't assigned, but you haven't had anything on this topic in the last six months, at least, and let's face it, you don't have to worry about the size of the news hole."

"Maybe — we'll see. Where are you on the petting zoo series?"

"It's coming. But I actually just handed you a piece of news and I'm asking what you're going to do with it."

"Sit down, Lily," he said, pointing to one of the wooden chairs facing his desk.

He looked like he'd rather be doing anything else. It confused me, because I knew I was one of his favourite employees, and he didn't usually look like that around me. I sat.

"Why is this news?" he asked me.

"Because it's happening, it's important, and nobody's talking about it."

"Why do you think no one's talking about it?"

The question floored me.

"Listen, Lily, every few months someone comes into my office with this story. Sometimes they've already done the interviews, sometimes they've already written the stories, sometimes it's just the raw idea. This is a great interview with McDuthie, she's someone who doesn't usually come up in this context, and the tie-in with Sweetwater's task force is a good one. But I can tell you this — the regency doesn't want this kind of article published."

"Why on earth not?"

"Because they see any suggestion that their methods have unintended consequences as a giant step down the slippery slope to anarchy. For them, this isn't an article about fertility — it's a criticism of the BLT laws. It's one thing if they decide the laws are no longer working, it's quite another if the news outlets they subsidize start saying it."

I sat back in the chair and considered Bob's half-covered face, his familiar, heavy-set body. He hated having to say this out loud. I knew it went against everything he held dear as a journalist, to have to base news coverage on what the government said could or couldn't be reported.

"If I print this," he continued softly, "I get in trouble, you get in trouble, Dr. McDuthie gets in trouble, and the article disappears almost immediately."

"But there's a task force," I protested. "Sweetwater gave me an interview. Why would he do that if the regency didn't want anyone talking about it?"

"Sweetwater's gone a bit rogue on this, and no one's talking about the task force, either. How'd you find out about it?"

"The pandemic history."

"Well, forgive me, I know you work hard on it, but I suspect the audience for that is small and specialized."

I shook my head.

As I got up to leave, my mind racing about how I could give one of the characters in my current story a fertility issue, Bob added, "And get me the first installment of the petting zoos thing soon, will you? I need to get graphics and photos on it. I don't suppose your contact would agree to having his picture taken? Or a picture of his zoo?"

"Not a chance." I laughed. "I'll get it to you by the end of the week." I stopped by the door, struck by a thought. "Why will the regency let you publish a story about nice petting zoos? Isn't that something they'd prefer to keep covered up? Rich people getting away with it while poor people get sent to work camps for the same thing?"

Bob sat back in his chair and shrugged. "Honestly, I don't know. I've had it at the back of my mind for a couple of years that I'd like you to write about them — I can see the layout for the piece in my head. But I was never able to get it past the editorial board. Then, suddenly, just after the Christmas holidays, I got a call giving me the green light, which means the regency changed its mind. I didn't stick around to ask why."

"Wow. Maybe something to do with the scuttlebutt you were hearing about a trafficking operation?"

"Maybe. Something happened to make them want to go public. I've got my ear to the ground for that, too — I'll let you know when I know."

"All righty, then." I opened the door, and stopped again. "By the way, do you and Ardythe want to come to dinner? Not this weekend, but next?"

"Sure," he said, surprised. "That would be lovely."

I nodded and left his office. I sent my spiked article to the colleague working on that part of the pandemic history, along with the raw transcripts of my interviews, and set to work finishing my petting zoo series.

In the end, I handed in three articles: one about the ring of elite zoos that Kaz ran; one contrasting the TTCs, the original zoos, and Kaz's; and one that talked about the need for human connection that led to all three. Bob seemed pleased enough with what I'd done, although if he'd had any idea about how many punches I'd pulled, or how many details I'd left out, he would have given me hell. He'd asked me to write about the underground world of petting zoos and I'd told as much truth as I could — although my desire to tell even that much truth was tempered by his straight talk about what the regency would or would not publish.

I'd given him some thoughtful articles about the nature of isolation and the human need for connection, and Bob gave them back, asking for more detail that highlighted the near-nudity of the players, the coming together of strangers in the permutations offered by the various chocolate levels, the illegality of the whole enterprise. Sex sells, that never changes, but it still hurt my feelings to write about them that way.

Stockholm syndrome, maybe. I'd started to think of the zoos as my safe haven, and the prospect of people salaciously drinking in the sexy details without appreciating the good the zoos did offended me. But the changes served Kaz's purpose by emphasizing that the people who went to these zoos weren't losers on a downhill slide: they were the well-off and powerful who were going after the same thing the lesser zoos offered.

I never let on that I'd visited the zoos as anything other than an observer, although I was abrogating my own journalistic ethics by not offering full disclosure. I consoled myself by thinking that Bob had sent me as a storyteller, not a reporter, and I'd given him a whale of a tale.

Coming to Dinner

THE PETTING ZOO series out of the way, I fell to planning my first post-pandemic dinner party, with gusto. I'd never hosted one without Sophie, but was newly confident that I could pull it off alone.

After going out to restaurants, dinner parties had been Sophie's favourite thing, as much for the opportunity to throw people into a mixing bowl and see how disparate personalities would coalesce as for the performance of dinner itself.

Sophie and I had created and cooked the menus together, making sure that the courses were complementary, each bite a delight. I was the detail person who imposed order on Sophie's chaos, and she rounded the square edges of my formality, and somehow it worked. We brought together artists and performers, writers and personalities in events that lived on in legend — like the time the pop singer had led a conga line of guests around the block, members of a local brass band on their way to a gig providing the rhythm. Or the night the painter spilled both gravy and red wine on the linen tablecloth and had been so inspired he'd insisted that we clear the table so that he could continue experimenting with his new form. Sophie had the tablecloth framed after it dried and sold it for something close to five figures. Even on ordinary nights, the conversation was the kind of thing you would keep revisiting days and weeks later. One night we held a party for Sophie's grandmother, who had just turned eighty-five. She turned out to be a master storyteller who spent the evening regaling us with memories about being a teenager in Europe during the Second World War. We all sat silent, reliving with her the whistle of falling bombs, the adrenaline of fear, and the urgency of stolen romantic moments.

The guest list for my first solo dinner party was a little more quotidian: Eleanor and Dan; Bob and his wife, Ardythe; Breaking-News Steve from my lunch crew, along with his partner, Lyle. And Kaz, who was a desirable dinner companion because he could round out the numbers, if nothing else. But having interacted with him primarily on a professional level — apart from when we'd met at the zoo — I was eager to see and get to know him in a social setting. I'd already been intrigued by him before Eleanor's suggestion that I ask him out became a tickle at the back of my mind. I was surprised and a little excited when he accepted the invitation.

"How are you going to introduce me to your other guests?" he asked when I called him at his office.

"Well, two of them already know you, or know of you." I explained about Eleanor and Dan. "My editor is coming, but he doesn't have to know you're my zoo contact. I don't think I've ever told him your name."

"Right. Eleanor and Dan. They'll have origin stories, too."

"Origin stories?"

"Stories we tell the straight world about what we do." He thought for a moment. "I'd rather you not tell them who I am. Tell them I'm a former art dealer and that I consult with the regency on the art they find."

"Are you an art dealer?"

"I have been."

"That could work. I could have met you through Sophie ... we could have just reconnected."

"Let's go with that, then."

"There are layers and layers to you, Kaz."

"You're peeling me like an orange." He laughed and signed off.

Ever since that first visit to the market, and then the farm, I'd been consumed by the amount of fresh food available, and by the desire to buy it and prepare it and share it with others. Lily's Lunches assuaged only some of that craving. I asked for recommendations for new markets from everyone I met, and received more from people who wrote in after seeing my columns. I did the rounds to see what might be available before carefully planning my menu. I also drew on the helpful advice and services of my new butcher friend, who'd sold me the best bacon I'd ever eaten, and a winemaker Valerie had recommended.

And I deliberately chose to go to my first semi-sweet zoo the night before the dinner party so that I'd be too busy the next day to beat myself up about what a bad girl I'd been.

Public nudity didn't come naturally to me, but how wonderful it had been to be stripped of that form-fitting leotard, to meet another naked body with mine from head to toe. At this level, it started to feel unnatural not to touch back. I had almost Pavlovian responses to certain sensations. My tac was about my age, lean like a runner, with a well-trimmed beard that felt like a soft brush against my skin. When his lips touched my nipple, it felt strange not to run my fingers through his hair, to hold his head there. His erection was a near-constant presence, but he didn't seem to expect me to do anything with it. All I had to do was lie there and receive pleasure. He was somewhat methodical. He spoke very little and got straight down to business, but that was good — I didn't want to be distracted from the other things he was doing with his mouth, which travelled the length and breadth of me, providing me with the first sexual pleasure I'd had at someone else's hands since Matt left. I'd forgotten how intense the orgasm could be with oral. It was obviously something my tac enjoyed giving as much as I liked receiving it. After I came a couple of times, he masturbated into a condom, and that was that.

He wasn't a cuddler, so this strangest of evenings ended earlier than usual. As sexual experiences went, this had left some things to be desired, but I went home happy and satisfied.

My skin was still zinging and singing from the zoo when I started preparing dinner, and all my senses were awakened to the sensation of the food, the crisp green crackle of lettuce, the heft of the chef's knife in my hand, the wet thunk it made as it slipped through a deep-red greenhouse tomato and hit the wooden cutting board. The sound of the knife sawing through a crusty baguette, and the yeasty, floury aroma that hit my nose when the bread opened to the blade. I washed my hands thoroughly, then used them to mash a ripe avocado. I smelled of garlic and lemon and herbs; my nose and my eyes and my hands and my ears swam in the sea of the sights and sounds and textures of dinner. I rolled some red wine around in my mouth as I surveyed the devastation in my kitchen and hoped my guests would be even half as enchanted as I was by the feast I was about to put before them.

I laid the table with pretty china and crystal, set out candles, glass flowers, and paper napkins where once I would have used linen, just in case any of my guests retained a fear of fabric. For the same reason, I didn't put a cloth on the table, instead using hard place mats and coasters to protect the finish.

A shower and a soft pre–Henny Penny dress, Yo-Yo Ma playing in the background, delicious aromas wafting from the kitchen, and I was ready for my guests.

Bob was all friendly bonhomie in a crowd. Ardythe was a little stiff — probably because she was going bare in front of so many strangers at once — but she loosened up after a couple of the cocktails I'd devised for the evening: vodka, sparkling wine, and syrup from a bottle of cherry preserves. I'd spent very little time with Dan, not much more than a quick hello and some small talk when I dropped in to see Eleanor, but he turned out to be a perfect foil for his wife's sly humour. Steve and Lyle were obviously veterans of dinner parties and social gatherings: they had anecdotes for every occasion so that a silence never became uncomfortable, and awkward comments could be glossed over and forgotten quickly. Sophie would have loved them for their ability to emulsify the different personalities around the table. Kaz moved around them all quietly, stepping a little back but not so far as to arouse attention. And when he was asked about himself, or was invited to participate in a conversation, he spoke knowledgeably and engagingly.

I sat at the head of the table — Sophie's place, I thought when I took my seat — surveyed my guests, made sure they had food and wine and water and were not left out as others talked around them.

"This wine is excellent," Steve said. "Where did you get it?"

"I made friends with a vintner — recommended by my hair stylist — who chose all of tonight's wine pairings," I said, running my fingers through my still-unfamiliar haircut. "I'm glad I found him. I know the very smallest bit about wine — my best friend in university once dated a guy who was a sommelier. Sophie found him deadly boring outside of the bedroom and a powerhouse in it, so she'd leave him to talk to me until bedtime. He seemed okay with it. He'd bring a bottle of wine, and we'd drink it, and he'd tell me why it was good, and then when Sophie beckoned, off he'd go and leave me with the bottle."

"And did you find him boring, too?" Lyle asked.

"As dirt. But he did know his wine, and I learned a bit about varietals. I'm nowhere near an expert, but Pierre is helping me take what I know and build on it with what's available locally."

"What's the vineyard?" Kaz asked, and I told them the name of the place, and where to find the winemaker.

"You're obviously going to a different market than the one I showed you," Eleanor said. "I couldn't tell you the last time I saw an avocado."

"Yes," I said, "this place in Greektown has some very limited import business. I'll take you the next time I go. Valerie told me about it."

In these early days of a renascent farm scene, we were all preoccupied with food. We talked a lot about what was available in stores, the kinds of imports that were starting to show up, and what was coming up next in the growing season.

"Remember when the hundred-mile diet was a goal and not a fact of life?" Ardythe sighed.

"Eating local is all well and good, but I suspect I'd be just as happy to walk into a soulless supermarket chain right now and buy out-of-season cherries from Chile," Eleanor admitted, and we all laughed.

"Well, I don't have cherries from Chile, but I do have strawberries from down the road," I said, getting up to clear the plates to make room for dessert.

Kaz helped me carry the dishes to the kitchen, and added dollops of whipped cream to bowls of strawberries while I made tea.

"This is a very different home than it was the last time I was here," he said softly. "I'm beginning to see you in it."

"It's a lot happier," I agreed. "I partly have you to thank for that."

He smiled and started carrying bowls into the dining room.

"Didn't you work on a farm or something like that last summer for your regency hours, Lyle?" Bob asked. "I seem to remember Steve going off somewhere with you."

"I wasn't farming — I was doing a farm inventory," Lyle said.

"How did that work?" I asked.

"The regency set me up with a car, satellite phone, camping gear, and maps and sent me out to count farms, herds, output, acreage. I had to see what they needed and help them figure out how to get it. It gives the government a better idea of what food resources we have and how much we have to trade."

"How were the roads?" asked Dan.

"Rough in places, and sometimes it was a long, lonely ride between towns, at least until Steve was able to join me, but it was a great experience. Have any of you ever done a regency road trip?" We all shook our heads no. "Well, I'd recommend that any of you, if you don't know what you're doing with your regency hours this year, ask about what's available."

"What kind of things can you do?" I asked.

"Well, there's inventory, like I did. Not just farms, but business and manufacturing. The regency knows about all the major manufacturers, but there are a lot of little start-ups, too — many of whom don't want to be found, because they're working on the black market, doing things like making untreated fabrics, for example, so there's some investigative work. And the regency is always on the lookout for itinerant professors. They're sending a lot of those out these days — people with knowledge of a specific area can go out and teach one- or two-week units and then move on and teach it again somewhere else. You could teach journalism, Lily, or storytelling. That sort of thing."

After dessert, someone mentioned board games. I got an old edition of Trivial Pursuit out of the closet — it'd been nuked, I assured my guests — and we played one riotous game, and then another, before people got up to go.

Ardythe fretted about leaving me with the dishes, but I just smiled. "To the victor go the spoils," I said.

Kaz was the last to leave. "I could stay and help you clean up," he offered.

"No, really, it's fine. I find it soothing to do dishes — it helps me come down from the evening."

"I see you went to a semi-sweet zoo last night," he said, smiling at me as I walked him to the door. "How did you like it?"

I blushed at a sudden vision of the tac's face between my legs.

"It was fun," I said, my memory of it distracting me from wondering how or why he might have known I'd gone.

"I like that one, too," he said, and I raised an eyebrow. "As Aziz and I said, it's part of the quality control. Sometimes we're short a tac — not often, but sometimes — and we'll step in rather than turn someone away. And sometimes it's fun to just go and blow off steam."

"In a manner of speaking." I laughed, and he joined in. "Well, maybe I'll see you there one night," I said, and was surprised at the little tingle the thought of it gave me.

"Maybe," he answered, and kissed me on the cheek before he left. "I really enjoyed the evening. Thank you for inviting me." He touched my hair and said, "I like this. The colour has movement. You look lovely."

"I'm so glad you came," I said, and opened the door for him, then added, "Oh, and the first article's being published tomorrow," before I closed it softly behind him.

I collapsed into my sofa, and looked around the room at the dishes that needed to be washed, the food that needed to be put away, and the spot on the table where someone had set a glass without using a coaster, and smiled. I'd forgotten what it was like, to be with people whose company I enjoyed, eat good food, drink good wine, have good conversation — and fun. I'd had fun. I couldn't wait to do it again.

Semi-Sweet

AFTER MY FIRST visit to the semi-sweet zoo, I stopped worrying about what good girls might do. I had a very good idea of what I wanted and where I could get it — and was pretty sure I deserved to have it. Even so, I gave myself a week before booking my next visit. I wanted to draw out the anticipation. I didn't want to develop a tolerance for the zoo too quickly.

I was late getting home from work that night, so I raced upstairs and had a quick supper, then brushed and flossed carefully before heading out. I had just enough time to shower and dry my hair at the zoo before the seven o'clock start.

I was still slightly damp when I took my place in the line with a dozen other fauna, my toes curling against the soft wool of the carpets, drinking in the fresh smell of soap and feeling the hum of anticipation. I put on my blindfold and closed my eyes, seeking my Zen space, calming my heartbeat.

The hand that fell on my shoulder slipped down my arm and clasped my fingers. I took the strip of fabric away from my eyes. "Kaz."

"Kate."

My blood rushed to my head and my knees trembled. I'd had it in my mind that he might come, but had steeled myself to expect a stranger. And now, as in my first zoo, I wasn't sure I could go through with this with someone I knew. I stood stupidly still for a moment, looking at him with his blindfold on.

"Aren't you going to invite me into your parlour?"

Sheepish, I led him to my blanket.

"Is that a see-through blindfold? How did you know it was me?"

"Magic. Take it off me," he said, and I reached up, touching his face for the first time, his hair, as I slid it up off his head. His hands came up and trapped mine behind his neck, and he leaned down to kiss me. I unconsciously lifted my lips to his so that it wouldn't take so long for them to meet.

I whimpered when his mouth barely grazed mine before moving away.

"Tell me what you want," he said.

"I want ..." I hesitated, unused to asking.

"Look at me," he said and my eyes met his. "Tell me," he repeated, his knee insinuating itself between my legs, throwing my body a little off balance, the way his presence had knocked me off my mental axis.

"I ... I want you to kiss me."

"Is that all?"

I thought of the first night at the milk-chocolate zoo, where Aziz had kissed me for hours. "No."

"What else?" He lifted his knee slightly so that it stroked the inside of my thigh. "If you can't say it, you're not ready for it."

I died a thousand little deaths inside as I said, "I want you to touch me."

"Where?"

"Everywhere."

At that, his lips came down on mine and I was jolted by the force of the kiss, by that bolt of electricity I'd only really ever felt once before, with Matt. But that had been gentler than this. This was raw, needy. It took my breath away.

He released my hands, his palms skimmed down my raised arms to my shoulders, down my back to my buttocks, lifting me up and closer. I shuddered against his warm skin, breathing in his soapy scent. My head started reeling as my brain tried to process all of the sensations my nerve endings were relaying.

My mouth left his. "Dizzy, Kaz, dizzy," I said. He picked me up and I wrapped my legs around his waist. He knelt on the mat, leaning over so that I could lie flat, then he joined me.

My whole body had become an erogenous zone. Everywhere he touched was hyper-sensitive. The leotard left a trail of delicious chills as he slid it from my body.

"Everywhere," I said again, and he did as I asked — frustratingly avoiding my nipples and between my legs until I picked up his hands and placed them there. And then he kept touching me with his hands and lips and tongue until I begged him to stop, so that I could calm down, catch my breath, slow my heartbeat to a more manageable pace.

"Oh god, Kaz," I said as he wrapped his arms around me. I could feel his heart pounding as hard as mine, his breathing as ragged.

He kissed me again, as if he couldn't stop. "You taste so sweet," he said. "I knew you would taste sweet."

Later, when our hearts had stopped racing, I said, "I don't know what the rules are here. We're still fauna and tac. I don't know how much I'm supposed to touch you, or how much I'm allowed to."

"It depends on the fauna — and on the tac. Some tacs take their job very seriously and don't want to be touched. Some fauna just want to receive."

"And you?"

"For now, this works for me. I'm enjoying giving you pleasure. But if you wanted to help me remove my bodysuit, I wouldn't argue."

I leaned over and kissed him, then brought my sweaty hands to his shoulders and pushed the straps of his bodysuit down his arms, rolled it over his torso, revelling in the feeling of his soft skin under my palms. I rose up and, kneeling in front of him, manoeuvred the bodysuit over his erect cock, leaning over to drop a kiss on it as I slid the fabric down his legs and off, before lying down beside him once again, enjoying the feeling of his skin against mine, drinking in the smell of his body.

I asked, "Is this thanks for dinner?"

He laughed and pulled me closer, and I buried my face in the hair on his chest, breathing deeply, before I asked the question that had been at the back of my mind for a while.

"Did you know I would be here tonight?"

"Why do you ask?"

"It never feels accidental when we meet. You know when I've gone to a zoo." This was the first time he'd chosen me since that first vanilla zoo, but I'd seen him at others.

I'd had a sense for some time that he watched me at the zoos, although it was embarrassing to say it out loud, to suggest that I thought I had earned special attention.

He didn't tell me I was wrong. "The first time wasn't accidental."

"I didn't think it was."

"But do you want to know why?"

"*Droit de seigneur*, you said. I thought maybe you went first with all the fauna."

"I thought you might be an informant, working for the police. I didn't really believe you'd show up of your own accord, with no agenda beyond the article. Which was very good, by the way."

"Thanks. But why did you let me in — let me know where the zoo was — if you thought I'd tell the police? That was risky."

"Sometimes I take risks. I liked you before I met you, to tell the truth. I liked you as a writer. And when I met you, you felt honest. I weighed out the consequences and decided I'd see what would happen."

"And how were you going to tell if my purposes were nefarious?"

"I don't know — I was going to go by gut feeling. I figured I'd be able to tell by your reactions."

"And ..."

"You did not react like someone who thought the police might burst in at any minute. You were pliable as wet clay."

"Lovely image. So it wasn't my imagination — you have been paying attention, to me."

"I check the guest lists sometimes. I've been enjoying watching you change and grow. I like the idea of you being moulded into something here."

"But you don't always want to be the potter moulding me?"

"I think maybe I'm providing the wheel. The shape you're taking is entirely of your own doing."

"So on the other nights when I see you, are you working on other pet projects?"

"Pun intended? No, no pet projects — at all. Not even you." He paused, then answered my first question. "But I am keeping an eye on the shape you're taking, and it occurs to me every now and then that I would enjoy keeping my hands on it, too."

With that, I took his hand and slipped it between my legs. "Keep them there, then," I whispered, reaching up to kiss him, starting the exhilarating cycle of building excitement and coming down all over again.

Falling for Kaz

WEEKS HAVE SO many days in them. I was trying to slow down my zoo experience, to delay the inevitable moment when I would start wanting to move on again. As Kaz and Aziz had said months ago, public nudity was one thing; public sex still another. For nearly a week after that night with Kaz, I went to work during the day and at night I stayed home, cleaned my pristine apartment, did my laundry, bit my fingernails, cooked delicious meals, and thought about going back.

Not quite a week later, I made another appointment at the semi-sweet zoo. My tac wasn't Kaz, but that didn't matter. My body was remembering things it had forgotten — or that I'd made it forget — a long time ago, and it didn't need Kaz's

hands to make it feel good. Neither did the brain that was processing all of these new-old feelings. A nerve ending is a nerve
ending, regardless of the fingerprint of the person touching it.

When I left, I was certain my glow could have lit my way
home.

And despite my fear that I would build up a tolerance too
quickly, I was unable to come up with a good argument for not
going again two days later.

"So, how are the zoos? You tried semi-sweet yet?" Eleanor
asked me over Friday night drinks at our favourite bar.

"Yeah," I answered.

"Yeah?"

"Oh yeah."

"Girl, you have to stop playing in the zoos and just get yourself a date. Have you thought about asking Kaz? I was watching
you two at dinner the other night. He likes you, and I'm pretty
sure you like him."

I grinned. "He's been at the semi-sweet zoo, too."

"Yeah?"

"Ooooh yeah."

Eleanor laughed. "Robbed you of all vocabulary, did he?"

"Yeah," I said, and we giggled like two sixteen-year-olds
talking about the cute boy at school.

"I'm guessing that by the time you actually have sex, you're
just going to be able to communicate in grunts and sighs, if
that's how you are after a night of heavy petting. So how many
times have you gone?"

"Semi-sweet? Three. Going again tomorrow."

"Get out of here! Once you decide to do something, you
just do it, don't you? So was he there each time?"

I shook my head.

"You slut!" Eleanor whispered in mock outrage over her ersatz Singapore Sling, then slipped the straw under her mask and took a big drink. "Tell me everything. Was Kaz the first person at semi-sweet?"

"No, he was the second time."

"And?"

"He was fabulous." I took a sip of my Sling. "Did you ever make out with a guy in your misspent youth, one you thought you might just have sex with, who took you as far as you could go with your clothes on ..."

"There might have been one or two before Henny Penny made me reconsider how I was spending my youth."

"That was Kaz. No pawing, no force just ... a lick and a promise, to coin an old phrase. That's what that guy had when we were teenagers, right? The promise of a really, really, really good time if we ignored everything our mothers taught us about guys like that."

"I remember the feeling," Eleanor said dreamily. "Dan was one of those. And, may I say, promise fulfilled, which is why I married him." She smiled at a memory for a minute, then said, "So, will you see him again? I don't understand why you don't just ask him out."

"There's something going on there. I like him a lot. And he's not uninterested — he all but admitted he's been keeping an eye on me. But I'm not sure Kaz is a guy you date. And I don't think he's looking for entanglements."

"So ask some other guy from the zoo and be done with it. If I were you, I'd be sick and tired of the zoos by now."

Although she had a point, it must be said that not all the guys I'd met in the zoos were people I would have found attractive outside of that environment, and there wasn't a lot of talking, so I had no idea whether we had anything in common. But in the zoos, it wasn't about attraction, exactly — I didn't have to find tacs interesting to enjoy being touched by them in the short amount of time we'd see each other; I could close my eyes and just feel. It didn't seem to me that the experience was transposable — outside the zoo, it would have been a relationship, and to develop a relationship required attraction plus interest plus time and energy. And relationships left a person open to rejection and loss, and I wasn't a fan of either.

The zoos were a way to feed my skin hunger, and right now that was my primary objective. It wasn't to say that if someone invited me, I would have turned them down. I had grown up in an age where men asked women out, not the other way around, and as an adult, it had been pretty clear to me that the kind of men I liked didn't want to be chased. If they were interested, they'd let me know. But beyond that, there was also just the fact that I liked what I got from the zoos — and that was probably the only place where I could legitimately seek and receive it.

I tried to explain this to Eleanor. "If Kaz — or someone else — asked, I'd probably say yes."

"So you're waiting for Kaz to pick you out of a line both in and out of the zoo," she said, and I shrugged. "At the zoo you can be one or the other, right? Picker or pickee?"

"Yes."

"So why don't you be the picker? Do you think you'd know him? Is he in your nose yet?"

"I think I could pick him out, maybe."

"So?"

"He rarely goes, and he's never in the fauna lineup."

"That twain's never going to meet, then. Have you ever been, what do you call it, a tac?"

"Not yet."

"Why?"

I drew my cold gin and cherry brandy through my straw to give myself time to think about how to phrase my answer.

"I think it's because … For however long I'm there, I'm allowed to just be. I don't have to make any decisions about what will happen, don't have to think about when and how. Somebody else looks after me. And they get out of it whatever they get out of it, but that's not my concern. That person is focused on what I want, what I need. It's unequivocal. It's about me."

"You're like a goddess receiving offerings from your acolytes."

"A little bit of worship never did anyone any harm." I laughed.

"Kind of selfish."

"Self-centred, sure, I'll give you that. But not selfish, because I'm not saying give me pleasure at the expense of your own."

"Because the picker likes picking."

"Exactly. For most of my life, with a couple of brief exceptions, I've been the person who takes care of me. At some point, I just want to put myself in someone else's hands."

"So can you imagine a point where you will want to change sides?"

"Anything's possible — that's not me, that boldness of approach. But I can see a point where I'd like to be able to give back to the person who picked me."

"Don't you do that now?"

"A little bit — especially in the semi-sweet zoo, giving back is unconscious. I want to touch. I asked Kaz about it — he says it's all up to the individuals there. At the other zoos, I don't think it's allowed," I said. "They told me you choose to be one or the other, I assumed you weren't allowed to change positions in the middle of the game."

"You should try it sometime."

"Maybe I will."

Coming to a Decision

THE WISDOM THAT comes to you in the shadowy places between sleep and awakening is sharp and cuts deeply.

Sometimes I wake up in the middle of a thought, or even
an argument I'm imagining with another person.

My first thought on waking one morning in early June was,
"What am I doing here?"

The question wasn't about geography, or even an inquiry
into the reason for my existence — I'd long ago accepted that
I was no cog in a grand scheme; that I, along with every other
soul on earth, was a happy accident. I had no purpose and
needed none, except for what I set for myself.

But it had been a long time since I'd set myself a purpose.

After Matt was killed, I blamed stupid wars, and then I blamed Henny Penny for derailing whatever grand scheme I might have dreamed for myself — career, husband, children, happy home, friends, life — but the truth was that I'd been none too successful at any of that before the plague hit. My relationship with Matt had been an anomaly, and a short-lived one, at that. We'd met just as I had started to be concerned that I'd never meet my soul mate, and we'd been together for less than a year when he was killed. The years I'd lost to Henny Penny were, biologically speaking at least, pretty much the last ones I could have counted on to make it all come true even if he had lived.

Now here I was, happier about my life than I'd been in a decade, and yet there was still some little stone in my shoe, irritating me, keeping me from actually being satisfied, and I couldn't figure out what it was. Nothing seemed like quite enough. I wanted more, but more *what*, I couldn't tell you.

My epiphany that morning was that I'd spent far too much time on other people's interests and not nearly enough on my own: editing when I wanted to write, doing for others instead of myself. I had fallen into things — taking a job because it offered security, instead of challenge, for example — rather than taking the time to think about what I really wanted and how I might work up the nerve to achieve it. I applauded and admired people like Sophie, who didn't seem to worry about their lives meaning nothing — everything meant something to them.

The world had changed during my long sleep, and as I awakened to the possibilities that change offered to me, I finally acknowledged that if I was ever going to accomplish anything, I had to decide what I wanted and take it instead of accepting whatever fell into my lap.

And I was going to start with my job. It had carried me through the worst years, and I'd made new friends there over the last several months, but with the clarity of 5:00 a.m. wisdom, I realized I hadn't felt challenged by it in a long time. I wanted to bang myself up against something unknown and feel resistance.

After the dinner party, I thought a lot about what Lyle had said about doing a regency road trip. I started checking out the job boards to see what was available. There were lots of openings for clearance teams — in the big cities, that work was going to continue for years — and there were quite a few requests for farm labourers which, despite my renewed appreciation for farms and their puppies, was never going to be my cup of tea. I'd done farm labour as an adolescent and had no desire to revisit it.

Lyle had mentioned itinerant professors, people with skill sets to fill in the holes left by Henny Penny, and those were the openings that did catch my eye. The regency was looking for people to spend one to two weeks teaching modules on various subjects. Preference was, of course, given to people living near each school, but I noticed that quite a few universities between the capital and the coast were looking for sessional instructors in topics that I could teach. I wondered if the regency would let me string them together and send me on a road trip.

Because I was a writer and because I'd been terribly weakened by my bout with Henny Penny, the regency didn't require physical service from me, even after I recovered. Since my work on the history of the pandemic and its aftermath could be done at any time, I'd never fulfilled my regency hours in the usual eight-week block — I didn't take time from work or go anywhere to perform the extra duty. But I always got the automatic notice, anyway. When this year's notice came, telling me that my two-month mandatory service was coming up, I decided that that would be my breaking point: I would quit my job and go on the road.

I sent my application to the regency's labour board, which immediately approved it. I would leave in early August and return in late October. But there was a lot of work to do before I could go anywhere.

First, I had to quit my job.

Bob wasn't as surprised by my decision as I thought he'd be. I'd imagined that he would beg me to stay and I was a little hurt when he didn't. And I said so, half teasing.

"Look, Lily," he said, taking me seriously. "You can write for me any time you want, you know that. You don't have to be employed here for me to publish you. I know you're a bit disillusioned about the work you're doing since that fertility story, and because of what I had to cut out of your piece on the zoos. Don't deny it," he said, holding up a hand as I started to speak. "I've actually been waiting for you to tell me you're leaving. If you were going to some other zine, I might try to keep you, but you need to find yourself, and I'm not going to get in the way of that. It's been lovely to see you come back to life this past year, but it's been obvious that something's still missing. I hope you find it."

And that was that. When he asked what I was going to do, I laid out my plans for the road trip.

"What would you teach?"

"There are a couple of schools looking for someone to teach journalism modules, and there's one looking for a history module. A few schools are even looking for someone to teach a module that's essentially home economics. I think I could manage that."

"But teaching? The Lily I know doesn't even like showing people how to use the coffee machine."

"Yeah, well, gotta try new things, right? They give you help preparing the modules, and suggestions for making classes interesting. What I really want is to get out of town, spread my wings a little. Here I'm constantly reminded of everything that's missing. In a new place, it will all be new because it's supposed to be new."

Fred at the regency became my constant companion over the next month and a half. Somewhere in his sixties, he was a bureaucrat by nature. He had worked for the government long before it was the regency. He was a short-sleeved-white-shirt-and-tie kind of guy, someone who knew all the right secrets because he made it his business. I had the feeling that if Fred ever decided to go public with the things he knew, he could probably have brought the government down.

For all that my nature was decidedly not bureaucratic — and he let me know early on that he wasn't a fan of my fiction or my reporting about the petting zoos — he and I got along. I've always had an affinity for people who do their jobs — whatever their job is — well and with pride, and Fred was one of those. I knew that with him planning my trip, I'd have everything I needed.

"The Board will provide you with a four-wheel-drive SUV hybrid that will take you where you need to go even if the roads are bad and you can't find gas," Fred told me during my first visit to his office, which was in a squat grey government building whose furnishings had likely been chosen by a particularly uninspired designer in the 1970s. "Do you want to know the particulars of how it works?"

"Do I need to know the particulars of how it works?" I

asked, imagining a baffling lecture on whatever they'd done to the internal combustion engine that would make such a miracle possible.

"No," he sniffed, as if he'd been looking forward to baffling me a bit, but wasn't entirely surprised that I'd turn down an opportunity to learn. "Although it's an amazing story about what can be done when oil and gas companies aren't involving themselves in automobile manufacturing. Ah, well. I hope you won't mind learning a few things, though."

He put me in touch with the education professionals who would spend June and July helping me prepare modules in the subjects that I'd teach to university students on my way to the coast.

Just setting up the travel portion of my trip took weeks. As Fred had said, they had a "few things" to teach me before I could set out. How to fix basic problems — flat tires, or the unthinkable: a dead battery. How to read a map. How to set up my camping equipment properly, light the lantern, cook on the stove, and use the water purifier. I had to learn how to create a fire pit and set a campfire using a variety of fuel, including damp wood. I had to have a full medical exam before I left, and to know how to use everything in the extensive first aid kit.

"Don't expect the same level of services that you have in the capital," Fred warned me. "You're going to be travelling through some fairly remote areas — would have been remote even in the before times. There won't always be running water or electricity. You're going to have to expect not to have internet service anywhere but in the cities, and phone lines are erratic. We'll put a radio transmitter and receiver in the vehicle and give you a satellite phone for emergency communications, so you call in any real problems you see on your way that you think shouldn't wait for your final report."

He looked me up and down. "You're small," he said. "I'll be honest with you, I argued against approving your travel plan. The crime rate is down across the country — even the real stats, not just the ones that get published — so it's probably safer for a woman travelling alone now than it was before the pandemic. But there's a lot of empty space between here and the coast where things can happen and there'll be no one around to help you. I'm not entirely comfortable sending you off on your own. I'm going to set up a self-defence course for you, and we'll provide you with a weapon to carry with you, just in case."

And I had to learn to use that, too.

Going Down the Road

THROUGH ALL THIS preparation, I kept going to the zoos, switching back and forth between milk chocolate and semi-sweet as I wrestled with the idea of going dark. It wasn't so much a question of sexual mores, although there was certainly some of that. It was more that I was starting to think that I didn't want my first sex in more than ten years to be with some random stranger who just happened to have the money to go to a zoo. At the same time, I wanted to just do it and get it over with so I could stop overthinking the whole process.

I couldn't bring myself to suggest to my tacs at either zoo that we just go home and have sex. On some level, I realized the cognitive dissonance — it made no sense that I welcomed anonymous intimacy in the zoos, but I needed a relationship to imagine doing the same things outside them. I had heard of people meeting and pairing off since the pandemic but I'd yet to meet anyone myself — outside the zoos or in — who intrigued me enough to overcome my ambivalence and put myself in a position where I could be hurt again.

I wasn't just ambivalent. When you go for a long time without something, you idealize it — or, at least, I do — and you start to think that only the ideal will suffice. It was why I never answered my fan mail, despite being starved for contact. I'd rather have none at all than get stuck in a correspondence with someone who wasn't a perfect fit. In the zoos, if I got someone less than ideal one night, chances were I'd prefer what came around the next. It was like renting cars — you get to try all the different models, the cars are always new, and breakdowns aren't your problem. In the zoos, I didn't need to talk and flirt or get to know someone, didn't need to build interest and trust, wasn't required to impress or entertain. The strict roles meant I didn't need to sublimate my desire, or be self-conscious about it or feel awkward afterward. In the zoos, it didn't matter if I wasn't beautiful or exciting or didn't have anything to say. That was tremendously freeing in a way that I was coming to appreciate.

I was working on my nutrition module when I got the ping of an incoming internet call. It was Kaz, looking concerned.

"Hi, Kaz, what a nice surprise," I said.

"Are you all right?" he asked. "Turn on your camera."

"Yes, why? What's the matter?" I asked, turning it on so he could see me.

"I sent you a note at the office — they told me you no longer work there."

"Oh, that. We haven't spoken for a bit, have we?"

"Not since the zoo after your dinner party."

"Well, I have a lot to tell you, then."

"Are you free this afternoon?" he asked.

"I could be."

"I'll meet you in front of your place in an hour."

"For what?"

"I'm taking you to lunch."

I quickly showered and changed into an Impermatex sundress — it was yellow and had started life as linen, before the treatment clogged its pores, making it feel like it had been dipped in industrial-strength starch. An hour later, I was waiting at the front door of my building when Kaz pulled up in a four-wheel drive.

"Where are we going?" I asked when I got in.

"On a picnic."

He drove out of the city and into the mountains. The minute we were past the outskirts and prying eyes, we both took off our masks and gloves.

"I really enjoyed your articles," he said. The last of my petting zoos series had been published a few days earlier.

"Did you? Didn't find them a bit ... fantastical?"

"Well, the titillation factor was exaggerated — rather more emphasis on breasts and bulges than on how we do our part to keep the bonnelly rate down, but I expect that's not how you wrote it," he said. "I think it was an honest representation of what I do. And it has created interest in the zoos, both from new clients and from the authorities, so in that sense they did the job I wanted them to."

"Bob cut a lot out — I don't think I ever realized how much we pandered to what the regency wants. I guess I was protected from having to worry about it when I was just writing my stories — or it didn't affect me because I wasn't writing about life as it is, I was writing about life as it was." I told him about the fertility article Bob had spiked.

The roads became narrower and bumpier as we made our way into the forest, eventually stopping on a rutted lane where faded signage proclaimed *MacArthur Lake, picnic area and supervised swimming.* He led me farther down the path to a sandy beach, carrying a blanket and a picnic basket to a flat spot under a tree where we could watch the water and the wildlife.

"What a beautiful place," I said. "Though, to be honest, if we'd gone any further into the wilderness, I was going to start to worry about your intentions."

He laughed. Brandishing the rolled blanket, he said, "Are you hungry, or would you like to swim and then eat?"

Swimming sounded wonderful — the day was hot and humid and although there was a breeze in the mountains, it wasn't as efficient as the air conditioning in Kaz's car had been. "You didn't tell me to bring a suit," I said.

"I wasn't sure we'd still be able to make it all the way here. But ... is that a problem? I didn't bring one, either. Wear your underwear if you want, but remember I've seen you naked — there's no need for modesty. And I have towels." He unrolled the blanket to show the two beach towels that had been wrapped up in it.

Sophie used to extol the virtues of skinny dipping, but I'd never had the nerve, would suffer the torture of wet underwear under my clothes rather than remove those final barriers between my skin and the eyes of the world if I was caught without a bathing suit. I'd never understood her casual approach to nudity, almost certainly developed during her training as a circus performer, when costume changes would have to be quick and relatively public. That sort of practice — plus a perfect body — helps you lose your inhibitions about being naked. Despite my experiences with nudity at the zoos — and with Kaz himself — I waffled about whether to remove that final layer.

"Fuck it," I said under my breath. When I quit my job, I'd made a pact with myself to stop saying no to things I wanted. And I really wanted to swim. So I said, "Swim first, then eat, then swim again."

He grinned and started stripping off his shirt and shorts. I took off my dress and then my bra and panties.

"There's a nice sandy bottom and a gradual drop to about your knees, then it falls away," he said. "No rocks."

He ran into the water and dove, then resurfaced farther out. As he swam, I walked in slowly, gasping at the shock of the water against my legs, then took my own plunge, refreshing my skin, sluicing away the heat and humidity of the summer day.

I came back up and shook my hair out of my eyes and wiped my face down. "That's cold!" I yelled at him.

"Spring-fed!" he yelled back, turning to swim toward me. "Refreshing, isn't it?" he asked when he reached me.

"It's lovely. How did you find this place?"

"Did you never come here? This beach used to be public. One of Aziz's cousins has a cottage over there somewhere." He waved vaguely back toward his vehicle. "He and Aziz had a falling out a couple of years ago, so I haven't been here in ages and wouldn't go near the cottage. The regency doesn't keep the beach up anymore, so it's pretty private now — only people who know about it come here, and they'd have to have a four-wheeler or be willing to hike."

"What happened between Aziz and the cousin that was bad enough for cottage privileges to be revoked?" I asked, enjoying the silky coolness of the water passing through my hands and toes as I lazily treaded water.

"It was at a licorice zoo — did I tell you about those? S&M. Whips. Not my thing. Anyway, we were invited and Aziz went because he was curious — he likes to observe people in all their weirdness." Kaz lay back on the water and looked at the sky as he lazily waved his arms back and forth to stay afloat. "The son of Aziz's cousin was about twenty-five. He was there, dressed in leather short-shorts and combat boots — a very bad look on a man with a belly as big as his, by the way — and wielding a whip. Aziz dragged him out by his ear, reminding him, as he put it, that since their ancestors had spent the better part of the last two centuries under the thumb of various powers, it was extremely bad form for him to be subjugating others."

I laughed; as little as I knew Aziz, I could see him doing that.

"Well, needless to say, it doesn't look good on someone who wants to be seen as a master to be dragged out of a dungeon like a child and scolded for his bad behaviour. Aziz ruined his son's reputation, so the cousin put a price on Aziz's head."

"He what?" I sputtered.

"No worries, it was a while ago. Aziz says that no one smart enough to actually succeed in killing him would dare try to collect."

"Oh my god! I didn't think things like that actually happened."

"You should ask him about his family sometime. Although I'm never sure which parts of Aziz's family dramas are true and which are the filigree he adds around the edges to make a prettier story."

"Do you come from a big family?" I asked.

He shook his head. "Only child. That's what makes Aziz's family so interesting. You?"

"Two brothers," I said. "Not much of an extended family."

Kaz dunked himself under the surface and came back up, whipping the water out of his hair. "You ready to get out?" he asked.

"Yes, I'm thoroughly cooled down now."

We swam to the shore and picked up our towels. I patted myself down, then slipped my dress on. I'd never been comfortable eating while naked. Kaz stepped into his shorts before opening up the picnic basket and showing me the feast he'd thrown together after he called — sausage, cheese, bread, pickles, some hummus, carrot and celery sticks. Ripe red cherries. I joined him on the blanket as he poured ice-cold water from a canteen.

"Tell me why you're unemployed," he said, handing me a glass.

I told him about my upcoming trip, and how I'd come to the decision to go.

"I thought you seemed intrigued when Lyle mentioned it." He nodded. "Hell, I was intrigued, and I don't even do regency hours. I'd love to travel — I haven't seen much of this country outside of the city. Every few months, Aziz and I send someone to our other zoos to make sure they're working properly. If we didn't need the inspector to be anonymous, I'd love to do it. But I'd blow the cover."

"Maybe I could check out some of them for you," I offered.

He thought about it for a minute. "That's actually a good idea. Let me talk it over with Aziz."

We grazed for a bit, and he said, "But why not just do your regency hours? Why quit your job?"

"It felt like the right thing to do," I said. "I've been ... unsettled for a long time. Dissatisfied, even before Henny Penny. Part of that was Matt dying, but even with Matt, and before Matt, I always felt like something essential was missing, some vital part of myself, the key that would unlock my true nature, the part of me with purpose and passion. It's been almost a year since I went back to the office, and what with that and coming out of the depression I was in for so long, I've started to feel happy again, but there's still that piece of grit in my oyster, you know? And I decided that I could just be irritated by it, or I could turn it into a pearl. I didn't love my job before the pandemic, when I was an editor — it was something I did well and enjoyed, but I didn't love it. Telling stories has been fun but I think I need to go live some life."

"So you're happy but discontented?"

I shrugged. It was more that I was getting contented and was unhappy about it. Contentment was easy, and I was tired of easy. "I've always waited for things to come to me. I think it's time to act."

"Interesting." He dipped a carrot stick in the hummus and said, almost off-handedly, "Do you think it's time you stopped being fauna at the zoos, too?"

That question stopped me short. "That's an unexpected connection to make."

"Is it? You're saying you've been a passive observer in your life. In the zoos, you've been a passive participant longer than most people are — usually people will have moved on to the other side by now."

"Do you think it's a failing that I haven't moved on?"

"Not a failing so much, but it suggests that you're still ... out of balance a bit."

"You're calling me unbalanced?" I threw a cherry at him and he laughed with me.

"There is a natural equilibrium to life — give and take. We each give and we each take and in a perfect world we do so in equal measure. You have been taking — which gives pleasure in some way to the people who like to give, I know — but until you give, and allow yourself to receive the pleasure of giving, those scales will not be balanced."

"Have you ever known fauna who never become tacs?" I asked.

"Yes." A shadow crossed his face.

"Are those your orphans?" I guessed, and he nodded.

"Some — not all, but many — become orphans. Some become something else."

"What?"

He was silent.

"What do they become?" I prodded.

"They become prey for people like the Colonel — and Violet."

"You keep mentioning Violet and her zoo in those dire tones, but you never tell me what your issue with her is. You promised to take me to her zoo, too," I reminded him.

"I'd hoped you'd forget. And you've written your articles."

"A girl never forgets when she hasn't received something she's been promised," I said. "Plus I'm curious about the thing that goes too far for you."

He dipped another carrot stick into the hummus and popped it in his mouth, looked out over the lake but said nothing.

"I'm guessing that whatever she's like now, she wasn't like that when you met."

"God, no."

"How did you meet?" I asked.

"Aziz knew her. Or had friends who knew her. I don't know. I was staying with Aziz, and she just started showing up wherever we went. She was bright and funny and scandalous and easy to adore. Everything around us was just monochrome, and she was a splash of colour and life. She was the centre of everything, mostly because she wouldn't allow anyone to ignore her. For a while, at least, that was very attractive." I nodded. I knew how easy it was to be drawn to that kind of effervescence.

"How long ago was that?"

"Ten years? Nine? I arrived eleven years ago, and I'd been here for quite a while before I met her. She moved in with me and Aziz and the three of us became inseparable. We were having fun, we were adults but living like kids, daring each other to do crazier and crazier things just to stave off boredom. That's why we went to the petting zoo in the first place, on a dare. And then she suggested we start our own, and there we were. It gave us something to do. And then the zoos took on a life of their own." He popped a cherry into his mouth, chewed, then spat the pit onto the beach, where a bird quickly found it. "By the time we opened the mocha zoo, it had been over between us for a while. The zoos had become a job and she wasn't interested in having a job. She got bored, started looking around, and found the Colonel, and that's when we parted ways for good." He was quiet for moment. "I barely even recognize her now — she's almost literally become a different person. She had some cosmetic surgery, changed her hair. Her personality changed, too. I can't deal with her anymore."

"But you've gone to her zoo?"

"I went once." He took a drink of water. "I don't recommend it. But if you really want to see it, I'll try to arrange to take you before you go on your trip."

Other than that, we didn't talk about the zoos. It was a perfectly pleasant day. We swam and talked and ate and swam some more before he dropped me at my place.

"I'll get back to you about visiting my zoos, and maybe Violet's as well," he said, kissing me softly on the cheek. "And I hope to see you again before you go."

"I'd like that, too," I answered.

I'd kept waiting all day long for him to touch me, to instigate the kind of intimacy we'd shared at the semi-sweet zoo — and maybe take it to its natural conclusion. It seemed like a perfect time and place, and we'd spent half the day naked. But he'd been a gentleman. I wondered if I was in his friend zone. I had no idea how he'd receive an advance from me if I made one, and I hadn't wanted to spoil an otherwise lovely day by finding out he wasn't interested.

• • •

Given our hands-off picnic, I was surprised to see Kaz there in front of me the next time I went to the semi-sweet zoo. And again three nights later. I had waited with my eyes closed, but I knew it was him even before I opened them.

"Kaz."

"Kate."

"I'm happy you're here."

"I wasn't sure I'd come back this soon."

"Did you think I would?"

He didn't answer, but of course he'd know if he wanted to.

I led him, still blindfolded, to my blanket. "So, keeping your hands in again? Was this accidental?"

"I knew I was choosing you, if that answers your question."

"It does and it doesn't."

"Do you want to talk about it?"

"Not right now, no."

"Tell me what you want, then."

"I want you to leave the blindfold on," I said in a playful voice, growing bolder with experience of him.

Then I told him what I wanted him to do next.

I didn't even notice when I started unconsciously touching him back. I ran my fingers through his hair, held his head just there, stroked his back and along his arms, wrapped myself around him when we both needed to regroup.

"Will you do something for me?" he asked, late in the evening when we were lying still in each other's arms, enjoying the contact, soft skin to soft skin.

"Sure," I said, moving my hand between his legs.

"Not that," he said, "or at least, that wasn't what I was going to ask." But he didn't take my hand away, so I left it there, brushing the delicate skin with feather-light strokes.

He said, "Next time, I'll come here and wait for you. I want you to be the tac."

"Really? Why?"

"It's just something I'd like you to do."

"It's not my style."

"I know. But I'd like you to try."

"Because you're worried about me becoming an orphan?" He didn't answer. "When?"

"Let's not plan a night. Let's just let it happen. Let's say I'll come here four nights in the next week, and you come here four nights, and so at least one night we'll be here together."

"So you don't mind if I work out my technique on someone else for three out of four nights?"

"That might be best." He laughed.

"What if I don't choose you?"

"Then you don't."

"I'm not a tactile, Kaz."

"Sure you are." He smiled, stilling my hand with his own.

"But if I can do this as fauna, why do I need to be a tac? Why isn't it the same thing?"

"Everyone needs to learn how to share."

"Is that what you do?"

"You tell me."

Nearly alone in the dimly lit zoo, we wrapped ourselves in a blanket and talked softly about my preparations for going east, and I reminded him that we'd discussed me checking out zoos. What I didn't say was that his offer had been the solution to a dilemma and there was no way I was leaving town without finalizing the agreement. I'd had no luck finding zoos on my own, didn't know the first place to look, and if I was going to be out of the city for two months, I would need my fix.

"I'd forgotten about that. Yes, I still need to talk to Aziz. I'll get back to you. When do you leave?"

"In a couple of weeks."

He wasn't there the next night I went, or the night after.

It was strange, being the blind one filing in, instead of the one waiting. It gave a completely different flavour to the evening. Even the atmosphere in the changing room was different. There was always a buzz of excitement in the fauna changing room, but it was interior, expectant. I never paid attention to the other fauna other than acknowledging that there were people around me. Getting ready with the other tacs, that aura of excitement was laced with testosterone — and not just because they were mostly men. The feeling was more urgent, more physical, and competitive. I could sense every man and woman in the room sizing each other up, as if they were wondering who they'd have to fight to get the prize, and who among us might win.

There was a moment of helplessness after I put on my blindfold and walked into the zoo. Pheromones? I couldn't say I smelled them. I waited for a twitch, an audible movement, something that could catch my attention.

Finally, on a signal I couldn't have explained seconds later, a movement in the air, a breath, an imagined tap on my shoulder, I reached out and claimed my fauna.

Funny, when I was fauna, it never occurred to me to think about my level of attraction to the tac who chose me, but now that the choice was mine, now that I was the one who would be making the advances in a zoo that took you right to the door of sexual intercourse but not through it, I found myself sending up a prayer that I would find something attractive, something to make me want to make love to this person. My body, it must be said, was ready for the encounter, but my head hadn't completely accepted what was about to happen.

Fortunately, my fauna had no qualities that I found offputting. He was average — middle-aged, middle height, a little heavy, still had most of his hair. I panicked for a moment, not really knowing where to start.

I borrowed Kaz's line: "Tell me what you want."

"No one's ever asked me that before," he said, and thought for a moment. "Just touch me."

That didn't give me much to go on. And I stood there for a moment, wondering where the hell to begin. None of this came naturally to me. *This isn't me*, I thought to myself in despair for the hundredth time that day. And then it hit me — it wasn't me, so I would be someone else. I would wear the skin of someone to whom this came more easily. I would perform.

I took his discarded blindfold and put it on him, then walked around him as he stood on his blanket, lightly massaging his shoulders and back, reaching up to graze his cheek with my lips but dancing away when he tried to kiss me.

"No touching," I whispered.

Using the palms of my hands, I skimmed his bodysuit down his body, lightly caressing as I went, until he stepped out of it. I took my blindfold and used it to tie his hands behind his back, removed my own bodysuit and then, like a lap dancer at a very permissive strip club, I first used my body to touch his, then my hands, then my lips.

"Get a condom," he said, and I reached for one from a nearby basket. I rolled it down just in time — he came almost immediately.

I enjoyed the performance, and as always, my skin drank in the sensations I was feeding it, but I was astonished by the amount of effort it took to pleasure this man over the course of the evening. I wanted him to enjoy himself, but it was work to be the only one touching. I briefly felt bad for the men and women who'd been my tacs.

I was surprised, too, to find his passivity a turnoff at some level. Even with Matt, and before Matt, I'd rarely been the seducer, always the seduced, and so far, I decided, I didn't like this new role — at least not in this venue. It took a lot of energy, and while there was a payoff — it can be gratifying on a certain level

to give pleasure to others, especially those you care about —
pleasing a random stranger who didn't reciprocate left me entirely unfulfilled. As a fauna, I found this zoo frustrating but also
enjoyable; as a tac, I could see why people quickly moved on.

Still, all in all it wasn't the worst experience ever, and
whatever else it was, it was touch, it was feeling, it was a re-
grounding in my sense that I was a living human being with
tastes and appetites and the wherewithal to satiate them.

I went back the next night, thinking Kaz wouldn't want me
to drag it out, and again he wasn't there. I started to wonder
whether he'd make me wait three nights.

The second night, the fauna I chose was female.

That was another possibility that hadn't occurred to me.
Even though I'd had plenty of female tacs at the vanilla zoo,
and some at the milk-chocolate and semi-sweet zoos — and I
knew that there were always more female fauna than male —
somehow I'd assumed that I would only choose a man. My
female tacs in the chocolate zoos had lit the same slow fire
under my skin that the male tacs did — which I put down to
the fact that touch, anyone's touch, was so rare and strange that
the pleasure centres in my brain welcomed it, and my body
responded the way it did to pleasure. As Bethany had said to
me nearly a year earlier, I am a sexually healthy woman, and
once past the vanilla zoos, the touch was supposed to be sexual.
My body was reacting naturally, unfettered by anyone else's
conception of wrong or right.

I had had fleeting attractions to women in the past, usually
a reaction to a quality — self-confidence, raw sexual power —
that I also found attractive in men. I'd just never found myself
inclined to act on those feelings. And now I removed my blindfold to discover that I was in the position of having to do so

with a woman who, it must be said, wouldn't have sparked even what little attention I'd have paid in the real world.

"Hi, I'm Kate," I said to the woman, a little older than me, whose eyes were wide as platters — obviously I wasn't what she'd expected, either, I thought. "So, you new to this, too?"

"This is my first time here," the woman said.

"Ah. Well, it's not my first time, but I'm not usually a tac, and you're my first woman."

"My mother is rolling over in her grave right now," the fauna said with a hint of a smile.

"Because you're here, or because a woman chose you?"

"Both."

"But you've had female tacs before, haven't you?"

"Yes, but … this zoo …"

"I understand. Listen, we don't have to get naked — we'll only do what you feel comfortable doing. You'll be my guide, okay? Let's lie down."

We lay side by side on the mat the woman had laid out earlier. I leaned in and kissed her lips and she gave a little whimper and squirmed beside me. I paused to give her the chance to back out, but she lay still, so I gathered her to me, stroked her back and arm, and eventually she gentled under my touch, relaxed, opened to my hands and lips.

"What's your name?" I whispered.

"Guinevere," she answered.

"Tell me what you want, Guinevere."

• • •

The next time, I chose him. I was making my blind, unsteady way down the line, aware of the tac ahead of me and the one behind and the fauna to my right, so close I could almost feel their breath on my skin. The tac in front of me stopped and picked someone out of the line, and as I stepped forward, I smelled him, and I sensed him as well, a quality of heat, of expectation. I knew he smiled when I reached out to him, that he knew it was me even before he took off his blindfold.

He led me to his mat, and we knelt facing each other.

"Keep the blindfold on," he said, repeating my request to many tacs before him.

"What do you want me to do?"

"Touch me."

That request was far less compelling when someone was asking me instead of the other way around. "Yes, of course, but ..."

"What does your hand need to know?"

"Silly question."

"Ask it anyway."

With my eyes removed from the equation, every other sense was brought into focus. I found my hand needed to know the sinews and papery skin at the back of his knees. The exact line of his hair. The delicate bone at his wrist. It needed to know the fold of his elbow, and so did my lips, which tasted there, and then traced a wandering path to his mouth.

My hands needed to know everything there was to know about him, where he was rough and where he was soft, how the skin of his belly quivered under the scratch of a fingernail. My ears drank in the rasp of my hand against the hair on his chest and navel, my nose absorbed the soapy musk of his hollows and valleys.

"Your hands are very curious," he said later.

"They had a lot of questions they'd been meaning to ask," I replied.

We were quiet for a while. My fingertips revelled in the whorls of hair on his chest, enjoying the play of it against his soft skin. Hearing him catch his breath when I brushed his nipples made me smile in delight.

"Does this make you happy?" I asked.

"How do you mean?"

"It's almost begun to feel like we're dating, that there's an intention behind our meetings, yet there can't be because the meetings are always accidental."

"You would have gone with another tac — or tonight, would have gone with another fauna — if it wasn't me."

"That's what I mean — you told me to meet you here, but you were okay with the idea that I wouldn't choose you."

"I wanted you to choose me. I knew you might not. I left it up to Fate and Fate rewarded me."

I worked up my courage, thinking back to him telling me that if I couldn't ask for it, I wasn't ready for it. "I enjoy seeing you."

"I enjoy seeing you, too."

"I'm starting to feel ..." I searched for the word. "Frustrated."

"Do you want to move on to another zoo?"

"Not in that way. Well, not just in that way."

"Oh?"

"I'm going to ruin this, aren't I, if I say I'd like to see you outside a zoo. I like spending time with you. I enjoyed having you at dinner — I enjoyed our picnic."

"You probably want to know my real name, too," he said.

"That would be a place to start."

"Tell me — the other tacs, do you find pleasure with them?"

"Of course, or I wouldn't keep coming."

"And you would give them up for me?"

"Probably. I don't know. I don't enjoy them in the same way."

"So it's a matter of technique?"

The question took me by surprise. "No … with them, that's our only connection. I feel a connection to you that doesn't have to do with the zoo. Because we met outside it, probably, and because we've talked to each other. Ever since that first time — I've always hoped you'd be there, that you'd pick me."

"Are you falling in love with me?"

"I don't know. Would you be okay with that? Are you falling in love with me?"

"I don't know."

"If I said yes?"

"Why do you come here?"

"Is that why you're hesitant? Because I come here?"

He was silent for a minute, that frustrating way he had of ignoring questions he didn't want to answer. He asked again, "Why do you come here?"

"For the touch. I need the touch. But it's not all I need."

"When did that change?"

"With you. Talking to you. Being here with you. Is that love?"

"Maybe infatuation. You said it's been a long time."

"I haven't become infatuated with any of the other tacs, though there are several I've had a number of times and have enjoyed quite a bit. There haven't been any I've hoped to see again."

"I think I've been selfish," Kaz said thoughtfully. "You have ten years to make up for, and I'm afraid that by choosing you as often as I have, I've not let you get those years out of your system. You should experience others." He nodded, as if he'd decided something. "I'm going to take myself out of the equation. I want you to come here as often as you can before you go on your trip, or move on to the other zoos. Visit zoos everywhere. I'll give you the introductions like we planned. Experiment. Test yourself. Be a tac. When are you back?"

"Middle of October."

"Call me when you come back. Tell me what you've learned. And if you still want to have this conversation, then we'll have it."

"Avoiding the question?"

"Giving you space. Okay?"

It looked like I wasn't the only one who was ambivalent about a relationship. It gutted me in a way, that I'd worked up the nerve to say something, only to be pushed back, however gently, and however much promise was in that deflection that wasn't quite a rejection. I wondered if he was happy with what he found in the zoos, too, and I'd read into his attention an interest that wasn't there. If I didn't call him when I came back, would he notice? Would he call me? There was just enough of a carrot at the end of the stick to keep me from being completely heartbroken, just enough to keep me guessing.

But what could I say?

"Okay."

"Okay."

I didn't expect to see Kaz before I left. I thought he'd send me the information about the other zoos in an email, so when I found the familiar heavy stationery slipped under my door a few days later, that was what I thought it was.

Instead, I was surprised to find an invitation to a summer cocktail party at his place.

Going Dark

I'D JUST VISITED Valerie to get my hair cut and coloured before my trip. I dressed and made myself up carefully, then walked to Kaz's penthouse condo, which I'd been surprised to discover was nearby, a couple of blocks closer to the river.

A doorman keyed in the code for Kaz's penthouse when I showed him the invitation, and I rode up alone in the elevator, which dropped me in a slate-tiled foyer rich with light and colour.

Kaz stood near the entrance and greeted me warmly. "Kate," he said. "Thank you for coming."

I had been afraid this would be awkward after our last conversation, but it felt natural to be with him.

"Hi ... Kaz?" I asked, noting that he was using my pseudonym. What was his name?

"Yes." He smiled.

"There's no nuker?" I asked.

"It's in the elevator," he said.

"Oh, I didn't notice it."

"I know. Turns out that light doesn't have to be blue."

Kaz wasn't wearing a mask or gloves, and neither were any of the guests, so I slipped mine into my handbag and then handed him the light jacket I'd worn despite the heat of the day, to hide the fact that I was wearing an illegal dress.

Kaz took a minute to admire me. "You look beautiful," he said sincerely, and I knew it was no empty compliment.

I felt fabulous. I was wearing an iridescent-blue knee-length tunic that hugged my body in all the right places, its nubby raw silk an open invitation for fingertips.

"You're going to make me blush if you don't stop staring," I whispered, finally.

"I find it bizarre to see you in clothes," he said with a coy smile. "Who knew you'd look as good in them as you do without?"

He looked pretty good himself, in a form-fitting black T-shirt and ivory-coloured linen pants, slim black belt, leather loafers. Sleek, Kaz was, in clothes and out.

He reached for my hand and his lips approached my ear. "I've missed you," he whispered, then before I could answer, he leaned back and said, "Let me take you in and introduce you around. You're Kate Matthews tonight, and if anyone asks, you're in insurance."

"What if they ask me about insurance?"

"They won't."

"How do you know?"

"Because they're all in insurance, too," Kaz said.

"Saying it like that, it sounds as if we're in a gangster movie," I admonished.

"We *are* all criminals," Kaz reminded me.

I laughed, a flirtatious tinkle that turned heads our way.

"Now come with me. All the world's a stage tonight," Kaz said, leading me into the crowd.

No one in the room was wearing treated fabric, a sign that either I wasn't the only one who had squirrelled away a few pieces from a previous life, or they had access to the kind of black-market supply Lyle had mentioned — something I'd like to find myself.

This had been one of Matt's favourite dresses and, like Matt, Kaz was not immune to the allure of silk; his hand kept going to my back, ostensibly to guide me around the room, but his thumb stroked as well, and his palm rested a bit too long to be merely polite. When he left my side — and he did, once he was satisfied that I could hold my own — his eyes continued to follow me.

There were maybe thirty people, most of whom seemed to already know each other, milling around between the comfortably furnished room and the patio beyond the French doors at one end. Like his zoos, Kaz's home was filled with tactile opportunity, textured furnishings, carpets and drapery in rich colours to please the eye, as well.

Despite my workplace lunches, I hadn't seen so many bare faces so close since before the pandemic. Most of the kids at the rave had been a blur of activity. I hadn't really picked out individuals. And while everyone went bare at the zoos, I paid no attention to the mass of others, was never as close to them.

Here I found myself staring at lips and noses, mesmerized by teeth as people mingled on the rooftop patio in the early-evening sun.

The guests laughed and drank freely, but although waiters clad in burgundy T-shirts and white shorts circulated, carrying plates of appetizers, no one really seemed to eat. It was as if everyone, having lost the habit of eating in front of others, was self-conscious about taking it up again. I took a shrimp from one tray, and a cracker with pâté from another, and felt the eyes of the room upon me as I chewed. I wondered if Kaz would be offended if I asked for a doggie bag.

"This is the oddest party," I commented to Kaz when the ebb and flow of the crowd brought us together again.

"How so?"

"Well, since we're all 'in insurance,' I'm guessing that every-one here is making up the life stories they're telling me."

"Any intriguing ones?

"A surprising number are superheroes," I said, raising a skeptical eyebrow, earning a laugh.

"And are you making up your own?"

"It took me a few tries to come up with a good one. But I've decided that I am a modern-day adventurer, travelling the world and saving those in need."

"Sounds like you're having fun," he said with a smile.

"I am! I am. It's just odd. It's as if we're all our own avatars."

"Are you saying we're not?"

"Now there's a question for philosophy class." I laughed.

"You could say that we've always been our own avatars, deciding a course and following it but presenting to the world only the face that we choose."

"And your avatar, Kaz? What does he do in his spare time?"

"Seeks world peace." He smiled, signalling to a passing waiter to take his empty glass.

"You're one of the good guys, then?"

"Did you ever doubt it?"

"We're all outlaws, you said. And I still don't know why you were on the run."

"You can be on the wrong side of the law and the right side of justice at the same time. You should know that."

"Is that how you see yourself?"

"I believe a perfectly well-meaning law can be unjust," he said. "For example, the law would strongly disapprove of your dress, yet I couldn't bring myself to if I tried."

I smiled at him, and he smiled back, then another guest joined us, and soon the gravitational force of the crowd moved us out of each other's orbits again.

What did it mean that he'd invited me here, I asked myself, not for the first time. He had told me he was going to leave me alone, but tonight he was flirtatious ... I wished Sophie was here to read this for me. Or Eleanor.

Then Kaz was at my elbow again. "Come, you have to meet ..."

I was on the patio, laughing with Aziz, enjoying the first evening breeze from the river, when I heard a raised voice from inside, and Aziz frowned.

"What's going on?" I asked, turning to look inside and finding that the glare from the sun on the glass prevented me from seeing anything.

"Uninvited guests," he said. "Excuse me."

He went inside and I followed at a distance. Kaz was speaking to a man and a woman whose backs were to me, and he looked furious.

"— did you get in here?" I heard him ask.

"Dick let us up. I told him I lost my invitation — though, of course, it was you who lost my invitation, wasn't it, darling?" the woman asked.

"I want you to leave now. Just go."

"Oh, just let us in for a few minutes, Kaz. I know Ramon is here and I want to say hi."

"Violet, Colonel," Aziz said as he approached the two, holding out his arms as if to greet them, but effectively herding them to the elevator, where Kaz held the door open.

I recognized the Colonel from my visit to his zoo. The woman beside him was medium height, with jet-black hair cut into a precise bob. She was wearing what looked like a vintage flapper dress, red, covered in bugle beads that clicked against each other when she moved. She turned to greet Aziz, but a pair of oversized sunglasses obscured her face, so I couldn't see what she looked like.

"*Et tu*, Aziz?" Violet asked, pursing her blood-red lips but inclining her head so that he could kiss her cheek. Her voice did have an arch Katharine Hepburn–ish delivery, as Eleanor had mentioned. I wondered whether she came by it naturally. "You know my favourite parties are the ones where I'm not invited. And you used to enjoy crashing them with me — you both did. So don't act surprised that I'm here."

"You know your guest is not welcome here, Violet, and never will be. You insult me by bringing him to my home. So I'll ask you to leave with him," Kaz said tightly, obviously working to keep his anger in check, to avoid alerting the guests to the contretemps at the door. It was a valiant effort, but I could tell that it hadn't gone unnoticed, although so far no one had tried to intervene.

Violet looked briefly past Aziz into the room. "Smaller crowd than usual, Kaz, and very sober. We could liven the place up for you. You never could throw a party without my help."

Violet remained focused on Kaz. The Colonel looked around with a smirk on his face, obviously enjoying having disturbed a happy gathering. He caught me watching. I felt a chill run down my spine as his half-lidded eyes appraised me the way he had that night at his zoo. There was no question that he recognized me. Smiling as if he felt my discomfort, he bowed slightly before turning back to Kaz and Violet.

"Come, my dear, there are other parties in other places. We've paid our respects — let's go." With his palm at her back, he guided Violet to the elevator, and she moved gracefully but reluctantly toward it.

"Just to show you there's no hard feelings," Violet said, "I'm having a party of my own on Thursday — silent auction. You're more than welcome."

A nerve jumped in Kaz's cheek but he said nothing, just saw the pair into the elevator and watched the doors close, then stayed there with his back to the room, visibly trying to calm himself down, breathing deeply and slowly. Aziz spoke a few quiet words to him, and he sighed and nodded, wiped his face with his hand. Aziz gave him a quick hug and moved back into the party. Those guests who had noticed the disturbance at the door gathered around Aziz; he shrugged and smiled, said something funny to make them all laugh, and moved on.

I watched Kaz until he, too, turned and moved back into the party, the anger gone from his face but not his hands, which were clenched into fists until someone came up to him and gave him a brief hug, whispered something into his ear. Little by little he relaxed. Then he looked up at me and smiled, and came over to me.

"Sorry about that."

"You can't do anything about uninvited guests. So that was Violet?"

"Yes. She enjoys making a scene. They knew they wouldn't get past the door, but it made them happy to try."

"Are you okay?"

"I am." He paused. "I am working on it. I will be."

The sun had started to go down when the first guests started leaving and I watched them depart with regret. I'd have to leave soon — I didn't want to be one of those unfortunate people who can't tell it's time to go and have to be ushered out by an impatient host.

When about half the guests had left, I went up to Kaz. "I should be going," I said, and the smile left his face for the first time since Violet had made her exit.

"Why?"

"The party's ending."

"Stay," he said. "*This* party's ending."

I felt a lurch in my stomach, the kind that comes with speed and flying.

After the last guests had gone, Kaz took me by the hand. "I have something for you."

He led me to a room whose door had remained closed throughout the party. He opened it to reveal a library — bookshelves lining every wall, comfortable armchairs, a gas fireplace, a beautifully carved wooden desk that was obviously not just decorative. He turned on one of the many lamps and walked over to the desk while I went straight to the shelves to see what was on them: a mix of fiction, biography, political science, historical analysis — a lot of the books I'd once owned, and some of which I still did.

"Where did you get all of these?"

"I started collecting after I arrived here. The regency was putting everything online and destroying the books once they'd been scanned. I made a deal with the people paid to destroy them that I'd get to see them first."

"But where did they come from?"

"Public libraries, university libraries, personal collections."

"I had to leave most of mine behind when I moved." I ran my fingers over the spines, marvelling at the abundance.

"But this is what I wanted to show you," he said.

I turned to find him holding out a small, wrapped parcel. "Here," he said, "this is for you."

I took it from him and carefully unwrapped the same linen-finished paper that he'd used for his letters to me, folded this time into an intricate pocket. Inside was a slim volume covered in red cloth with gold-embossed letters that read *Serialized, by Lily King.*

"What ...?"

"I took some of my favourites of your stories and had them printed and bound," he said with a shy smile.

I opened the book and saw familiar titles in the table of contents.

"This is stunning, Kaz — what a wonderful present. Thank you." I hugged him and kissed his cheek. "But I don't understand — where and how and what made you ...?"

"I know people, and I thought it would be nice to be a part of your first book. And to give you back some of the pleasure you've given me. Now, let's have dinner."

I was torn between the desire to talk to him and a longing to curl up in a comfy armchair and read my stories for the first time in book form. Kaz won, but only just. I put the book in the pocket of my jacket and joined him in the kitchen.

A wall of windows looking over grassy riverbanks framed the full moon in a sky that wasn't quite dark.

"So now I know you're a reader. But I don't know anything else about you. What do you do in your spare time?" It was odd, watching him move around his kitchen, to realize how two-dimensional he still was for me, despite our hours in the zoos and the time we'd spent together outside them. I couldn't imagine him shopping for groceries. I had no idea what kind of present might mean something to him.

"I like wandering around the city, like you, looking for signs of regeneration, new markets, new construction. I like to go hiking. I spend a lot of time with Aziz's extended family — there's always a project or something to do, and they're great people. His parents were close friends with my parents, so I'm welcomed like one of the family."

I looked out the windows as he put a light meal together, watching the darkness take over. "You have a tremendous view here, the sky unfolding in front of you like that."

"When the moon's full, I like to watch the moontrail move down the river."

"I used to hate not being able see the stars in the city. It's not so bad now."

"Did you grow up in the city?"

"No, I'm a country girl at heart. You?"

"City born and bred." He smiled. "The country is something you visit briefly, to go swimming or camping, or visit a farm where they make good cheese."

"I've always had a foot in both camps, I'm afraid. When I'm in the one, I miss the other. Less so now, of course, with the city more like the country all the time."

Kaz laid a linen tablecloth over one end of the butcher-block island and set two places. He pulled out one of the bar stools and indicated that I should sit. He ladled a delicate gazpacho into small cups and passed a basket to me. I lifted the linen napkin to find rolls warm from the oven.

With the candles lit and the lights turned low, we looked out at the moon and the city, cast into relief below us. We talked about reading and books and our favourite authors.

"Were you a chef in your former life?" I asked, after several small but exquisitely composed courses — cherry tomatoes stuffed with herbed goat cheese, cucumber involtini with a light mustard dressing, poached trout with wild rice. "I'm glad I didn't eat anything earlier — you didn't say I was invited to dinner."

"I wasn't sure you were," he answered. "I was afraid it would be ..."

"Awkward?"

"As you say."

"But it's not."

"No. That makes me happy."

"Me, too."

Replete with good food and wine, I laughed when Kaz set up a small chocolate fondue pot.

"My little brother loved chocolate fondue for seduction," I said. "Swore he could always seal the deal after feeding a date a strawberry dipped in chocolate."

"Do you want to be seduced?"

"Do you want to seduce me?" I asked coyly, dipping a slice of peach into the precious chocolate before laying it on my tongue and closing my mouth around it, the sweetness of the syrup making my salivary glands cramp in pleasure. "Oh my god," I said, "if you don't want me, I'll make love to that all night."

Kaz laughed. "Please, don't let me interrupt." He dipped his own slice and savoured it as I prepared another piece for myself.

"Where on earth do you get chocolate? It's probably been two years since I last had a piece."

"Did you meet Ramon tonight? He visits every summer from South America. He always brings chocolate for me and coffee for Aziz."

I remembered a Spanish-speaking man who'd spent most of the evening in intense conversation with another guest. It didn't seem like the kind of conversation a stranger should interrupt.

"Is he in insurance, too?"

"No, import-export." Kaz laughed.

When the peaches were gone, we washed the dishes, then he warmed two cognac glasses before pouring a finger for each of us. He suggested moving into another room with more comfortable seats, but I liked the coziness of our spot in the kitchen, so we stayed there, looking out at the river and the city and sipping quietly.

"This whole evening has been a wonderful surprise, Kaz. Thank you."

"You're welcome."

"So do you do this a lot — throw a party, then seduce one of the guests with peaches and chocolate?"

"Throw a party, at least."

"Does that mean you're not big into seduction, or that you're not seducing me?"

"What do you think?"

"I think you're cursed with a touch of ambiguity, a smidgen of ambivalence," I said, a little testily. "A girl can hope — she can't always tell. You said you were going to leave me alone."

"I thought it would be nice to see you before you left, see you off in style. I wanted to give you your present, and I wanted to spend time with you. I missed you." He held up a hand. "I know that not seeing you in the zoo was my choice, and I stand by it. I still think you need a lot more time away from me before we revisit that conversation. But I am also selfish, and this seemed like a more controllable environment than being naked together in a zoo."

"What do you think I'm going to find in the zoos that I haven't already found?"

"In zoos — and also in the world — I would hope you find choice."

"I can still make choices. Or are you so fabulous in bed you think you'll blind me to all other possibilities?"

"It's not just that. My world is a bit chaotic right now. I know what I want, but I'm not in a position to make it happen. And I'm not sure whether that's even what you're looking for."

"You should stop telling me what you don't think I want and ask me what I do."

"What do you want?"

"I think I want you, even though I'm not liking the paternalistic side of you. What do you want?"

"I want you to be free of questions about what you've been missing."

"There you go again — making assumptions about what questions I need to have answered. Let me show you how I feel," I said and, taking his hand, placed it over my heart, let it pound against his palm.

He stood up, moved to stand beside my stool and mirrored the motion with my hand over his heart, which if anything was racing faster than mine.

"I haven't been ambivalent about this from the moment I met you," he said, locking my eyes with his own, pupils growing, evidence of the arousal he'd been trying to repudiate.

"So what's stopping you?"

"I guess Aziz's strange sense of honour has rubbed off on me." He sighed and went back to his stool.

I sipped my brandy and tried not to choke on it. I didn't know what was happening, but I suspected the night wasn't going to end up as I'd hoped when he'd invited me to stay.

"Aziz was supposed to stay for dinner so we could go through the zoo information with you, but he insisted on leaving."

"Don't tell me Aziz was hoping we'd end up sleeping together, too."

Kaz nodded. "He's a born romantic, and I didn't say I didn't want to sleep with you — or better yet, stay awake all night long."

There it was, that delicious lurch in my stomach again. "You are such a tease, Kaz. Do you want me or don't you?"

"Oh, I do. But I don't want to be the first thing you have since your ... Matt. You've been living in a cocoon since the pandemic, in your beige apartment, and you've begun to moult, but you're not a butterfly yet. And I live in a bit of a cocoon, too — no real contact with the straight world. Nearly everyone I know, quite a few people I like an awful lot, and everyone I'm likely to meet, is a criminal, greater or lesser."

He stopped and considered his next words carefully.

"I don't want you just exchanging one cocoon for another. You should fly a bit in between."

"You want me to live a little," I said flatly.

"In so many words, yes. I mean, don't you want the same thing? I've been watching you take shape for months now. If you had any idea how different you are from the nervous, tentative woman I met last winter, looking for something she couldn't find anywhere else ... I want to see what you turn into when you realize the world's in front of you. I want to see your colours. I want to know what you can become on your own without me adding my own shades to who you are. And I think you need to find that out, too, for yourself."

I got up from the table and walked to the windows, gathering my thoughts as I looked out on the moonlit streets and buildings, the river.

Kaz had obviously given this more thought than I had — all I was doing was feeling, stuck in a well of need, drinking in the sensual overload that the zoos provided, not considering the long term, the ramifications of my actions. On the other hand, who the hell was he to decide what was best for me?

What would Sophie do? I asked myself. But that was foolish, wasn't it? With Sophie, the question would never have come up. Sophie had taken what she wanted, made the outside conform to her will. There was a power in that attitude, I thought. I'd watched Sophie work her magic more than once — I wondered if I could appropriate even a tiny bit of that sorcery.

Looking out at the streets below, and at Kaz's reflection in the glass, I could see that he was watching me. I said in my best imitation of Sophie's husky voice, "And I can't have sex with you even once in mid-moult? Would that be so devastating to my evolution?"

Kaz laughed but was wary, too, at the shift in my tone. "I worry that it could slow your metamorphosis."

"Afraid that I'll lose my taste for what life has to offer once I've had a taste of you?"

"Maybe."

"Such hubris." I smiled, walking back to where he was sitting at the table.

"Not just hubris," he said, a grin tickling at the sides of his mouth as he watched my approach. "There's been some question of infatuation ..."

"I've been enjoying other men — and women — since that question arose," I reminded him, arching an eyebrow. "Do you think this," I placed my hand at the junction of his legs and squeezed lightly, "will rob me of that capacity?"

"Lily ..."

"Come now, Kaz," I said, increasing the pressure while at the same time leaning in to kiss him. "We don't want to disappoint Aziz, do we?"

Part of me stood back and watched in awe as for once in my life I took the seductive lead, asserting my desires without worrying about rejection or looking foolish.

"Where's the bed?" I asked between kisses, and he took my hand and led me to his room.

"Undress me," he said, and I helped him out of his shirt and pants, then he unzipped my dress and I stepped out of it and we stood there for a moment in our underwear, which seemed strangely seductive, given the amount of time we'd spent naked in each other's company. We stayed partly clothed for a while, playing with the new paradigm, enjoying the tease that the fabric offered.

The hymen doesn't grow back, but I cried out like a virgin when he entered me. We weren't children and we'd come to know each other's pleasure spots in the zoos, so this was not just a crazy mad coupling for which I wasn't prepared — I was as ready as it was possible to be, but even so it came as a shock, this profoundly neglected part of my body finally being called on once again to do the thing it was made for. It was an age-old motion and still brand new, and I struggled for a moment to let go, to open up, to feel and to enjoy the feeling.

"Are you okay?" Kaz whispered in my ear. "Is this okay?"

"Yes," I said. "Yes, just …"

He rolled us over without losing the connection. "Do this in your own time," he said.

I sat still for a moment as my body adjusted itself around him, closed my eyes, and just experienced the feeling of his cock inside me, my clit riding his pelvic bone. He stroked my breasts with his left hand. He licked his right index finger and used it to inscribe obscenities on my belly. When I was ready to move, he was ready for me. I was hungry, but his appetite matched mine. Slow, frenzied, hard, tender. We'd sleep briefly, then wake to begin again.

"You're right," I said to him at one point, drawing a question mark on his navel with my index finger. "I have a lot of questions for myself. And you might not be the answer to a lot of them. But you're a very satisfying answer to a few."

• • •

"What did you do before the pandemic?" I asked him the next morning as we sat at the butcher block island, wearing silk robes that pooled around the legs of our bar stools to the floor.

"A little of this, a little of that," he said.

"Uh-uh, mister, you know everything worth knowing

about me. Time for you to give up your own secrets. For instance, what's your name?"

"Kaz."

"No, your real one."

"That's it," he said. "Well, one of them. My family is European, religious. I have several. But that was always my favourite."

"What did your mother call you?"

"Son. Darling." He grinned, and I threw a roll at him. "She called me Mischa."

"Russian?"

"She was. My parents defected after I was born. We lived here and there after that."

"You said you had no concerns about money — oligarchs or mafia?"

He laughed. "Neither. But you're not the first person to ask. My father invented some terribly important software and made a fortune, which I inherited. I've never actually had a real job, one that I had to make a go of or face ruin. I stayed in school far too long, studied things guaranteed never to get me an honest day's work, ran an art gallery for a while ... I've owned a few restaurants, nightclubs ..."

"You don't really strike me as a dilettante. It doesn't sound like you lived the kind of life you'd need to escape from."

"It doesn't, does it?"

"So? What were you escaping from?" Because I could — because I wanted to — I ran my foot up his bare calf, enjoying both the tickling sensation on the sensitive arch of my foot and the look of pleasure on his face.

"Listen ... I rode the edge of some bad things. Knew some bad people and looked the other way because what they did didn't involve me. I realized too late that I was a useful idiot to them. I saw some things I shouldn't have seen and eventually I saw too much, something horrifying, and they found it problematic that I'd witnessed it. I needed to disappear. I managed to get my money and myself out, and hid in a refugee camp where no one would think to look for me. I got a message to Aziz, and he helped bring me here through some back channels his family keeps open. So was I a criminal? No. Was I a good guy? That's relative."

"You're a criminal now. Are you a good guy?"

"I am trying to be. My motives are purer than they were when I was young and stupid, anyway."

He got up from his stool to take the omelette he'd made out of the oven. Cheese oozed out when he cut it in half to put on our plates. He brought it to the table with more of last night's warm rolls. We were quiet for a bit, enjoying the food.

"So why don't you have a licorice zoo?" I asked as I used a piece of my roll to sop up cheese from my plate. "You'd think, with your blindfolds and your strict rules, that you'd have more sympathy for a little BDSM, but you get a look on your face every time they come up, like you've just smelled something rancid."

"Dominance and subjugation — Aziz and I decided that we've seen too much of the bad places that can go to find it appealing. We want to celebrate the skin, the body, not desecrate it with whips and other instruments." Kaz picked up our plates and took them to the counter, returning with a bowl of sliced peaches and blueberries. "But my problem isn't so much with the zoos themselves — as long as everyone consents, who am I to say whether some kink is more acceptable than any other? My problem is with the zookeeper. The Colonel is the only one of us with a licorice zoo. He's an objectively bad person. And I'm not going to ruin breakfast by talking about him."

I stabbed a peach slice with my fork and said, "Okay, then, let's talk about how we'll know when I'm a butterfly. What's the signal?"

I'd asked the question flippantly, but he was thoughtful for a moment before he answered.

"I don't know. For all we know, you're already there. You're not as passive as I thought, and I'm obviously not as ambivalent as I'd like to be." He drew a finger down my cheek the way he had the night we met, and I felt the same thrill.

"Obviously. In fact, I bet I could seduce you right now with both hands behind my back," I said, eyeing the knot in the belt of his bathrobe. He sat up straighter. "There, not feeling ambivalent at all now, are you?"

I jumped off my stool and, to his immense pleasure, was using my teeth to undo the knot when a voice came from behind me.

"Well, hello, Katie!"

I stood, confused, and spun to see Aziz in the doorway of the kitchen, an espresso pot in his hand, smiling ear to ear, dressed in a bathrobe exactly like the ones Kaz and I were wearing.

"It's called knocking, Aziz," Kaz said, drawing me protectively to his side, not realizing that he'd pulled my robe aside and left a breast exposed.

Aziz approached us, leaned in to kiss me on the mouth and at the same time pull my lapel into a more modest place.

I was too shocked to protest — or even to decide whether I wanted to.

Then he kissed Kaz on the lips and moved to the counter. "This calls for espresso," he said, "and not whatever weak tea you were no doubt feeding your guest."

"Knocking, Aziz," Kaz repeated. "It's practised in many civilized societies when one is confronted by a locked door."

"I knocked," Aziz said, gathering espresso cups from a cupboard. "And there was no answer. So I used my key. I heard voices, so I went back to my place, made some espresso, put on the appropriate attire, and returned." He turned to face us. "A fabulous time was had by all?" He turned back to his pot, as both of us blushed, and began to pour.

"You see, Kaz? There was no need to be hesitant. Our Katie appears to have overcome her passivity, as I have been telling you for some time now she would."

"Aziz ..."

"You've been telling him what?"

"Kate, my dear, I keep a close eye on what goes on in my zoos. And who goes on in my zoos. And knowing you were a particular interest of Kaz's, I've been keeping a close eye on you, too, and I've enjoyed every minute of it."

I was speechless.

"As we've established, he's a voyeur," Kaz said tersely.

"We are all voyeurs to a certain extent, so there's no need for that tone, my friend. Sometimes I am in the room, sometimes I am not. But tell me, who would you rather have watching? Me, or some anonymous, slavering security guard? Not to mention that once the vanilla walls have been breached, we are all voyeurs — and exhibitionists, too, am I correct?"

He raised an eyebrow at me, and I blushed again.

"As I said," he concluded, serving each of us a tiny cup of espresso.

"Now, no more need for blushing. Well, maybe one more thing." He untied the belt on his bathrobe and shrugged it off, did a pirouette in the middle of the kitchen floor, struck a number of different poses so that we could admire his form, well-muscled but going a bit paunchy, then bent to pick up his robe and put it back on.

"There. We've all seen each other naked. Now there truly is no further need for blushing. Let's discuss your trip."

For a minute I looked at him, astounded, and then laughed out loud. Aziz was audacious and outrageous and I was utterly charmed. The two men looked at each other and smiled before joining me.

"This is why I love him," Kaz said to me, shrugging.

"I completely understand." I laughed.

"I'm guessing time for talking was short last night?" Aziz asked, raising a sly eyebrow at Kaz.

"Kaz mentioned that you had a list, but didn't elaborate."

"It was perhaps absurd of me to think that he might have on a night so obviously made for love."

"I love you, but will still smack you if you don't cut it out," Kaz warned his friend, who appeared not at all contrite, sipping his espresso with an innocent smile on his face.

"So if you're willing to do some quality control for us, we have zoos in three of the cities where you'll be spending a couple of weeks, which will give you time to work your way through all the levels, to see whether they're working as they should," Aziz said.

I looked at Kaz. "All levels?"

"All levels." He nodded. "Vanilla to mocha — if you want to. No worries if you don't. But if you want to do it, it will be good to get a woman's perspective. We'll give you a recommendation that will help you accelerate the time that it takes — you won't have to do five nights at each level."

"We have contacts outside our syndicate as well," Aziz added. "We've put together details of zoo owners in other cities, but we can't vouch for all of the names we're giving you, if you wanted to visit a zoo in a city where we don't have one"

"You're a grown woman and know how to look after yourself so I don't need to tell you to get out as quickly as you can if it doesn't feel safe, or if they give you a bad vibe at the door," Kaz said.

"Okay."

"Don't expect the ones outside our syndicate to all be as clean or as comfortable as ours, and they may have different rules regarding clothes and sexual activity — and how you're all put together. They should all be of a higher standard than the zoo I showed you next to your place, because they all charge membership fees and screen the clientele, but after that, no promises."

"Understood." I thought about what I was agreeing to, and wondered if I'd have the nerve to do it. I said, "Vanilla to mocha. I've never had actual intercourse in the zoos, you realize. Not sure I'd ever move on to mocha at all, left to my own devices. That's not something I've spent much time thinking about."

Aziz smirked. "Kate, my darling, if ever a woman was built to go mocha, it was you."

"What the hell does that mean?" I jerked back from the table, stung.

Aziz reached across the butcher block and took one of my hands, stroking my palm with his thumb. "It means you give yourself over to tactile pleasure with an abandon we don't often see. You drink it in, soak it up, and keep coming back for more. A mocha zoo might be just enough to satisfy you." He lifted my hand to his lips and kissed my palm in a way that made my feel warm all over as Kaz watched us.

I didn't know what to say, caught short both by his words and his actions. He put my hand back on the table and looked at me smugly.

"Aziz was a psychology major, did I mention that?" Kaz said, stroking my back. "Psychology and philosophy. It's one of the reasons he watches — he says he's studying the human condition."

"And you think my condition is insatiable?"

"To use an old term, Kaz does look a little like he was ridden hard and put away wet. And yet, when I walked in, you were going back for more," Aziz pointed out.

"I did do that, yes," I said. "But you must remember I have more than a decade to make up for."

"Understood." Aziz nodded. "All the more reason to get the kinks out of your system in the zoos and then come back here for something more ... finely tuned."

"Kaz seems to be afraid that I'll get lost in the zoos. You don't think I'll become an orphan? You think I'll be able to control this need?"

"That is always the gamble when you taste a powerful drug for the first time. You obviously enjoy the high. The question is whether you'll allow it to rule your life."

"I'll help bring you back to earth if you need it," Kaz promised.

"I don't think you'll need it, but I, too, am willing to anchor you," Aziz affirmed.

We sipped our espresso quietly. Aziz hadn't been bragging when he said he made good espresso. I felt the caffeine zinging through my bloodstream.

"You should go to the dark-chocolate and mocha zoos before you leave," Aziz suggested. "Just to see what you need to measure your experiences against."

"Do I need to participate, or could I watch with you?"

Kaz and Aziz looked at each other, and shrugged. "You could watch. That might be better, actually, because we could tell you what to look out for," Kaz said. "And then if it turns out you don't want to go dark — well, you'll know what you're missing."

"Why don't we do that?"

When Kaz and Aziz went to work, I returned to my place to continue preparing for my trip. Every so often, while I carried out mundane chores like laundry or packing, a wave of happiness would build and crest over me as I remembered the words he'd whispered — and those he'd shouted — or when a random movement would employ an unusually tender muscle, or trigger a memory of him touching me there. My skin — I — glowed from the inside out. Joy pulsed with every heartbeat.

• • •

I didn't see Kaz again until two nights later, when he picked me up and drove me to the dark-chocolate zoo where Aziz was waiting.

As they'd done months earlier, when I met Aziz for the first time, they led me through the empty zoo to the darkened alcove hidden behind the intricately carved wooden screen that would separate us from the fauna and tacs who would soon arrive. We sat in the comfortable armchairs facing the screen.

They quietly pointed out to me the particulars of the zoo setup, things I should check for to make sure their zoos were working as planned. There were beautiful rugs, as in all of the zoos, with piles of blankets and cushions strewn about a space about the size of a classroom. Like in the vanilla and milk-chocolate zoos, baskets with small bottles of lotion were placed around the floor; and as in the semi-sweet zoo, there were bowls of condoms, too, piles of towels and boxes of tissues, as well as lidded garbage cans.

The lights in the zoo dimmed and the fauna filed in, laid out their blankets. At this level, they no longer wore the form-fitting bodysuits but instead wore silk bathrobes like the ones the three of us had all sported for breakfast two days earlier.

Kaz leaned in and whispered in my ear, "Because there should be some mystery, some element of seduction, even though the question of whether there will be sex has already been answered."

He stroked my arm as if he'd known that having his breath in my ear would raise goosebumps there. We hadn't talked about it on the ride over, but I wondered whether that particular question had been answered for us as well — he was sitting rather far away.

Although the ages of the participants at the vanilla zoo had ranged from eighteen to eighty or older, I had noticed the age range progressively narrowing as people made their way through the chocolate zoos — tonight they probably went from twenty-five to sixty.

As Kaz and Aziz had explained to me, at this level, participants were divided by gender, and not by role, although on this night, the women were the ones lining up, and later this week they would be the ones filing in blindfolded.

It was strange, observing from a distance the familiar ritual. I found myself calculating which tac would choose which fauna, and when the choosing was done, watched with interest as they met and mated, surprised at how quickly the seemingly shy ones got down to business, heartened by the tenderness strangers showed to strangers.

I was also surprised at how aroused I felt. I'd never been a fan of porn, but there was something compelling about watching fellow humans, in all their shapes and sizes, engage in the most natural of acts even in the most unnatural of situations. My breathing quickened and Kaz and Aziz both glanced over at me knowingly, but avoided catching my eye. Neither spoke, neither moved.

Suddenly, when only one or two couples remained, someone came in through the door behind us and whispered something into Kaz's ear. The man left and Kaz stood up, reaching for my hand. He pulled me gently from the couch and we went out the same door into a hallway, Aziz following.

"I have to go," Kaz said. "Aziz, can you take Kate home?"

"Trouble?" Aziz asked.

"Not one of ours," Kaz said. "The Colonel's making a nuisance of himself again."

"Will you have time?"

"I hope so." He turned to me. "We'll talk later, I promise," he said, taking me into his arms and kissing me fiercely before walking quickly down the hall through another door with an exit sign above it.

I looked at Aziz. "What was that about? What does it mean that the Colonel's being a nuisance, and why is it Kaz's problem if it's not your zoo?"

"Kaz is a man with a mission," Aziz said inscrutably. "It is not my story to tell." He nodded his head toward the zoo. "I think we can safely leave them to it now. Let me drive you home."

As we sped through the dark streets back to my place down-town, Aziz asked me what I'd thought of the experience.

"It was ... it would have been nice if the night had ended a different way."

Aziz laughed heartily. "It's a tease, isn't it, to watch and not to play."

"So you're not immune, then, even after all this time?"

"Oh, no, not at all."

"And Kaz?"

"Not as far as I know," Aziz said. "Neither of us go so often as to become jaded by watching this beautiful sport."

Aziz saw me chastely home, where I worked off my frus-tration on the rowing machine. Even so, I had a restless sleep.

Kaz called me the next day to make arrangements for the mocha zoo that night.

"What happened last night?" I asked. "What was the Colonel doing that you had to go look after it?"

"It's a long story," he said. "I'm sorry I had to leave you there."

"Not nearly as sorry as I was."

"Never assume," he said softly. "Aziz has already spent the better part of the morning explaining to me the many ways in which I am an idiot for running off and leaving you there."

"So come over here and let me smarten you up."

"I'd love to, but I really can't — there's a nervous old dear sitting out in the waiting area right now, and if she's left to pon-der her decision too much longer, she's going to walk right out."

"So I'll have to go crazy by myself, then."

"You're getting ready for your trip. That should keep you occupied."

"As if that's what's on my mind ..."

"I know, I know. I'll be thinking of you, okay? And I'll see you tonight, before the mocha zoo."

Kaz called again later and asked me to make my own way to the zoo, saying he and Aziz would both be tied up there until it was time for them to go in. Jane led me to a smaller, more intimate space than either the vanilla zoo two floors down, or the dark-chocolate zoo on the floor above, where we'd been the night before. She pointed me to the screened-off alcove where I would watch the proceedings. Kaz was already there, sitting at the chaise longue end of a generously proportioned sectional sofa, which was the only furniture. His eyes were closed, his head resting on the back of the sofa, but he looked up when he heard Jane's voice.

"Here you go, Kaz. Take it easy on her."

"Thanks, Jane. Go home now — we can take it from here."

As with the dark-chocolate zoo, which also separated by gender instead of role, the men and women would enter the building by separate side doors, which streamed them to sex-specific changing rooms, and not the front door, where I had come in. Jane had waited just to see me in.

After she left, I asked, "Does Jane ever come to the zoo?"

"She did once." Kaz chuckled. "Met the man of her dreams at her first vanilla zoo and never came back."

"Wow."

"No kidding. It happens every now and then, but more often at the chocolate levels."

I sat in the middle of the sofa, and Kaz turned to look at me. "Why are you all the way over there?"

"I thought you were all about keeping a polite distance," I said.

"Except right now, I'd like to kiss you, if you wouldn't mind coming a little closer."

"No, I think if you want to kiss me, you should come over here."

"Meet me halfway? I'm tired, I didn't get much sleep last night, and it's been a long day."

"No, I don't think so. I'm done making it easy for you."

With a grimace, Kaz scootched over to sit beside me on the couch. "How can I make it up to you?"

"Right now, you can kiss me. Later, we'll discuss your other options."

Kaz did as he was told, taking my face in his hands and kissing me softly, while communicating a far more passionate intent.

Aziz coughed gently from the doorway behind us. "I'd say get a room, but this does appear to be the right place for that," he said with a twinkle in his eye. He sat on the other side of me and kissed my cheek.

Seconds later, the lights in the zoo dimmed. The men and women filed in carefully through their separate doors, their eyes covered. Suddenly, the lights went out and a voice said, "Blindfolds."

I realized each of the robes had a small red light, so that participants could see where there was another, and I watched the dots come together in the dark. A minute later, the zoo's dim lights came back on, showing that each of the participants, now without blindfolds, had matched up with another — or others. They seemed to all be somewhere between thirty and fifty in age, the narrowest range of any of the zoos I'd seen so far.

"Oh," I sighed softly as I watched one threesome strip off their robes and start caressing each other directly in front of the screen. I found it hard to take my eyes from those three, but finally looked away, to the other pairings of two and three and four, watched as they formed and reformed, touched and kissed and sucked and fucked each other. I lost myself in their sounds of consummation, exultation, and satisfaction, so much louder, more vibrant than the other zoos.

I was deeply regretting my decision to watch and not participate when Kaz started kissing my neck, unbuttoning my blouse. I turned toward Aziz, to see if he'd noticed, and he took the opportunity to claim my mouth.

"Oh," I whispered, aware of the need to keep our presence secret, as Aziz kissed my neck and Kaz's lips and teeth found my breast. Soon I couldn't tell which one of them I was kissing and which one was pleasuring me elsewhere, and whom I was fondling in return. We were a tangle of half-removed clothing, lips and fingers and hair and limbs, a tango with three. Our voices rose to join those in the zoo. I would later swear that together the groups on both sides of the screen built to a simultaneous orgasm, rested and then started building again.

I didn't know what time it was when we slept. When I woke, it was to the pleasant sensation of being sandwiched naked between two men, and the very delicious memory of how we'd come to be that way. Without turning my head, I could see that the zoo was empty. I wondered idly what time it was.

"Good morning," Aziz said sleepily, kissing my back and stroking his leg down the length of mine.

"Hello, sleepyhead," Kaz said.

"Have you two been awake for long?"

"No," they said together.

I wriggled between them. "What a lovely way to start the day."

"I think it's better than espresso," Aziz said.

"Now there's something I never expected to hear you say." Kaz laughed.

I marvelled at their ease at finding themselves together in the morning after, with me between them. And at my own lack of self-consciousness about it.

"You two have done this before," I said, as Aziz sat up so that Kaz, who'd been squeezed into the cushioned back of the couch, and I could find a more comfortable position.

"We've been friends a long time," Aziz said, smiling.

"Good friends," Kaz added.

"And when did you good friends decide to share me?"

They looked at each other, surprised. "We didn't discuss it," Kaz said finally.

"It seemed like the right thing to do at the time," Aziz agreed.

"And now?"

"I stand by our decision," Kaz said. "How about you?"

I probed my psychological well-being, like a tongue feeling out an achy tooth, flashed back to the night before, scenes that in a previous age might have filled me with a sense of chagrin or guilt at my wanton behaviour, spurring a lifetime's worth of self-recrimination.

Ever since that first zoo with Kaz, my brain had been humming, my body throbbing with all the colour and texture and life and flavour in the world. I'd been waiting for that tingling under my skin to moderate, but it had just kept intensifying. I felt like I was on speed, I wanted to see and do it all, and do it all at once. Last night had calmed that buzz, but it was still a low hum, a subcutaneous vibrato.

"I think I'm okay with it." I smiled.

We showered and dressed, and met back in Kaz's office for espresso.

"Do you still want to go to Violet's zoo?" he asked me.

Aziz shot him a sharp look. "You're not going to take her there."

"She wants to see it." Kaz shrugged. "I think she should."

"It's not a nice place," Aziz warned me.

"I'm curious," I said simply.

"We can go tomorrow night, if you still want to go," Kaz said, and I nodded. "Okay."

"Isn't tomorrow her auction? You want to take Kate for that?" Aziz protested.

"It's black tie, no Impermatex," Kaz warned, ignoring Aziz. "Will you have something to wear?"

"I'll find something," I said.

. . .

Back home, I rummaged through the boxes in the storage room and found a simple black cocktail-length dress, and in one of Sophie's boxes, I discovered silk stockings and a garter belt, and a colourful, embroidered silk shawl to top it off. I spent extra time on my hair and makeup. I was aware that Kaz was taking me to meet someone who had once met a great deal to him, and I didn't want to be found wanting in comparison.

The zoo was in one of the gorgeous brick Victorian houses that stood on well-treed streets just to the east of downtown, close enough to walk but too far away to interest casual riff-raff. Any of the rich owners who survived had managed to avoid the regency's demand that buildings with a certain square footage be divided into apartments to house refugees from the suburbs.

I'd reported on some of the debate that had gone on at the time — the owners argued the houses had heritage value that should be preserved for after the pandemic; that the time and materials it would have taken to convert them were better spent elsewhere. In the end, some of the houses were requisitioned for regency use — partly to house regency members — but the regency finally decided that on the whole it was too much effort for too little result, and looked elsewhere for housing opportunities.

A tall cedar hedge and wrought-iron gates set inside a stone wall hid the mansion from the street.

In the foyer, there was a butler who directed us to a small table with baskets of masks — not the surgical type required by law, we took those off when we entered, but eye masks: some ornate, others strips of leather or silk that would cover enough of the face to provide plausible anonymity without impeding any activity the guests might want to engage in.

"Are these necessary?" I asked and Kaz shrugged.

"They're required. They're part of the performance. And some find them useful."

The black satin strip he chose was the perfect accent for his dinner jacket and crisp white shirt, giving him a James-Bond-as-Zorro appeal. For fun, I chose a gilded Venetian carnival mask made of stiffened leather, which covered most of my face. The colourful crystals scattered across it matched the embroidery of my shawl.

One of the first things I noticed was a plaster figure on a low plinth just to the right of the entryway, covered head to toe in purple satin, including a blindfold of the same material. I spied another inside the great room and wondered if they were part of an art installation. The mannequin in front of me was exquisitely lifelike, with long black hair, a riot of shiny curls, strong face and neck, glossy, dark skin.

Kaz saw me staring, so he led me to the figure and pointed to a small hole in the fabric at about hip level. "That is where you may touch this exhibit tonight."

"This exhibit?"

"She doesn't call them people. It ruins her fun."

I tried not to show my shock that this was a person and not a plaster figure.

The exhibit gave no sign that it noticed us.

"Go ahead," Kaz said, so I put my finger to the spot and felt soft, moist skin and the edges of the rough surface of the paint that covered every other part of him except his hair. His warmth and the slightest quiver under my fingertip were the only indication that he wasn't bloodless.

Kaz took my arm and we walked together into the great room.

"We'll discuss it all later. I can't bear talking about them as if they're not there."

The black and white marble floors of the foyer gave way to hardwood, covered in places by lush carpets woven with intricate designs. The walls were wainscoted in gleaming dark wood; the walls above were covered in wallpaper whose bold colour and pattern was made bearable by the twelve-foot ceilings. There was art on the walls, and chairs and occasional tables, as in any proper parlour. Every room also held at least one or two cages, made of beautifully wrought iron, with bars far enough apart that it was clear their purpose was more to impose on the eye a sense of separation than to keep anyone in or out. The exhibits sat on mats on the floor or stood next to the wrought-iron bars so that partygoers could reach in to pet them, if the sign on the cage said that was allowed, or they could reach out, although I saw one exhibit get his fingers slapped for doing so.

In the great room, people milled about, drinks in hand, exclaiming over the exhibits on their plinths or in their cages.

After half an hour or so of wandering around the main party, Kaz led me down a quiet hallway and paused in front of a tapestry. He looked to make sure no one was watching, then twitched it aside and hustled me through a hidden doorway and up a back staircase to a door on a private landing. He reached into an urn holding an assortment of dried grasses to find the key for the lock.

The circular turret room called to mind a library, but instead of having books on display, it had people. After my experience downstairs, I knew they weren't mannequins, but for one heart-stopping moment, I worried they were dead. I wasn't terribly reassured to discover that they were alive.

"What the hell —" I started, but Kaz shushed me just as a woman came through the door at the other end of the room, tying a silk mask around her eyes. There was a soft whoosh and thump as all the naked people in all of the recesses in the walls of the room came to stand at attention.

"Excuse me, the auction doesn't begin for another hour — you shouldn't be in here," she said as she approached.

"Hello, Violet," Kaz said.

"Oh, it's you." She stopped halfway across the room. The black bob I'd seen the other night was gone, although she was wearing a cap to go under a wig. We'd obviously caught her as she was preparing for the evening. She tightened the belt on her robe. "What's this — I crashed your party, so you're crashing mine?"

"You're not at your party."

She waved her hand in the air as if shooing away fluff. "The interesting people won't arrive until much later. Only the dull normals are out at this hour." Behind her mask, her eyes moved from him to me and back again.

"I heard you had a new girl you were taking around to all your haunts, inviting to your parties." She looked me over. "Not your usual style, Kaz. A little ordinary — I can always tell their personality by the mask they choose. You used to like women with more flair."

Suddenly, the mask I'd thought was so pretty seemed like cheap artifice. I was mortified. In one line, she'd made me feel small and unsophisticated.

"Kate, meet Violet." There was my pseudonym again. Was he protecting me?

Violet squinted at me, then crossed the room and offered me her hand. I took it. It was soft, well manicured, warm. A delicate perfume followed in her wake, and there was another smell, something familiar that I couldn't quite place, underneath.

"Kate? Delighted. Where *did* you get that ensemble?" She fingered the shawl for a moment but didn't wait for a response, turning to survey the room from our vantage point.

"I thought you'd sworn never to return, Kaz — that you didn't like the entertainment. Did you come back just to show off to your new girlfriend? Introduce her to the dangerous people you used to know?" There was a glint in her eye and an edge to her voice.

From Kaz's party, I remembered her clipped, mid-Atlantic accent. She could have been delivering lines from some 1940s film noir. She turned to me and as she spoke, I tried to place the voice — the accent underlying the one she'd adopted.

"I invited him to my Christmas Eve show last year. I knew he'd come — Kaz's moral outrage will always lose in a fight with his natural curiosity. At midnight, all the animals started lowing at a bright light that magically appeared in the ceiling, and a choir sang 'Away in a Manger.'"

Kaz snorted in derision. "And then the Colonel —"

Violet cut him off. "I'm going to have to move that key," she said. "Except it's so damned convenient when you have no pockets."

The tie on her robe loosened and the robe opened, exposing her naked body underneath. Eleanor had described her as ropy, and that was accurate — not an ounce of body fat, muscle definition a much younger woman would have killed for. She took her time tying it again — her near-nakedness didn't diminish her arrogance at all; on the contrary, she seemed fully armoured and ready for battle.

"So, did he promise you a tour, Kate? Or were you interested in bidding?" She didn't wait for me to respond but slipped into a docent's carefully rehearsed speech. "Downstairs, we have the kids and calves and lambs of your everyday petting zoo — the best of their kind, of course, the finest examples of their species, but common. They'll go up for bid first. The punters see them and are titillated by the zoo and maybe they'll enter a bid — never enough to buy, of course, they leave that to collectors, but they can go away feeling like they've done something *scan*dalous." Scorn dripped from her scarlet lips. "Still, what can I say? Their membership fees pay the bills. Kaz has a lifetime membership, which I gave him for free — not that he's used it lately, or shown the appropriate gratitude for my generosity." She paused for a moment, perhaps to see if he'd rise to her bait, but when he did not, she continued.

"Private viewings are another price still. Membership comes with certain privileges; private viewing prices pay for a more intimate experience."

I looked at Kaz and he said, "Explain what you mean by intimate experience, Violet. Kate is a bit naive — she thinks you mean sex."

Violet tittered. "No, dear, every membership comes with sex, as long as all parties are willing — that's part of the contract the exhibits sign."

"And the animals are not allowed to be unwilling — it's also part of their contract," Kaz said.

Violet continued as if he hadn't spoken. "I'm like a library, or a museum — I lend out my collection to people with the right credentials. Private viewing pays for all-access passes to the exhibits, including my exotics in this room, without purchase. They can be removed to the viewer's home and treated as the viewer's personal pet for an agreed-upon period of time. I ask no questions, only that they not be marred."

"And if they are marred?" Kaz asked. "Or, say, if they're killed?"

They were talking in light, airy voices, as if they were discussing cheese at a cocktail party, but beside me I could feel Violet's body tighten like a bowstring. I realized, to my horror, that Kaz was not speaking hypothetically.

"Well, of course I wouldn't want my animals to get killed — especially my exotics, they're hard to come by," Violet answered, her words clipped. "But when they do, the prices rise, like insurance. Really, Kaz, are we going to start this tiresome nonsense again?"

"He still has a pass." Who was he talking about?

"Of course he still has a pass."

"And you still seek out particular exhibits for him, when he asks. Is the Colonel coming here tonight? Do you have a nice, juicy orphan for him?"

They glared at each other for a long moment, as if daring the other one to push a little harder.

"Up here is where I keep the exotics, the truly rare specimens that constitute my private collection," Violet continued to me, as if the argument had continued into the silence, and something had been settled.

She took my elbow and led me slowly down the line of exhibits. "I've been gathering them for a while now. As you can see, there's something special about each of them — their beauty, their height, the texture of their hair. Feel this one," she said and waited until I reached out, reluctantly, and touched the hair of the exotic in front of me. Gossamer, almost pure white, it trickled through my fingers like water. "I just got her. I have to buy special products to keep it from going yellow. And this one — have you ever seen skin that colour? Chocolate! I just want to drink it."

We moved on to the next exhibit, a man with long, flowing brown hair, but none on his body. She licked his stomach just below his rib cage and watched with delight as he sucked his belly in and his penis grew to porn-star proportions. Smiling, she stroked with her thumb the spot where she had licked until it was dry. She took my hand and wrapped it around his penis, and he quivered. "He's not allowed to cum until I tell him to, and this," she tapped the sensitive head of his penis and he winced in pleasure, "is also not allowed, but I'll let him get away with it this time because every woman should get a chance to touch his glorious hard-on. If you'd like to give him a try, I can offer you a good deal."

I dropped my hand and stepped back, and she stepped back with me.

"All of these treasures, of course, command a much higher price than those below."

"Price?" I asked.

"In the auction, dear — weren't you listening?"

"You ... sell them?" I asked, knowing I sounded hopelessly naive but unable to help myself.

"Even an excellent collection needs to be weeded out every now and then, to make room for new exhibits."

I was appalled, at the idea of auctioning off people; at the suggestion that one of them had been killed. Violet stood to the left of me and Kaz to the right, and the tension hanging in the air between them was strangling me like a garotte. I could have left, but their personal drama needed to play out and, god help me, I wanted to watch it happen.

"Do they just stand there all day?" I blurted out the first thing I could think of, needing to make noise of some sort.

The exhibits stood motionless, but there were brackets set in the walls for them to lean on, chairs to sit on, and each recess held a table with a carafe of water, a glass and a plate of food.

"They are required to be here for performance hours, but must only be at attention when I am in the room, or a private viewer is here. They have breaks written into their contracts. They each have a room with a bed and a chair, whatever they want to eat, and books and music and other things to occupy their time, as well as their own bathrooms and showers."

She surveyed her menagerie with a proprietorial gaze. "I think the makeup of a menagerie says as much about the tastes of the owner as it does about the exhibits themselves, don't you agree? What do you think this says about me?" she asked me.

"That you like to have slaves around you?" Kaz suggested.

"Well, they are all a little submissive, darling, or they wouldn't ask to be here."

"That's not what I meant, and you know it. You buy and sell people."

"They've all chosen to do this, Kaz."

"All of them?"

She shrugged. "Some provenance may be sketchier than others, but you're the only one I hear complaining. I pay good money, give them food, clothes, a roof over their heads ..."

"Are you paying your exhibits or the other collectors?" Kaz asked. "Who gets the money?"

"You are being deliberately obtuse, hoping to score points off me. I won't have it."

"You like to think of yourself as a good employer, but if you're not paying the exhibits for their service, and instead paying other people for access to them, you are trafficking in humans, not providing employment. And if you're handing them over to paying customers for sex, you're a whoremaster as well as a slavemaster."

"You've become such a prude, Kaz. I left the vanilla zoos far behind a long, long time ago. And I thought you did, too. I would have thought a man who has taken the joy you have in the chocolate zoos would have a more open mind." She turned back to me. "Have you seen him in a mocha zoo? He's a wild man."

"I draw the line at people being held in cages, and bought and sold for others' pleasure. And why don't you tell Kate what happens to them when rich collectors no longer care to bid on them."

I watched, mesmerized, as they drew nearer to each other with every new accusation and defence, the better to aim and hit their targets.

"These are not your orphans — they have free will. They are turned on by the very idea of their captivity — captivated by it, you could say. Money might be a lure for some, but not as many as you'd think."

"If you wanted to gather trophies, why didn't you do that? Keep them for your own enjoyment, if the thought of it doesn't make you ill. Why provide them for others? Why the auctions?"

"Because it's all about the performance. A zoo without an audience is just a jungle, and I've never enjoyed those. I cannot perform as zookeeper and audience at the same time."

They were nearly toe to toe. She closed the gap and kissed him hard on the mouth, brought a hand between his legs and stroked him there. By the look of victory on her face, I could tell that his body had reacted to her touch, but his arms remained at his sides, and eventually she moved away.

"You need to loosen up, darling," she purred. I was fascinated by her, and repulsed at the same time. I couldn't take my eyes off her and I also wanted to slap that smug smile from her face.

Kaz stared at Violet as if he was looking for some faint trace of the woman he'd fallen in love with years earlier. But whatever it was he would have said was lost. She'd taken the air out of him, and knew it.

"Now I think it's time for you and your friend to go, Kaz. You've come, you've made your scene, your point is taken, la la la, go off to your little bourgeois world with your ordinary girl and bask in your righteous indignation. Your hostility is giving me wrinkles."

We went down the stairs, were out the front door and nearing the gate when it hit me, where I'd heard that line before. Startled, I tripped on a flagstone and fell to my knees on the grass.

"Are you okay?" Kaz asked, reaching down to try to help me up.

I waved him away.

"Kate? Lily? What's wrong?"

"Just … just give me a minute."

She'd changed her hair. She'd always been slender, but was now painfully — fashionably — thin. Her voice, her vocabulary, even her hair and clothes — it was a performance she was putting on, like an actress in one of those old black and white movies she'd always loved.

Sophie used to say that all the time, "Your boredom is giving me wrinkles," "Your lack of imagination is giving me wrinkles." Everything unpleasant gave her wrinkles, although from the look of things, she'd had access to some great skin treatments — or, wait, Kaz had said that day on the picnic that she'd had plastic surgery. She didn't look a lot like the woman I'd known, a different nose, higher cheekbones, and she certainly didn't look a day older than she had when she'd left me sick and alone, with food for three days, eleven years earlier.

I stood up and dusted myself off.

"Let's go," I said.

My mind raced as we drove the short distance back to my place in silence. Could it be that I'd ever been friends with this woman? How was that even possible? She had moved so far from anything I would have imagined attractive in person, even when I was younger and less discerning about who I spent time with. "All about the performance," she'd said. Well, yes, it always had been, hadn't it? Did she know she'd been performing for an old friend tonight?

I invited Kaz in and poured us both a glass of wine. We sat on the sofa and drank for a moment. I realized I'd torn a hole in my stocking when I fell, and left the room for a minute to take them off, along with the rest of my finery. The shawl that had seemed so lovely at the beginning of the evening now felt cheap and garish. I threw it in the garbage. I put on a T-shirt and shorts and sat on the edge of the bed for a minute, taking a few deep breaths to calm myself. I'd found Sophie after all this time and part of me wanted to be happy, but most of me felt revolted and in some way betrayed. And angry. I was very angry.

I went back to the living room, where Kaz waited, and joined him on the sofa — him at one end, me at the other, our tension and misery creating an energy field pushing us apart. I finished my wine, then poured another glass.

"Thank you for taking me. I'm glad I've seen it but I'm sorry. I didn't know ... I didn't realize how hard it would be, why it would be hard for you."

He nodded but said nothing, just stared into his wine.

"Remember I told you I had a friend who left me after I became ill?"

"Yes."

"I found her tonight."

"Where? Is she one of Violet's trophies?" He looked alarmed.

"No. She's Violet."

"What?"

I nodded.

"Why didn't you say something?"

"I didn't realize it until we left. There were a couple of clues, but anyone can wear that perfume, right?" I should have known — that other, underlying scent that I'd smelled. Of course, that was why I recognized it. "Her voice is deeper, and she didn't look or talk like a 1940s movie queen when I knew her." I told him what had tipped me off in the end, and he nodded. Her favourite way to express disappointment.

"Are you going to go back and talk to her?"

"No!"

He was taken aback at my vehemence.

"No," I said more quietly. "Or, at least, probably not. That is not the person I knew, or if she is, that's not a side of her I ever expected — or admitted to myself, if I suspected — could exist."

"Do you think she recognized you?"

I wondered if she'd had any idea that Kaz's Kate was her Lily — my hair colour had changed, too, and unlike her, I'd aged since the last time we spoke, plus my mask had covered most of my face. It's possible she hadn't known.

"She recognized the shawl I was wearing, or at least she would have remembered that she used to have one just like it." One of the reasons I'd worn it had been to try to adopt some of her flair. "Whether she figured out it was me wearing it — hard to say. But if she did recognize me and put on that show anyway ... well, there's a good enough reason not to seek her out, right?"

Kaz shook his head and emptied his wineglass.

I refilled it, then said, "I have a lot of questions."

"I thought you might." He waved his wineglass. "Ask away, I'll give you all the answers I can."

I paused for a moment, then asked, "Who died?"

"Excuse me?"

"You said someone died at her menagerie on Christmas Eve. Who was it? What happened?"

He looked at his glass and said, "You have anything stronger?"

"I have some vodka, but nothing to mix it with."

"I'm Russian," he reminded me.

I retrieved the bottle from my freezer and picked up a pair of shot glasses on the way back. I poured a measure into each. We both winced as the rough alcohol went down. Kaz poured two more.

"That Christmas Eve performance was … horrifying. I knew it would be, I knew I shouldn't have gone, but she's right — it's like picking at a scab, you know it will bleed but you do it anyway, just to prove that you were right. The place was crowded — she'd invited nearly everyone she knew, it seemed, including the Colonel."

He downed his second shot and poured a third.

"I've never liked him. You met him — there's something … reptilian about his eyes. He takes too much pleasure in humiliating his marks, in inflicting pain. He's also into erotic asphyxiation."

"And on Christmas Eve, he passed the point of no return?"

He nodded. "Violet had set up a manger scene, and one of the exhibits was wearing a long blue scarf, as Mary." He paused, looking at his third shot of vodka, holding it up to the lamp to see how impurities in the alcohol refracted the light. Then he downed it, too.

"Why didn't you stop it?"

"Because at first I thought it was just part of the performance. When I saw that the woman was in distress, I tried to step in, but Violet had her security guards put me in a cage." Two tears carved a slow path down his face.

"I'd been hearing for years about the Colonel. Always rumours, nothing anyone had ever seen, that every so often his little kink would go too far, maybe on purpose. Then I heard Violet was setting aside delicacies — orphans — for him at her zoo. I went that night to prove to myself that it wasn't true. But I think Mary was scheduled to die on Christmas Eve. And Violet liked knowing I was there to watch him choke her to death with a host of angels looking on."

"Angels?"

"That was the dress code for the night, Oriental kings and angels. As I said, it's an open secret that the Colonel's a predator — he's not exactly discreet about it. Years ago I started looking out for the orphans, people who had no one to miss them, saving them before he could find them, but I couldn't even save the one he killed with me in the room." Kaz looked indescribably sad. "I told you that I had to go into hiding, twelve years ago. Well, the thing that I witnessed ... Christmas Eve was not quite a re-enactment, but very close. And Violet knew it. I'm sure she told him. And I hate to admit this, but I wouldn't be at all surprised if they orchestrated it so that I would be watching, so that he could show me how helpless I still am, in the end."

"Why on earth would she do that to you?"

"Listen, I wish I could say I knew. As far as I know, my worst sin was that I bored her, the zoos became work, I stopped being amusing, and because of Henny Penny, there weren't a lot of options. My shortcomings made her angry, and she took her anger out on me."

We drank in silence for a moment.

"What happened to the woman who died?" I asked, finally.

"People turn up missing or dead all the time. Her death was probably staged as a suicide, just another bonnelly by a woman who couldn't take the isolation anymore."

"So when you worried that I would be an orphan, you were concerned that I'd be prey for the Colonel? Exquisitely submissive and no one in my life to miss me?"

Kaz shrugged. I remembered the way the Colonel had looked at me, and wondered if he'd been able to read that in me.

"Who was the Colonel before? Surely he didn't spring fully formed from Henny Penny." I tried to mentally dress the man I'd seen in a businessman's suit and tie, but he didn't quite fit.

"I'm told he ran a string of elite gyms — high priced, personal service, but he had a side hustle running BDSM clubs. He'd pick marks from his gym clients and groom them for his other thing. He's a psychopath — they can be charming."

"Why did you take me there?"

"Fuck," he said bitterly, jumping up and pacing, the heels of his shoes clicking against the hardwood floor. "I hadn't even meant to tell you about the place, but when I did, I hoped you'd forget about it. And then when you didn't … I thought maybe it would be an eye-opener for you. You love the zoos so much, you don't really see the bad side of them. You don't see the shit that they become."

He poured and drank a fourth shot. Then he sat down in the chair facing me, holding the vodka bottle by the neck.

"I thought I'd just show you the zoo and then we'd leave before she came downstairs. I didn't want to run into her. I knew it wouldn't go well. But I needed to show you the trophy room."

"So tonight was supposed to be a lesson for me?"

"Maybe. I don't know. I thought you should see how far zoos could go, how far orphans could fall." He closed his eyes, wiped at his face. "Each time I see Violet, I think I'll be able to find a good person inside her and make that person see the

error of her ways, and set her off on a better path. The zoos
started out as a good thing, a business venture with a humani-
tarian side effect, but it all goes to hell."

Kaz had always had an underlying edge that I'd put down
to ennui. I thought he was just jaded and tired of what he was
doing. It had never occurred to me that he was disgusted by it
as well.

"Next question?" he asked, rolling the vodka bottle between his hands.

"Why didn't you take me before I wrote my story?"

"I wanted you to *like* me." He laughed, a sharp sound in
the quiet room. He kept his eyes on the bottle, not looking at
me. "I didn't want you to know that I travelled with people
like her, people who could do those things. Besides, it was too
dangerous for both of us. Because there's no way you wouldn't
have written about it."

I thought about something else he'd said to Violet. "What
happens to those people when the collectors no longer want
them?"

He sighed. Covered his face with his hands. "If they've been
in a collection for a long time, many forget how to take care of
themselves. They ... founder. They become lost. The Colonel,
or someone like him, sweeps them up at a bargain price, and
they're never heard from again. I have heard that they get sold
on to different kinds of collectors. The kind you don't come
back from." He twirled his empty shot glass on the arm of his
chair, then set it on the table.

"Your next question is why I didn't turn them in," Kaz
said. "It's complicated, but it's partly self-protection. If I turned
them in, they'd know who it was and come after me. And I'm
more vulnerable here than I was twelve years ago."

"So you let them get away with it."

"For now. Aziz and I are working on a way to get rid of them without ending up dead ourselves. We have a plan. It takes time."

"Was talking to me part of your plan?"

"When you finally replied to me in January, I thought it was a sign. And talking to you became part of the plan, yes." He shook his head. "It's not as easy as just calling the police. Some authorities were there on Christmas Eve, you know. They know full well what happened, and they're okay with it. You straight people, you trust your regency because life has nearly gone back to normal — the Sickos have been dealt with and Henny Penny isn't killing people by the millions anymore, but it is wrong to trust everyone who works under the regency's banner." He poured another shot, drank it. "I started writing to you because I live in the underworld and you're in the daylight. And after Christmas, I wanted you to write a story that would focus a little sunlight on what's going on. I don't think my zoos are evil, but I think they open the door to the rest of it."

I remembered Bob telling me how the zoo story had suddenly received a green light after years of rejections. Maybe someone there that night hadn't been okay with it.

Before I could tell him, Kaz stood up suddenly. "I need to go. Is that okay? I need to punch something."

"No, it's okay. Go. Do what you have to do."

"Do you hate me now?"

"No," I said slowly. "But ..."

"But?"

"But I think you need to do something about this so you can stop hating yourself."

He touched my cheek, like he had the first night we'd met, and left.

I put on my sweats and spent an hour on the rowing machine, back and forth, trying to work off some of my anger, and instead I built it up. I was angry for the way Violet had treated Kaz, knowing that she'd deliberately set out to humiliate him for my edification, hoping to make him smaller in my eyes. I was furious to know that she was alive and she lived so close and had never checked in on me. I was pretty sure she'd known who'd been with Kaz tonight, and had enjoyed shocking me. I choked on that thought. I was incandescent with rage at that thought.

I got up from the rowing machine and decided to start on my trip in the morning, a day early. The apartment couldn't contain my anger. Maybe I'd find a place for it on the open road.

Going to the People

IT WAS HOT driving through the mountains to my first teaching gig. A drive that would have taken four hours pre-pandemic now took a day and a half, thanks to the detours necessitated by unsafe — or even fallen — overpasses. The regency hadn't put much effort into highway maintenance in the last decade, and it showed. Maybe now that trade was coming back, it would become a priority again.

There was air conditioning in the SUV, but Fred had warned that using it would be a drain on the battery, and I preferred to leave the windows down anyway, feeling the wind on my face and in my hair. The unfamiliar scenery and having to concentrate on the road helped take my mind off seeing Sophie again. My decade of experience in ignoring my feelings also enabled me to compartmentalize my emotions while I drove. But I couldn't help replaying the scenes from the night before, and reliving episodes from our past that in hindsight were clear indicators that she had it in her to become the woman I'd met the previous night — episodes that shone a spotlight on my complicity.

"Stop!" I yelled at myself, to try to break the loop. And for a while it would work, and then it would come around again.

Fred had booked furnished apartments where I would stay for the one or two weeks that I'd spend teaching in the cities. He'd also identified potential billets along the way — towns where I'd be able to find a bed for the night — but because the uncertain road conditions made it impossible to know when I might arrive somewhere, he hadn't made reservations in any of the towns en route. That first night, at least, not being expected was a blessing — I was too angry to deal with strangers.

I pitched the tent in a dry, uncultivated field behind some trees, the four-wheel drive taking me safely off road and well out of sight of any passersby, although given the small number of cars I'd seen all day, I wasn't expecting any. Perhaps because I was so angry, I was surprisingly unconcerned about my safety. I figured if I was careful and didn't advertise my presence to anyone happening to pass by, I'd be all right. I kept the gun Fred had given me close to hand and went about setting up my camp.

I inflated my queen-sized air bed and laid my sleeping bag out on it in the tent, then wrote my daily journal entry for the regency and reported in using the radio transmitter they'd provided for me. The SUV had a small fridge attached to the battery and I'd stocked it, and a cooler, full of food. I made myself a light supper and ate in comfort using my folding chair and camp table. I had brought along a few bottles of wine, so I poured myself a glass and sat back to watch the drama of the clouds and the setting sun, the darkening sky.

Music from the player in the SUV had been a soft accompaniment to dinner, but as night approached, I shut it off to enjoy the silence — or as silent as a late-summer field ever gets: there were always birds and bees and various animals and insects to make noise, but there was a complete absence of sound originating from human activity. I'd been alone for a long time but never in a place so completely still. I had always been reminded that there were others nearby. The lack of noise filled the air around me; I could almost hear the rhythmic thump-thump of my heart, the whoosh of blood through my veins and arteries. I was aware of my breath in a way I'd never managed to be in yoga classes. Breath in, breath out. Breathe in, filling the lungs, raising the diaphragm, breathe out, collapsing the chest. Pause.

As a teenager, I used to lie out in the middle of a field on summer nights with my brothers and our friends, patiently turning the AM dial on a transistor radio, moving through static until we found the sudden clarity of music being broadcast from stations a thousand miles away. We had had long, rambling conversations those nights, working out our adolescent philosophies and wondering what the future might hold for us. I was mesmerized by the stars. I remember watching a meteor shower one night with my friend Mary, trying to decide whether a boy from our school who'd died that summer was sending us messages via the celestial bodies shooting across the sky. We were starstruck in those golden years, those ebony nights before light pollution and adulthood.

Sitting in the dark with the memory of decades-old music on a tinny transistor radio, I started to probe how my life had become so wrapped up in Sophie's to begin with. I'd lost myself long before Henny Penny. I'd been a person to whom things happened, rather than someone who made them happen. That had always been my tendency — even before my mother left, I'd been a shy girl. Afterward, I wouldn't say I wasn't cared for, I was fed and clothed and housed, but I was constantly reminded that I had nothing to offer the world. I wasn't beautiful and shouldn't try to be. Did I think I was smart? Shame on me. I shouldn't speak up if I had nothing intelligent to say. My fear of rejection was paralyzing. I held on to a certain sense of self in spite of it, but was always ready to cede the floor to louder, prettier people. And for the most part I hadn't minded doing so, because I could bask in their glow without ever having to face the embarrassment of failure. I got the benefit of being part of a scene without any of the responsibility for making it happen, or making it happen again. When Sophie came along, it was okay for both of us that she was the star and I was the friend of the star — I never expected to be her equal. I became a bit lazy with it; even when I was able to draw someone like Matt, I lacked confidence in my ability to maintain whatever glamour had attracted them in the first place.

If I thought about it — and I did, now that I had time and sky — although I'd been raised to think of myself as lesser-than, Sophie had given me permission to be content with that, encouraged the little voice in my head that told me not to try too hard lest I fail and be humiliated. She had gently pushed me to take that secure editing job instead of going down a less certain path, where I might have scrambled to pay the rent but would have freed my time and mind to concentrate on the writing that made me happiest — and thus subtly undermined my confidence in my ability to write. She never pushed me to try for something more. She needed so much sunshine that she had to take some of mine, even if in doing so she stunted my growth.

And I had let it happen. I had had a friendship that made me part of something exciting, and all that was required of me was to reflect the brightness back at her, absorbing none of it for myself.

I realized with a start at some point that long first night — after I went to bed but lay awake, jumping a little at every noise in the dark — that every time I tried to think about myself and what I wanted, I thought about the way I'd been with Sophie, as if the two of us were inextricable parts of a whole. I'd let her be my personality for so long I'd missed the chance to develop one of my own as an adult in the real world, although I wrote the personality I imagined for myself into my characters. I'd started to see glimpses of it in my cocktail nights with Eleanor, my lunches at the office — and that dinner party. I'd sat in Sophie's chair and hosted a great evening without her hoarding all of the attention or worrying that I might get punished for making too much of an impression.

I also, for the first time, became fully conscious of how angry I'd been for the better part of my life — at my mother for deserting us, at my father for taking it out on me, at my brothers, and at Sophie, and not just for leaving. Last night's fury had found a familiar home with all of the anger I'd been storing up for years. With no safe way to express rage, I had annealed it into depression; instead of striking out in anger, I became passive with despair. I used my transformed blocks of rage to build a protective wall around myself. That process was what had kept me sane during my lost decade, but it seemed to me that when my wall came down in the zoos, when I opened the door to emotion, I'd lost my control of it. Maybe it was the thing that was making me feel unsettled — I no longer had a safe place to put my anger.

And maybe Kaz was right about my preference for being a fauna over a tac. Maybe it was time to move on, rise above my upbringing and assert my claim to personhood, to my right to take up space in the world. And to start taking responsibility to give back. Maybe that was what I was doing out here, after all. Going to the zoos, quitting my job, and heading out on the road were the first active choices I'd made in decades. And I'd made all of those choices because they were good for me, even though others might question them — or condemn them.

With that realization, something heavy lifted from my soul, and I finally drifted off, drunk on starlight and the night air, sensing a hint of the freedom I'd hoped to find on the road.

• • •

Bob had been right: I wasn't a born teacher, but I really enjoyed those two months, going from school to school and presenting my three modules: one on writing, another on the history of the pandemic, and one on nutrition. None of the country's once-famous colleges and universities was operating anything like they'd been before the pandemic — too few academics to provide full degree programs, too few students to take the courses. Home-schooling took care of grade-schoolers, and after that they were on their own. But about five years earlier, the regency had started cobbling together post-secondary curricula, finding local academics and professionals with the expertise to teach some subjects, and using itinerant professors like me to travel around and fill in the holes because the internet still wasn't reliable enough for remote teaching. Sometimes students themselves would travel from school to school to find scholars who could teach the subjects they were interested in pursuing.

When I wasn't teaching, I explored the cities. The absence of a typical academic community — and the antisocial nature of cities in general — meant I rarely got to know anyone but my students. I also didn't encourage friendship because I was saving my nights for the zoos on the list that Kaz had given me. The one or two times that I accepted an invitation for a drink with colleagues or students, I made it clear I would have to leave in time for an "appointment."

The zoos were an escape from loneliness and incipient depression, and the anger that had been simmering since I'd gone to Sophie's zoo. Kaz had sent me a couple of emails asking if I was okay, and I'd answered briefly that I was, told him a bit about what I was doing, and if I'd gone to one of his zoos, I reported in as promised, but otherwise I wasn't all that interested in talking to him yet. I hated the complicity I'd seen in myself and I didn't find it all that attractive in him.

I told myself that if I met someone interesting, I'd explore that possibility instead of going to the zoos, but no one came close enough for me to do so. And I was okay with that. In the zoo I put myself out there, but in a safe way. I didn't have to worry about being molested or raped or hurt if it didn't work out. And I didn't have to go through a mating ritual, using time and energy only to find out that he was a Star Wars aficionado, or that we were sexually incompatible. For once I was taking what I wanted when I wanted it and as I wanted it, and for now at least, it was satisfying on most levels. There was still a small space that the zoos couldn't fill, but I didn't let myself think too much about it, didn't look too hard at it.

When I could I used references to jump the line so I wouldn't have to do the mandatory five days in each level of zoo before moving on. The zoos gave me something to do in the evening, but I'd have been lying if I said I was going for any reason other than that my body craved the feeling of fingers against my skin and in my hair, lips on mine, orgasms that were no less strong for happening in a stranger's arms.

I worried over my first dark-chocolate and mocha zoos. Public sex, even with a loved one, had never been my fantasy, and until that night with Kaz and Aziz, I would have never thought that sex in a group would have been to my taste, either.

So it was surprising — educational, even — to realize how much I enjoyed it. A lifetime of socialization about men's and women's supposedly vastly different attitudes toward sex had been eroding as I'd made my way through Kaz's zoos, and completely disappeared in the strange cities. Knowing there was no one who could shame me removed that last inhibition.

My feelings for Kaz had put a certain patina on the nights I'd spent with him, but that hadn't stopped me from losing myself in Aziz's body, and neither of them were on my mind when I walked into my first dark-chocolate zoo — or the mocha zoo a few nights later, where I revelled in watching and being watched, in feeling the warm bodies all around me, taking and giving in equal measure. It was less bacchanal than buffet; I found I wanted to taste every experience that came my way.

I'd expected my skin hunger, my aching need, to moderate once I knew physical contact was available when I wanted it and once I was satisfied sexually, but that never happened. The fire was banked somewhat in what I began to think of as my

straight life, when I was presenting my lectures and otherwise
behaving like a respectable citizen of a germophobic society,
but it quickly reignited the minute I walked into a zoo. I didn't
burn just for sex, although a couple of times when I wanted
chocolate but was forced to go to a vanilla zoo in a new city
where I didn't have a reference, the process dragged intermin-
ably. Other times, vanilla was just what I needed, and I went
back to it after a couple of nights of dark chocolate, because just
having another's hands on my body was what I craved.

Coming on Primal

I COULD WRITE a book about the towns I stopped in as my trip progressed — for a pit stop or to spend the night — and the people I met there, some of whom welcomed a visitor from the capital and some who didn't.

I was about twenty miles from a town where I'd planned to stop for a rest when I got my first glimpse of the ocean. Oh, how I'd missed the ocean.

I love fields and streams and mountains, but the ocean exerts a visceral gravitational pull on me, and has done so since the first time I laid eyes and toes and hands on it as a child. I would watch it for hours and listen to it when I could no longer see it. To be near the living water with the moon and stars above me makes my soul sigh with satisfaction.

It was one of those hot mid-September days, the sun creating diamonds on the wavelets raised by a slight breeze, when I came to a place I remembered, a track that I knew would take me to a once-favourite beach. It was deserted, and it appeared to have been a long time since anyone had come that way. I drove the SUV in as far as it felt safe. I made a sandwich and set my folding chair on a flat rock above the tide line. I ate my lunch staring out over the water. The air was clean, and a fresh breeze on the incoming tide blew away the late-season humidity. I wanted to swim but single-person-alone warnings in my head kept me from doing anything more than wading after lunch. This had been a popular beach, but there had always been a swimming area marked out with buoys, warnings about the dangerous currents beyond them.

The shore birds and the water made the only sounds. There wasn't much between here and the next town, and I hadn't seen anyone on the road for hours; I was as alone as I could be. I started to sing a fragment of a song that had been in my head all morning — softly at first, then louder. It was my private concert, after all. That felt good, so I sang a few more before falling quiet again. I stood in the cool water, waves tapping my knees. I moved back as the water rose higher, but maintained my connection with the tide.

As often happens to me in a place so serene, I felt an urge to scream — not to destroy the peace, but to impress myself upon the place's memory. To let go of the childhood indoctrination that said proper girls don't draw attention to themselves. To give voice to my inner self, to the rage that I'd carried beneath the surface of my skin since childhood and didn't know how

to express without exploding. In the past I'd always been in-
hibited by the possibility of someone being within earshot who
could hear me and worry that I needed help, and come running, which would have been mortifying. People who come
running when others call aren't generally the ones who understand the need to scream for no visible reason.

I took a look around me to make sure there could be no
one near, and then I cried out, a thin, pitiful squeak that made
me laugh. I used to have nightmares about not being able, not
having the voice, to scream when I needed to. But it had never
occurred to me that screaming — yelling — would be difficult. Part of my inhibition was feeling that I should use words,
but not knowing what to say. I yelled, "Hellooooo!" and "I am
Lily," and "I love the ocean," but while it was satisfying in a
certain sense to yell, to make noise, it wasn't what my soul was
looking for, which was a vocal expression far more primal.

So, having warmed up, I tried it again, and again, loosening
up enough to pour my frustration and my pain into it, telling
the ocean in tones it might understand about the last ten years,
and the years before them, ripping off the Band-Aid that the
TTCs and then the petting zoos had placed over my scars,
exposing them to the light.

I stood in the ocean up to my knees and watched the waves
and screamed my heart out, and out my heart, and out my pain
and depression and frustrations. And Sophie. I screamed her
out, too, the beautiful, glorious friend, my chosen sister, who
had failed me in so many ways, by pulling me into her world
instead of demanding I inhabit my own; by being a reliable
crutch for the me who was too afraid of failure to try standing
by herself; by making me dependent on her and then deserting
me, the way my mother had. I screamed out my realization

that she hadn't *become* someone who preyed on weaker people in the years after she'd left — she'd always been that person, she'd simply refined her technique. On some level I'd known that and loved her anyway, and I cried out because I despised my weakness.

I screamed and screamed, and the ocean was inexorable, just like time. It kept coming at me in waves, and the sea birds kept circling, hoping for a snack.

When I was hoarse, and hot, when my lungs hurt and my diaphragm allowed no more compression and my skeleton was folding in on itself because the rage that had been holding me upright for years was eased — temporarily, at least — I took off my clothes, threw them onto the beach, and sat down in the shallows, letting the healing water lap into my hollows, wrap around my curves, cool me down again. I sat facing the horizon and let the salty ocean scrub me clean, chill me to the bone.

I won't say I felt at peace but, just like on that first night when I had slept under the stars, I felt like I'd rid myself of another piece of an invisible burden — something I'd never been able to see or weigh but had nonetheless carried with me for far too long.

Just defying the inhibitions that had kept me from being able to give my soul voice made me feel triumphant. I had announced myself to the world, had imprinted myself on the water. I was ... in this space, where my voice began, taking my essence with it across the waves, to that headland, to the birds and animals — and maybe people — beyond. I was staking my right to the space I occupied. I'd minimized my self and my needs and my place in the world for most of my life. The first TTC had helped me to remember the extent to which I was a physical presence; this day in the ocean reminded me that my influence reached farther. I wondered if there was a butterfly effect for voices, if a scream here would be felt days or weeks later somewhere around the world, and how it would manifest there. Would it be a harbinger of peace or of chaos?

I don't know how long I stayed in the water — long enough to be covered in goose pimples, skin nearly blue, teeth chattering. The tide had reached my clothes, so I picked them up and carried them to the back of the SUV. I found a blanket and wrapped it around myself while I set up the camp stove and put water on to boil, then rooted around in my bags for clean, dry clothes that created an instant warmth against my cold skin. I made tea and drank it staring out at the ocean, enjoying the calm, warming up.

And then I got back in the car and moved on. My last teaching gig was ahead of me, and after that, a new life of my own choosing.

Going Feral

WHO WAS IT who said that in leaving what you know, you find yourself? I lost myself and found myself at the same time — found that little, bright, burning spark inside of me that had been longing to turn into a full-scale conflagration, to burn away the fears and old habits and behaviours that kept me from being the fullest version of myself.

Looking back at it now, I can see that it was inevitable. The first time I stepped foot in a petting zoo was my first step on the path.

I'd been teaching the nutrition module, which always brought me closer to my students than the history or journalism courses, because of the shared meals and conversation around the table with all those bare faces.

During those two weeks, we'd talked a lot about petting zoos. A number of the students had read my articles and wanted to know more about them.

This little city on the coast seemed to have fared better than some since the pandemic. It was bustling in ways that even the capital was not, with people on the sidewalks at all hours and traffic in the streets. There were fewer boarded-up windows in the downtown core, and a lot more goods in the stores because distance had sheltered people here from the virus during the pandemic and they were able to benefit from what little maritime trade there was after it.

Maybe it was because there was more life in the city itself that the atmosphere in the first zoo I went to was so different. It was one of Kaz and Aziz's zoos, smaller than their places in the capital but clean and as elegantly appointed as their other spaces — the ubiquitous rugs, blankets, and cushions, low lights.

In the change room before the vanilla zoo, some of the dozen or so fauna seemed to know each other — they acknowledged each other in a way I'd never seen fauna do before. I could feel them staring at me, and some clearly whispered about the cuckoo in their nest. They made no space for the outsider. Fair enough, we weren't friends, didn't have to pretend to be.

Inside the zoo, after we'd all laid out our blankets, though, they arranged themselves deliberately to put me at the end of the line. Newcomers, it was clear, got the leavings.

That lack of respect carried through to the tac who chose me. Aziz had been more careful with his hands in the milk-chocolate zoo where we'd met than this guy in a zoo where that kind of touching wasn't allowed. As fauna I had always thought of the zoo as being about my needs; for the first time, I had the feeling of being a means to the tac's end — and my tac that night didn't care whether I got anything from it. I felt the eyes of the room on me, creating an unpleasant tingle in my skin. It was the first time I hadn't felt safe in a zoo.

I left after an hour or so, angering my tac. I waited in the change room until several fauna came back at once and left with them, afraid he'd be waiting outside. After that experience, I had no desire to return.

So I simmered for two weeks. I enjoyed teaching and getting to know my students, who ranged in age from late teens to late thirties, but I missed the ability to let off steam through my skin. Whatever pressure I'd released on that lonely beach was starting to build again.

I'd even toyed with the idea of taking one of my students home. It would make sense, I told myself; in fact, it would have made more sense to go that route in the first place instead of going to a zoo. After all, if the reason I was going to a zoo was that I didn't have anyone in my life, wouldn't the solution be to bring someone into my life instead of to commune with strangers?

Ryan, one of the older ones — although still a good decade my junior — was tall and lithe, handsome, with a ready smile, smart enough to banter intelligently, able to make me laugh. In another time, I would have been half in love with him after our first meeting. We flirted together for two weeks and even went out for drinks a couple of times after class. But while I was his professor, it felt wrong to act on that impulse, so I didn't. And since he didn't bring it up, either, it felt like the right choice.

On the last day of class, he waited until all the other students had gone and then approached me. Because I had spent the day trying to figure out a way to get him to stay after class so I could ask him out, the fact that we appeared to be on the same wavelength made me very happy, and I was ready to say yes when he asked me. Maybe I'd invite him home, cook dinner, open up one of my last bottles of wine.

Instead, Ryan invited me to check out a zoo he knew.

Part of me was paradoxically hurt. It was a bit of a kick in the pants to find out Ryan was no more interested in creating a deeper connection with me than I was with him, or anyone else. But it was a zoo — not an elite club like Kaz's, but one of the originals. Ryan was a regular there. He assured me it was clean and that I'd be safe.

There were many reasons not to go, of course, far outnumbering the reasons to give it a try. No one in this city knew me, so it would be days before I was missed if something bad happened. On the other hand, no one in this city knew me, so if there ever was a time to give an original zoo a try, this was it. I'd been intrigued by that first zoo Kaz had shown me, more than I'd admitted to him and more than I cared to admit to myself. Not the debasement of the animals, but the freedom they'd felt to seek out what they wanted in a less civilized way than those in the clubs with screening, memberships, and other safety precautions. After two weeks of no touch at all — and the prospect of at least four days on the road before I was back in a city with a zoo I knew — I was ready to take a few risks. Was a little giddy at the prospect.

I told Ryan I'd meet him at the zoo, which was about a half-hour walk from where I was staying, at 6:45, which would give us time to get ready before it started at 7:00. First I went back to my billet and started packing for my trip back to the capital. My plan was to head out in the morning. When it was time to leave for the zoo, I left a note on the table saying where I was going and with whom. Just in case.

The setup was completely different from the zoo Kaz had shown me. It was an old school gym, albeit a small one. Instead of a corral, there was a hardwood floor covered in vinyl mats. Mats were also attached to the walls to a height of about six feet.

You didn't enter the gym directly; instead, men and women went into separate changing rooms to undress, locking clothes and valuables away in numbered lockers.

"When you get the signal," Ryan had said, "everyone goes into the main room. It is pitch black except for a bit of emergency lighting, which illuminates the alert buttons you can push if you need to. You can always leave, find the doors and go out, but they're constructed so that light won't spill into the space and disturb the others. Once every seven hours, the lights come on so they can clean the place. You can get a shower, get something to eat, or get dressed and leave. And then an hour later, it starts again."

"So it's all in the dark?"

"Yeah, this isn't a zoo for voyeurs — everybody's in. It's all about being ready and open for whatever happens in the dark. It's not separated by gender or fauna and tacs like the zoos you wrote about. This is a fully tactile experience."

I found the idea of swimming around in the dark like that thrilling.

I put my clothes in a locker, set the lock, and lined up with about thirty other women, some my age or older, and quite a few who were younger. There were nukers at the doors, but as long as you had the fairly low cost of admission, anyone could

play — there were no psych evaluations, or tests for Henny
Penny, which added to the danger of the experience, but at this
point I needed that contact so badly I was more excited by the
danger than wary of it.

The sensory deprivation in the dark zoo chamber was urgent and pressing, and for a moment or two, I couldn't breathe
through the panic. As my eyes adjusted to the gloom, however,
I could see that it wasn't pitch black — there was the occasional
glow of an infra-red emergency light set low on the walls, just
enough to let me see shadowy figures moving around.

There was really no need to see them, though — there were
enough people, and the room was small enough, that it was
hard to move without touching someone somewhere on their
body. Electronic dance music played, reminding me of Eleanor
and Dan's rave, and the kids all rubbing against one another as
the music and lights pounded out a racing pulse.

The crowd — someone in the crowd — started chanting
"Turn! Turn! Turn!" and other people took it up. We started
to spin in the dark, each one of us a bead in a stygian kaleido-
scope. I turned in slow circles, unsure of my footing at first
and fearful of getting dizzy without a point of reference. I held
my arms out and as I turned, I touched those nearby, and they
touched me, a whisper, a glancing caress, and then we turned
and moved on. As we spun, we all drew in closer and pulled
in our arms so that it was our bodies touching, not hands and
fingers but breasts and stomachs and legs — hairy, smooth, fat,
bony, like fish in a sea of pure sensation.

Kaz's zoos, as they became progressively more intimate, had
each given me a hint of something like this, but this was the
first time in or out of a zoo that, for me, anything had been just
about the experience of touch, without sex, without voyeurism,

without all of the accoutrements of society and its mores and its sense of shame. This was Adam and Eve in the garden, before the apple, before the fall, just enjoying their bodies, learning the texture of skin on skin without too much intrusion from the other senses. Yes, we could hear and smell each other, but touch was paramount. My whole body sang with it, my skin tingled, I was warm in the cool room. My skin hunger was entirely satiated for the first time in more than a decade. And I lost myself in the feeling of repletion.

When the lights came on, hours later, I was curled up in a pile with half a dozen men and women, young and old, snuggled together like kittens.

We smiled at each other and I tried not to be embarrassed by my nakedness, to be as comfortable with it in the light as I'd been in the dark.

Ryan was nowhere to be seen — who knew when he'd left, or if we'd ever come together in the dark.

"Are you going to the three o'clock?" one of the women who'd been curled up with me asked.

"Hmm?"

"I'm going to go to the three o'clock. I'm going to have a shower and get a bite, and then come back for the next one."

I was in, pulled by that powerful beginning, when we had all floated like molecules in the dark, looking for connection. And also by the opportunity to be held as I slept. In my previous life, I'd sought my own side of the bed as often as not, but with Kaz and Aziz, I'd slept the sleep of the dead in strong arms. It was only an hour or so into my second zoo that I curled up with companions and fell asleep again, not hearing the music, just surrounded by a womb of flesh that gently rocked and sheltered me.

I had some lunch before the next seven-hour shift started. The locker rooms supplied toothbrushes and toothpaste, soap and shampoo, razors for those wanting smooth skin, deodorant. There was a 24-7 buffet next to the change rooms. Most of us didn't bother to put on clothes to eat. There was no need to get dressed. There was no need to leave.

Those seven-hour intervals were the only way of telling how much time had passed. Most of my original companions left after the second zoo, but after three or four, I noticed that I wasn't the only one who was staying. As long as you didn't leave, you didn't have to pay again, and it was possible that some people were freeloading — paying once, taking advantage of the buffet and drinks and naked flesh, maybe as a weekend bender or perhaps even as a way of making ends meet. It would suit management's purposes to have people who stuck around, as there would always be someone there. I was astounded by how many people arrived for each new shift: 3:00 a.m. or 11:00 a.m. or 7:00 p.m., it didn't seem to matter, there were never fewer than forty people in the big room, even after the weekend was over, during what should have been a normal working day.

Eventually I stopped counting. Nothing mattered outside of the seven-hour increments. In the free hours, even as I showered and ate, my body ached to be back in the room. I talked a bit with others, got to know the staff, but I really had nothing to say. I wanted to be in the dark again, I wanted to be part of a swirl of skin and hair again, wanted to feel beautiful and free again. Three eight-hour increments made a day, but days had lost their meaning. The next opportunity to be part of that tactile experience was what was important.

I didn't know how long I'd been there when Kaz found me. And I still hadn't had enough of that warmth and comfort, pure sensation. The freedom to allow my thoughts to swim around in the dark like my body did, not worried about finding a focus.

I remember that I'd woken up reluctantly when the lights came on. I'd been dreaming about a puppy. In the dream I was both puppy and the person petting the puppy, and about as pleased as a person-puppy could be to be on both ends of the love. Fur under my fingers and fingers under my fur, stroking the velvet of my ears and forehead, skritching my cheeks. I didn't want it to stop.

Seeing Kaz in the doorway when I went to get a snack was like a splash of cold water in my face. For the first time in days? weeks? I felt the need to cover myself, the first time I'd felt so naked in front of him.

"Lily, can I get you something to drink?" he asked as if we saw each other every day and I was always naked, and I nodded, letting him lead me to the windowless room where they laid out the buffet.

"How've you been?" he asked, after getting us both a sparkling water with lemon.

"Good — you?"

"Good. A little worried when I couldn't find you."

"You looked for me?"

"Everyone's looking for you. Fred at the regency contacted Bob, wondering if he'd heard from you. Bob waited outside your apartment building for Eleanor, hoping she'd had word, and she contacted me. Everyone was worried you'd had an accident or come to some harm on the road."

"Why is everyone so concerned? I'm only a few days late. What day is it?"

"You don't know how long you've been here?"

"Since my last class ... A week, maybe?"

"No one's heard from you since the end of September — a month ago. You were supposed to be back in the capital two weeks ago at the very latest," he said.

I sat down on one of the metal auditorium chairs arrayed around the edges of the room, and he pulled another one up and sat beside me, resting his elbows on his knees.

"Sorry," I said, "I lost track of time."

That understatement surprised a chuckle out of Kaz, but time is slippery. For someone who had let ten years go by without much in the way of human contact, losing a month to sybaritic joy was unremarkable.

We talked for a bit — or Kaz talked, and I wondered what was going to happen next. I could feel the clock ticking toward the next zoo and it took everything I had not to just get up and get ready to go back in. But on some level, I knew it wouldn't happen, that the zoo was closing for me.

So when Kaz suggested that I get dressed and return with him to the apartment where I'd been staying, I didn't argue.

It was daylight when we went outside. The sun burned my eyes, and even though Kaz had told me it was the end of October, I realized I had no conception of the time of day, day of the week, or month of the year. I was vaguely aware it was autumn. I was like one of those gambling addicts in Las Vegas, used to living in an artificial environment. I felt a literal wrenching as I left the zoo.

"You can come back any time you want to," Kaz said gently as I hesitated at the threshold, feeling that magnetic pull, my new circadian rhythm telling me the zoo was about to begin again.

The mask cut into my face and the gloves suffocated my hands; the Impermatex clothes were sandpaper against my skin.

Kaz sent me to bed when we got back to the apartment. The short walk in the fresh air had left me exhausted after weeks of moving within a confined space, and sleeping only a few hours at a time.

I woke up after dark and showered before joining Kaz in the living area. He'd prepared a light dinner.

"Don't worry, I didn't use the chicken you had in the fridge."

I dully remembered that my fridge had been quite full — I had been expecting to leave for home the day after my last class and had shopped for what I'd need for those days on the road.

"Did you go out?" I asked. I hadn't heard a thing, I'd slept so deeply.

"Just to the market."

"You weren't worried I'd get up and go back?"

"You have free will. If you'd gotten up and gone back, that would have been your prerogative."

"I didn't want to leave. Why am I here, then?"

"Eat, and then talk. Talking deeply during meals interferes with the digestion."

"That sounds like something Aziz would say."

"And so it is."

We finished our meal at the table without speaking about much of anything at all. It was just as well. My brain felt full of sludge. I hadn't had to put a sentence together for weeks, and it took energy to do so. Food helped.

"Did you ever go walking in the park down the street?" Kaz asked.

"Not after dark," I answered.

"Let's go now. There's a harvest moon, and some solar-powered lamps along the path. Walking's good for the digestion."

"Aziz told you?"

"My mother."

"Oh."

We walked quietly for a while, but unspoken words strung a taut line between us, weighing on me as heavily as the unfamiliar mask and clothes.

"How did you know about the park?"

"I've been here for a day or two," he said. "I came out here last night — it's peaceful and pleasant."

We walked some more while I arranged a more complicated sentence in my head.

"It seems to me like you invited a conversation and now you're avoiding having it," I said with difficulty, but pleased with myself that I'd managed it.

"Does it? I guess maybe … I was just thinking how normal dinner felt, preparing a meal and eating it with someone familiar, and I wanted that feeling to continue. There's a chance that you or I might become angry or upset when we talk, that one of us might storm off, say or do something irrevocable. I wanted a nice feeling of companionship first."

"Even if the person you were feeling companionship with wanted to be somewhere else."

"Even so."

"What's normal?"

"Hmm?" Kaz turned to look at me.

"You said it felt normal at dinner. When was the last time that was normal for you?"

"Ha," he said. "I think I meant the kind of normal that you read about in books. The kind of normal your soul yearns for. My soul yearns for."

"Was life with Violet normal? Love? Companionship?"

"My relationship with her was an explosion, a roller coaster. It was fun and exciting, and in the end all about her and not much about love."

"Sounds familiar," I said.

"A relationship, I've come to realize, has to be at least a little about me."

"Can't argue with that," I said.

"Can't you?"

"What do you mean?"

"You in the zoos. It's always about you."

"I'm a tac sometimes," I protested.

"But not because you want to be. This place you love here, it's all about receiving. It's more symbiotic in this place, less of a strict division between give and take than in my zoos, but there's no participation in any real sense. You stand there or twirl there and receive sensation — if you give, it's accidental."

"You were there?" Had I met him in the dark and not known him?

"I was there. Your landlord let me into the apartment. When I saw your note, where you had gone, I talked to the zookeeper and he told me how long you'd been there. I wanted to experience what you were experiencing. I can understand why it draws you. But you're addicted to it. You can feel it pulling you back now, can't you?"

It was true, as much as I was enjoying the walk, that now I'd slept and been fed and watered, all I wanted to do was go back and be among the anonymous throng again.

"You were wrong about me," I said. "You said I'd know when to stop."

"I guess I didn't understand what you were looking for — or how desperately you wanted to find it."

We walked a little further in silence.

"So my question is: what are you looking for, Lily? What do you want that you're finding in this zoo — or, more to the point, what are you failing to find, so that you keep going back?"

He didn't press me to answer. We just kept walking, enjoying the breeze, the stars, the moon, the distant light sounds of vehicles moving, the awareness of people on other paths around us. As we walked, I could feel the experience of the zoo leaching out through my pores, leaving my system. I quietly mourned the return of self-awareness.

What am I looking for? I asked myself. *What do I want?*

And why was what I was getting so very, very far away from enough? For as much as I got from the zoos, there was always an empty space left at the centre of me that they did not touch — even this last one, which was as close as I'd ever come to the frictionless existence I'd always thought I wanted.

Not naming the empty space was the way I'd survived alone for all those years. A thing left unnamed is the pit into which uncomfortable realities fall and themselves become indefinite and vague.

We came to a bench and I considered leading him to it and sitting down and telling him about the hole inside me, but as much as I coveted the mask of the night to conceal my confession, I also feared that exposing my inner self to it would be an invitation for the darkness to rush in and fill me up again.

"Let's go back," I said, and we retraced our steps to the small apartment.

He poured us each a drink and we took chairs out to the balcony, wrapped ourselves in blankets and sat there staring out over the harbour, watching the moonlight dance on the wavelets.

"I thought it was about the contact," I said after a while. "The first few times, it was such a high just to be touched, and I thought that was enough, I thought that was it, but then it stops being enough, so you go to a different zoo and touch more intimately, but it's still so proscribed — you can only touch here during these hours and when and how we say. So you start thinking it's all the restrictions, that's why it's not fulfilling — or maybe it's the fact that your head still has rules about what you should or should not do, maybe if you could just let those go, be anonymous, embrace the wildness, it would be enough."

"But it's not."

"But it never is." I took a drink of my wine. "You've obviously seen this before — it's like a drug that you're pushing. You're doing what you can to protect the users, but you're also protecting yourself, telling yourself you're just giving us what we ask for, what we say we need, and knowing all the while you're treating the symptoms, not the disease, leaving us just sick enough that we'll keep coming back."

"Not all of you. Some people get what they need and don't come back."

"But not me."

"Not you."

"When did you know I was going to be one of your orphans?"

"I never knew for sure. I thought maybe since you'd had such control for all those years — well, it could always have gone either way."

We sat quietly in the moonlight, sipping our drinks, watching the moon and the waves.

"That's not true," he said after a moment. "I knew it would happen but was hoping against hope that I was wrong because I wanted to be wrong. I see this stream of needy people coming through the door — all they want is the zoo, all they think about is what they're getting. I didn't want you to be one of them, so I refused to think of you that way. I could talk to you. I wanted to talk to you. I've been reading your stories since you started publishing. I saw this recurring character — this strong, funny, smart woman who'd show up in every story, and I pretended it was you. I wanted to get to know her."

"The author is not the character," I said, thinking of all the fan mail I'd left unanswered, not wanting to have to face the disappointment on readers' faces when they discovered this truth — or my own disappointment at not having reached the person I was looking for.

"No, not entirely, but I said to you once that we're all our own avatars, and I think that's true. We're all at least partly the people we decide to create. And I wanted to meet the person who wrote those stories, connect with that imagination. And when you wrote your TTC story, I got the idea to introduce you to Kaz the zookeeper." He kicked softly, absently, with the toe of his shoe at the wrought-iron balcony railing. "I loved it when you were working on the series because we could meet and talk and finally there was someone in my life other than Aziz with whom I could share conversation and ideas ... Dinner at your place, seeing you in your element, with normal people around you, talking intelligently about interesting things. It was everything I loved about my old life. We played a game! Do you know how long it had been since I'd played a game that didn't involve moving people around my own little chessboard?" He stretched forward in his chair, holding his hands out to the air.

"I had touch, Lily, all these years — I had touch any time I wanted it, any way I wanted it, but I didn't feel. I had no contact. Being with you gave me hope that this life I've come to abhor didn't have to be this way, that I had options."

"You abhor it?"

"A zoo is a prison for animals. It mutates their nature; they change their behaviour in it. It also changes the zookeeper's nature. He either comes to enjoy imprisoning others, or he comes to despise the prisons and the animals in them."

I got up and leaned my elbows on the balcony railing, considering what he'd said. It had never occurred to me that sleek, suave Kaz, who seemed to have it all and to know just where he'd put it, was missing anything in his life. That he had written to me in the first place because he was empty inside, too.

"I can't have been what you expected."

"You weren't what I expected, no," said Kaz, "but what you were was even more disarming. And I so desperately wanted you to like me."

I mulled that over. The foghorn on some far-off point sounded twice before I responded.

"In a way, this last month, this is something I've been dreaming about for years," I said slowly, cautiously, aware that with every word, I was showing him parts of myself that I kept hidden, parts that were vulnerable if exposed. "Well, not this exactly, of course, but I've longed for a space without rules, the ability to be me without the trappings of civilization, not worrying about who was watching and what they thought, or how I was going to pay my bills or if the roof was leaking. I was free to just be in a way I've never been. Even for ten years alone in my apartment, I played by what I believed were the rules."

I finished my wine and threw the glass over the railing, listening for the tinkle of glass breaking on the pavement below.

"The last month in the zoo, I just lived. I ate when I wanted, slept, fucked, bathed, and groomed entirely at my whim — or not even at my whim. I wasn't making conscious choices. I was feral. I was doing what came naturally. Although, since I was being housed and fed, I was more house pet than wild creature. Still. I didn't ask anyone's permission — I became one with my surroundings. And I loved every minute of it. Waking up in a random pile of people was bliss. Except ..."

"Except it wasn't enough."

"All this time, I've been thinking what I want is to escape everything, when maybe what I want is for the ... the ... cosmic everything to embrace me, gather me in. I've even fought true connection when it was offered to me, just because I was afraid it would find me wanting and move on. For years I've been yearning for something — physically, of course, but spiritually, too. And I don't mean God — I don't need an all-powerful creator to legitimize me, but for community. For welcoming, for open arms, for acceptance and approbation, and for knowledge that none of that will be withdrawn arbitrarily."

I looked over the balcony railing to see my broken wineglass on the pavement below, sparkling in the moonlight. I sighed deeply.

"Those ten years alone were perfect, in a way. There was no one to say no to me, no one to tell me I wasn't good enough, that I didn't deserve to have what I wanted. And the zoos — they're set up specifically so that no one says no. It's unconditional acceptance, love I don't have to work for."

"I don't think it exists, love you don't have to work for," Kaz said softly.

"I wanted to will it into existence. Everyone I've ever loved has either died or left me, Kaz. Or left me and then died. You and I have danced around the idea of love, but you pulled me close, then pushed me away. And maybe you had good reasons for that — I'm not saying you're wrong. But ... in some ways, the zoos are more trustworthy. It doesn't matter who I am or what I look like, or whether I feel like talking or being amusing. I can just go and be — be welcomed, be enveloped by them, be subsumed. Just me, as I am, in all my flawed wonder. They're exactly what they say on the box. They don't promise to be anything but temporary physical respite. This much and no more."

I breathed in the fresh night air, smelled the salt and seaweed of the nearby ocean.

"Except that big empty space inside me wanted this ... and. This and someone to talk to who already knew me. Someone I had a history with — or could create a history with. Touch, as you say, plus contact. Contact plus ... love."

And there it was, the name, the acknowledgement of the big empty space.

And the darkness rushed in to fill it, as I'd known it would.

"It's not enough!" I cried out. And I howled, having learned beside the ocean how to do so again, adding my darkness to the black of the night.

Kaz stood and drew me up beside him, and held me while I cried, like he'd done so many months ago at my first zoo, when his fingers on my hand had made me tremble and weep. And he wept with me this time, two empty souls on a seaside balcony.

Later, he led me to the bed and we lay down together, spooning for comfort. I slept again. Maybe he did, too. He was still there when I awoke.

Coming Home

KAZ HAD FLOWN east to find me, hitching a ride with a friend who had a small plane and a business providing fresh seafood to the capital, so we drove back together. A drive that in perfect times would have taken about twenty hours all told — and had taken me the better part of weeks in between longer stops, as I made my careful way east — took four long days with both of us sharing the driving from dawn to dusk. The road conditions made driving after dark unsafe. We avoided towns and used the camping equipment, even though the nights were cold. I wonder if Kaz worried that I would seize on any opportunity to ditch him in a crowded place and make my way back to the zoo, although he needn't have. Now that the empty space had

been named, knowledge had been shared, the zoo had lost its
hold on me.

We added more blankets to the already generous pile that
the regency had provided when I started out in case I needed
them for my scheduled October return, and we slept together
for warmth. We didn't speak much — I was still coming down
from the zoo, and he was lost in his own thoughts. The miles
were long and quiet, the early November scenery showing a
faded glory, leaves falling, green grass dimming to brown.

"What are you going to do when we get back, Lily?" Kaz
asked as we approached the capital, our largely silent trip coming to an end. "Normally when I rescue an orphan, I set them
up somewhere, make sure they have a support system."

"Is that what I am to you now? An orphan? You don't like
them much."

He was silent for a moment. "It's what you could be, but
it's not all you can be. Will you accept help from me to come
down?"

"Do you think I need it?"

"It kind of depends on how you think you might spend
your time when we get back. I'm a little worried that you don't
have a job, don't have structure. It would be good to know you
have a plan."

I'd actually given that question a lot of thought before my
road trip derailed at the zoo. I had enjoyed meeting people
in the small towns where I'd stayed, getting to know them,
seeing how they lived. I'd also liked teaching more than I'd
ever thought I would. I'd started checking the regency's job
boards and realized there was a world of opportunity for me as
a teacher or doing some sort of outreach for the regency, and
my thoughts had started to take me that way.

"I don't know," I said. "Maybe teach for a while — there's lot of work for part-time professors."

"Is that the passion you were looking for when you left?"

"No." I laughed. "I enjoy it, but it's not … no. No, I still want to write, but I want to write a book. Books. About life and people and how we live and love and hate and fight and die. I want to add to the volume you gave me."

"Is that the butterfly finally moulted?"

"Maybe. You tell me — you're the one who had the idea that I wasn't fully formed." He said nothing. I shrugged. "Well, I suspect I have some development left to do."

He stopped the SUV in the middle of the road. There was no traffic, no need to worry about anyone coming along.

"You and I talked about love once," he said, turning to me.

I looked out my side window, uncomfortable under his direct gaze. "Yes, we did."

"Do you want to talk about it again?"

"Not really."

"So was it just infatuation?"

"No." I turned to face him. "No, it's not that. It's just … I have a lot to process. I don't know how I feel about you. You were so damnably ambivalent for so long, I didn't want to let myself think about anything more with you. And I worry that if I have fallen for you, it was because you were there and looking at me." I looked out the window again. "I'm not stuck in the past the way I was. I'm no longer grieving what I lost. The penny dropped in that last zoo — I was able to experience a freedom from my own … self, in a way. And it was really fucking hard to leave because I liked that feeling. But I left, and while I want to go back, understanding why it had a hold on me kind of breaks that hold in a weird way. I don't think you need to worry about me becoming an orphan again. I don't think I need it anymore — or not in the same way."

I turned back to him, needing him to see my eyes, to know what I knew deep down, that I was tame again.

"I need to build a life that incorporates that feeling somehow, but doesn't rely on it. I need to build a life where I am an active participant. And that might include you. If you don't hate me because I turned out not to be strong enough to resist the addiction."

"I don't hate you. I think we've both had a good look at each other's flaws now — it's hard to claim any kind of superiority." He leaned back in the driver's seat and closed his eyes.

"If you want me to, I'll add you to the list of things I might like to have, then."

Without opening his eyes, he reached out and took my hand. "I want you to."

"Okay, done. But you have to give me time. I need to know that I can thrive on my own, with the tools that I bring to the table. Right now you would be a crutch, the way Sophie was a crutch in my past life. I don't ever want to depend on someone else for my happiness again. So give me time. Let me find my way back to you."

"How much time do you need?"

"How long will you wait?"

"How long would you want me to?"

"Give me a year — is that reasonable?"

"That's reasonable."

"Okay, then."

We stopped at his place first, and he took his stuff out of the back, then kissed me on the cheek and went into his building

without waving goodbye. I told myself that that was all right —
he was just doing what I'd asked him to.

I contacted Fred to let him know I was back in the city, and
we set up an appointment for me to return the SUV and gear,
and to debrief. And then I slept. And ate. And walked.

I went to Valerie's, and she tutted over my hair but didn't
ask what I'd been doing that I hadn't taken care of it. I decided
I liked Valerie. She didn't need me to talk.

Unlike Eleanor. She wasn't letting me get away with the
silent treatment. I went to her place the day after I got back and
invited her over for a glass of wine. She was concerned, then
angry, then concerned again.

"Are you sure you're okay? Are you sure you won't go back?
There's a zoo right next door ..."

"I think the zoo next door is safe from me. The zoo out
east was a very specific experience, and I don't know whether
I'd find it anywhere else. Kaz had never heard of a zoo like it,
and if it was strange to him, it might be one of a kind. But even
so ... I think I learned from it what I needed to learn."

"And what's that?"

"I learned it's okay just to feel. And that I have a space in
the world where I belong."

"But doesn't having to come out and leave that zoo behind
tell you it's not okay to just feel?"

"I just need to find a different way to do it, is all." I smiled.
"I might need to leave the city, go to a place where I can have
animals and untreated fabrics and ten people to sleep in a pile
with. But I'm never going to deny myself the pile again for fear
that someone will think I'm a bad person for wanting it."

· · ·

One of my top priorities was to find a new condo. It was time to move. I'd stayed here because it was easy — under the terms of the move, it was mine for as long as I wanted, with ownership returning to the regency when I left — and because I'd always had it in my head that Sophie would be able to find me if she came back. Knowing that she'd been so close all this time — the night she, Kaz, and Aziz had gone to the zoo next door, she could have looked up at the lights and seen I was home, come in and said hello — made me angry all over again, but I forced myself to let it go. I'd found myself; I didn't need her to find me anymore. Buying my own place was like divesting myself of the last bit of the cocoon I'd been bound up in for so long. I was making a new start, living life my way.

My friends helped me move, and I thanked them by inviting them to Christmas dinner in my new place on the river, where my favourite art hung on the walls, colourful rugs — sourced with help from Jane — covered the floors, a small tree with lights and old treasures hanging from its branches warmed up the cozy living room. I didn't think about taking Sophie's place at the head of the table — I took mine.

I settled into my new place, with my art and my things around me, and started writing again: about Henny Penny, about Sophie, about the zoos, and about myself, pouring myself out onto page after page.

• • •

"Kate! Hi!" Jane exclaimed, drawing me in for a hug. "I wasn't expecting you. How have you been?"

"I've been well, thanks. You?"

"Good, good. Some big changes since the last time you were here," she said.

"I know — Kaz has become quite the public figure." I had been amazed to see him running for election in the spring, campaigning on opposition to the BLT laws. As a business owner — in addition to the zoos, he'd bought the market where my favourite vintner had a stall, it turned out — he was able to stand for election even though he wasn't a citizen, although apparently that was in the works, too. Even though he'd lost, a bill to repeal the mask and glove laws was now making its way through the legislative process.

It had been almost exactly a year since we'd come back to the city. A year of teaching, writing, rebuilding a life with people in it, working out for myself who I wanted to be and how I wanted to live. I even went to the zoos every now and then, but no longer needed them in quite the same way. My experience in the zoo out east had made me examine what it was I had been looking for when I went. I was like a former stress eater who had learned to eat only when I was truly hungry.

I'd started teaching at the university in March. It had finally found enough academics — itinerant, like me, full-time, and some distance professors — to start offering a limited number of degree programs again.

And teaching had made me a part of a community of interesting people with whom I was able to build friendships over food and wine and monthly movie nights. On Tuesdays, one of the theatre professors held table readings. He'd cast me as Maggie the Cat in *Cat on a Hot Tin Roof*, after which the men cast as Brick and Big Daddy both asked me out. I hadn't expected much from either first date, but to my surprise, I'd ended up liking each of them for different reasons — one because he forced me out of my shell, and the other because he didn't. When I went to the zoos now, it wasn't because I needed human contact — I was getting as much of that as I wanted — but to get it without strings, without expectations. Each of my lovers had started to press me to make the relationship official, to move in and set up a life together.

And I'd thought about it, thought maybe it isn't always a love story. Sometimes it's an "I like you a lot and maybe that's enough" story. Sometimes it's a "You're what I need right now and we'll see where it goes" story.

I could have been contented with either of them, had the world and my experience of it been different. They were both lovely but unrelentingly straight. Neither of them knew I was seeing the other, or that I went to the zoos. I knew they'd react badly if I told them about my secret life, would feel threatened and wouldn't understand why they weren't enough for me. I resented and felt a little scornful of them because of that. And in the end, I had no interest in being contented.

Kaz knew me and accepted me — I didn't have to explain my yearning for wildness; he'd seen me feral and still wanted me. And I'd seen him at war with himself, and that fight had not diminished him in my eyes.

I still didn't know what kind of relationship I wanted to have with him. But I knew that I wanted him more than I wanted other men.

I'd no sooner decided it was time to contact him, however, when I realized I couldn't. His old email address didn't work, and the letter drop I'd used before had been at the office — I didn't know whether he was still using it. I'd tried going to his place, but his doorman was less than helpful — he wouldn't even admit Kaz lived there. He'd no doubt been given an instructive earful after letting Violet and the Colonel into the party the previous summer.

I went to the zoo as a last resort. I'd caught Jane just as she was leaving.

"You're in luck," Jane said. "I know he's been waiting to hear from you. And he's here tonight, observing a mocha zoo."

"I would have thought he'd stopped coming to the zoos once he went mainstream. In fact," I said, looking around me at the familiar carpets and panelling, detecting the faint aroma of coffee on the air, "I'm a little surprised the zoo is still open."

"Oh, this is a rare sighting. It's the first time for a member they're a little concerned about, and Aziz couldn't make it tonight. As soon as the BLT laws are gone, I'm out of a job, they tell me. He's still in his office — let me buzz him for you."

I looked at my watch. I had time to shower and get ready if I wanted to.

"Is there room for me?"

Jane grinned. "In the alcove or in the zoo?"

"In the zoo."

"It's mocha — there's always room for one more, and tonight men outnumber women, so I know you'll be welcome. Go on in. I can't wait to hear how he handles this!"

I went to the change room and showered. I dried my hair and donned a robe. In the other zoos, fauna and tacs were grouped into separate changing rooms, so no one paid attention to anyone else — none of them were going to end up together. But the change rooms for the mocha zoos were divided by gender. Anyone could end up with anyone, so yet one more layer of privacy was removed from the proceedings as eyes surreptitiously slid around the room, stopped or moved on, evaluating the potential. Finally I pulled the blindfold down over my eyes as I walked through the door behind the others into the zoo.

After a moment, the voice said, "Blindfolds," and I removed mine, then looked around at the little red lights in the darkness. A hand slipped down the silk covering my back, then an arm pulled me close. By the time the lights came back on, my eyes were closed and I was kissing the man who'd chosen me, helping him shed his robe as he helped me with mine. A woman came up to us and we warmly welcomed her into our embrace.

I had already forgotten about Kaz behind the screen. It was only later, when I found myself holding on to it while another partner entered me from behind, that I thought about him. I looked into the black, knowing he could see me, knowing he'd be watching me. My heart raced even faster as I felt him approach. I could barely see his outline in the gloom. His fingers peeked out through the holes in the screen, touching my fingertips, tiny triangles of skin pressed against it. He brought his mouth close to my ear, whispered softly, "I missed you, butterfly." He stayed there, a silent presence bolstering me from the front, and when I came, I felt him feel it with me — it was as if I'd been making love with him, and not the stranger behind me.

"Come home with me, Lily," he said, as my partner turned me to face him and kissed me. I could feel Kaz's tongue touch my back through the screen.

In a while, I made my way back to the changing room, where I showered again and dressed, then used the hidden door that he'd shown me months ago to enter the office suites where he waited for me.

"Lily," he growled and suddenly I was in his arms and I felt the difference between being with the one I loved, and loving the one I was with. The men and women in the zoos had excited me, had touched every erogenous zone on my body and brought them alive, but Kaz made me feel, just as he had in my first zoo.

"Kaz. Take me home," I whispered between kisses.

We walked quickly to his car. Kaz opened the door for me to get in, then he got behind the wheel and we raced through the dark night to his place by the river. We didn't speak. He took my hand and didn't let go; when he needed to shift gears, it was my palm on the gearshift, his hand on top guiding it.

At the elevator, Kaz keyed in the code for his penthouse. We stood side by side, not touching, not speaking. When we arrived at his floor, he took my hand and led me to his bedroom. He slammed the door behind us and only then brought me close. "My god, I've missed you," he said.

In response, I just kissed him back, unbuttoning his buttons, unzipping his zipper, stripping him of layers of fabric until I came to his skin, pale in the low light of the room, cool and smooth against my palms. I helped him take my clothes off, no tease, no style — all I wanted was to align my body with his, to touch skin with skin, as if there had been nothing and no one in the months since I'd last seen him.

"I nearly went through the screen when I saw you there," he told me later. "Why didn't you tell me you were coming?"

"I didn't expect you to be at the zoo. I was just hoping Jane could help me find you when you weren't at home. When Jane said you were there, I decided to surprise you."

"Well, you did that, all right. Surprised me, bemused me, turned me on, told me what I'd been missing. You're a very effective communicator, doing all that without talking."

"Teach you to go to a mocha zoo without me."

"Never again."

We got up and made a snack and sat at the kitchen island to eat it and drink brandy out of warm snifters.

"So," I said. "You've been busy."

He laughed and then got serious. "Violet's gone."

"What do you mean?"

"We put some pressure on her to close her zoo and leave town. Her and the Colonel."

"Who's we?"

"Aziz and me — most of the other zookeepers. And some others, people who owed Aziz's brothers a couple of favours."

"Well, it's not quite life in prison …"

"Life in prison isn't life in prison anymore," he said. "She might have gotten ten years on a work farm, and you and I both know it wouldn't have taken her long to turn that to her advantage. We sent them packing. We more or less blackmailed the regency officials who were there on Christmas Eve to get them to freeze most of Violet's and the Colonel's accounts. And we sent the word out. If either of them tries to set up shop again somewhere else, they'll have difficulty."

"I'm stunned," I said truthfully. "All that worry about how it would affect you, and it happened just like that? Aziz's family puts on some pressure and it's done?"

"That was the short version — I left out a few steps. Aziz and I started putting a plan into play even before I met you. But everything was accelerated after I took you to Violet's zoo — that's when we brought Aziz's family in. Seeing the look on your face — I didn't ever want to disappoint anyone as much as I'd disappointed you that night."

"Do you still worry about them coming after you?"

"No. They'd have to come after all of us. And Aziz's family is enough to discourage anyone crazy enough to try."

"What does Aziz's family do?"

"Insurance," he said, and we both laughed a little.

"And then you went legit?"

"I talked to a lawyer and found out I could turn myself in to the regency as a displaced person. I have personal resources and a plausible back story, so while they rapped my fingers for not coming forward sooner, there was no lasting damage."

"Going straight and going mainstream all at the same time, Kaz." I shook my head. "I was proud of how you did in the election, and that you're still working for the cause."

"Yeah, I surprised myself a little with that," he said sheepishly. "But it seemed like propitious timing."

"And you don't think you'll miss all this?"

He paused. "I always liked living a little dangerously, a little on the edge. I liked the adrenalin of running with a bad crowd. But it was never really my style to be one of them. But enough about me. What about you? What have you been doing?"

I told him about moving, about the book. About other things I'd been thinking about.

"I want to do another road trip, a longer one, maybe do some more teaching. I don't want to stay here anymore — at least not all the time."

His face fell. "When I saw you, when you came back with me, I thought …"

"Shhh, shhh, I think so, too." I took him in my arms and kissed his temple. "I've been thinking for the past year about what I want my life to look like, and what — and who — I want to have in it. You're still on my list. If nothing else, this last year has shown me I'm not interested in settling down and

becoming Mrs. Middle Class, worried about keeping up with
the Joneses and whether I have the right car. I don't want to sit
still and accumulate things — I want to move and gather experiences, life. I don't want to be content; I want to be happy."

"So where does that leave us? Is there an us?"

"Were you thinking you wanted to be Mr. Middle Class
with me?"

"I was willing to give it a try, if that's what you wanted."

"I want you — I don't want the person you think I want
you to be. I think we need to spend some time working out
how we fit together without the zoos acting as intermediary."

We talked a little, made love a little, slept a little, woke up
and started all over again. The sun was well into the sky when
Aziz burst through the door, fully dressed, waking us.

"I thought you were just observing last night, not playing,
Kaz. Espresso is ready and will go to waste if you don't soon
drink it."

He raised the window blind, then turned to see us in the
bed. "Oh, ho, I thought you'd stopped bringing your darlings
home. Sharing?"

I raised myself up on my elbows. "Ask nicely," I said, and
Aziz's grin widened.

"Kate!"

"Lily, actually."

"Whatever — it is a pleasure to see you." He sat beside me
on the bed and kissed me good morning.

"Knocking, Aziz," Kaz said sleepily. "It's called knocking
and is practised in most civilized societies ..."

"Since when has this place been a civilized society?" Aziz
asked, hugging me and stroking my back. "You smell delicious,
like sleep. I want to climb in there with you."

"Why don't you?" I asked.

Aziz looked at Kaz, who shrugged and smiled. "Lady's choice."

Aziz stripped quickly and climbed into bed with us.

"My ego is taking a bit of a beating here," Kaz admitted wryly, kissing my shoulder as I turned to hold Aziz. "I thought I had some reason to believe you wouldn't be looking for variety quite so soon."

I looked back and stroked his cheek. "Not looking for variety, but greeting an old friend. And I'm beginning to suspect that loving one of you means loving both."

"Excellent," Aziz said, throwing an arm and a leg over both of us, to include everyone in his embrace.

I watched Kaz's face as Aziz's hands disappeared under the blankets.

"You wanted me to moult, Kaz — you shouldn't complain about the kind of butterfly I've become."

"I'm not complaining," he protested. "I'm awestruck."

"Are you two still talking?" Aziz asked. "We are not wearing enough clothes for that — there are rules about that sort of thing. There is far more pressing business here to attend to."

"What about your espresso?" Kaz asked.

"When a beautiful woman invites you into her bed, the least you can do is destroy a pot of espresso for her."

My first time with Kaz and Aziz had passed in a blur — I had been so surprised by it, and so distracted by the sights and sounds in the zoo on the other side of the screen, that it all bounced around together in my memory, and I couldn't have said the next day with any clarity what had actually happened. I remembered Kaz being a soft warmth at my back while Aziz and I made love, and vice versa.

That night, I'd been the focus for both men separately; this morning, we were a threesome. There was no point at which one of us was not pleasuring another, lips, tongues and teeth, hands, fingers and nails finding the soft, tender parts of each other's skin and exploiting them for our own pleasure as well as theirs. As the fluidity of sexual roles in the zoos they created suggested, Kaz and Aziz took pleasure in each other as well as in me. They were two different people, different shapes and sizes, different styles and approaches, but together they completed a circle. And I felt like the treasured centre of it.

We were drinking from a fresh pot of espresso when Aziz asked, "So, are you staying?"

"That's still under discussion."

"We'd like you to stay," Aziz said.

"Do you live here?" I asked him.

"I have the other penthouse," he said. "And there's an adjoining door, to which I have the key."

"For now," Kaz said darkly, but softened his intent with a smile.

"I know, I know, knocking, civilized societies, et cetera." Aziz grinned. "There is generally more freedom of movement between our two homes. Kaz talks about civilization and closed doors only when you are here."

I turned quickly to see Kaz's response to that statement, found him staring at Aziz, smiling, but there was an undercurrent of tension as their gazes met and held.

"Just admit that you love her and want her to stay forever, Kaz," Aziz said softly.

"What if she doesn't want to?"

"She might like to have visiting privileges when she's in town and see what happens from there," I said.

Aziz and Kaz broke off their staring contest to look at me. "And what about Kaz's new closed-door policy?"

"What was your arrangement before?"

"Arrangements change to suit the occasion," Kaz said.

"That's not really a fair question," Aziz admitted. "At other times, the question of willingness to share has been answered definitively by this point either in the affirmative or the negative. There seems to be some grey area here."

I looked from one to the other. "I don't want to come between old friends."

"There's yet another grey area — because to the contrary, it seemed you quite enjoyed it." Aziz smirked, and Kaz laughed.

"Maybe that's a question for another mood," he said. "If you want to visit — often — that would be excellent. If you want to stay, then I'd love to have you," and seeing Aziz about to speak, he added wryly, "As would Aziz, who is suddenly my straight man. And if you go, I'd love to come with you, and maybe he would, too."

"We'll work something out, then," I said, sipping my espresso and feeling its warmth overtake me in that sunny kitchen, feeling that last little bit of doubt flee from my mind. This was my life now. And life was good.

Acknowledgements

I'D LIKE TO thank all of the people, too many to name, who listened to me talk about my great idea for a novel, and agreed, and then agreed again a few years later, and again a few years after that. My earliest readers: Maggie, who didn't like it; Dave, who did; and Annamarie, who helped me see the need for a major plot change (thriller!); as well as the folks in my Ottawa writing workshop, who encouraged me back in 2009 when I was just starting.

Thanks to Lucas Crawford and Zoe Whittall for accepting my application to a writing retreat at the Banff Centre for the Arts in March 2020, and to my cohort at the abbreviated retreat for making me feel like a real writer and being enthusiastic about my story (especially Jane, who wasn't taking any of my shit, and Austen, who saw future success in my cards), and of course Keith, who emailed me while I was in Banff saying something to the effect of, "Now would be a good time to finish that goddamn book!"

Zoe never did get a chance to mentor me, but she did something better — she introduced me to her agent, Sam Haywood at Transatlantic, who agreed to take me on, along with Laura Cameron. Thanks to all three of you for your encouragement and support.

My beta readers are all fabulous, including Maggie (who still doesn't like the book) and Dave (who still does), Katya, and especially Nicole, whom I met in Banff, and who provided the best notes a first-time author miserably unsure of her structure and pacing and story arc could have ever hoped for.

Thank you to Russell Smith at Dundurn Press for taking a chance on a book about a pandemic in the middle of a pandemic, to copy editor Vicky Bell for cleaning up my tenses, and to Jenny McWha and everyone else on the production team who have helped me realize my dream of becoming a published author.

Gros bisous to all of you.

About the Author

K.S. COVERT WAS born in rural Nova Scotia, the only girl between four boys. Growing up in the country, she dreamed of living in a city, where people did exciting things at all times of the day or night (or so the books said), but when she's in the city she yearns for sunny days and quiet, starlit nights in the country. She's a pluviophile who loves curling up with a good book and a cup of tea on rainy days, and thunderstorms make her heart pound with excitement. As a reader she's an omnivore, though she prefers fiction to non-fiction, and is a lapsed member of Mensa. She's on her third career, after secretary and journalist. She lives in Ottawa with one of her brothers and two cats.